THE AGE OF
DISCRETION

Also by Virginia Duigan

NOVELS
Days Like These
The Biographer
The Precipice

FILM
The Leading Man

VIRGINIA DUIGAN

THE AGE OF
DISCRETION

VENTURA

First published in 2019 by Ventura Press
PO Box 780, Edgecliff NSW 2027 Australia
www.venturapress.com.au

10 9 8 7 6 5 4 3 2 1

National Library of Australia Cataloguing-in-Publication entry:
ISBN: 978–1–925384–66–6 (paperback)
ISBN: 978–1–925384–74–1 (ebook)

Cover design by Christabella Designs
Internal design by Working Type
Printed and bound in Australia by Griffin Press

To Anne and the friends she shared:
Annie, Caroline, Catrine, Kathy and Mary.

'There is nothing in the world that does not have its decisive moment, and the masterpiece of good management is to recognise and grasp this moment.'

– Jean-François Paul de Gondi, Cardinal de Retz 1717

1

THE SENTENCE

Certain decisive moments, Vivien Quarry would say, are like being struck by lightning – and staying alive. And as a result, having a life-changing tale to tell. Such cataclysmic moments are rare, but she experienced one this morning when her husband of thirty-two years let slip an unguarded sentence.

His delivery, typically, was almost offhand, but the remark didn't come out of the blue. Viv had once again raised the subject of sex; the vexed subject of its absence from their lives for the past two years. The departure, too, of simple gestures of affection that might have done much to compensate.

It had been a one-sided conversation like all its predecessors. These lopsided exchanges used to be quite frequent in the first year of their sex drought but they never got anywhere, and her husband's refusal to regard this as a problem or take it seriously – to discuss it at all, for that matter – has been an ongoing source of conflict. Today, however, he has come up with a double whammy: the ultimate conversation-stopper that also happens to be an unstoppable provocation.

His sentence was: 'Men are hard-wired to not find older women attractive.'

Viv's husband Geoff Mayberry is not an insensitive man, on balance, nor is he given to extremes. He has never said anything like this before and it takes a moment before it sinks in. Not long, just a few seconds in which nothing further is said and the words hang between them. Invisible words, full of portent.

Viv and Geoff are still lying in bed, side by side. When he clambers out without a backward glance and pads across to the bathroom, Viv realises she has not drawn breath since those words were uttered.

When she does she feels a sharp spurt of rage, but by now he is safely in the shower. Later today this will be dismantled as the bathroom renovation begins. She imagines the hot water cascading over his balding head and lean white limbs. He's in pretty good shape, she has always thought, give or take minor touches of wear and tear. Until now she has been kindly disposed to these, finding them endearing. Conscious of her own facial lines (fine, not overly intrusive) and bodily imperfections, she has rated the two of them as well matched in the visible-signs-of-ageing department.

What Geoff has said doesn't change this. But it changes everything else. Once Viv has digested his sentence, she sees this in an instant.

They are officially retired now, although neither likes to use this word. Geoff used to be a boffin, a top scientist in a global pharmaceuticals company. Rewarding, but high-stress. Viv was a senior editor in a small publishing house where the stresses, mercifully, she told her friends, were less macho.

After two of Geoff's colleagues were felled by catastrophic cardiac events, Viv had talked up the golden handshake. Just think of all that leisure to do the things you never had time for. The decision was made, the handshake received – it may well be relevant – just over two years ago, when Geoff was sixty-seven. Think of all that time to do things *together*. Now she regrets it.

In the immediate aftermath of his bolt from the blue, his harsh, sexist bombshell (out of character, she'd once have thought), Viv has an urgent desire to get out of the house. She is badly in need of counsel from a trusted non-professional. And providence has arranged for just such a one to be on hand.

Three hours after hearing Geoff's words, Viv feels them inhabiting her body like some malevolent growth. She imagines them seared on her forehead, visible to all the people she passes on this frigid October day. Yet nobody on the Tube flinches from her presence. No one even catches her eye. When she emerges from the Underground she flutters like a moth among the lunchtime crowds on the pavements. I don't register on their radar, she thinks. Is this something to be grateful for, or to resent?

This Monday in her diary is written and underlined: *Bloomsbury 1-ish lunch J.* The perfect distraction, and in the normal way the perfect confidante. J is for Jules, better known to the world as the great operatic soprano Julia Jefferies, who happens also to be Viv's one famous friend. Viv is aware that Julia too may be facing a crisis, though of a markedly different nature. This may not be the normal way for either of them.

It's not that Julia is an out-and-out red carpet star – at least, not according to the gossip magazines that measure popular celebrity. Most of their readers couldn't give a stuff about ageing sopranos. But in opera it's another story. Here, in one of the most exacting and least merciful branches of the arts, she has achieved at the highest level. Her distinctive, soaring voice has brought audiences to tears. Over the course of her long career there are hundreds of thousands of people around the world on whom Julia Jefferies can truthfully be said to have had a profound emotional effect.

And Viv counts herself lucky that her friend is even in the country; she has only just returned to London from Australia. A career at Julia's level is lived largely in hotels and serviced apartments close to the great opera houses of the world. Those of Paris, Milan and Vienna, of New York and Buenos Aires, Sydney and St Petersburg.

And whenever possible Viv has answered Julia's call and flown in to visit her.

Small publishers are not renowned for high salaries. Until Geoff's earnings rose it was Jules, more often than not, who covered the shortfall. 'Nothing to do with generosity, Viv, I promise you. It's self-interest, pure and simple. I'm footloose and fancy-free, which translates as unmarried and childless and alone in a strange city.'

Viv has seen enough of Julia's life and at sufficiently close quarters to wish to qualify this, in certain respects. She has seen at first hand the glamour and luxury that come with diva status, together with its fair share (and more) of extravagant admiration. Obsequious fawning, I can take it or leave it, Jules has always declared – any amount of it. But the single life lived out of suitcases has its downsides. Especially, Viv knows, in the latter stages of a brilliant career.

And even in the middle stages, when the consequences of decisions made much earlier in life begin to bite. Tough choices put in place in the first flush of an exceptional singer's working life. Strategic decisions to let nothing get in the way of advancement; such major hindrances, for example, as marriage, and children. Viv has always assumed that her friend made these choices, and made them deliberately.

Now, at a time when many of their friends (but not Viv herself) are involved grandparents, she feels a need to tread carefully around this subject. However well she thinks she knows Jules, there remains an area where she's up against the proverbial brick wall.

The area is love, the mysterious arena of relationships and sex, a subject on which Jules is not known either for reticence or squeamishness. I don't have a prudish bone in my body, Viv, she says. As you might testify before a grand jury, if required.

Viv would testify to that, and it explains why she will feel free to air her present problem, in due course. But over the years she has come to accept that Jules has an interior chamber to which she alone has access. She has contrived to keep it that way over the course of their long friendship. It is at odds with everything else in her personality, and Viv has concluded it must be linked to something innate and profound – a private sadness or regret, perhaps – that Jules could never bring herself to share.

There have been passing hints of dalliances, plenty of them, but Julia's name has never been publicly linked with anyone. *Miss Jefferies was accompanied by*—. *The legendary singer was on the arm of*—. This has been the extent of it. Never more than a paragraph or two, here and there.

In her heyday, Julia's diary would be filled with engagements three and four years ahead. Her heydays may be gone, Viv reflects, as she strides with the velocity of a much younger woman towards Julia's flat, but she is far from being forgotten. She has just sung an acclaimed Dido at the Sydney Opera House. Sydney is her home town.

Before this gig, though, there was a hiatus of several months when her calendar was empty and her agent had no offers to report. Does she have anything lined up after her small but starry turn? Viv suspects she may not. For the first time in her life Julia Jefferies may be without any forward engagements. It is just possible that she is staring down the barrel at the end of her career. The implications of this temporarily override Viv's own pressing concerns.

With Julia's handsome red brick building looming in her sights, Viv pauses on the street corner to gather herself. There is no predicting quite what mood her friend will be in. She may not be best placed to assume a counselling role. Appearances are deceptive, and of the two of them it's Jules, the international success story, who is the more vulnerable. Viv, who knows that she herself is at bottom a grounded and resilient woman, has no real doubt of that. Even though she is aware of fielding, right now, a body blow of monumental (and unpredictable) proportion.

One thing, though, is sure. Whatever Julia's state of mind and whatever the hour, she will answer the door in full fig and war paint. You show up tarted up, Jules says, because that is your brand. These unforgiving days you can't rely on talent alone, however prodigious. You can't afford to let yourself go. Or, she adds, to *go off*. To put on undue weight, to appear in public tired and emotional – anything like this would be artistic suicide in one's profession, at one's age.

One's official age, and today this is right at the forefront of Viv's mind, is sixty-six. Personable, yes, and formidably well groomed, with clothes and demeanour exuding success, but sixty-six nonetheless. Which happens to be a year this side of Viv's rather more raffish sixty-seven.

It also happens, as Viv recalls with an attitude more complicated than before, to be three years this side of Julia's real age. Her real age is sixty-nine, and Viv is one of the few people privy to this small but telling fact. She can keep secrets; not even Geoff is aware of this one. Not that it would cut much ice with him, she thinks. A few years here or there – you're still an *older woman*. With all that this may (or may not) imply.

In the recesses of her mind, concealed behind immediate concerns about Julia, Viv is studiously attending to what it may *not* imply. She is in the early stages of formulating an action plan which she may (or may not) disclose this afternoon, depending on the lie of the land.

2

AT BLOOMSBURY

It's starting to rain as Viv hurries down one side of the massive Edwardian block to the far end. She computes, soberly, that it's nearly forty years since she arrived here for the first time to find her friend in a state of euphoria.

Jules had disinterred the most captivating abode, Viv, and was about to rescue it from the jaws of death. Irrelevant that it was murderously dark and the sunken baths were tiled with hieroglyphs and demonic figures – she could see the bones, and the bones were *divine*. Two bedrooms and two bathrooms and it faced south and west! Ultra-convenient, too; walking distance to the opera house as well as the theatre district, Soho and the British Museum. A zest for life, together with a sporadic tendency to plumb the depths, was typical of Jules then. It has not diminished in either respect.

Viv always has a feeling of time travel when she comes to Bloomsbury, but rarely has it been so specific or whisked her so far back. Today she is twenty-eight and has recently met Geoffrey Mayberry (the problematic young man who is still her husband). She is entitled to put the letters PhD after her name now, and just getting used to it.

Her friend Julia Jefferies has not yet put her age back and is therefore thirty-one. After several years of playing small parts to rave notices she is midway through a season at Covent Garden singing the plum role of Violetta in *La Traviata*. She is already used (it's not hard) to being lionised.

When she suggests they share this grim apartment Viv is hesitant, but only briefly. Jules is persuasive and strong-willed. She's earning a lot of money for the first time in her life and itching to spend it. She has already worked out how to transform the interior; within weeks the transformation is achieved.

Stripped and redecorated, the creamy high-ceilinged rooms maximise the London light, as she predicted. The tall sash windows are framed with silk and linen curtains in shades of ivory and parchment. On the polished floors are rugs in the ochre colours of the outback. On the walls are luminous Australian landscapes from early last century: gum trees, hazy blue hills and winding rivers, evocative of the wide open spaces Jules once roamed with her brother Max. The paintings may be out of fashion these days, but she is scathing of trends in just about everything.

Viv will go on to share the flat with Jules for a mere six months before Geoff Mayberry moves in, for what becomes another year, or even two – exact times are blurred at this distance – until they can scrape together the down payment on their first house, a dismal terrace in Battersea.

But that, as Viv is painfully aware today, was then. Way back then, in our youth. Who could have known we would still be together? Still an intact couple, and rather remarkably still in our first marriage (even if a little precariously, these days) unlike most of our contemporaries. Although I am officially now an older woman and therefore, according to my husband, men no longer find me attractive.

Is Jules aware of this fact of nature? Does it extend to famous, high-achieving women for whom adulation is routine? Is it, indeed, even a fact? Should one include all men in this equation, as Geoff would have me believe, or is it merely the view of this particular man? Of this particular husband?

Viv presses doorbell number twenty-four. Inside Julia's apartment the intercom shows a blurry image of a woman of middling height and build with a mass of refractory, windblown hair. She is wearing a voluminous overcoat, and dancing a little jig on the spot. Her appealing, triangular face is upturned towards the security camera with visible anticipation, even on the fuzzy screen.

The lift delivers her to the landing opposite the flat, where her old friend has flung the door wide, and she tumbles in, almost tripping over her maxi coat – a genuine relic, somewhat the worse for wear but more or less intact – from the swinging sixties. They hug closely and kiss, then hold each other with an appraising fondness at arm's length.

What Viv does notice right away, and it gives her pause, is that Julia's hair is less immaculate than usual and she appears to be wearing no make-up. While she herself doesn't always bother with it, this has never been Julia's way. She usually wears a great deal, applied with professional skill. Viv suspects that Jules has never looked truly dishevelled in her life, but today her hair is nearly (but not quite) untidy. It has altered in colour many times over the years and is currently tawny with discreet highlights. She's had variations on the same theme, a shoulder-length bob with the hair swept sensuously over the right temple, for decades.

Her clothes, though, are as stylish and carefully put together as ever. A cream cashmere sweater over charcoal trousers with ironed creases, chunky silver bangles and sassy buckled ankle boots – which Viv immediately (but not too immoderately) covets – in pearly suede. And the customary scarf to protect the throat, a body part always capitalised in Viv's mind. Most singers are neurotic about The Throat, and Jules is no exception.

In her company Viv is accustomed to feeling unkempt and rather radically underdressed, but she never feels overwhelmed or inadequate, or propelled to make more of an effort than usual. From time to time she has wondered why. She has concluded that she is happy in her own skin, and that this is surely a good thing. That she is, overall, a confident woman.

Confidence has come in part from a fulfilling career, a daughter she loves and a stable long-term marriage. In another it derives from having, without false modesty, a passably attractive personality. And being, furthermore, a passably attractive woman. Not a beauty like Jules, or anywhere near it, but a woman men have liked and responded to. Some of these long-term assumptions are suddenly under threat.

As Jules assembles lunch, which can be a lengthy operation (it's never thrown together here; she likes to do things well, and do them herself) Viv takes off her boots and sinks into a white, feather-filled sofa. As she plants her stockinged feet on the ottoman she experiences a strange sensation. The feeling is unprecedented; it's almost as if she were someone else, an interloper, whose connection to the old Vivien Quarry (the original, younger model) is vaguely fraudulent.

This feels like an obscure form of treachery that must be resisted. She is in her old stamping ground in a warm, inviting flat, with the resources of a friendship that has stood, triumphantly, the test of time. And to endure with such success, friendships need flexibility, involving at times not mere give-and-take but also a degree of selflessness. Viv decides to hold off on her own revelation while she tests the water.

Usually Jules watches her weight and rarely drinks at lunch, but today she dismisses this as too sensible and grown-up. She has a toothsome little rosé she wants her friend to try. No, not at all sweet. Dry and remarkably full-bodied. They settle on one glass. One at a time, to start with. Always a risk to be too grown-up at our age, they agree.

They will lunch under the window at a small card table spread with a cloth, circa 1950s, whose borders are hand-embroidered with sprigs of wattle. A bunch of dahlias is on the table in a vase with a kookaburra handle. Jules, who is not averse to a spot of kitsch, collects old ceramics featuring Australian flora and fauna. Mugs and plates are displayed on the dresser of Viv's kitchen, along with other colourful items sourced from Julia's visits home.

As they sit opposite each other, Viv sees at once that things are as she feared. Julia is convinced she's facing down the spectre of redundancy.

The topic is not untrodden ground between them. Not by any means – Jules has incubated doomsday predictions ever since the curtain fell on her final, spine-tingling performance as the Marschallin in *Der Rosenkavalier*. She had made this bittersweet role her own, and she milked it for all it was worth, continuing to sing it around the world for more than twenty years.

The character is a woman in her early thirties, indulging in a doomed fling with a seventeen-year-old boy. Julia may have been legendary and one of the world's best-loved sopranos, but audiences could only suspend their disbelief for so long. Six years ago she turned (officially, that is) sixty, and the door closed forever on what was perhaps her greatest role.

'And now I'm on the scrap heap. It's not even a *voluntary* heave-ho, Viv. Not like Geoff's. Geoff retired at a moment of his choosing, when he'd had a gutful, didn't he? He was fed up to the back teeth.'

She helps Viv to poached salmon from a platter, with steamed asparagus and home-made basil mayonnaise. Viv makes an appreciative noise, followed by a doubtful one. 'But I encouraged him,' she says.

'Because you were thinking of what was best for him, after those colleagues fell off the twig. And what was best for your marriage. You wanted to have quality time together, before it was too late.' Viv suppresses a negative reaction.

'It's not like that with me, Viv, as you well know. Performers get off on adrenaline, but Geoff's not a show pony. People like him find stress oppressive. He always did, right?' This is a reference to past incidents both can identify. She raises her eyebrows interrogatively.

Viv shrugs. 'Yes, but I'm not so sure about that now, I think he actually—' She pulls herself up. This is not the time. Julia's slender, artistic fingers are curled round a long-stemmed glass. She holds the pale pink wine against the muted light from the window.

'It's not just the singing itself I'll miss, it's all the creative scaffolding. Costumes, fittings, make-up. The scurrilous gossip. The building blocks of every production.'

She replaces her glass so it covers a faded stain on the tablecloth, and leans forward, lowering her voice confidentially. 'Do you know what I'll miss most? It's being part of an ensemble. Being an *insider*. And knowing that, from this time forward, I'll be an outsider looking in. Just like everybody else.'

Viv tends to accept from Jules statements she might have trouble with if they came from other people. Usually they are seasoned with astringency. Not this time. She thinks, Jules is going through the motions of talking to me, but this is a painfully honest conversation she's having with herself. And she's entitled to say these words without irony; she has earned the right.

A gust of wind rattles the windows. Jules smooths her hair, an unconscious gesture. She looks at Viv through half-closed eyes. 'To contribute to an art form that at its greatest is so life-enhancing. To be part of occasions that are so awesome, to use a much-abused word.' The well-known voice drops. 'That can be so goddam *sublime*.'

She falls silent, then remarks, 'I've never, ever taken it lightly, you know. Not once. Any of it. It's been a rare gift. I know that.'

This is what it must be like to be a priest in the confessional. 'You've been blessed with a rare talent, Jules.'

'No.' A vehement shake of the head. 'It's a privilege I've been blessed with. But it spoils you. For the future.'

Viv watches her with a prickle of unease. Something else is coming. Julia is gazing at an enormous vase of full-blown yellow roses on the piano. Then to the right of it, a silver-framed, black-and-white photograph that always sits in the same prominent position. Jules and her brother Max when they were teenagers, posed with theatrical formality as in an old-fashioned studio shot. Jules with her dark hair in ringlets, demure in a long-sleeved dress, sitting up straight; Max in a dark suit and tie, similarly curly-haired, leaning against the armchair. His elbow bent, chin resting in his hand.

The likeness between the two serious, conspicuously beautiful children is strong, and Viv has always found the photo affecting. Jules has cupped her chin in her hand, echoing her brother's pose. She seems to be staring at the view. A London expanse of leaden skies and wet grey roofs, glimpses of tall buildings, a church tower, the swaying tops of trees. The autumnal monochrome-inducing melancholy, Viv supposes, to someone raised in the sun. She says nothing and waits.

Jukes says conversationally, 'Where was I? Oh yes, the sweet hereafter. The bloody *afterlife*. The life you have when you're not having a life. And I'm shit-scared of it, Viv. The prospect of the afterlife scares me half to death.'

Viv can't recall her ever making such an admission. Its weight is only imperfectly camouflaged by the throwaway manner of its delivery. Jules has rarely alluded, except in a coded, playful way, to her deepest fears or her solitary state. Viv had no notion this was coming, and she doesn't question its significance.

Then, an abrupt change of tack. 'I've been spoilt bloody rotten. You know that better than anyone. Which is why I'd do almost any damn thing rather than give up the perks of the job. I'd drone on into mewling senility, God knows.'

Viv, along with God, knows this very well. She also knows that Jules needs to go on saying it to get it off her chest, although she can't see any possibility of that happening anytime soon. Right now she can see no solution to this predicament, which must eventually confront every great singer – and which all those on the outside have their own version of, and must face one day. Including Geoff and me, she thinks. Together, or apart.

But Jules faces specific professional issues, not to mention the personal ones. Acutely aware of the existence of these (whatever they may be) Viv murmurs, 'Because it's been your whole life.'

Jules looks up. 'I can't pretend I haven't known the sky would fall in some day – well, you'd have to be a real dill not to know that, wouldn't you? There's probably not a night in the past ten years when the dread of it hasn't crossed my mind. It's occupied my bed like some kind of hideous *incubus*, Viv.'

Viv thinks it wiser not to take this too seriously. 'There have been plenty of other less fiendish occupants. Admit it.'

A volcanic sigh. 'I can't let myself descend into a public embarrassment, screeching on into my dotage like some we could—' She pauses, but chooses not to name names. 'That really *would* be grotesque. No, my public has given me the order of the boot and I must grin and bear it, just like everyone else.'

Her friendship with Jules has given Viv a nodding acquaintance with the state of opera politics around the world. 'It's not your public's decision, you know that very well. It's those ageist apparatchiks, and bean-counters.'

'A bad excuse is better than none,' Jules says lightly. 'No, it's the age and the voice, that's the bugger of it. You can't rewind either of them. Singers don't last – unlike the fucking conductors and directors; they can go on forever. No, I've had a dream run and I can't complain if oblivion's formless ruin beckons.'

Her rich, infectious laugh rings out with apparent conviction. Vitality radiates from her, along with a certain feverishness. I know you're sixty-nine, thinks Viv, but you don't look it. Even without make-up and in a good light. Even in the spotlight.

She leans forward. 'Jules, listen, you still have the voice. You know you do. There are roles. Be realistic. You can't be *sure* it's the—'

'Vivi darling, shut up. You know the ending of the Purcell, don't you? *Dido and Aeneas*. Dido's lament?'

She gets up and goes to the piano, lifts the lid. 'Here's what they just heard me sing in Sydney.'

Jules rarely practises, but she keeps her piano tuned and is capable of accompanying herself in songs and arias at a basic level. She sings Dido's brief but devastating farewell.

When I am laid, am laid in earth
may my wrongs create no trouble, no trouble in thy breast.
Remember me, remember me!
but ah, forget my fate.
Remember me! but ah – forget my fate.

The signature Julia Jefferies voice envelops the room. To Viv it is instantly recognisable, a mature soprano, lower now than in her prime. But it retains the poetic purity, the intelligence, the knockout capacity to transmit emotion that has entranced legions of fans.

When the piano lid is replaced they sit for a long, meditative moment. Viv finds she is shaken, she has tears in her eyes. She focuses, blinking, on the vase of yellow roses. There is a delicate perfume in the room. Julia's flats are always filled with flowers, a badge of residence appearing magically the moment she flies in.

Her speaking voice, which Viv thinks has acquired more roseate notes itself over the years, breaks the silence. 'Then Dido kicks the bucket. It's very moving, isn't it? Quite beautiful. A few high Gs there. Quite tricky. *Remember me!* I felt I was saying goodbye, Viv. And I felt the audience knew it. There was an outpouring, and then a standing O. Every night.'

Viv imagines the sold-out auditorium. The hush, followed by the ovation. The tears flowing from women and men alike. They must indeed have thought that this was Julia's swansong. That, unannounced, she would choose the Sydney Opera House for her farewell appearances.

'Jules. It must have been beyond draining.'

'Too right. I was put through the wringer and hung out for all to behold.' She leans back, using both hands to lift her hair above her ears then let it fall back, a characteristic gesture, and then in another lightning change of mood (also characteristic) she throws Viv a conspiratorial look.

'My Aeneas was dear old Vince Farr from the olden days.' A reminiscent laugh. 'He proposed to me once.'

Encouraged by this less toxic topic Viv goes on to ask, 'Did Max come? The family?' She knows Julia is close to her brother, who is married unhappily, Jules has always said, to Patricia, a no-nonsense Englishwoman from Paignton. Jules is circumspect about family, on the whole, but she has never bothered to hide her dislike of her sister-in-law, dismissing her as prissy and suburban.

'Yes, they came. Of course they did.' She looks thoughtful.

Max and Patricia's two children are married and in their thirties. The unmarried and childfree Jules is a devoted aunt and great-aunt. Viv has met them all, and most often Max, who owns art galleries in Sydney and Melbourne and who contrives to juggle his schedule in order to attend, unfailingly, Julia's premières. Invariably on his own, as Viv recalls. She has often sat next to Max, and seen his face run with sweat from the tension of watching his sister sing. She has always thought him a strikingly attractive man, if somewhat distant.

'He's talking about getting divorced, at long last. He sent me those roses.'

'Divorced? *Max*? But he must be, what – seventy?'

'Mm. And it might be just talk. But you know what he's like, overflowing with rude health. And *joie de vivre*, which Pat did her level best to nip in the bud.'

'Isn't it a bit late in the day? For something so – so dramatic?' Viv considers the implications. 'I mean, think about it.' She thinks about it herself, in relation to her own situation. 'All that shared history. The children. The companionship. All that *stuff* to sort out.

All the spoils to divide. It would be so exhausting, apart from anything else.'

'Oh, give me patience! Late in the day? Is that how you think of yourself – sitting in the departure lounge?' Jules has jumped up and started to clear the table. 'The *companionship?* They don't have any companionship, they never have.'

Now she sounds positively irate, realises it, and says in an altered tone, 'Sorry, but people can get divorced at any age. Give themselves a chance to rock before the rot really sets in.' She has moved from irritation and impatience to lightheartedness in seconds. This is unusually mercurial, even for Jules.

'Well, you may be right. Have they separated?'

'I am right. No, they haven't. Not as yet. But I think it might happen.'

'And it would be a good thing, you think? On balance.'

'On balance?' Jules bristles again. 'Of course it would be a good thing. On any reckoning.'

Viv had been thinking they might be moving towards an appropriate moment to bring up the trouble with Geoff, but decides it would be prudent to stay with her earlier decision. Jules, understandably, is in a febrile state. Another depressing topic of conversation about the consequences of ageing might be one too many.

And anyway, they will see each other again very soon. Jules is keen to see Geoff, they have taken out their diaries and made dinner and theatre plans. There are shows at the National Gallery and the Royal Academy that Viv has been saving for Julia's arrival. Jules likes to keep up with everything when she hits town. The autumn opera season is up and running. Viv assumes she will want to keep up with that too, then wonders about it.

The light is fading fast as she leaves the flat and heads for the Tube. As she waits on the platform she goes over Geoff's incendiary sentence once more. She will live with it for a day or two while she decides what is to be done. Something must be done, of this there is no doubt. Something radical. Preferably something that is also constructive.

She reflects on the other meaning of the word sentence: a punishment for an offence. In Geoff's eyes I am guilty of the offence of being an older woman. But I'm a free agent. The rot has not set in, and Jules is quite right to react the way she did. I'm not parked in the departure lounge, or anywhere near it.

And as it turns out, Viv will not live with the sentence for a day or two before deciding what to do. The very next morning she will embark on a course of action that might be described as both radical and constructive. It might also be described as asking for trouble.

3

DISCRETION

Viv always did have an unpredictable streak. She would concede that in her youth this was teamed with a reckless tendency. As maturity kicked in, recklessness took a back seat. When her daughter was born it bowed out altogether and responsibility took over.

But, as she would be the first to acknowledge, the building blocks of personality never go away. They are always lurking in the background, awaiting some impetus, some provocation. And after two years of frustration, Geoff's sentence has provoked her to the point of doing something her closest friends, even Jules, might think was outside the square. Might think was imprudent. This surprising action will happen in twenty minutes' time, when she makes a telephone call.

Viv and Geoff are having two bathrooms renovated. While their Victorian house in West Hampstead couldn't be called elegant, it's a substantial four storeys and worth a great deal now. The improvements currently underway will highlight the flaws, but Viv isn't bothered by that. Anyway, she couldn't see Geoff agreeing to the financial and psychological assault of anything further.

There's been no progress today. Piotr, the young Polish plumber, is taking time off. Not that he's unreliable; his son was born just before dawn this morning, three weeks early. When she heard this news Viv urged him stay home as long as he needed. She said this in the face of her husband's opposition. Geoff can't bear the mess, disruption and dust. He is fundamentally good-natured, but not as laid-back as he used to be. These days his low tolerance level often takes her by surprise.

Her face stares back from a mirror streaked with grime. She takes a flannel and scrubs at her reflection, then holds up a hand mirror to view the back of her hair, the roots, twisting under the light to get a good view. Geoff looms up behind her.

'What on earth are you doing?'

'I'm overdue for a hair appointment.'

I've let it go, it's almost entirely grey now, she stops short of adding. Best not to bring it to his attention. He would probably say, why bother? Why not make a feminist statement and let it all grow out? Much cheaper and no hassle. He's probably thinking: no point is there, *at your age*, let's face it. Viv suspects that she is more concerned with what Geoff is probably thinking than what he's actually saying, just now.

To embrace the grey or banish it is a long-standing topic. Viv is well acquainted with Julia's views on the subject. Nuke the mothers, every last strand, is her advice. Jules has offered to call her personal colourist: I'm sure she'll squeeze you in if I say the word. Just now Viv is more inclined than usual to be swayed by Julia's views on matters of appearance, while making allowances for a degree of celebrity overkill.

Geoff says, '*Another* hair appointment? It looks perfectly all right to me.'

Viv can't remember the date of her last visit. 'Most women have their hair done every few weeks, Geoff. And that includes most *older* women.' She doesn't look at him as she drops this little barb, but thinks: you don't see my hair because you don't look at me anymore. Nor have you for two years.

'You're just jealous that I've still got mine,' she adds and regrets it, but only a little, when she sees the shadow of hurt. Geoff is sensitive about his hair loss. She veers away from him. 'I'll be in the shed if you need me,' she says. In the past they might have touched. Physical contact used to be an essential part of the relationship, in small, everyday ways. A hand on the shoulder, a pat on the behind. Not anymore.

It was Geoff who christened Viv's workroom her shed. He leaves her to it and rarely sets foot up here, on the top floor. The width of the house, with exuberant turquoise floorboards and a small bathroom, it was their daughter Daisy's den until she left home.

Now, lined floor-to-ceiling with Viv's overstuffed bookshelves, it exudes a bustling sense of purpose. Trestle tables piled with material scraps, computer and printer, sewing machine. A sheet of paper is pinned to a cork board, displaying a geometric grid of pencilled lines. This is a design for a patchwork quilt, Viv's second. The end product is intended – over-generously, she now thinks – for the matrimonial bed.

Since she left publishing Viv's recreational reading has, if anything, doubled. But she has also surprised everyone by taking up the craft of quilting. Her first effort was smaller and less ambitious: a cot quilt. This was done on spec, and since she was unsuccessful in concealing it from Daisy it has been a source of mortification. It is hidden away now in the back of a cupboard, out of sight if not of mind. Daisy is thirty-eight, and her five-year on-again–off-again relationship with Marco would seem, as far as her parents are concerned, to have stalled. Daisy and Marco will be returning to London soon after a week in Rome.

The design of the new quilt resembles a jigsaw with squares and triangles of material pinned up in experimental positions. To Viv, it's a puzzle awaiting her solution. An intricate puzzle with multiple solutions, rather like life. Viv's friend Joy believes that everything in life happens for a reason, but Viv believes in pre-emptive action. Certain actions are inherently adventurous and involve taking risks. She has decided she is not averse to taking the odd risk, even at her age.

And today, as chance would have it, the latest copy of *The Economist* is lying next to a jumble of colourful material cuttings. Lying right there in front of her nose. And Viv's hand is moved to flip it over to the inside back cover, to the personal columns.

But to call this chance is being more than a little disingenuous, and she knows it. For a start, Geoff likes to go out every Sunday morning and pick up the papers and a magazine or two along with fresh croissants. He likes balance, and often comes back with *Private Eye, New Statesman, The Economist* or *The Spectator.* Viv has had occasion to study the various personal columns on and off for a while, and can repeat verbatim the wording of a particular advertisement. It's a short ad, hardly more than a paragraph, and no matter which periodical it appears in is always the same.

It reads:

DISCRETION

Are you heterosexual, in a committed relationship that is not, for personal reasons, meeting your needs? At **Discretion** we enable individually screened introductions that are appropriate, intelligent and feasible. Ring Martin for more information and an initial, confidential interview.

There is a website, which Viv has looked at more than once, and a London phone number, which she knows by heart. She picks up her mobile, then replaces it in her pocket and switches the radio on. It happens to be playing an aria from one of Julia's operas.

She turns the music down, looks at the door (which is closed) and then takes out the phone again, balancing it in the palm of her hand. The sequence of movements suggests a kind of ritual. It suggests the possibility that she may have performed these actions before, perhaps a number of times. This time, however, she doesn't put the phone away.

The call is picked up on the first ring. Don't give them time for the cold feet to kick in. Her heartbeat has speeded up. A man's voice says, 'The Discretion Agency, Martin Glover speaking.' He has a pleasant, classless accent.

Viv had expected some sort of intermediary. 'Oh yes, hello. Hi. I'd like some information please,' she says. She hears herself sounding less assured than usual. Sounding slightly flustered. 'I mean, I know it's all there on the website, Mr Glover, but—' What she means is, what kind of a business is this? And more to the point: who do you do business with?

'What would you like to know? Just fire a few questions at me and I'll do my best to answer them. Please call me Martin.'

'What would I like to know? Well, let's see. Is the agency designed for women as well? Is it for any age group? How do you check people out? I mean, you know, how does it all work, exactly?' She's pacing around the workroom. 'Sorry, that's too many questions being fired at you already. I'm not usually like this, I think I'm a bit – off balance.' Fending off a panic attack, more likely.

'You haven't done this sort of thing before. Don't worry, most of my clients haven't either.'

'Really, they haven't?' Viv is surprised to hear this. It's heartening.

'No,' Martin says, 'they certainly haven't. For most of them, men as well as women, this is the one and only time they will have anything to do with an introduction agency. And for most of them it's a bit of a last resort.'

'Before giving up on the whole damn thing?'

'Well, quite possibly. But we have no age restrictions, and you'd be surprised how many people don't give up.' Before a client is signed, there is a preliminary, in-depth interview. This helps screen out people with other agendas. The interview is obligatory, and on a no-obligation basis on both sides. That's the deal.

Martin conducts these interviews himself. He set up the agency with his wife; it's a small, personal operation. Maybe that's why it seems to work rather well. But he likes to think it's thoroughly professional, nonetheless.

'So, you think there might be a chance for me? Or an off-chance of one?' Martin is amused, she thinks, but in a nice way. By which she means non-patronising. Before they make a time and date for the interview, he says, he should bring the housekeeping side to her attention. There is the small business of the fee. Which turns out to be not inconsiderable, although the women's rate is a quarter of that of the men.

Viv approves. It sounds like a very gallant way of doing things. Not exactly, Martin admits; it's to try to attract more women. There is always an imbalance. Well, that's better still, isn't it, she says, from a woman's point of view. Martin adds that they also offer a cut-price rate for three months, with five intros guaranteed. But this is for men only. Women get a whole year for the same investment.

Investment. An interesting word to use. Viv notices words, and she's feeling more relaxed. 'When you say there are no age restrictions …'

'Well, we have clients on our books from every age range. But the majority are middle-aged.'

'Oh.' All their friends think they are still middle-aged. But Geoff wouldn't agree.

'Well, middle-age is often the period when problems within a marriage commonly tend to emerge, if they're going to. And when people have significant investments, such as children, and more compelling reasons not to divorce. Illness of a partner causes others to use our service. Or incapacity – for whatever reason.'

'Yes, I see,' says Viv.

'May I ask your first name?'

She does a quick mental toss-up and comes down on the side of honesty. 'Vivien. And by the way, I suppose I'd better tell you that

I'm sixty-seven,' she says. It sounds ominous. Jules wouldn't have said that. And Jules would have given a false name, like Germaine. 'Might that squeeze in as middle-aged? Is it too old, Martin? Seriously, I mean.'

Not necessarily, is his reply, which while no doubt truthful doesn't fill her with, as Jules might say, ineluctable confidence. Still, they make a date for the obligatory, no-obligation interview. There is a slot available this Thursday afternoon, which is very soon. In three days' time, in fact. He suggests the coffee lounge of a hotel near Victoria Station. Most people can get there and it's nice and quiet, Martin says. There's a useful screen of ornamental plants at the far end. He generally takes up a tactical position behind that.

'In hiding?'

'Well, only if it seems advisable.' A smile in the voice. 'But I promise to come out.'

Viv is feeling slightly light-headed. 'Can I ...'

'Ring me if you change your mind?' The voice is reassuring. 'Of course. No worries.'

She puts the phone in her pocket and sits down to take stock. She finds she has a stiff neck, and rotates her shoulders. The particular nature of the conversation makes her think of her mother. Judith Quarry is ninety-one, and still living in her own home.

Until recently, Judith wouldn't have been seen dead in what Viv is wearing today: old jeans and T-shirt over a long-sleeved top. She'd have worn something she deemed more alluring to the opposite sex. When Viv saw that her mother had stopped dressing with the opposite sex in mind she realised that Judith had crossed an invisible line. She was now, in anyone's language, an old woman.

Viv's jeans may be old too but she can still get into them. Unlike some of her friends she hasn't put on weight – well, no more than a few pounds. She rides her bike to the shops against safety-conscious Geoff's wishes, and since last spring she also rides to the local gym to work out. This was prompted by the slogan of a chain of fitness clubs, plastered all over billboards in the Tube: *Look Better Naked*.

Geoff works out too. He used to play cricket, but since the arthritis in his bowling arm he's taken up croquet, which has proved to be a ferociously competitive sport. He is lean and fit; his lack of interest in conjugal relations can't be put down to incapacity – one of Martin Glover's words. For a while Viv had wondered whether Geoff's interest might have been tweaked if she looked better naked, and had signed up for a course with a personal trainer.

The desired outcome did not eventuate, but she has kept it up. She goes to the gym two or three times a week to do cardio and weight-training exercises. The need to be *toned* is a pressing one among Viv's friends. Women who lift weights live longer and have a superior body image, is the prevailing wisdom. Everyone subscribes to the theory, if not quite so often to the practice.

The only women of her acquaintance who don't care about it are members of her friend Joy's quilting circle. Joy, originally from Louisiana, is also a successful writer of children's picture books; she was one of Viv's discoveries. But she's forty-four, a whole generation younger, and she assures Viv coyly that she gets more than enough exercise the natural way. Joy has lived in London more than half her life, but she likes to play up her Southern drawl for Viv's benefit. 'Maybe I'll start tangling with my body image when I get to your age, honey. That's if I haven't *passed* already.'

Viv knows she only says this to keep her quiet, and has no intention of tangling with it. She accepts that Joy's body image, forged in the flat river country outside Baton Rouge, has a different template from her own.

Viv's mind fast-tracks to two o'clock on Thursday afternoon. Martin Glover, an indeterminate figure, will be waiting to meet her from behind a screen of plants at the far end of a hotel coffee lounge.

Through the gaps in the screen he will see her approach before she can see him. She has no illusions about the coming interview: it's an exam, a *viva voce* she will have to pass in order to go any further – should she wish to do so. No obligations on either side. That's the deal.

First impressions are important. This woman of sixty-seven is an unknown quantity to Martin Glover. How does she appear? There are a handful of things Viv is powerless to change even if she wanted to.

Gender and age are what a stranger will see first, and process automatically. And – thinking of Joy – skin colour. Age, gender and race, pure and simple. But there is a fourth item on the stranger's internal checklist, and Viv can't pretend otherwise because it's as true of her as of anyone else.

That complicated item is sex appeal. The accidents of birth that make up your level of attractiveness, and that of the unknown person coming towards you. Your pulling power. Everyone has an internal gauge. *Men are hard-wired.*

But like the small matter of the fee being not so small, there are other components in the not-so-insignificant matter of one's package. Over some of these elements Viv knows she has some control. Even if, she tries to stop herself adding, they are limited *at my age.*

There is the matter, for example, of the hair. Like it or not, grey (or – horrors – white) adds *aeons*, in Julia's opinion. Is that what you want? Viv inspects her hair once more. It's grey, it's shaggy, it needs remedial surgery. Anyone can see that. A man like Martin Glover, accustomed to summing people up and assessing them, would certainly see it.

Well, when you want something done well and in a hurry, go straight to the top. She remembers Julia's offer, and picks up the phone. Jules is coming to dinner tonight, but Viv will suggest they meet for a coffee first. Or perhaps a drink. Viv doesn't want her husband to be anywhere in earshot when she acquaints Jules with Geoff's sentence. And the specific action the s-word has prompted her to take.

Julia's curiosity, a dominant trait, is piqued by the urgency of Viv's request and by her refusal to elaborate over the phone. She agrees to lean on her personal colourist Ramona, an angel she has known forever. And within five minutes Jules rings Viv back.

The gods are smiling, the angelic Ramona has buckled under pressure (the ranks of those who have buckled under Julia's pressure being considerable, and ever-growing) and agreed to give up her lunch hour today. *Today*, Viv! That's all right, isn't it? You did say it was urgent, didn't you? This is the one and only time she can fit you in before Thursday. Take it or leave it, adds Jules, with an undertone of warning.

Jules once remarked that it was harder to get an appointment with Ramona than a table at The Ivy. Oh, I'll take it, Viv says, looking at her watch. She runs downstairs full pelt, like someone half her age. In ten minutes flat she has thrown off her work clothes, picked out something more respectable (better trousers, smarter shirt) put on some make-up, and grabbed coat, scarf and bag from the bedroom.

Geoff has made himself a study in a cosy nook off the sitting room. He has a worn leather armchair in which he likes to sprawl and read science fiction and books on the origins of the universe. Viv looks in. 'I'm off.'

'Where to, poppet? Why are you in such a hurry?' Geoff asks, without looking up. He has always been verbally affectionate and hasn't altered much in this regard. Viv thinks the endearments are automatic, they must have rusted in.

'Hair appointment, like I said. And I'm meeting Jules later. We might shop for a bit.'

'I thought you didn't like shopping.'

'No, I hate it, but I need something for winter. I've got to go, or I'll be late.' She heads into the hall, calling, 'And don't say my clothes look all right to you.' And don't dare think, what's the point of buying new clothes at your age?

'You seem to have plenty in your cupboard,' Geoff calls back, mildly. 'You're taking over mine, remember? But it's true, you always look perfectly all right to me.'

'I'm aiming higher than perfectly all right.' The door slams, then opens again. 'I nearly forgot, Geoff,' she shouts, 'Jules is coming for dinner.'

That's good, she hears him say. Can I do anything to help?

Since the sentence, which has not been mentioned again, Viv has noticed a tendency in Geoff to be more helpful than usual. Only a tendency; nothing else has changed. Nothing, or everything.

4

SELF-IMPROVEMENT

You don't ride your bike when you're going to get your hair done, and certainly not to Julia's hair salon. Vivien takes the Tube to Holborn and arrives in Sicilian Avenue where, after some preliminary discussion, she will proceed to have the grey nuked by Ramona. Ramona is not the style-Nazi of Viv's imagining. Instead she is a buxom Scot in her early fifties whose attitude towards the older Julia is indulgent and motherly.

'Ah well, I'm part of the accoutrements where our Julia is concerned, you see,' she says, as if this explains everything. 'I'm one of all the wee pieces of furniture in Julia's life.' Viv likes her on sight and is charmed by the metaphor.

She hadn't intended to have a haircut as well, necessarily, but upon setting eyes on her, Ramona is moved to observe that a wee trim wouldn't go astray. Her last trim now, when might *that* have been? Viv is unsure. It might have been, let's see – well, it might have been a few months ago. Perhaps even several months, Your Honour, she is tempted to append. Such an admission in this very high-end temple of self-improvement rings like a guilty plea in the dock.

Ramona nods. We do have to work at keeping our hair tamed, do we not, or it'll start thinking it rules the roost. Especially your headstrong kind, dear. Give it an inch and it'll take a mile! And she beckons Danni over. Ariane, Julia's personal stylist of choice, is *not* available – she's fully booked, as per usual, but Danni is new and very good. Ramona leans over and whispers, Don't let the presentation give you the willies; Danni's a pet, and she knows what she's doing.

Danni is very young and short-skirted, with multiple piercings and cropped gamin hair. In comparison to half the clientele, and certainly to Viv's eyes, she appears dangerously thin. She appraises Viv's bushy locks and makes several rapid observations. Although offered in a neutral way and in a down-to-earth Yorkshire accent, they come embellished with authority. Some thinning out, some shaping, and let's take a look at the length. Like, how it is now, it's a bit heavy and draggy, right? And all those split ends and straggly bits, we'll get rid of them, yeah? Nothing massive, not really, just a tidy up. Yeah? A really *good* tidy up. It will look *sooo* much better, trust me.

Viv decides to trust Danni, although she is under no illusion that she has made a decision on the matter. Being in a salon such as this one reminds her of having a surgical procedure: you consign yourself to a total stranger's capable (you hope) hands. Danni's small hands, sporting black nail polish and diamante studs, prove to be deft and capable. When Viv is out of them she is passed on to Ramona's. But it doesn't feel like an impersonal production line. The process is accomplished with professional attention and panache.

Three hours into the afternoon she is pleased with the result; her revamped hair now has a discernible contour, thanks to Danni – mid-length, between jaw and shoulder. To complement the shape of your face, right? It has reverted to a discreet mid-brown, much like its old colour. Only now it has texture and interest rather than being plain mousy, says Ramona, because we want to avoid the boring old mouse, do we not?

Viv agrees that we want to avoid this, although she wonders aloud about the qualifications of an interesting brown. Something that is neither drab nor timid, Ramona explains, as this is not your personality, dear, and our hair should always be an expression of

33

our personality. This is one of the advantages we ladies have over our menfolk, age-wise. Ramona wears her dark auburn hair tellingly, Viv now perceives, in a French roll.

She has impressed on Ramona the need for the colour to look natural (as far as this is possible, age-wise) and to be sure to leave in some artful hints of grey for verisimilitude. I know, pet, you don't want your wee hubby to notice a thing, Ramona says cheerily. Oh, I'm sure my hubby won't notice, replies Viv, not a thing. And anyway, she adds, *sotto voce*, it's not for him. Ooh, is it not, then, says Ramona with an upward inflexion, *I* see. But she is experienced enough to see that Vivien is not inclined to go there. Nor does Viv yet know where she is going, as she would be the first to admit.

The bill seems astronomical, especially with the tip for both Ramona and Danni that Jules said was mandatory, but Viv has to admit the end product is an improvement on that wrought by her local salon. A distinct upgrade. She might even make it a habit, once every four to six weeks, like some of the smarter, more elegant women she knows. But what an expensive habit that would be. Perhaps once every three months is more like it.

Jules, meeting her outside a wine bar in Belsize Park, performs an operatic double-take. There, she says, didn't I tell you Ramona knew her onions?

She said my hair needed to be tamed, Viv tells her, or it would end up ruling the roost. She also said, unprompted, that my personality was neither drab nor mousy.

Of course it's not, says Jules. I've told you that, any number of times. She examines her friend, walks round her in the street, head on one side. Jules herself, in gradations of pink and black today with a fuchsia scarf and pert black fedora, looks as if she is off to a photo shoot.

'Yes, it's a big improvement, Viv,' she says. 'Not that it didn't look all right before, but it's got *style* now. And the colour's great.'

'Years off my age?'

'Years off. Absolutely.'

'You'd never know?'

'Never.'

Viv says that's just as well, because the whole operation could have bought a month at the Waldorf Astoria. They enter the wine bar, very chic, very upmarket. Just as Jules has contacts who can wangle a table at The Ivy and practically every hot ticket in town, Viv imagines she also has a network of informers whose business it is to suss out exclusive little haunts like this. She feels she's living, albeit temporarily, an alternate life. A diverting life of daily luxuries, great and small, and one in which her name and face are recognised on the international artistic circuit.

Viv often has this feeling when out with Jules. It is not at all unpleasant and sometimes quite heady, although she has always returned without a thought to her own less ritzy existence. Still, Julia's life, seen from close quarters, has been a source of wonderment.

Do you ever cease to be a celebrity once you have been one? Not in your own eyes, she suspects. There must be an enduring part of your self-image that sees you as more special than your fellow humans. That sees you as a creature apart. Though Jules does not give herself airs, and never has. And we are all creatures apart in our own eyes, aren't we, as Viv has said to Geoff.

Julia's demeanour is subtly different today. Viv was expecting this. In her own flat, in an intimate one-on-one situation, surrounded by her own possessions, Jules tends to be more toned down. More real, Viv might have said much earlier in their acquaintance. She now thinks that the other side of Jules, the public aspect, is just as genuine. It's the flip side of her personality.

She toys with the idea of asking Jules how she is feeling about the future, and decides against it. She doesn't want to risk altering her mood too dramatically, not before she has had the chance to air her own edgy revelation. Jules hasn't referred to their last meeting. She seems upbeat, or relatively so. Her agent called earlier to schedule a lunch tomorrow. Jules feels that he may have something up his sleeve.

What's your poison, Viv, she asks as they commandeer a couple of armchairs in a dark corner of the bar. Jules always goes for the dark corners and the far tables. Viv prefers to be in the centre of a room, in the thick of the action. How curious, to prefer to be in the middle where everyone has a good view of you, when you are, from the point of view of a smart restaurant, a non-event no one is interested in watching.

'I'll have a dry martini with a twist,' she says, surprising Jules, who has never known her to order anything other than tea, or at a stretch white wine, at the relatively early hour of four in the afternoon. But Jules had selected this wine bar over a cafe for good reason. I thought you might need a drink to loosen the lips, she says complacently. All right, out with it, I've been on tenterhooks all day. Stop dropping coy little hints and let's have the full disclosure. What is it with Thursday?

'With Thursday? An appointment is scheduled,' says Viv. Her stomach flutters. 'An in-depth interview with an agency offering discreet personal introductions.'

Julia's expression undergoes some rearrangement. She wasn't expecting this. Is that right? she says slowly. You don't say.

'For those whose carnal relations are a thing of the past, and for whom rumpy-pumpy is a distant memory. For those, in short, whose intimate relationship is not meeting their needs.'

As one of a select few in the know, Jules is up to speed with Viv's personal difficulties over the past two years. Her eyebrows shoot up. 'Good god, Viv. You daredevil.'

Viv prefers to call her action a constructive response to criticism. She is pleased with Jules's reaction. Both pleased and, if she is honest, a touch more destabilised than she was already feeling. Julia's mobile face is unusually eloquent. At the present moment it is communicating, as Viv correctly identifies, an element of admiring surprise together with some perturbation.

What brought this on? I mean, Jules says, is it just two years of accumulated frustration boiling over? Or, and she regards Viv with a keen eye, has something else happened to change things?

'Well, you might say that.' Viv takes a deep breath. 'There has been an unforeseen development. Words were said. A sentence was uttered. A sentence of some – of some *import*.' She stops. She is finding it surprisingly hard to get to the point.

'Viv, you know you can tell me,' Jules says, gently. And then, when this fails to do the trick, 'Come on. Spit it out.'

Another deep breath. 'Geoff said: men are hard-wired not to find older women attractive.'

'*He didn't*.' Viv can see that Jules needs no assistance in processing the implications of this. She gets them, in their mind-blowing entirety, right away.

'I'm afraid he did.'

'*Geoff* said that? To you?' She drums her feet on the floor. 'But that's terrible. That's a truly terrible thing to say.'

'It is, isn't it? It happened a few days ago. Out of the blue, really. Although I had brought up the subject yet again. I suppose he could have just said it out of exasperation. But that doesn't excuse it.'

Why the hell hadn't she said something about this before?

'Because it seemed a bit of a bridge too far when I saw you. On top of, you know, your own problems. Which are really much more—'

Jules cuts her off with a snort. 'You mean my interminable whinging and ghastly self-pity? You should have told me to shut up, Viv. You should have told me to shut the fuck up in no uncertain terms.'

She glances down the bar. It is thinly peopled at this hour, two singletons and three other couples their own age or younger conversing in low voices. At least one of those couples in a bar like this at this time of day, Jules thinks, is probably having an affair, and it is just as likely to be the oldest couple of the three.

'Let me tell you something, Viv. It's quite absurd to say all men are like this. I can vouch for that personally.'

They exchange a droll glance. Viv knows that Jules will not elaborate. She thinks, but you are a famous woman. In certain elite circles, at least. One cannot pretend that's not going to influence things.

She says, 'You also know perfectly well, Jules, that given the choice of two, and all things being equal, a man would prefer to shag the younger woman.' Viv has always grappled with the word fuck, and uses it sparingly.

Jules has no such reluctance. 'Answer me this, then. All things being equal, who would *you* prefer to fuck, given a one-off choice with no repercussions: a paunchy old misery-guts or a gorgeous young hunk? Excuse me, Viv, but an assertion like Geoff's is balderdash. It puts all men in the same basket. It takes into account nothing about anything.'

She draws breath, sensing that Viv is unconvinced. 'It's on a level with those hoary old claims they used to make about women. You know, how *all women* were biologically geared to have babies and so they were too emotional to fly planes and too dim to vote. You can't assert that *all men* are hard-wired to do anything much, except the basics.'

Jules, who has ordered a slimming white-wine spritzer, pauses to sample it. 'Besides, they don't talk about their feelings, hard-wired or otherwise, so how would anyone know? From a scholarly point of view the statement is grossly sloppy, for a start. As someone who's supposed to be a scientist, Geoff should know that.'

Viv thinks there may be a grain of truth in it. She also thinks that Geoff was really talking about himself, and not necessarily about every other man in the world. But apart from whether it's scientifically accurate, there is the fact of it being said at all. They both agree on one thing, that the sentence is an example, a comparatively rare one, of something which, once said, can never be taken back, or forgotten, or even overlooked. It's a point of no return.

Jules is still dealing with the point at issue. As she sees it, this is the matter of Geoff's holistic competence.

'You know him better than me, but it's unlike him to say something as unkind and hurtful. He's a bit depressed, isn't he? You've suspected that for quite a while. It could be hormonal. Men have hormones too, they tell me. Is he having mood swings? It might be the *mano*pause. This has always existed, as we know, but could this be a new strain, in which a sophisticated, tertiary-educated man relapses into the chauvinist attitudes of his youth? Well, a *moderately* sophisticated man. Or a strain of Tourette's, where he emits offensive statements without warning? A blokey version of the hot flush? It could well be that.'

Viv is rapidly regaining her equanimity, under the influence of the martini and Julia's particular approach to deep and meaningful conversations. Julia's temperament is buoyant, overall. Conversations rarely get bogged down in depth and meaningfulness for long.

Rather late for the hot flush, Viv observes, bearing in mind Geoff is sixty-nine. Well, it could be a rare *mani*festation, says her friend, undeterred. 'Or, perhaps even more likely, it's a midlife crisis that's been developmentally delayed. All men being developmentally delayed to a greater or lesser extent. As is well recognised in the literature.'

'Since we're in the business of non-evidence-based generalisations.'

'You know it makes sense.' Jules shakes her head. 'What on earth was he not thinking?'

'I can only assume he finds my ageing self physically repulsive.'

This pulls Jules up, hard. She lifts her hair with both hands and lets it drop abruptly. 'Whoa, Viv. You look great for your age. Great, period. Don't say that, please. Of course he can't.'

'Why ever not?'

Jules breathes out through dilated nostrils. '*Why?* Because it's crap, that's why. Because it's not true. Because you've had such a good relationship. Because he loves you.' Her shoulders sag. 'Because any bloody number of things.'

'He doesn't touch me anymore. He's definitely not incapacitated. What more proof does one need?'

An affair might explain it, Jules supposes, at last. They have worked this painful idea over, well before now. Geoff has denied it, of course, but it's quite possible. There are obvious candidates. Geoff belongs to an eccentric circle of sci-fi buffs. Mostly men, but the odd bright young woman. There are mixed teams at the croquet club. It can't be ruled out. All in all, it seems the most likely scenario.

But it still doesn't quite add up, Viv says. I mean, I think I'd know. Although they all say that, don't they?

'You're both out a fair bit, what with his sci-fi loonies and croquet. And your quilting circle and refugees, and so on.'

'Yes I know, but even so ... Maybe it's his roundabout way of saying he wants a divorce.'

She can see that Jules has thought of this, but hasn't wanted to say it. Nor does she want to talk about it now.

'Listen, Viv, I think we may be barking up the wrong tree. We may be looking for some esoteric explanation when it might just be a straightforward case of loss of libido. As simple as that. A consequence of age, let's face it. For *some* people, that is. I believe some people experience a *consummate* loss of interest in sex as they get older, pardon the pun. Not you, obviously.'

And what, Viv thinks, about you? On this subject you are as opaque as always.

'Men don't like it when it happens to them. Death blow to their masculinity, and so forth. And the whole thing's got Geoff down, so to speak. He's not himself anymore.'

'I've only told this to one other friend, so far,' Viv says. 'A younger friend. She told me on the phone that I had four options. One, ignore it and do nothing. Two, leave him. Three, murder him. Four, have an affair.'

Which friend is this?

'It's Joy. Of all my friends she is far and away the most practical. I think it comes from writing for children.' She thinks about this. 'Although that does sound counter-intuitive.'

Well, Jules thinks Joy's advice is spot on. And the fourth option does have a lot going for it. The others are less immediately appealing. And bumping him off could land Viv in very hot water.

Jules sips her drink delicately. 'So, an affair it is. I could probably rustle up a tenor or two, but they're always travelling, so they're not ideal liaison material. Why not select a nubile male of your acquaintance? Wouldn't this be a more sensible way of going about it? Cheaper, too, presumably.'

Viv says she doesn't know anyone suitable. Or anyone suitably nubile who is also unattached. She doesn't want to cause any ructions. She'd rather everything was organised and above board.

Above board? Jules gives her a jocular look. She wants to know about the agency. 'Since the subject will be off limits at dinner, I take it. What have you found out? I'm mesmerised, Viv, to put it mildly. I'm also mildly trepidatious. Have you checked out their bona fides? It might be a mistake to assume they recruit purely from rarefied literary catchments.'

'The clientele might not all be pseudo-intellectuals, you mean?'

'There could be a danger of undesirable blow-ins is what I mean. Eager to sample the genteel erotic wares of the literati.'

Viv is inclined to think the literati's erotic wares might be a fictional creation. In any event they're unlikely to be a stand-out attraction. Jules shakes her head. 'You could get any senile, out-to-pasture old fart foisted on you, mark my words. The bottom line is, you have to be a bit careful at our age, to be brutally frank.'

This will not be music to Viv's ears, she knows, but it's strategically sensible in these matters, where she is proposing to pick up total strangers—

'At *our age?*' Viv interrupts. 'I thought you were keen to convince me we were not yet parked in the departure lounge?' Anyway, she doubts if a person's degree of social desirability would be among her criteria at all. How would one even measure such a thing? 'And furthermore, Jules, I am not proposing to pick up total strangers, that's the whole point.'

Julia hears her out with growing disapproval. Viv really *does* need to keep a sensible handle on this issue. I'm being your mother, she says firmly, and telling you to be careful who you choose to go to bed with. How *is* Judith, by the way?

'My mother wouldn't be seen dead saying anything so bourgeois.'

'Well, there are basic safeguards to adhere to. It's not like the sixties, when you could jump in the sack with whoever you fancied, by and large, and all you had to fear was herpes or crabs. Or a mild dose of the clap. These days the dangers are a lot less benign.'

Please don't get on to drugs and safe sex and women being dismembered and disembowelled, Viv murmurs. Please don't go down any of those roads. I didn't come down in the last shower, and I'm not a spring chicken. Which is part of the problem.

But Jules is in no mood to be put off. Take *vetting*. Viv needs to know that people have been thoroughly checked to weed out the con artists, as well as the weirdos and psychos. She looks sideways at Viv as she says this, wishing to put the wind up, but not wishing to put it up too much. What Viv is contemplating doing is unorthodox, it's under the radar. What she must never do is lower her guard. She shouldn't imagine that an agency like this one is a form of insurance. It cannot buy safety.

Viv says, 'Just to please you I shall be on the lookout for unwashed, depraved Lotharios who prey on foolish old women.' She throws fortune hunters into the mix for good measure, although anyone who looked at her and imagined she was harbouring a fortune would need their head read.

They take an Uber to West Hampstead, where Geoff has laid the table for three, put some Hendrick's in the fridge and opened a bottle of red to breathe. He greets Julia with a bear hug, which Viv thinks is more than she has scored herself for many a month. Jules is looking as glam as ever, he enthuses. Eternally youthful.

This is an unfortunate slip, as matters stand. An undercurrent passes between the three of them. No one, however, bats an eyelid.

The lapse prompts Geoff to recall that Viv has been to the hairdresser. He is complimentary. It looks very nice. 'And the colour, Geoff,' prods Jules. Yes, that's nice too. But it sounds perfunctory to Viv's ears.

The women know that Geoff knows something (although by no means all) of what they have been discussing over the past couple of hours. And Geoff is perfectly well aware that his wife will have shared his contentious sentence, word for word, and that the wider implications will by now have been thoroughly dissected. Both women know he is aware of this, and Geoff knows that they know.

This is how it is when old friends have shared a flat in their youth. But in order to be relaxed and convivial together, as is their way, the subject that is uppermost in everyone's mind will not be aired this evening. They will enjoy each other's company and recycle a number of old jokes. It will seem, on the face of it, as if nothing has changed.

Viv makes a pasta sauce while Julia and Geoff drink gin and tonic at the kitchen table, and catch up. This is largely focused on what Jules describes as the big fat full stop in her career. Geoff, shaking the vinaigrette in a jar, is sympathetic. Empathetic, even. He knows what it's like to have your life behind you and bugger all to do.

'But you chose to leave,' says Jules. 'You weren't given the bum's rush.'

Geoff shrugs. 'No, but it would have happened. One just got in first in a vain attempt to hang on to one's self-respect.' Viv is surprised to hear him say this. He and Jules nod sagely. Self-respect is something they feel strongly about. It has been a central driver of both their careers.

Jules looks at him. 'All that time. How to kill it? Meaningfully, I mean, not just belting balls through hoops and droning on about little green men.' It's a tease that usually gets a rise. 'You don't have any problem, do you, Viv?'

'But I'm not killing time. I like what I do.'

Jules tweaks the table settings. 'The blade of the knife should always point inwards, Geoff. Didn't your mother tell you?' She sighs. 'It all boils down to finding a substitute for something you've given your life to and adored.' Viv sees she is worried this may be too close to the bone.

It's not lost on them that this is a privileged conversation. They are lucky to have the prospect, says Geoff, of having a retirement, let alone of living into it. And of living into one's *old age*, Viv adds sharply. To defuse this, Jules raises another matter that concerns them all: the continuing saga of Daisy and her boyfriend. She takes seriously her position as godmother to Daisy Julia Mayberry.

Neither she nor Daisy's parents like Marco very much – not much at all, really – but what can you do? Daisy is getting (rapidly) on for thirty-nine, and it's her life. But if she is going to have a baby, and they know this is what she wants, she needs to get her skates on. Marco is not keen to procreate and has thus far been successful in avoiding it.

For a while those on the outside looking in had rated this fortunate, since Marco and fatherhood were a discouraging mix to contemplate. But the march of time is forcing a re-think, and it may be a case of making the best of a bad job. At least Marco has one. And not a bad one, either. A former ace computer hacker, he's now high up in IT security, an area none of them has much of a clue about. He earns enough to subsidise Daisy's more challenging career as a painter of miniature portraits.

And neither does Marco have any transmittable genetic defects, as far as anyone knows. Other than his disastrous personality, says Geoff. This is something of a family joke, though not one ever made in Daisy's presence.

The conversation moves on. Easy, comfortable, and substantially evasive.

5

THE INTERVIEW

Viv and Julia share the same GP, tucked away in a small street near the British Museum. Viv has been friends with Nerida Clifford since they were at Oxford. She thinks it's quite possible that Nerida knows her better than her husband does; certain intimate details about herself, at least. Geoff was always squeamish about medical matters, even though he worked in pharmaceuticals. Today is a case in point.

'Greetings, m'dear. Long time no see. What would seem to be the problem?' This is Nerida's standard intro, however recently Viv may have been in, after they have greeted one another with a kiss on both cheeks.

'The pesky problem would seem to be pelvic-floor dryness.' And today Viv feels bound to add, 'Age related, no doubt.'

'No doubt, but we have cunning potions with which to tackle it.' Nerida looks at her computer screen. 'We might kill two birds while we're at it. You're due for a pap smear. Debag, and let's have a dekko at the nether regions. Is this a recent phenomenon?'

Viv doesn't think Nerida talks like this to all her patients. It's a throwback to their time at Somerville.

'Not really. One has just lived with it; you know how it is.' As usual, Viv reverts seamlessly to the same lingo.

'One just hasn't felt the need to do anything about it until now.' Shrewd, Nerida, and super-tactful. She has made connections and drawn conclusions without having to be told a thing. She remarks, 'Good hair day, btw. Been having a bit of a makeover, have we?'

From her prone position Viv can't see Nerida's face, but she knows how it will look: bland and innocent. Ditto with her follow-up question about Geoff's state of health.

'Geoff is quite well, thank you.'

'Busy? Or, perchance, not busy enough?'

'That's just it, really. I think he may have a mild case of depression.' She hadn't anticipated this subject, but Nerida always did have a sixth sense.

'They all get it when they retire.' Nerida goes to her desk. 'It's all ship-shape down there, you can cover up now.' She rips off her latex gloves and peers at the computer screen. 'These high-flying men. Don't know what to do with themselves when they're no longer top of the heap. Won't seek help. Won't talk. Won't do nothin'. *N'est-ce pas?*'

'*Exactement.*'

They exchange an expressionless glance. 'Well,' says Nerida, tapping out a little rhythm on the desk, 'a woman's gotta do what a woman's gotta do.'

Viv nods. 'How true that is. Jules is in town.'

'Yes, her nibs has been in touch. Talking about drowning her sorrows with an end-of-career wing-ding. I egged her on.'

Julia's parties, bringing together a mix of friends from all periods of her professional life and outside of it, are highly esteemed. No skimping on booze or catering. At a period in their lives when most people's interest in these activities has undergone a steep decline, Julia's has, if anything, increased. This is not unconnected, her friends imagine, with the fact that she is unattached.

Keeping in mind the bulging waiting room, Viv steals a few more minutes with Nerida. It is sober talk, today. They have a mutual friend with late-stage lung cancer, and another with a case of early breast cancer only recently diagnosed. Well, at least that case is eminently treatable. We have to expect things like this from now on at our age, they agree, as they have agreed before.

'All the more reason to make hay,' the doctor says negligently, glancing out of the window at the grey skies and switching on her desk lamp. 'Needs must. Isn't that what they say?'

'And who am I to disagree? Women must work and men must weep. Isn't that what they also say, these days?'

'In increasing numbers, *believez-moi*.'

Viv gets on her bike and heads for Marylebone High Street, where she intends to spend a couple of hours checking out clothing shops. Sometimes this tedious task can't be avoided. Tomorrow is the interview with Martin Glover, and given the importance of first impressions she has been thinking about her own.

There's nothing to be gained by trying to look like someone she is not. This precludes most of the clothes Jules might wear, and those of her friend Joy, who has a penchant for gypsy skirts with tight boleros and cowboy boots.

She drops Nerida's prescription into a chemist, and while she's waiting buys some face cream. A pricier one than usual. It describes itself as a concentrated serum, and the box states that in a trial of this product, eighty-two per cent of women reported an improvement (significant to very significant) in their fine lines and wrinkles, after four to six weeks.

Viv doubts if the trial had much scientific rigour, much like Geoff's sentence. She feels a significant to very significant increase in her personal gullibility rating as she plucks the package off the shelf, but goes ahead with the purchase nonetheless. The accepted wisdom among her friends is that none of them work and you'd do just as well with the cheap crap. However, she is fairly sure few of them actually buy the cheap crap in practice. Instead they go on shelling out on the off-chance of some barely discernible effect.

Viv enters a large popular store with racks of clothing in all directions. The tops look as if they're made for midgets, and there's deafening rap music blaring. She turns and walks straight out again. Small shops, boutiques, are less off-putting. She is in a branch of a French chain looking at their jackets, which are shorter this year, when her mobile rings. It's Daisy, on a crackly line.

'Daisy! Are you back? How was—'

'No, back tomorrow morning, and I'll have to be very quick – okay if I come over?' There is tension in her daughter's voice, even on the bad line. This is not unusual. During the five years Daisy has been with Marco, Viv has become inured to domestic dramas.

'Tomorrow, you mean? Of course, darling, yes. Whenever you like. Any time, let me think – any time after six should be fine.'

'I'll come in the afternoon, when I've dumped my stuff.'

'Well, actually I won't be there in the afternoon, I've got to go out.' Pause. Daisy says something inaudible. Viv moves outside against the wall of the shop. 'Come for dinner. I'll make the green chicken curry Marco likes, and we'll hear all about Rome.'

'No! He's not coming,' she hears Daisy shout. The line is worse in the street, so she ducks back inside.

'We'll have you all to ourselves? We needn't have the curry, we can have fish instead. Does fish pie work for you?'

'Mum – listen, I've got something—'

Did she say something *on*, or was it something *to*? Viv can't be sure. 'Have you got something to tell me, darling? Some *news*?'

Daisy's voice curdles in Viv's ear. 'No. *No*. Nothing like—'

The line cuts out, but Viv presses on in case Daisy can hear. 'Well, we can talk it all over when you get here. Six-ish, or later. Look forward to it.'

She returns to the rack of fine-wool jackets. A sales assistant comes over. Daisy's age, French, thin and elegant, helpful without being over-intrusive. Some are in navy. Not so predictable, *oui*? The lapels and the pocket have this little denim stripe, the tiny but important detail that brings them alive. Very clever and *très* cute, *non?* And they mix and match. The jacket, it teams up with these trousers or those skirts. And these tops, they work very well too.

There! You will have a whole new wardrobe. The young woman demonstrates, holding the garments up against each other with a flourish. Viv sees she is in danger of being sold half the shop when she thought she was only after a jacket. The subtle touches on the collar and pocket make it very Frenchy and chic, but isn't it a bit short? You must try it on to find out, says the assistant knowingly.

As Viv goes into the fitting room a text shoots in from Daisy. *Cant do evng. Come str fr gatwck & meet u 4 lunch islngtn at 1?* Daisy says she can't be arsed with predictive texting.

Viv shrugs into the jacket as she stews over this. Her appointment with Discretion Agency is in Victoria at two-thirty. Why Islington? No way could she have lunch there and get back to Victoria in time. But the Gatwick Express goes to Victoria. She could meet Daisy's train. But then she would have to extricate herself from her daughter in order to get to the hotel alone. To do this she would need an excuse. A little white lie, she thinks.

In the mirrored cubicle she quite likes the look of the jacket. The length is fine; in fact, it makes the one she was wearing look dated. Quite liking an item of clothing is about as good as it gets these days. The period when you loved how something looked on you is long gone.

An armful of items to team with the jacket has materialised in the cubicle. The above-the-knee skirt is rejected. But the wool pants have slanted pockets with the same single denim stripe. Far too long, as always, but well cut, and she can turn them up tonight at home. What about the top? Pale blue dots on light cream wool, with a scoop neck.

The assistant looks in, nods approvingly. 'Ah, yes. You see? *Voilà*, a new ensemble!'

Viv voices a fear common to all women of a certain age (or past it) when about to splash out in such a boutique. 'It's not too young, is it? Be honest. Pretend I'm your mother.'

While her own mother mightn't be at all fussed about whom Viv is sleeping with, her fashion sense, on her daughter's behalf, remains keen.

But this was an unrealistic ask. 'Too young?' the assistant looks horrified. '*Non, pas du tout, au contraire*! It is *très, très élégant*. You like?'

And yes, Viv really does quite like. It's a bit extravagant, but how often these days do you find a more-than-passable outfit in one fell swoop? It looks – what is the French word? It looks *insouciant*. And understated, without having tried too hard. Is that how I wish to appear to Martin Glover? Yes, it is exactly how I wish to appear.

With her mother on her mind, Viv goes into a cafe and makes her daily call. Judith Quarry is a former Oxford don, and fiercely independent. A small squad of visiting carers, heroic in Viv's eyes, are helping to keep her in her own home. Her home being a high-ceilinged ground-floor apartment in North Oxford, part of the old family house Judith converted into two flats after her second husband died.

Viv tells her that Jules wants to see her soon, maybe next weekend, reassures her about various small matters and describes what she has just bought. She winds up the call with the usual twinge of anxiety. Judith has been showing a few cracks lately, after a lifetime of forceful competence. So far, and fingers crossed, they are only hairline cracks.

Another text arrives. Daisy again: *Not dinnr. Lunch 2moro ok?*

Will be in Victoria so could meet Gatwick train, Viv replies, without wasting any more energy mulling over the advisability of this. *Ok*, comes the reply. The flight gets in at ten. Daisy will text when she's on the train. Plenty of time between now and then to concoct the white lie.

The Rome flight is late, predictably. When the Gatwick Express trundles in well after midday Viv has had enough time to check out the location of Martin Glover's hotel, which is large and unremarkable (suitably discreet, she supposes) and find somewhere for lunch.

She has also had time to stress out, both on account of the coming interview and getting to it punctually. With this in mind she's tossing up between competing stories. She has even, briefly, flirted with the idea of confiding in Daisy. Neither Jules nor Joy thought this was advisable. Are you losing it or what, Joy had demanded. Which was roughly Julia's response.

Viv has only to see her daughter striding towards her pulling her luggage while speaking forcefully into her mobile to know that Daisy is under pressure. Slender, tall and vibrant, with a mane of Celtic hair, Daisy attracts attention wherever she goes. Her body language was always eloquent, to her mother's eyes. And as Viv anticipates with a stab of apprehension, today Daisy is eaten up with her own all-consuming problems. She doesn't remark on her mother's new outfit or her revamped hair. She's pumped with fight-or-flight adrenaline.

Daisy and Marco have split up. The baby issue has been a wedge between them all along. It has happened before, more than once, but this time Viv senses something different. An air of finality. Now that it looks as if Marco has been given his marching orders, Viv is surprised to find herself ambivalent about it.

Daisy holds back until they have settled themselves into the Lebanese restaurant and ordered from the waiter (male, early forties, swarthy). Then she lets rip. The break-up is irrevocable. There's a reason for this, Mum. Worse than you'd ever guess. A flick of the head. Much, *much* worse.

A selection of dips arrives promptly. Daisy seizes a piece of flatbread and tears it into small pieces. There's something Marco had never told her. Something fundamental. Something shocking. Marco is incapable of fathering anything. Anything of *any description*. He's had the snip.

'Without consulting you? But – when?' Viv feels appalled on her daughter's behalf. On her own behalf too, it must be said. Her heart constricts as she looks at Daisy sitting opposite, her face stony. She quells the impulse to take her daughter in her arms. She knows it would be unwelcome. Daisy is a grown woman, facing a very adult crisis.

It transpires that the procedure was performed after Marco's previous relationship broke up, following an abortion. He'd been firing blanks, says Daisy, wide-eyed with disbelief, for *our entire relationship*. That's six years, counting the year before they met when no doubt he was fucking anything that moved.

'And he never told you?' Viv is transfixed by the injustice of this. 'But how did you discover—'

The answer hurtles like a missile across the table. The truth emerged yesterday morning in Rome, over breakfast in Trastevere, in response to an ultimatum from Daisy. She couldn't wait any longer: Marco must agree to start a course of IVF immediately on return to London, or they were history. Well, it turned out they were history there and then because there was no point in shelling out squillions for IVF when it never had a hope in hell of working, was there?

The waiter is looking worried. Daisy has hardly touched her meal. Instead, she has made a pattern on her plate of torn pita topped with different-coloured dips. Like a patchwork quilt, Viv thinks. She starts eating more, and more rapidly, to compensate.

'He'd kept it a secret from me, when I should've been the first to know. All those wasted years and he'd never admitted it. He said he didn't want to lose me. Isn't that criminal behaviour? Isn't it beyond *unbelievable*?' She directs an accusing gaze at her mother.

Viv agrees, it is an unforgiveable betrayal of trust. But she is also processing this information. There's something about it that doesn't quite add up. It's the contraception issue. Why had Daisy decided IVF was going to be necessary?

'*Why?* Because I hadn't got *pregnant*, Mum. Why do you *think?*'

Viv feels as if all the fury, distress and exasperation in Daisy's voice is aimed at her. She is reminded of episodes of projectile vomiting when Daisy was a baby.

It emerges that Daisy has been trying to get pregnant for the past two years. Or thought she was trying. 'Little did I know there was fat chance of *that* happening.' Two years was how long they said to give it, when you're already in your mid-thirties, before seeking medical intervention.

So, Viv is still working through this, you went off the Pill two years ago?

'Mum, try to *concentrate*, okay? I just *told* you that. I went through it all. Jesus.'

Without telling Marco that's what you were doing?

'Well, he was never going to change his attitude, was he?' Daisy demands, gesticulating. 'And *he* hadn't chosen to reveal the crucial little *nano* fact of the vasectomy to me, had he? Obviously I had to be proactive. I thought he'd change his mind when it happened, when we had a baby, whatever he *thought* he wanted. I was sure he'd actually really like it.'

She tosses her long curling hair. Her mother's hair, brown but not mousy, with highlights for added interest. An expression of Daisy's personality, which like her mother's is neither drab nor timid. Instead it is sometimes wilful and can be fiery. Her parents had hoped these traits might tone down somewhat when she took up with Marco. Instead, they seemed to intensify.

'I even thought he'd turn out to be a good father. How fucking stupid was that?' Daisy's eyes brim with tears.

Viv strokes her hand. 'If you had told Marco what you were doing two years ago, it might have all come out then, when you were thirty-six ...' She knew full well this was an unwise thing to say when she was halfway through saying it, but it's too late. Her daughter's welling eyes flash with an outrage that is all too familiar.

'Shit, Mum, shove that up your bum. I'm not in the mood to be moralised at.' The tears spill over in a rush. She buries her face in a pink damask napkin. The sudden lull is pierced by the raucous catcalls of a now defunct punk band, the ringtone of Daisy's mobile.

She springs up and rushes away from the table, scrubbing at her eyes and narrowly avoiding crashing into the good-looking waiter. He is old enough to be a father, although not old enough to be hers, and he looks after her with startled concern.

Is the caller Marco? Viv is in turmoil too, wanting to wrest the phone from her daughter's hand and give him the mother of all roastings. But it's not Marco. She sees Daisy become more effervescent and animated, a sign that she's talking to one of her friends. From the character and duration of the call, it's most likely her best friend, Alyse.

Viv is very aware of time ticking by. She will have to make a decision soon, whether to leave Daisy or cancel her appointment. The decision is made for her when Daisy returns to the table, having been to the loo and repaired her face. She is going to Alyse's. With any luck she'll get to her place before the older kids get home from school.

Viv is relieved but also torn. Is Daisy sure she will be all right? What about tonight? Would she like to come—

It's *okay*, her daughter says with weary emphasis, tonight she's having dinner with Adrian. Adrian is a gay friend of long standing. Daisy and Adrian have seen each other through various calamities, more or less equally apportioned.

No, Daisy doesn't know where Marco is, nor does she care. No, she hasn't a clue where she's going to live. She is too stressed to even think of all that stuff now. All she knows is she couldn't bear to set eyes on that slimy little turd ever again. She gives her mother a desultory kiss and heads off, towing her suitcase.

She takes a few steps and looks back. 'Thanks for lunch. Cool threads, Mum.' Daisy has always had a tendency, lovable to her friends as well as her mother, to undercut her self-absorption at the most unlikely times.

'Oh—' Viv is caught unawares. 'The suit? You don't think it's too young?'

'Too young? Of course not. You're in your *prime*, staggeringly youthful, Mum!' A laugh, even. This is a running routine of theirs. 'Good hair day too, hey. So, where are you off to?'

Viv is caught short. Just now, the little white lie couldn't have been further from her mind. And which one to choose? The friend in hospital? College reunion? Dentist? 'Well, I—' But by now Daisy is well out of earshot.

Alyse has a responsible lawyer husband and three attractive, lively children. Collective arrows in Daisy's heart under the circumstances, her mother can't help feeling. Daisy has often compared her bestie's luck in love with her own lack of it. And Adrian, while undeniably funny and charming, is a fey and feckless drifter, Viv has always thought. She hopes he will be up to dealing with this latest catastrophe.

She feels she herself has been inadequate, though not for want of love or care. Motherhood has been a joy overall, but it would be inaccurate to claim it has been an unmitigated one. Like old age, it is not designed for sissies. Viv thinks most of the mothers she knows would concur with that.

She looks at her watch. Eight precious minutes of calm before she has to go. She slumps back in her chair, eyes closed, and tries to empty her mind. In this she is unsuccessful. Worry about her daughter supersedes anything else. When she beckons the waiter over for the bill, nothing is said but something passes between them: a shared acquaintance with the perilous shoals of parenting.

One of many useful habits fostered by a career in publishing is punctuality. You don't keep authors and agents waiting. With two minutes to spare, Viv is outside the hotel. She dives into the powder room and makes an attempt to spruce herself up. Jolly herself up too. She examines her reflection in the mirrored wall, striving to recapture the impression of insouciance. It feels lost and out of reach.

She sees an anxious-looking Caucasian woman in her sixties in a red trilby hat. There are parallel lines (fine, but visible) around the corners of her mouth and radiating from the corners of her eyes. Laughter lines; when she tries out a smile her face creases into them. If she moves out of the direct overhead light, are they more unobtrusive? One should seize every opportunity to be backlit, is Julia's advice.

The person in the mirror is quite snappily dressed, however. Beneath the hat her hair has life and texture. That's something. The insouciance flutters like an elusive butterfly. She thinks: I can capture it. I will bring it down.

And on the dot of two-thirty Vivien Quarry can be seen strolling, but with a spring in her step, through the sparsely populated coffee lounge towards the screen of climbing plants at the end. She knows she is being observed by someone behind the screen. As she approaches she sees his profile (male, sixties, Anglo). He is tucking a folded newspaper away into a briefcase.

He gets up and holds out his hand, smiling. 'Madam Vivien, I presume? I'm Martin Glover.' Medium height and balding, pleasantly unremarkable face, tortoiseshell glasses, slight paunch, grey suit, open-necked blue shirt. He is appraising her in turn, while appearing not to do so. She tries not to guess at his assessment.

'Let's bring on the sustenance before we fade away,' he says, signalling the waitress. 'Tea or coffee? And we'd better have a plate of their delicious biscuits as well. Chewy oatmeal or chocolate? Hmm, difficult. Both, I think, don't you, to be on the safe side?' He is practised at the skills of putting people at ease and drawing them out. Viv recognises the techniques. She has dealt with many introverted authors, and before she knows it he has elicited this very fact from her. Does she think of herself as retired, then?

'My husband is but I'm not. I mean, I've left publishing, but I'm doing other things and I don't have any more spare time than I used to. Less, if anything.' She tells him a little about the things. He shows interest, and she thinks it is genuine. Occasionally he writes in a black Moleskine notebook.

So, she's not bored. That's good, he says. A lot of people are looking for sex on the side as a way of filling in time, although they may not see it that way. Mainly older people, it's true, but not exclusively.

'Oh, I'm certainly not bored,' Viv says. 'That's not my problem at all.'

Many people are looking for excitement, to spice things up a bit. Or even for love, at a pinch. To recapture those heady, youthful feelings. What is she looking for? Besides sex, he adds. Lightly, with a sidelong smile.

What an interesting question. *Is* she looking for anything besides? She hadn't anticipated being asked precisely this.

'Well, I'm not looking for love. I'm certainly not looking to recapture that first fine careless rapture; I couldn't handle that again.' The answer arrives of its own accord. 'I want someone – a man – to notice me again.' Preferably with desire, she thinks. Is this out of the question? Is it so outlandish? 'With a little affection. If possible.'

And you're not getting that from your husband, Martin says. A statement, not a question. You want sex within a relationship, of some sort.

Of some sort, yes, Viv says. I want my sex life back. I've been very frustrated for the past two years. My husband seems to have lost interest completely, and won't talk about it.

On one level she is amazed to hear herself say such things to someone she has only just met. Someone who is not much more than a perfect stranger. On another level there is something about the matter-of-fact way the conversation is unfolding that negates the personal. Or is it more that it removes the burden of the intimate from the personal, so that what would normally be private can be put on the table in a businesslike way.

'But you don't want a divorce.'

'No. No, I don't.' She is positive on this score. A divorce at her age – at *their* age? It is somehow unthinkable. And yet, of course, people do it. They take that step occasionally, as Julia has pointed out in relation to her seventy-year-old brother. What has prompted Max to bite the bullet at this stage, so late in his married life? Although Max and Patricia's relationship was never happy, according to Jules.

'We've got such a history together. To break it all asunder, over something like this, like having no sex – it just doesn't seem necessary. We're very companionable together, on the whole, and we have a good life.' And we have our daughter. Viv has decided not to mention Daisy unless asked.

Martin is listening intently while eating, with evident enjoyment, a chocolate bath oliver. He doesn't respond, and Viv is aware that this is deliberate. He has gleaned there is more to be said on this subject. She decides to say some of it.

'We've had – we still *have*, really – a pretty good marriage. But this issue is undermining it on a daily basis.' She thinks of the events of last week. 'It's already done that, quite severely, and I think it's up to me to stop the rot.'

'Up to you alone?'

'Well, it doesn't seem to affect my husband. I've tried everything, all the usual suspects. He says he doesn't need testosterone, for instance, because there's nothing wrong with him. And couples therapy would be moving deckchairs on the *Titanic*.'

Martin, munching his biscuit, has been scribbling in his notebook. He nods. Viv guesses he has encountered this scenario in a wide arc of variations.

'No doubt you've heard all this before, many times. But maybe more often from the other side of the fence? I mean, from the opposite gender.'

He smiles. It's true that men are more likely to do something about it, and use the internet, or perhaps escorts. Neither of these options holds any appeal for his particular clients, however, which is why they enlist the help of a targeted introduction agency such as his own. He thinks it would be a mistake to assume that this sort of situation does not impact women in the same way as men. But society's norms mean there are fewer options, and women are more hesitant about seeking solutions.

Women are less likely to take remedial action, I suppose, says Viv. Or they have been, until recent social changes. She likes Martin's attitude.

He leans back with his hands behind his head. So you want to maintain your marriage, while conducting an occasional discreet, no-strings liaison. What kind of person do you have in mind?

'Is there a choice?'

This time he laughs. 'Ah, we should be able to come up with more than one option, with any luck. Thinking about possible candidates, we might start with the non-starters. Something about a chap that would be a deal-breaker in your book. Have you thought about your priorities?'

Viv is thrown. She was unprepared, quite so early in the piece, to be given the news that she has passed the exam. Or at least that she has been given leave to advance to the next stage. Well, I'd like someone in the same boat, ideally, she says. Or a comparable boat. Perhaps with a mad wife in the attic.

Martin looks up. What about age? Would she consider meeting a younger man?

'Younger? I hadn't thought. How much younger?'

He counters with his own query, flipping back two pages in his notebook. When they spoke on the phone, how old did she say she was?

Julia had strongly advised putting her age back. Sixty-seven, Viv says, rejecting this advice again, with misgiving. She realises she has not seized control of the interview in the way Jules suggested. It hasn't seemed necessary.

'Yes, that's what I wrote down, but I thought it might be a mistake. You could pass for quite a bit younger, so I think it might be preferable for us to list you as late fifties. Fifty-seven or eight, or so. It's easier for me to find chaps who want to meet someone that age.'

Viv's confidence has not recovered from the blow dealt by her husband. Her pleasure at hearing she looks younger is tinged with disbelief.

'You can always tell them when you get to know them,' adds Martin, 'if it makes you feel better.'

'For instance, if we're about to jet off on Ryanair for a weekend in Rome? So he doesn't keel over when he sees my passport and call the whole thing off?'

'Ryanair? They haven't upped their game that much. I'd hope it was BA.' He proffers the plate. They both take another biscuit. Viv finds she is beginning to enjoy this. The interview has acquired a slightly playful quality, now that she has pushed Daisy's problems to the back of her mind.

'I don't know about younger,' she says. 'I might feel uncomfortable.' She thinks it over. 'I've never had a boyfriend who was younger than me. Not even in my twenties, in that post-Pill period.' When everyone was fucking everything that moved, as Daisy would say.

Well, maybe it's time to give it a whirl, says Martin. Anyway, don't worry about it. You can see how you feel on the day. In my experience, you can't predict how any two people are going to get on, not with any great accuracy. Whatever they may have said in the privacy of the confessional, chemistry tends to override it.

Personality pheromones, auras – call it what you will. But having said that, let's get back to your preferences.

Yes, Viv can see the logic, or the wilful *illogic*, of chemistry. But in that case, is there much point in asking me – in asking any of your clients – what they think they'd like or wouldn't like?

'There's some point,' Martin says. 'There are certain fundamentals many people feel strongly about.' He ticks them off. 'Age can be one. Colour is another. Nationality, too. Habits such as smoking and drinking. Then there's education level, religion, politics and, dare I say it, class.'

All the ingrained prejudices. 'Chain smoking might be a dealbreaker, I suppose.'

'And we haven't even started on the whole matter of appearance. Fat, thin, tall, short. Receding, balding, dreadlocks, tattoos. You name it, people will have strong views about it. Or think they do.'

Of course. 'The level of attractiveness. How can you quantify an enigma like that?'

'And is it even relevant? Have another biscuit. Don't mind me, I just tick the boxes. Try to locate what you really feel. I'm only doing the maths, I have no opinions.'

'I doubt that.' She takes another biscuit. 'You know, as well as never having had a younger boyfriend, I've never slept with anyone black or Asian. I'm boringly middle class, and I don't think I've ever dated a blue blood, or even a blue-collar blood. Or, now I come to think about it, anyone who didn't go to university, at least for a period. Lordy' – a word she has picked up from Joy – 'how shameful is that? What a shockingly narrow life I've led.'

'Well, we were both young in the sixties,' Martin says comfortably. 'There may be a few things we don't remember. Don't worry, I'm afraid we all tend to surround ourselves with a comfort zone of like-minded people. It's the way of the world.'

'Yes, but it shouldn't be, should it?' Martin is right about the fog of the sixties. She has just recalled a certain young Turkish musician, a classical guitarist who serenaded her outside her bedroom window. He was self-taught, brilliant, and lived in other people's beds. Including, for a brief period, her own. He also took hard drugs. What happened to him? Whatever was his name?

Before she has had time for second thoughts, or for any cautionary thoughts at all, she reaches a decision. 'Let's forget about my prejudices. I'm sure I've got the full board, but I'm not entirely sure what they are. And I think I'd rather make up my own mind about a person, not rule him out in advance because of the packaging. That gives you more scope, doesn't it?'

'It does widen the catchment area. And nothing's set in stone. If you find I'm way off the mark with any of the introductions, if you suddenly find you can't stand excessive weight, or specs or baldness, you can let me know at any time.'

She likes his self-deprecation, and she finds this encouraging. Any of the introductions; this must mean he envisages more than one. Possibly even several?

He agrees to forget about her preferences for now. Or her prejudices, as she prefers to call them. 'But we can't overlook those of the chaps. They're not always quite as accommodating, sad to say. We should talk a little more about your background and interests.'

Oh. She thought they had been. 'Wouldn't their prejudices boil down to one? I'm not a beauty, not even a faded one. What I'm getting at is the problem of my age. Given that men are hard-wired not to find older women attractive.'

She bites her tongue. It just slipped out. Enunciated here in the coffee lounge of an impersonal hotel, it sounds oddly out of place. And it carries more than a whiff of what her mother would call the unexamined idea.

'Now Vivien,' Martin says, leaning forward. 'You seem to have a bit of a bee in your bonnet about this. You can rest assured that anyone who contacts you will know in advance your—' He pauses, and the puckish look on his face becomes, she thinks, even more so. 'Your *approximate* age. And they will be fine with it.'

He removes his glasses for emphasis. 'You can be quite sure they are fine with it, otherwise I won't point any of them in your direction. Men come in all shapes and sizes, you know.' She suspects he has been prompted to say this before. 'In my line of work I see all types with all manner of druthers. There are widespread tendencies, certainly, but there's no one size fits all. Any more than there's one size for all women.'

Viv feels a little reassured. Also more than a little foolish. 'Which is fortunate. Yes, of course you're right. It's silly to generalise. It's just that my husband has a problem with me being the age I am.'

'Well, I think I can come up with some chaps who won't have this problem.'

'You think so? You're reasonably confident?'

He appears to consider, looking serious. 'I think there are grounds for guarded optimism.' They laugh. 'I can't guarantee anything – least of all, of course, whether you will approve of any of them enough to want to take things further.'

Relating salient points of the conversation to Jules later on, Viv describes Martin's eyes, at this point, as twinkling. He is a decent man, she has decided. If they weren't much of an age, she might have described his attitude to her as protective. Paternal, even. Which given the situation is diverting. She is fairly confident that her own father would have reacted to this situation with incredulity. As, no doubt, would Geoff himself. Martin though, she feels, would take any human foibles and deviations in his stride.

And this is probably why, as they reach the end of the interview, she has become sufficiently trusting of Mr Martin Glover, whom she has known for just under two hours, to write him a cheque for a few hundred pounds.

Jules had advocated forcefully against this. A cheque or credit card would create a paper trail for Geoff to trip over, which should be avoided at all costs as it could come back and bite you on the bum. When contemplating having an affair – and Jules thought the activity Viv was proposing qualified as such, and could well involve multiple affairs – one should always err on the side of caution.

6

TRIALS AND TRIBULATIONS

Before shaking hands with Martin (warmly) in the cold air on the pavement outside the hotel, Viv has also signed a brief form in which she engages the introduction services of the Discretion Agency, hereinafter known as the Agency, for the period of a year. During this time, the Agency will do its best to introduce her to a suitable range of clients from its books. However, it makes no binding commitment in this regard.

Moreover, Vivien absolves the Agency absolutely of any responsibility or liability (moral, legal or financial) for any occurrence, accident or misadventure of any kind or description that may occur as a result of any introduction facilitated by it.

'It's more of a gentlewoman's agreement than a formal contract,' Viv admits to Julia in a rushed phone call later that afternoon. While the wording has a semblance of legalese, she senses the principal input came from Martin Glover himself.

Viv is obliged to confess that not only did she neglect to do anything that Jules recommended, she went ahead and did the opposite. She did not subject Mr Glover to the third-degree, or anything like it. The subject of vetting was never mentioned. Nor was the nature of the pool of suitable clients. She committed herself on the spot, handing over a cheque with her own name printed on it.

Having railed against this raft of actions, Jules, who is about to go out and has her regular minicab on the way, homes in on what she sees as Viv's gullibility and general attitude of compliance. She has no hesitation in finding this attitude bogus.

'As for the baloney that you don't have any likes or dislikes,' the voice on the phone is rich with exasperation, 'you know you can't abide slip-on shoes with tassels, or socks with sandals. Or gaudy Rolexes. Or phrases like: *In this day and age*, or *Young people today*, and—'

'Are you quite finished?'

'Nowhere near, but I think I've made my point. Now, I simply must go or my poor driver will go AWOL. No, the list of your prejudices is endless. As are those of anyone our age, don't get me wrong – it's not just you. I too have the odd bias. I tend to shy away from tenors with steatopygia, as you may remember. And dribbling basses. But to give that poor man the idea that you'll happily take home anything that happens to have a functioning penis – it's asking for trouble, Viv.'

Viv pictures Julia shaking her head, shapely nostrils dilated. She knows Jules is already pacing the floor, by the way her voice keeps dipping in and out. Viv is keen to change the topic, and acquaint her with the details of Daisy's plight.

'Be that as it may, Jules, I thought it was better not to queer my pitch any further than it already probably—'

Before she can say a word about Daisy, there is an explosive guffaw in her ear. '*Be that as it may?* What fresh bullshit is this? You're kidding yourself. You're just after a bit of rough trade. Talk tomorrow after you've slept on it. You can always cancel the cheque.' And Jules hangs up.

Viv, who is up in the shed with the door shut, has been doing a bit of pacing herself. She needs to go downstairs and get the dinner on. She needs to talk to her husband about their daughter's problems. Geoff was out playing croquet on this unexpectedly dry afternoon, and he usually comes home in a good mood. He doesn't yet know that his chances of becoming a grandfather have suffered a major setback.

This subject is not as fraught as that of Viv and Geoff's moribund sex life, but it has its difficulties. There are uneasy parallels, not exact but analogous, with their own history as parents. For several years after Daisy's birth they had fought over whether to have a second child.

Both find this hard to process now, but Daisy's very existence was an accident, coming at a stage in their lives when they were still establishing their careers. Her conception was a matter of a missed pill or two for which Viv, perforce, took the blame. And after this inauspicious start the pregnancy itself was plagued with problems. Midway through it, they moved out of Julia's apartment into a deceased estate untouched since before the First World War.

Julia's flat, if nothing like the luxury it would become in later years, was a daily pleasure. They would have left eventually, but the imminent – and, it must be said, unwelcome – prospect of fatherhood had a galvanising effect on Geoff. It propelled him out of there. He'd had enough of Bloomsbury women and their managing ways.

Jules diagnosed this as a primeval instinct, the drive of a hitherto slatternly and undomesticated male to provide for his family in his own cave. Too bad that the cave of choice happened to be unfit for human habitation. Viv opposed the move too, but saw it differently. She saw it as Geoff taking revenge on her for the unplanned pregnancy. Perhaps it was entirely subconscious revenge; perhaps not entirely.

Julia Jefferies, Covent Garden's rising young star, had followed up her success as Sophie in *Rosenkavalier* with a triumphant Juliet in Gounod's *Romeo and Juliet*, and offers were now coming in from opera houses around the world. Before long they would be flooding in. Her absences were likely to become more frequent and prolonged. She liked to come home to raucous companionship and a well-stocked fridge. Her friends could ramp up the size of their deposit to a more realistic level and have their baby in comfort.

Viv was sympathetic. She suspected this was a roundabout way of saying Jules didn't want to be alone. But Geoff had just been given a modest raise and he forced the issue by slapping down a deposit on a renovator's dream in Battersea.

Following Daisy's birth, a period that was rarely less than tense lurched into chaos. After burst pipes and rodents came the discovery of asbestos. Bloomsbury was no longer an option as Jules had just engaged a new tenant. Viv leant on her mother for temporary crisis accommodation in Oxford.

Judith was busy negotiating new domestic arrangements of her own. She had just embarked on life with her second husband, Stefan, Viv's excitable new Czech stepfather. Stefan was an electrician and amateur jazz violinist with whom Judith had been having an affair (quite widely known in academic circles, although not by Viv's father) for some time.

Geoff dug in his heels. The temperature of their relationship, Viv wrote to Jules (singing Juliet in Hamburg) reached new levels of fraught. It threatened to soar off the scale after Viv took the baby to Oxford for a few weeks that turned into six months. The fact that she stayed on with a fractious infant in circumstances that were not ideal (Stefan's children were grown up, their babyhood a distant and evidently mixed memory) said a lot about the difficulties back in Battersea.

Things changed when she brought Daisy home. Viv and Geoff had missed each other. They were reconciled. Geoff saw big changes in his daughter, who didn't know who he was. This was a shock; Geoff couldn't remember his own father, who had walked out before his third birthday. He discovered in himself a powerful desire not to revisit this script.

Many of the difficulties in their parents' marriages had related to domestic chores and child-rearing. Viv and Geoff divided their responsibilities in a more equitable way. But Geoff was adamant that any talk of more children should be postponed.

They continued to postpone it until Viv, like Daisy now, reached her late thirties. In these years of declining fertility their best efforts didn't do the trick. Nor did several gruelling cycles of IVF. The inability to have a second child became their biggest disappointment.

What has now befallen Daisy, therefore, will resonate in ways that are painful and complicated. Memories will surface. On Viv's side they are likely to be tinged with resentment, as she recalls those years of possibility squandered. On Geoff's, they will be coloured by guilt. But Viv reminds herself that while the memories may be different for each of them, the upshot is the same. The whole subject is touchy and to be tiptoed around.

She decides to wait until they've had their usual pre-dinner cocktail in front of the TV news. Geoff likes to make these; he mixes them strong and better than most. His mojitos, ever since a holiday in Mexico, are particularly good. He makes them tonight, adding handfuls of mint from the garden.

He tells Viv about this afternoon's croquet game. She listens to this on one level, while going through the interview with Martin in her mind. Geoff's team won today. They tossed, and he was the outright winner of the monthly jackpot. She enthuses. How will he squander it?

Geoff thinks he will splash out on a new jacket. A corduroy one with elbow patches he has seen in a local shop. Viv is intrigued to hear this, since he rarely buys clothes. She usually has to bully him or buy them herself. Could this be a sign he is having an affair? What colour, she asks.

Geoff ponders. Dung colour, he thinks.

'Very smart,' says Viv. 'Most of your trousers are in shades of dung, aren't they? You won't have to worry whether it goes with them.'

'That was my reasoning. I won't have to worry, I thought.'

'I had lunch with Daisy,' she tells him, as they sit down for dinner at the kitchen table. Sesame chicken stir fry with Thai vegetables. 'You could have come if it weren't for croquet, of course.' This is not quite true. Today was strictly mother and daughter.

'Daisy's back? Couldn't she have come over tonight?' Geoff stabs a baby corn. 'Or should I say *they*,' he adds darkly.

'She's having dinner with Adrian.'

Geoff doesn't like Adrian either. He gives a grunt of distaste. 'How was Rome?'

'Rome was not good.' Viv takes a sip of wine. It's an unoaked Australian chardonnay, one of Julia's recommendations.

'Why not? Marco being more of a shit than usual? Or just being his usual shitty self?'

Viv puts down her knife and fork. She's not quite sure how to tell him. He continues to eat hungrily until he realises something is up.

'What is it, then? Have they split up again?'

'Yes, they have. Only this time it's for good.'

'You can't know that.' Geoff pauses, the persistent Daisy and Marco baby disagreements uppermost in his mind. And Daisy's age. 'Well, maybe it's for the best ...' It sounds uncharacteristically tentative. The subtext is all too plain. In recent years he too has discovered a visceral desire for a grandchild.

'But I can know it's for good.' Viv takes a deep breath. 'You see, Daisy discovered Marco had a vasectomy done six years ago. A fact he'd never seen fit to disclose.'

Geoff utters an exclamation that includes a strong element of satisfaction. 'I always knew he was an arsehole.'

'*We* always knew.'

They glance quickly at each other for the first time in the conversation, then look down again and go on eating. Each is also chewing over the ramifications. How is Daisy taking it, Geoff asks. Badly, he assumes.

'Badly, yes. Very. She's violently angry and upset, as you'd imagine. She—' Viv hesitates. She has been in two minds whether to tell Geoff about the other salient fact, Daisy's attempt to get pregnant without telling Marco. It's relevant, in a roundabout way. She goes ahead and tells him.

Then she says, 'It's a bit of a moral conundrum, isn't it? Not that it affected the issue, in the event. But Daisy wasn't to know that.' She wavers, but only briefly. 'Still, I can understand why she did it.'

There is an extended pause in which Geoff, knowing nothing useful can be said, says nothing. Viv experiences an upsurge of strong emotion. 'I should have done the same, shouldn't I? How I wish I'd done it.' She didn't intend this.

Her husband inclines his head. It is a small movement, scarcely perceptible, but it's enough. It's an acknowledgement. It puts them on the same side. She brushes away a single tear.

Geoff sees it. He says, 'At least we have Daisy.'

For more than twenty-five years, on the other occasions, the rare other occasions when they have ventured into this territory strewn with landmines, one or other of them has ended up saying the same thing. Often using the same words. Geoff pours more wine, generous slugs. Julia knows her stuff on the wine front, as on other fronts.

When they are clearing up, and there has been a safe interval, Geoff asks Viv what she thinks Daisy will do now. Marco was paying the lion's share of their flat in Docklands. Daisy won't be able to keep it on unless she gets someone else in. And if she were to do that she would lose her painting studio in the second bedroom.

'I'm worried about her,' Viv admits. 'Apart from anything else, she may be tempted to rush into another relationship on the rebound.' Daisy has rushed into rebound relationships before, and made unsuitable choices as a result. Marco is a case in point. 'Or …'

'Or?' prompts Geoff, cautiously.

'It did occur to me to wonder if she might decide she wants to go it alone. As a single mum. In some way.'

72

'Did she say anything of that kind to you?'

'No. No, she didn't,' Viv hastens to say, 'not at all. She said nothing like that, it was just me speculating.'

'Did you suggest it?' His voice is neutral.

'Oh no, and I don't think it's a good idea. At least, anyway – not ideal. Not *necessarily*. And I'm not suggesting it would happen. But if it did ...'

'If it did happen, we'd just have to support her decision, wouldn't we?' Geoff says.

They watch two gripping episodes of a Swedish detective series, part of a DVD set that Daisy and Marco passed on and they will in turn pass on to Judith, and go upstairs in a preoccupied but more harmonious frame of mind than they have for some weeks.

Not that there's anything to show for it, thinks Viv. Geoff has fallen asleep almost instantly but her mind is active. It's been quite a day, what with Daisy's news and then the interview. She listens to her husband's breathing. Should I feel guilty about what I'm contemplating doing, she wonders. In any case, what does *should* mean, in a situation such as this?

It's the kind of linguistic conundrum that her intellectual mother spent a large part of her academic life mulling over. Judith was skilled in identifying ways to determine what might make an action moral or immoral.

This did not, however, appear to carry any practical obligation, as Viv discovered when she became a teenager. She was shocked to the marrow when her mother told her she was having an affair with a post-grad – but not, Judith hastened to reassure her daughter (who was not at all reassured) one of her own students.

'I hope you don't mind, but I thought I should tell you,' Judith said. The thirteen-year-old Viv found her mother's choice of words here somewhat ironic. And she did mind. 'Well, *shouldn't* you tell Dad too?' she'd asked. She loved both her parents.

Definitely not, was the response.

'Why not?'

Because I need something he can't give me, her clever and sensual mother had replied. Viv's teenage instinct, and her preference, told her not to ask further questions.

Many years later, when she was in her twenties, Viv found she had much more of an idea what was meant when she met Stefan for the first time. She witnessed telling changes in her mother's behaviour. It was as if Judith had emerged from an emotional hibernation.

When Judith first revealed her affair with Stefan Kasproviak, Viv had again asked questions. What about Dad, aren't you going to tell him? *Shouldn't* you? This time the answer was different. Not yet, said Judith, but I will when the time is right. The right time had arrived a year later, precipitating the divorce of Viv's parents.

Whether or not I should feel guilty, Viv thinks, the fact is I don't. She suspects her mother would not be averse to discussing the subject even now, at ninety-one. Not averse at all. She might even consider bringing it up next time she goes to Oxford, before her mother's memory really starts to deteriorate. But she will not tell Daisy. Jules and Joy were quite right to advise against it. The knowledge of Judith Quarry's secret life had been a burden Viv would not wish to impose on her own daughter.

While she is drifting in this way between the past and the present, she falls deeply asleep. She dreams about Jules having a baby. It is a dream she has had before. Julia's age in the dream is unclear, and her reaction is equivocal.

Last time the dream just faded away. This time Viv thinks about offering to adopt the baby herself, but the dream drifts into another story before she can get round to it.

7

A REPRIEVE

Julia's long-term agent is Malcolm Foster. Of course, he's older than me, she tells people, but then – just between ourselves – Mal was always this age. When I first met him, she confides, he was only in his mid-twenties and he already had a face like a ploughed paddock full of wombat holes. *Yes!* Just like Auden.

What she neglects to say is that when they first met, Mal was two years younger than her. He became older only after she put her age back, an adjustment prompted by the imminence of her fortieth birthday. Malcolm had given this action his tick of approval. Back then, celebrities' ages were not noted with such alacrity. Julia Jefferies' age hadn't lodged in the public mind and she was able to get away with it.

So Malcolm is sixty-seven, and considered all the more distinguished for being stooped, lined and grizzled. Years of managing the careers of driven, talented people, some of whom were (still are) volatile, some needy, some delusional, and some (perhaps most) passionate and emotional, have left a succession of calling cards on his face. Not that he would have had it any differently.

Malcolm Foster's knowledge of the opera world is second to none, and his clients know it. Most of them, like Julia Jefferies, have stayed with him for their entire careers and like him they are getting on. He's been heard to refer to them as his problem children.

They may be grown up now (they certainly look that way) but they seldom make a major decision – and not only in their careers – without first canvassing his views.

Very few ever grow out of the need for Malcolm's astute and holistic perspective, his light guiding hand at the elbow. Rarely has one chosen to defect to a rival. They would be unlikely to find anyone else with such an intense, with such an *inclusive* interest in their lives. And that includes their partners, if any, in life.

Two or three times a week Malcolm can been seen lunching at Da Paolo, the small Italian restaurant close to his office in Fitzrovia and just a short stroll from Julia's apartment. With a client, or with a book, he sits at the far end. His table is never released to anyone else before one o'clock.

He's in place today, and rises to greet Jules as she arrives in a swinging royal blue coat and jaunty pillbox hat, causing a little stir. The proprietor and staff know her. She is overdressed for this casual restaurant, but no one is complaining. Julia can be relied on to meet any tone, and raise it. You look wonderful, darling, Malcolm murmurs, both youthful and regal. An equipoise few in *that* family can carry off.

Today Malcolm has a proposition to put to Julia. He's well aware that it is a tricky one, potentially, and may not be welcomed. It's likely to meet with an initial resistance he will need to wear down with all the wiles in his armoury.

No one understands better than him what Jules is going through at this late stage of her career, or the precarious state of her equanimity. She may talk carelessly of being happy to grab at any straw, but he knows better. And he is convinced that what he is about to put on the table is, to put it baldly (as he'd never dream of putting it to her) the best his client can reasonably expect at this juncture.

The Royal Opera House Covent Garden, Julia's old home, her alma mater as they call it, has been in touch. They've had a singer pull out of a small role in *The Queen of Spades*. The role is that of the Old (as she is usually known) Countess. Julia would be playing someone whose glory days are long gone and who expires on stage.

The offer is a hard sell and will need to be prudently stage-managed. To prepare the ground, Malcolm entertains her with a little divertissement, some sharp and sassy anecdotes about the hierarchy as well as the odd colleague and rival. He's not, however, into full-on scandal-mongering. Where shop talk is concerned Mal is adept at maintaining a few delicate balances of his own: between gentle and outrageous indiscretions, and flattering confidences that are not full-on betrayals.

Malcolm Foster is respected throughout the business for his precision in these areas. His clients know he can be trusted where necessary, and trusted absolutely. While he's not averse to telling stories out of school, the protagonists of his more colourful tales belong to other schools and other agencies. This is understood and highly valued. Certain secrets have been in the possession of Malcolm Foster since the early days of Julia Jefferies' career.

Julia has been away on the underside of the world for a while and is more than happy to indulge in some in-house gossip. But her interest can only last so long. She has guessed, as she told Viv, that Mal has something up his sleeve, but just in case he doesn't she won't demean herself by asking.

She will order with impunity, she declares, since she no longer has to worry about her figure. It can go to pot, Mal! Spaghetti carbonara it is, and don't hold the horses. Cream if they have it, and lashings of cheese. There have to be some compensations, don't there?

Malcolm puts out a cautionary hand. He has been waiting for this. She may want to rethink the carbonara. He has some news. *They* have been on the blower, he says, with a significant little pucker of the lips.

'The *Garden?*' Jules does not hide her incredulity.

'They are in a bit of a pickle for December. They've got less than two months. To cut to the chase – it's *The Queen of Spades*. New production. The Countess. The one who predicts the winning cards.'

Jules, energised, cuts to the chase in her turn. She can summon up enough of the plot to seize on several salient points. 'The *Old* Countess? The one who's lingered too long, whose career is finished? The faded beauty who *croaks* on stage?' She claps a hand to her heart. 'It's come to this, has it? Who left them in the lurch?'

Malcolm names a big American name. A (formerly) very big name. 'I hear cancer. I'm afraid it's throat.'

Julia's hand, inadvertently, travels from her heart to her neck. She has gone white with empathy.

'Yes. Terrible.' Malcolm is carefully assembling his arsenal. 'She is – well, what a blazing talent, I don't have to tell you. And a wonderful actress, which is why they wanted her in the first place, of course.' He pauses, to enable them both to reflect on this. And to allow his opening volley to settle, and sink in.

After an interval Julia's colour begins to return and he resumes. 'She sang it in Paris a few years ago and made quite an impact. So much so,' another staged pause, 'that since then, she's been doing it around the world.'

But this is not something Julia would *ever* have imagined singing. It's such an insignificant role, Mal. 'I wouldn't want to be accused of,' she drops her voice, '*reigniting the embers of a dying career.*' She knows that Mal will have read and noted this phrase in a newspaper review this very morning, in relation to a singer who, they both know, is younger than she.

'Not one of my clients,' Malcolm says firmly, 'and I'd have dissuaded her. This offer is in a different category altogether. Yes, the role may be small, but insignificant it most emphatically is not. When did you last see the opera?'

He knows she is unlikely to have seen it for years. 'The role packs a punch that is in inverse proportion to its size. The Countess is the pivot. The drama unfolds around her.' His client is looking unconvinced. He fixes his eyes on her. 'If you remember, she has the gift of second sight. She can foretell how the cards will fall. She is threatened with a pistol, dies of fright, and then in Act Three returns as a ghost to predict the winning cards.'

'How very Russian.'

'Isn't it? Pushkin, of course, with some dramatic licence. To make it work, you require a singer who is also a powerful actress. She must have both charisma and presence, controlling her scenes with a very strong stage personality. Which is why they thought of you, Julia.'

He usually calls her by the nickname used by her closest friends. Only when he has something he really wants her to do does he revert to Julia. This does not go unnoticed.

'They're rather desperate to get you. That's not putting it too strongly. They'd like you to go in tomorrow, so they can state their case.'

'Put the screws on, you mean.' Jules is wrestling with her demons, the ones telling her that this role is unworthy of Julia Jefferies. It would be a backward step. On the other hand, where would it be a backward step from? Realistically, is there any such thing as a forward step, in her position?

Reading her mind, Malcolm says gently, 'Think about it, darling, will you? New production, one of Tchaikovsky's greatest pieces. You could make a real mark, do something marvellous with it. Attract a lot of notice where it counts. And it could be the start of something—'

'Don't say something *big*, Mal, or I'll bite your head off.'

But he can see she's wavering. When she goes away and thinks it over, the odds are she will be persuaded. Which will be for the best; Mal has no doubts about that. When a great soprano gets to Julia's official age the available options – well, even a great agent is hard pressed to find many.

'On another potentially life-enhancing note, my dear,' he says, 'what are the prospects for Max's divorce? Should one go so far as to be cautiously optimistic?'

Julia's face relaxes. 'I think one could go that far. I think it's going ahead. At least Pat's not opposing, and they've got a chance to keep the lawyers' snouts out of it.'

Ever shrewd, Malcolm proffers another titbit. Might Max come over in December? In time to see her gracing the stage of the Royal Opera House once more. Something he is quite sure she will have convinced her brother he will never see again.

Malcolm has a sweet tooth, and Julia knows he will only have dessert if she agrees to share it. He lives alone, and lunch is a highlight. He has never put on weight; she suspects that if he has no evening engagement, this may be his only proper meal of the day. He orders panna cotta and she eats two dutiful teaspoons.

She leaves the restaurant humming an aria from *Traviata*. Full of good food, and full of food for thought. Before she has walked fifty yards she has decided to go to the meeting at Covent Garden tomorrow. When you're in the last-chance saloon …

Across town, Viv too has plenty on her plate as she strides towards West Hampstead Tube. She has heard nothing new from Daisy, but this doesn't surprise her. Daisy was always an erratic communicator, and her mother knows better than to bug her on this issue or any other. But Viv has received two thought-provoking text messages during the morning.

The first came from the Discretion Agency: *Please call Martin at your convenience.* He has someone who would like to meet her. When she calls, Martin says his client is a gentleman named Dev. He is a younger man, in his forties, Indian born, very dark-skinned, very presentable, in fact very handsome in Martin's opinion, and—

'In his *forties*?' Viv is dumbstruck. 'Doesn't he know how old I am?'

'In his mid to late-ish forties,' replies Martin, unfazed. 'Yes, he knows how old you are. I gave him the age you and I agreed on. Don't worry, he expressed interest in meeting someone older; he was quite specific about it.'

'But I'm not sure I want to meet *him*,' Viv says, brow furrowed.

'Maybe this is not something you ought to make up your mind about in advance though, Vivien.' Martin's voice is soothing and sensible. 'Why not give it a whirl? What have you got to lose, after all? You're not signing up for a life of penal servitude. If it doesn't work for either of you, then it doesn't work. Which is always going to be the case, isn't it, whoever you meet?'

'Yes, but—'

'Think about it this way. At worst, you'll have a one-off encounter with someone you need never see again. Perhaps it's best not to prejudge the issue? As you yourself did say.'

That's true, she did. What he says is reasonable enough, Viv supposes. And feels herself being coaxed into agreement, rather smoothly and expertly. She gives a mental shrug. May as well give it a whirl, as he put it. In any case, the unknown Dev may have second thoughts himself. That would seem very likely.

But Dev appears to have no such qualms. Within the hour she has received a text proposing they meet in a coffee shop near Liverpool Street Station at two o'clock on Sunday afternoon, if she should be so free, exclamation mark. She is not free, however. This is her regular date with Joy's quilting circle and she is not prepared to miss it. Especially not in order to meet someone she is dubious about meeting in the first place.

She texts a casual reply. *Sorry, Sunday not possible. Raincheck? Maybe early next week?* Within minutes another text flies in. Since it is the lady's prerogative to choose the day and time (?!) he is open to any suggestion! She avoids suggesting a venue, but offers three alternative times on Monday and Wednesday. Then remembers that Dev is considerably less than retirement age. Perhaps he'll be at work, and perhaps this will be for the best.

Even without an assignation, her own week is not short of action. Quilting is a flexible day job, if a day job can also be an affair of the heart. There's Joy's group, and the gym. On Tuesdays she teaches literacy to disadvantaged young people and refugees in Tower Hamlets. There are fortnightly visits to her mother in Oxford. There are family and friends.

On top of which, there is a husband. Geoff is an important part of your life: discuss. Easy enough, she thinks: affection and resentment in roughly equal parts, spliced with anger and regret. Where does he now reside on my list of priorities? Once a major player, he has been relegated. To the sidelines? Not quite, more to the second eleven. We still sleep in the same bed and see each other for most meals. We still spend most evenings together. But Geoff, as a concept, is swathed in a newly negative aura.

There is, though, the fact that we have lived together for close to forty years. Doesn't that assume a fair bit of harmony? Or is it merely that we have a combined history, a benign mutual tolerance? That tolerance has become less benign. Could it be in the process of unravelling altogether?

Geoff and Viv have always given each other space. This, she supposes, may be a singular advantage in a long-term relationship. It has never been a problem for them. Which is just as well, as another text wings in from Dev.

He suggests the earliest of her three proposed times. The same cafe at eleven on Monday morning. What kind of hairstyle does she have? And what will she be wearing? Can't risk making shome mishtake, right?!

Viv reads the text and its predecessors over again, several times. She finds these questions vaguely irritating. Aside from the clumsy attempt at humour. And the spelling and punctuation. Instead of replying immediately she decides to run the message past Joy on Sunday afternoon.

Viv's friendship with Joy is a by-product of a professional relationship. They first met five years ago when Joy sauntered off the street into Viv's publishing house with a bunch of pages in a Tesco bag. The receptionist happened to be in the loo; Joy had no appointment, and this was not how things were done. But Viv's office was opposite and her door was open.

The typescript was about a feisty trio of outliers, a badger, fox and squirrel who conducted daring raids on nearby kitchens from their base in a London square. The storyline needed tightening but it was fresh and funny, and accompanied by appealing watercolour illustrations by Joy's tenant Yasmin. Viv worked on it pro bono at first, as a sideline from her adult fiction, and the book became the first of a successful series.

Joy's quilting circle spills over from the double sitting room of her Brixton house. The participants are something of a revolving door, with sundry ring-ins who come and go. The permanent residents – Joy and her three tenants (none has left since Viv's first visit a year ago) – are all single mothers.

Joy strikes Viv as a benevolent landlady, with minor despotic tendencies. More than one member of the circle has confided that she allows her tenants to pay rent in accordance with their means. These are also revolving, but very often slender and occasionally non-existent, at which times Joy has allowed them to stay for free.

Viv hasn't yet worked out the precise number of children living in the house. The revolving-door policy works against an accurate head count. Joy has two teenagers, but younger kids wander in and out and there is at least one baby.

When Viv first joined the group the front door (painted a psychedelic rainbow) tended to be left unlatched. Since one memorable visit from someone's ex-boyfriend, however, the rainbow has been painted out and the door kept securely locked and equipped with a spy hole. Viv is scrutinised through this when she arrives late, after an unscheduled stop between stations on the Victoria Line (a suicide, she suspects). The door is thrown open by Riley, the dishiest of Joy's residents. It was Riley's thuggish boyfriend from Yorkshire who broke in and caused havoc. The whitey from hell, Hull and high water, Joy called him.

Nineteen-year-old Riley was pregnant with her second child at the time, the caramel-skinned charmer she's now carrying on her hip. Viv asks after her older child, a boy in kindergarten.

Hoisting her carpet-bag into the cavernous hall, she steps around coats, brollies and kids' sporting equipment, and a baby sleeping soundly (the same one as last week? she can't be certain) in a fold-up stroller. The circle is well patronised today. She counts eight others, including Joy's talented illustrator Yasmin.

'Listen up, y'all.' Joy has been waiting for Viv's arrival to make an announcement. A newbie is coming to join the group next week. A Mr Jackson Adeyemi. He's a rookie, right, so be nice to him, *okay?*

Mr? A current passes through the double drawing room. A ripple of surprise, and disapproval.

Yes, a nice, manly Nigerian gentleman they will all like. A security guard who works round the corner. Very quiet and well behaved. Ondine knows him. Ondine is gay, Joy has told Viv, but tends to be non-functioning, although she goes to clubs.

Everyone is aware that Joy's former husband, now vanished off the face of the earth, also happened to be a nice (initially) and manly Nigerian gentleman. Joy adds, 'We're not into discrimination round here, right?' A sly glance at Viv. 'We're multi-cultural.'

Viv thinks Joy probably made a similar announcement before she herself was invited to join the circle. She's older than the others by a considerable margin, as well as whiter, but she has never felt awkward. She hopes, rather fervently, that this new initiative won't imperil things. The quilting circle is powerfully feminist in its sensibilities. But it is not physically powerful, and nor is the household. She suspects that Mr Jackson's night job may have weighed heavily in his favour. Riley's ex is not the only disaffected dad to have shown up uninvited; there was another fracas only last week. A tame security guard down the road might have his uses.

Viv spreads a section of her quilt-in-progress on her knees. She unwraps the simple tools of her trade: needle and thread, thimble, embroiderer's hoop. With everyone hard at work the room assumes an atmosphere she has not encountered anywhere else and finds addictive. She has tried to describe the phenomenon to Geoff, but floundered in the face of his scientific scepticism. Jules, though, caught on completely. She says the same elevated mood happens in the rehearsal room.

Joy is a touch on the defensive when Viv shows her the text from Dev. She's still pumped after her controversial announcement, and not in the mood for dissecting spelling or punctuation.

'Just reply to the poor sod – he's only asking for a meeting. He's not proposing holy bigamy.'

'But he's years younger than me, Joy.'

'Half your luck, girl. Check out his credentials. If you don't,' a canny look, 'he'll think you're racist.'

This is persuasive. Viv thinks perhaps she has been a bit precious. She dashes off a reply, ignoring Dev's questions about hairstyle and outfits, but saying she will carry the improving book she's reading – Clive James' *Cultural Amnesia*. After pressing send she has a nasty feeling that this message qualifies as pretentious, which is arguably worse.

Still, it doesn't discourage Dev, evidently. He shoots back a cheery: *OK hope i can read the title! Look forward to seeing you tomorrow morning Vivien!!*

Joy thinks Dev sounds like a bit of a pet, full of beans like the big frisky puppy in her new book. Anything like your Mr Adeyemi?

queries Viv. Ever since the collapse of her marriage Joy has dallied with a succession of men, while contriving to keep them at arm's length. But it is a given that she will not disclose anything until she is good and ready.

Viv's mobile rings. Daisy wants to come over tomorrow morning at eleven with stuff. They can have coffee. 'Sorry darling, I've got an eleven o'clock appointment I can't change. And the afternoon's no good either – I'm filling in at the Red Cross.' A rapid calculation. 'I could probably do an early lunch, just. Or what about dinner tomorrow? Or tonight?'

'Jules said you're going to the theatre tomorrow – the Almeida. *Ghosts.*'

'Oh *yes*, that's right, of course we are, I forgot. Why don't you try to get a ticket?'

'I've seen it. It's great. Tonight's no good. So, what's the unbreakable appointment?'

'Appointment?'

'Tomorrow *morning.*'

'Oh, that. Doctor. Just Nerida. But there's no reason you couldn't come over and dump stuff, of course.' Viv catches Joy's eye. Joy is following the conversation with undisguised interest while stitching her wadding.

'Is something wrong, Mum?'

'Wrong? No, absolutely nothing. Routine, you know. Only a prescription.'

'What for?'

'Oh, nothing special.'

'Well, couldn't you change it, then? Make it another day? It doesn't *matter* which day it is, does it?'

'Another day?'

'The appointment, Mum, Jesus. *Concentrate.*'

'Ah, no, I'm afraid I can't, not really. You know how booked up she gets.'

Pause. 'Is there something you're not telling me, Mum?' Daisy's voice is studiedly casual.

'No, of course not, darling.'

'It's nothing to do with your—' Viv hears Daisy hesitate. But her daughter is nothing if not forthright. 'You're not worried about your *memory*, are you, Mum?'

Viv laughs, with a scintilla of unease. 'No, of course I'm not. Well, I shouldn't say of course, everyone I know is worried about their memory. Including Joy here,' she says, with a pointed glance, 'but I don't think I'm any more worried than anyone else. Listen, forget that, tell me how you're feeling. Have you made any decisions?'

But she can tell her daughter's keen antenna has picked up something. It was an unwise thing to say, that she had an unbreakable doctor's appointment. Joy agrees that it was a very foolish thing. And quite unnecessary.

I suppose I could have said I had to meet a suicidal friend, Viv says.

Such as the person who jumped in front of a train on the Victoria Line this afternoon? That's a dumb idea, Joy scoffs, because she wouldn't be able to meet you. And you'd already *know* that, right? Joy is nothing if not practical.

Next morning Viv is discomfited to find herself feeling distinctly apprehensive. She considers not going through with this nonsense and cancelling the meeting with Dev. If it weren't for that excuse of an unbreakable doctor's appointment, she could have told Daisy she was free after all.

What do I think I'm doing, she asks herself, not for the first time, proposing to meet a man who is twenty years younger than me and who uses copious exclamation marks? Proposing to meet a strange man, to get down to the nitty-gritty, with the object of possibly having sex? Isn't this a rather preposterous course of action for a woman my age to be considering?

But there is an inescapable problem. Joy was right. Dev may well feel insulted if she cancels, even if she insists it is because of his age. Viv has an ingrained horror of racism. She feels she can't risk such an outcome. And wouldn't it be one in the eye for Geoff... This thought tips the balance.

She'll just have to go through the motions with this one. Next time, she will be more assertive with Martin Glover. She's paid the piper; next time she will call the tune. Always assuming there is a next time.

She will treat Dev as a dry run. She'll be in and out of that coffee shop in twenty minutes flat.

8

DEV

All Viv's doubts and preconceptions become irrelevant the moment she walks into the coffee shop and locks eyes with the man sitting alone under the window. She is knocked sideways, she will relay later to Julia, left breathless. Both reactions, Jules will point out, were most likely on account of being late, and having just lugged her weighty tome down several blocks of soulless Bishopsgate in pouring rain, when there was a perfectly good cafe at the station.

The inescapable fact is that Dev is one of the most jaw-droppingly attractive men Viv has ever set eyes on. He is dark-complexioned and, equally plainly, only in his mid-forties. She was expecting that. She wasn't expecting him to be such an unmitigated knockout. Never in a million years, she will tell Joy, was she prepared for that.

She realises that she is standing mutely in front of him – slack-jawed, quite possibly – while he remains seated, openly inspecting her in turn. Not standing up, not even pretending to identify the dripping volume wedged under her left arm.

Viv gives a nervous laugh and immediately regrets it. She drags off her raincoat and drops the book on the floor, together with her scarf, bag and umbrella. She feels uncoordinated and burdened with a mountain of paraphernalia, all of it wet. The simple operation seems to take forever, and for its duration Dev continues to watch her intently, his handsome features unreadable.

She slides into the chair opposite him. Breathe normally, she tells herself, and don't let nerves cause you to avoid eye contact. Then, when this is patently not working: for *fuck's* sake, woman, get a grip.

Dev is dressed in a conservative dark suit with a white shirt and plain blue tie. Viv is wearing jeans and a bright-red cardigan, long and rather baggy, over a white cheesecloth shirt. She didn't pay much attention this morning because she hadn't taken this appointment seriously. She is feeling insecure enough already; this only adds another layer of discomfort.

Her hair is damp and windswept. She had forgotten to wield the firm-hold, high-gloss hairspray Ramona had urged her (successfully) to purchase. And her cheeks and nose will be red and shiny from the cold. She must look like a bag lady. Dev is probably thinking she's a gauche ageing hippy. But perhaps that's just what I *am*. Although I wouldn't say I was gauche, exactly …

'I am very pleased to meet you, Vivien,' he is saying politely. 'Very pleased indeed.'

The formal cadence sounds genuine to Viv's sceptical ears. She's on an all-systems alert for any suggestion of distaste or (horror of horrors) pity on his part. He has thick black hair, glossy without the aid of product, full sensuous lips and the kind of soulful brown eyes often described as melting. Viv has read the description many times, dismissing it as a cliché, but never before has she sat so close to someone whose eyes cry out to be so described.

Dev extends a smooth hand across the table. He looks dry and unruffled. Did it start raining after he arrived? How long has he been sitting here – is she very late? Not more than a few minutes, surely. Ten? She takes a surreptitious glance at her watch. No, twenty. How did that happen? She sees an empty coffee cup in front of him.

'I'm sorry I'm so late, and so bedraggled,' she says. She wipes her cold wet hand on her cardigan and belatedly shakes his, introducing herself, giving her full name without a qualm, even though

Martin had stressed this was not obligatory. She's finding it hard to equate the rather immobile person facing her with the chirpy texter. It shows how misleading punctuation marks can be.

'Yes, I had been looking through the window,' Dev says, still on his former train of thought. He is keeping hold of her hand longer than is normally considered best practice. 'I knew it was you, Vivien, even before you opened the door.' His voice is deep and resonant. Viv has a swift mental picture of the still depths of remote rock pools in the Kakadu National Park, which Jules has promised to show her someday.

'I knew it was you too, Dev, oddly enough,' she murmurs. 'Not that there were many other—'

'And even though,' he interrupts with emphasis, 'you had left me in the dark. You gave me no information about your clothing, or your hairstyle. Luckily this turned out to be quite unnecessary, because you were self-explanatory, Vivien.'

What was it Ramona called her hair? Headstrong. She tries to pat it down. Self-explanatory? What does that mean? Could it be a joke? No, Dev is unsmiling. Martin Glover must have given him some kind of description. If so, it might be cause for concern. But – here's another thing – Dev thinks I am only in my late fifties. Perhaps he thinks this is how Englishwomen of my age just *are* …

Dev, her new template of male beauty in its prime, is still holding her hand. His large and seriously melting eyes are fixed on her face. 'Your hand is *very* cold, by the way, Vivien.'

'Yes, I'm sorry about that. It's very cold outside.' How feeble is this?

'Sorry? You must not keep saying that. The English are very fond of saying sorry. Too fond of it. Cold hands mean a warm heart. That is how the English saying goes, I think.'

'Yes, it does go like that. It's probably rubbish, though.' Might this be construed as belligerent? 'Not,' she adds hurriedly, 'that I would want to cast aspersions on your choice of English saying.'

The humour sounds clunky to her ears, and it elicits no detectable response. Almost certainly a misjudgement. She casts around for something to say but finds that her capacity for conversation seems to have flown out the window. What could Martin have been thinking, introducing her to this paragon of pulchritude?

And Dev himself must be fuming, planning to give the Discretion Agency an earful the moment she leaves. Should she leave now? No, that would definitely be taken as rude. And probably racist as well. Which could not be further from the truth.

Awkwardness must not be allowed to set in. But she has never tried to make small talk in such an unlikely setting with such an unlikely man, with a subtext they both know but cannot mention: the reason they are here. The reason being hardly credible. We are checking each other out to see if we want to go to bed together, of all things. Of all the lunatic, deluded things. Of all the *unlikely* things.

Her eyes alight on an object on the floor. 'That's my weight-lifting done for the day,' she says, indicating her book, *Cultural Amnesia*. 'You must have thought I was striving to impress. When the truth is, I was trying to absorb reams of arcane knowledge by osmosis.'

This is worse still. Smart-arse. Perilously close to inanity. Present me with a young and ridiculously gorgeous man and I fall to pieces. Dev's expression hasn't changed. He is still expressionless. Could it be horror-induced paralysis?

Then he says, 'Vivien, do not feel you have to make conversation in order to entertain me, please. We must relax together, in each other's company. This is an important first step for us.'

First step. Could this mean he is envisaging a second? Dev leans forward. He has dropped her hand but hasn't once taken his intent eyes off her. 'That is a very beautiful pendant you are wearing.'

Her hand moves to her necklace. 'Do you like it? It was given to me by my—' It was a present from Geoff, when Daisy turned twenty-one. A sinuous, sterling silver pendant from Tiffany, set with an exquisite natural pearl. By far the most expensive piece of jewellery she owns.

'Yes, it goes with everything, no matter how ratty, so I tend to wear it all the time without thinking.'

It partners another favourite, the Mexican bracelet of beaten silver she clasped on her wrist, also semi-automatically, this morning. Geoff always had excellent taste in jewellery, and in the latter part of his career the means to indulge it a little. Viv feels a small pang in the pit of her stomach.

'Don't you think it is very strange indeed, Vivien,' she hears Dev ask, 'that I knew immediately who you were?'

'Well, there aren't many people in here …' It's not a very appetising cafe. Of course, it's made more alluring by—

'But even if there were a *great* many customers arriving, there was something about you, as you came through this door. Something that—' He breaks off. He has the most luxuriant dark eyelashes Viv has ever seen. There is another abrupt, alarming pause. It stretches out disconcertingly. She is struck by his statuesque stillness.

'Something that?' echoes Viv, faintly. She swallows, feeling herself wilt (melt?) under this steady beam of scrutiny. *The male gaze,* she thinks. I'm thrown by it. It's something to which I have become unaccustomed. I don't know how to read it anymore.

She imagines they are being filmed. They are in a scene from a movie, a comedy but not one of the witty, Cary Grant–Katharine Hepburn variety. A peculiar one, with two decidedly odd protagonists. This conversation, if you could call it that, has a distinctive, stop–start rhythm of its own. Dev is still waiting. Does he want her to finish his sentence?

'Was it something about me you recognised?' she says at last. 'Did I look like someone?' But who could it be? 'People have said I remind them—'

He shakes his head emphatically. 'No, not at all. Not at all, Vivien. You do not remind me of anyone. On the contrary. But, as

I was just saying, there was something – something very hard to put into words.' He is frowning in concentration, but hasn't shifted his gaze.

'Could it have been – you felt – something that *connected?*' Viv can't quite credit she is saying this. Daisy would explode. But it seems she has struck a chord. Dev exhales a long breath.

'That is it, yes. You are right. I cannot define why this should be, but I felt an *emotional* connection.'

Viv swallows. Since she arrived he has hardly moved. Apart from breathing and speaking, that is. Deeply, in both cases. Whereas she has twitched, and shifted—

'Yes, I feel drawn to you, Vivien. I hope you are not shocked. And I hope you don't mind if I tell you this straightaway, with no beating about the bush and no polite nothings. Because I think both of us have no time for that. Do you know what it is I am talking about?'

'Well, I – not entirely, no.' Viv is feeling gobsmacked, she has no other word for it, by the course events seem to be taking. Unless she is misinterpreting them, which is quite possible. She essays a nonchalant smile, but the muscles around her mouth have atrophied with no contribution from Botox. Dev is not smiling, and his delivery is even and intense. 'I mean, an unusually deep connection. A physical relation between us, Vivien, that I have sensed before you have even touched me.'

'Oh.' Viv's facial muscles spring to life of their own accord as her mouth drops open for the second time this morning. If only she had a secret device to record this riveting conversation. A miniature one, perhaps, inside a fountain pen.

'I would like you to ask yourself whether you too are feeling, or can come to feel soon, what I am talking about. It is an important principle to establish. Before we go any further.'

Viv feels an involuntary stirring of the loins. She may be perilously close to losing objectivity. Is she becoming delusional? She needs to keep her head, regain some detachment.

She unlocks her eyes from his. Their surroundings are indeed undistinguished. They are in a small coffee shop, the basic type, fast-disappearing, where you queue up to order at the counter. More of a sandwich bar, with few chairs and tables. There's a sprinkling of other people drinking coffee and biting into sugary buns. Perhaps they too might do this. She could give herself some breathing space. A minute or two to take stock.

'Shouldn't we – Dev, before we go *any further*, shouldn't we have a coffee? Or tea? If we sit here taking up space without buying anything they'll get, you know – rather peevish.'

She is annoyed with herself for getting so spectacularly rattled. It's very stuffy. Her mouth is dry. She has to project her words in order to pronounce them.

Dev looks indifferent. 'Certainly. I have had one already. While I was waiting for you. You must have whatever you like, Vivien.' He makes no move.

'Well, I think I need refuelling, even if you don't.' She suspects he may be affronted at the interruption. He remains motionless and impassive as she fetches her coffee, a flat white, the now widespread Australian style Jules introduced her to. And a jam doughnut. She feels in need of something comfortingly sickly, even though she rarely eats doughnuts. Geoff loves them, though. Dev appears not to have moved when she returns to the table, but she sees him observing it.

She gropes for a topic. 'Have you had many other introductions from Martin Glover, Dev?'

He shakes his head. 'This is my first time. You are the very first lady he has sent me, Vivien. And that is why it is such a remarkable coincidence.'

'You're my first introduction too.' She cuts the doughnut in half. The coffee is not well made. It's very weak; she should have asked for a double shot. Or a triple. 'Although I suppose – it's not such a coincidence really, is it? We both went to the same agency, after all.'

'Ah, but how likely is that occurrence? That we are both visiting the same agency, at the same time? Not likely at all, is it? And yet that is what we did, Vivien. It is the hand of fate, I am thinking.'

Is it possible Dev could be a Bollywood film star? His speech is well-enunciated and deliberate, rather like that of the late Richard Burton. Its impact is similarly hypnotic. And now he is gazing at her again, the melting brown eyes fixed and unblinking. She's finding the doughnut hard to eat. It sheds granulated sugar and jam everywhere. The debris is probably all round her mouth.

She scrubs at her face with one of the wafer-thin paper napkins, then worries that she has smudged her lipstick. Or did she forget to put any on? Too late to look for evidence; she has screwed the napkin into a ball.

She asks Dev what he does. He is in the hospitality business, he says, without enthusiasm or elaboration. He puts out a hand and touches her wedding ring. His fingers brush hers. A light touch, almost a caress. Her hand reacts.

'And I think you are married unhappily, Vivien?'

She looks down at her plate. Half a sticky doughnut, smears of jam, a scattering of sugar crystals, a screwed-up paper napkin. Hearing this question posed so starkly, she is unsure how to answer it without being disloyal to Geoff. Disloyal to Geoff, she hears Jules scoff, what do you fondly imagine you're being?

'In a way ...'

Dev responds with unexpected vigour. 'Well, Vivien, I am thinking you would not be signing up with the Discretion Agency and paying our Mr Martin Glover a great deal of money if you were in an ecstatic union. Is that not a correct assumption, exactly?'

'It's – well, I suppose so, yes.' Although how realistic is an ecstatic union in any long-term relationship? Not realistic at all, exactly. That's not what it's all about. It's all about long-term happiness and contentment, and entitlement to a—

'You are an independent woman, Vivien. I think you are want-ing exciting new experiences?' He pauses. 'I think you are wishing for someone with whom to enjoy a more physical life than you have been having. You are wanting to desire someone sexually. You are wanting someone to desire you.'

Viv has a sensation that compares, she imagines, with that of being hit by a train. She meets his eyes, this madly attractive man. This madly attractive, considerably younger man sitting opposite her, with more sex appeal than you could—

'I think that we are both wanting the *same outcome*, Vivien.'

And now she really is poleaxed. She nods dumbly.

'You will come to the house next week, and we will have an ini-tial assignation.' He sees she is about to prevaricate. 'In the country, near London. Don't worry, there will be no one there.'

'But what about your – your wife? Or your – partner?'

'She is not around. Don't worry.'

Viv looks down. There's a dusting of white sugar on her red car-digan. She brushes it off. She takes the bull by the horns.

'Dev, why did you go to the agency in the first place? After all, it's not as if you need—'

'*Why?* Surely this is obvious, Vivien.'

'Well, I'm not sure that it is.' Something must be said. It simply must. But how to put it? Straight down the line, nothing for it, no alternative. 'There is a big age difference between us.'

'A big age difference?' This seems to galvanise him. For the first time he becomes quite animated.

'But this is exactly what I wanted, Vivien. This is what I said to him,' his voice rises excitedly, 'find me an older, attractive, confident lady who would like to meet me! That was my order to Mr Martin Glover. An independent lady. And he has done it, first cab off the rank. He has hit the jackpot.'

Viv is aware that her misgivings are in steep decline. And this younger man with the film star looks and perfect, dazzling teeth, sitting less than three feet away, seems to be smiling for the first time. It's certainly not a beaming grin, but it is a movement of the mouth she has no hesitation in finding captivating.

She smiles back, thinking (like Alice in Wonderland) how very curious all this is. My body has parted company with my mind and my reflexes have taken over. It's as if I were a teenager again, in the back seat of a car.

'I hope you would like to meet me. Meet me biblically, I mean, Vivien. Because I, definitely, would like to meet you.'

Biblically? Viv barely hesitates. This is her surrender-to-chance moment, and she can't remember when one of those last came along. Not for some years, that's for sure. She knows, and knows full well, that chance is blind. It takes no care and no responsibility. This may not turn out well, but what the hell, she tells herself, if it doesn't? I'm of an age where I can choose to do foolish things. And do them just for the sake of it.

She is ready to suspend her disbelief. More than willing. Because she can't believe her luck. Jules, Joy, listen up, y'all! Just wait until you hear *this*.

9

A LATE COURTSHIP

Julia has her mobile turned off. She is sitting at a table in a smart Covent Garden eatery being wooed by two men. Two attractive men, as it happens, one around her age and one considerably younger. They are, respectively, the conductor and director of *The Queen of Spades*, a new co-production with La Scala, which opens at the Royal Opera House before Christmas. In less than eight weeks' time. Right now they are without their Countess, and they want, with a measure of urgency, Julia Jefferies.

Lunch orders are in but haven't yet arrived. No one has mentioned the subject in the forefront of all three minds. The elder of the two men is expecting the business end to be somewhat protracted. He has talked to Malcolm Foster, Julia's agent, and he knows that the desired outcome is by no means a dead cert. But he is a seasoned campaigner, well prepared, ready to bide his time and await the right moment. In this regard his restraint and urbanity are very English. The younger man is noticeably un-English, and is containing himself with difficulty.

Julia is enjoying the experience of being courted by two suitors. Milking it, as she would be the first to admit, for all it's worth. It is not a new experience; in the course of her career there have been many men – it has usually been men – competing for her professional favours. But the fact that it hasn't happened for a while (and she had feared it might never happen again) makes it all the sweeter.

On her right, in a pinstriped suit and silver tie, is the eminent British conductor Raymond Bayliss. She knows Ray from way back. They've worked together many times, most recently five years ago in Berlin on a production of Janacek's *The Makropulos Affair*.

The thickset young man on her left is one of the hottest young properties of the day, Emils Liepins. The polar opposite of an ascetic dreamer, his broad features radiate dynamism and intelligence. Passion and virility too; Julia would put money on that. His shot at sharp dressing involves an ancient herringbone jacket thrown over a shapeless sweater and jeans.

Already formidable at twenty-eight, Emils cut his directing teeth in Riga at the Latvian National Opera. He is unknown to Julia personally but his reputation is not; along with the rest of the opera world she has heard all about his triumph with *War and Peace* in St Petersburg. He may be the opera world's only wunderkind with a broken nose.

As the food arrives Ray steers the conversation towards the Sydney Opera House. Glorious from the outside, its cramped orchestra pit and tiny stage are notorious. A complete nightmare, Julia confirms, although there have been improvements lately. She is gloating over a grilled Dover sole, her all-time favourite and done very well here, off-the-bone with tartare sauce, new potatoes (a guilty luxury) and sautéed spinach. But it's remarkable what high standards Sydney manages to achieve on a regular basis, given those disadvantages.

Ray saw her *Dido and Aeneas*. 'She had them in a collective trance, Emils. It was sheer genius.' His pale blue eyes light up at the memory. Dear Ray, he's looking older, Julia notes. Since their last meeting his face is more lined and he's down to the bin-ends of his hair. But his vim and vigour are undiminished.

This is the signal for Emils to let rip. 'We need that genius!' He swivels round in his chair. 'We're on course for a ground-breaking production, Julia. But this is critically dependent on the casting. Because, you see, the Countess is an exceptional role for a singer who can act. It's *her* image that the audience will take home with them.'

Julia stirs mutinously. Small role, unworthy – the objections come crowding in. *Reigniting the embers of a dying career …*

Emils extends his hands towards her. 'Okay – the role is not big in terms of lines, we know that. But Julia – it is huge, *huge* in its implication. I can't stress this strongly enough.'

His English is fluent and idiomatic, with a pronounced American inflexion. She senses he would love to leap out of his comfortable chair and pace around. He grips the edge of the table, seemingly oblivious to his stylish surroundings, to the other people lunching in close proximity.

'You know the opera, but can I refresh your memory?' Rhetorical; he's off and running almost before he has finished the sentence. 'It's got the whole package: music, story, spectacle. Everything you could ever want in your wildest dreams, Julia.'

Oh, I wouldn't count on that, she murmurs, but he either ignores this or doesn't hear.

'Which makes it super-challenging, right? It's a suspense thriller, and that's fine, but along comes this paranormal stuff. We don't know how to read that.'

He is drinking his wine fast, fairly gulping it down. It's a Meursault, rich yet light, and selected by Ray with Julia's sole in mind. It is quite something, in her opinion, and deserving of more respect. She sips hers slowly, rolling it round in her mouth.

Emils drains his glass mid-sentence, but Ray catches the wait-er's eye and with an infinitesimal shake of the head deters him from a refill just yet. In any case the younger man has now switched to water and is swigging away with the same avidity. Water or wine, they're one and the same to him at this moment. What matters – in fact, the only thing in the world of any consequence – is this project. And Julia thinks: as long as he doesn't take himself too seriously, that bodes well. She suspects Emils works more through instinct than analytical reasoning. She has observed this before with certain directors.

He hasn't missed a beat. 'Fantasy in the movies we can do. But this is different. These people on stage are tangling with supernatural forces. Fate. Retribution. Premonitions of sudden death.'

He looks at Julia. 'Take *hell*. The prospect of burning in hell for eternity is very real here. And preying on the Countess's mind is what she got up to in her reckless youth – '

The back of Julia's neck prickles. She lays down her cutlery and sees that Ray has done the same. He's letting his young colleague have the floor. His arms are crossed, his high-domed forehead cocked attentively to one side.

The waiter, his eye on Ray, refills the empty water glass as Emils leans forward brandishing his fork. 'Here's where your acting ability will be critical, Julia. The audience needs to believe that you are an old lady. We need them to *totally* believe it.'

He flicks his hair aside with the fork and gives her a blatantly heterosexual look. 'This is one big ask in itself. But in your youth you were a staggering beauty,' another appreciative look, 'incredibly sexy. You were a femme fatale, the Venus of Moscow. It shouldn't be too hard to convince the audience of *that*.'

A pair of vigilant dark eyes are half-hidden behind a dishevelled clump of hair. The male gaze. Just as Viv has very recently (and unknown to Jules) been exposed to it, Julia is now on the receiving end of an even more potent delivery. Her eyebrows are raised. On a less calculated and entirely feminine level, she rewards this very unignorable young man with a glance of some intimacy.

He's not finished. 'And in your old age you're still magnetic. You command the stage at all times, Julia. Even when the Countess is not physically present, it's like she's still there in everyone's mind. All the stories swirling around her, all the rumours. She's a lady with one helluva past. She has a dark *aura*.' He uses his fork to sketch a halo around Julia's head.

'It's sinister and alluring. It attracts, it repels. No one's immune to it. Including the orchestra,' a broad grin at Ray, 'and the conductor. And every other male in the house.' He deals Julia a wide, disarming smile.

She smiles back. She knows exactly where her would-be director is coming from. It helps that he has his own aura, with sex appeal as a prime constituent. At this stage in her career, when it comes to sweet talk (both personal and professional) Julia is a dab hand at sorting the wheat from the chaff. And she's not immune to the allure of it, either. It won't be around forever, but today it's there for the taking. She can take it. She can take it in *spades*. Ray, suave, amused, catches her eye.

They can both see how this ardent young man has had such a meteoric rise. He has a natural authority and intensity that command attention. Most crucially, he has the power of intellectual seduction, which every director with vision must possess.

'Do go on,' Julia invites.

'As a young woman on the make, the Countess made a kind of Faustian pact with a sleazy Count. He had a foolproof gambling formula. If she could get her hands on it, she could set herself up for life, and hang the consequences. So, she agreed,' another speaking glance, 'to what was called in those days an *overnight meeting*.'

Fair exchange, some might think, Julia murmurs again, and they chuckle.

'But this is grand Russian opera, where bad deeds come back to haunt you. They come and hunt you down. Her scandalous youth will lead to three dramatic deaths in her old age. One of these deaths,' a pause, 'is hers.'

Something dark skitters briefly over the table. Julia has four decades on Emils. Ripples from the past have a resonance for her that is blithely absent from his mind. He senses it, and lays a light hand on her arm.

'But wait. She bounces back, as a ghost. And here's where we go places the Garden's never been.' A glance at Ray. 'I mean cutting edge. I mean *holograms*. On stage.' He leans towards Julia with an air of revelation.

'And let's not forget,' Ray backs this up, 'that the entire production will be filmed for cinema release.'

On film, the singer's voice can be amplified to envelop the auditorium. Earlier in Julia's career she wouldn't have been happy about this, but now it has a certain appeal. At this late stage in her career, could she perhaps become a film star? Malcolm Foster, her agent, had mentioned this. But holograms? She has never heard of such a thing.

Emils touches her hand. 'Julia, you do see how the entire story revolves around the Countess? How she is the real star of the show? With your voice, and your presence, you will be *mesmerising*.' He surveys the room as if to a listening audience.

And Julia thinks: you have all the drive and self-belief in the world, and a fair bit more besides. You have the world at your feet, as I did once, and as I continued to have for a great many years. Because you are young and talented and you know it. Just as I did. And you are charming and charismatic, and you know that too, and use it as the priceless asset it is. You know you can rely on it. As I did. And as – I must admit – I still do. To a lesser extent.

But in her mind this is not a done deal. The Countess is written for a low soprano, a mezzo. Julia has never seen herself as a mezzo. Her signature roles were all in the lyric soprano repertoire.

The older of the two men is far too experienced to believe the engagement is in the bag. Not yet. Not quite. Ray knows where his star is coming from, and where her insecurities lie. The professional ones, at least. For this betrothal to be signed and sealed, a trinity must be mobilised: negotiation, persuasion and reassurance. But the greatest of these is reassurance.

'It's too low for me,' Julia says quietly. Almost too quietly, but judged with precision. Julia's vocal skills, her refined diction, can cut through pretty much any level of ambient noise.

The reflexes of both men are in excellent repair. They leave the blocks and nearly collide. The younger man defers to Ray. This is his province.

'You are a soprano, Jules, that's true. But you have always had a rich middle range.' No change of expression, but a slight inclination of her head. 'And now your voice is lower than it was. If anything, it's even richer.'

Emils backs this with supporting evidence she cannot deny. 'You've just sung Dido – brilliantly, with no difficulty at all. And Dido is a mezzo role.'

Ray continues, with a delicacy finely calibrated, for this is a difficult balancing act. 'The Countess is not *too* taxing, vocally. Your middle register has always been strong; now it will be perfect for her. You have the skills of a lifetime at your disposal. Where singers fail in the role, it's almost always because their acting is not up to it.'

Jules knows these are telling points well made, by a man she esteems. When Ray says it's not too taxing vocally, he is spot on. The Countess only has three scenes. In fact, perhaps she should be more concerned that the role is *too small*…

'And the other cause for failure,' Emils now, 'can be that they are not magnetic or glamorous enough to be believable. We don't have that problem.'

'That will never be Julia's problem,' Ray agrees firmly. And then, in a voice to brook no argument, 'You'll lay 'em in the aisles, Jules.'

'You're the only one who can do it,' the younger man says, with a fervour verging on the messianic. The air around her thrums with masculine energy. Julia feels her resistance to this late alliance, this *ménage á trois* ebbing away.

And the key to reassurance is repetition. 'You are a great singing actress,' Ray repeats, 'one of the greatest. As you have proved so many times.'

Emils has been dealt the trump card. He remarks casually, 'Isn't the Met doing *The Queen of Spades* in a couple of years, Ray? They'll be checking on us. They'll be on the lookout for their Countess.'

This is a thought. A most enticing one. It's been some years since Julia Jefferies last sang at the Met. Her hands go up to smooth down her hair, but in the nick of time she remembers she is wearing a new confection, a little cap in olive velvet with net and feather. Her milliner called it a riff on Maid Marian, and Julia teamed it for this meeting with her flowing olive-green opera cloak, one of her favourites.

Her fingertips meet behind her ears and she raises her hair, fanning it out before letting it fall, gradually and softly. The men's eyes meet again for a second. They relax, imperceptibly.

She wavers. 'But I've already said my farewells …'

As a last hurrah, this is unconvincing. Her suitors are united in treating it with the contempt it deserves and, they suspect, she is most likely hoping for. Retirement, they scoff, *Julia Jefferies?* At this stage? Absurd. Don't even think of it.

'We're going to do great things together, Julia,' says Emils with a wink. He raises one unkempt eyebrow under an equally disorderly thatch of hair. 'Thrilling, intoxicating and very, very Russian.'

He is flirting with me, Julia thinks. It's always an advantage when there is chemistry with her director. Chemical attraction, she has found, is completely independent of age. It's not even related to looks, necessarily, although Emils has a rumpled, Slavic cast to his person and features she has always found appealing. Even if, or perhaps especially if, he has no interest in fashion and an evident disdain for the services of hair salons.

It's a special thing, chemistry between an opera star and director, and hard to pin down. It either exists or it does not. When it does not, she has found that there is nothing to be done by either party to bring it into being. When it does, the spark lights up a performance and influences the whole production.

Because this relationship is a love affair of sorts. A very public affair conducted on the stage, in the spotlight, with a rapt audience following every word, every note, and every gesture. It is unique and of itself, a special relationship that others, the *outsiders*, cannot fully understand. Over the years Julia has concluded that they would never understand it. Not even if it could be fully explained.

10

A BRIEF ENCOUNTER

Among the multi-national, multi-coloured early-afternoon crowds milling on the concourse of Liverpool Street Station this weekday is Vivien Quarry, a white European woman of a certain age. She's either past her sexual prime, or well past it, or conceivably *at it*, depending on which magazine article you read.

Today Viv has made an effort. She's wearing a navy jacket and matching trousers, black ankle boots with Cuban heels, a red trilby, leather gloves and a striped scarf. Hoisted over one shoulder is a straw tote with leather straps. Tucked on top and partially visible to the passer-by is a rolled-up trench coat, a small scarlet umbrella minus its sheath, a newspaper and a book. Not *Cultural Amnesia* this time, but one from this year's Man Booker shortlist, the writer's breakthrough book. Viv edited the author's first novel and took part in early discussions about this one. She is mentioned warmly in the acknowledgements.

Inside the tote, and concealed from prying eyes, is a roomy cosmetics bag that has seen better days. It contains a number of items, several of them new or travel-sized: mouthwash, toothbrush and toothpaste, hairbrush, spray perfume, pocket magnifying mirror, lip gloss, cleansing wipes, lubricant, and in a separate pouch more make-up than she generally carries in her handbag.

There's also a packet of condoms (unscented, unribbed), perhaps Viv's sole concession to sensible, grown-up behaviour. They were not bought at her local Boots, where she and Geoff are regulars and the purchase might have attracted covert interest, but at another branch.

While the contents of the bag might invite conclusions surprising to many, it's fair to say that no one in the crowd gives this woman a second glance. She appears, not nondescript exactly – she's more imaginatively dressed than most and has livelier hair – but otherwise unremarkable. There is nothing in her behaviour to suggest she is anticipating anything other than a pleasant afternoon's outing. But someone who has known her since student days and to whom she is not unremarkable in any way, someone like Julia Jefferies, or even Viv's own husband Geoff, might identify tell-tale signs of inner turmoil.

It had not escaped Geoff's notice that she'd made an effort when she passed his study nook on the way out. Where was she off to, all dolled up like that? Oh, just an upmarket tea, she'd answered vaguely, mentioning the name of a well-to-do friend she knew he couldn't stand. The lie surprised her with its ease and fluency. Geoff had raised his eyebrows and returned to the new issue of the fanzine he has printed out: *Cosmic Dust*, a digital monthly produced by his sci-fi circle.

It needn't concern you, Geoff, Viv had thought as she opened the front door, but what I'm really doing is this: I am about to take a train from Liverpool Street Station to Chelmsford, to meet someone I scarcely know, a darkly handsome man who is a whole lot younger than you, and with any sort of an even break I'm going to have sex with him.

In addition to a lurch in the stomach these thoughts prompted an array of mental pictures, a sequence that kept her occupied all the way to Liverpool Street where she may now be seen scanning the noticeboard for the next train to Chelmsford, Essex. This is not something she has done before. Viv has never been to Chelmsford, or indeed known anyone who lived there. Moreover, no one else knows about her imminent visit. No one, that is, except Dev.

Over the past forty-eight hours Dev has been on Viv's mind, a disruptive, unsettling presence. And because what she knows about him might be written on a postage stamp, he is an enigma.

She assumes he lives in Chelmsford, although when she dissects (yet again) their meeting she doesn't think he said this in so many words. It was more that he *intimated* it, she reflects, as she moves (having arrived a good ten minutes early) through the stationary train to a forward-facing window seat. Dev seemed disinclined to talk about himself, and she hadn't felt inclined to press him. She too had been reluctant to say anything personal, to give out any information about her husband, her family or her circumstances. Other than her name.

She doesn't even know Dev's surname, although she assumes the Discretion Agency has it on file. Or has on file the name he has given them. She experiences a fleeting tremor. Jules, if she knew what she was doing, would take a dim view. For a moment Viv toys with the idea of telling Joy where she is headed. But Joy turns her phone off when she is writing. Not that I know where I'm headed, Viv thinks, which is very much to the point. Apart from a house in the general vicinity of Chelmsford.

Dev had been quite forthright in other ways. They should strike while the iron was hot. Viv thought this metaphor, while inducing a mild panic attack, was rather well chosen. He suggested the day after tomorrow. Would she opt for the am, or the pm? The pm, I think, she'd responded without thinking, I've never been much of an am person. Later she regretted this; opting for the pm had meant enduring a morning that seemed interminable.

He had given her the time of his preferred train and told her to check the number of the platform because it was subject to change. It would take twenty-five minutes, he said, and she should text him immediately if she missed it. He would assume she was on this train unless informed to the contrary. He would meet her on arrival.

'I won't miss it,' Viv had assured him. 'I tend to be a very punctual person.' Detecting a doubt, she added, 'As a rule.'

In the immediate aftermath of the encounter with Dev, Viv had stopped short of full disclosure to her friends. She limited herself to a (fulsome) sketch of Dev's appearance. On hearing this, Joy urged her to strike while the iron was hot (Dev's very phrase, Viv marvelled). 'Grasp the nettle, honey,' she said.

The conversation with Jules was a rushed affair in the ladies loo of the Almeida, in the interval of *Ghosts*. Was I like this when I first met Geoff, Viv wondered. Jules, applying her lipstick, made an impatient move necessitating a repair.

What did Geoff have to do with this? 'You're not proposing to leave him, are you? On the basis of one meeting in a naff caf? This is just a little fling—' She was going to say, just an unwise little fling you're proposing to have, and more than a bit suspect as well. She reined herself in and powdered her nose.

But was it so different back then, Viv persisted. When they were on cloud nine? Young and foolish, and in love?

'You were young and foolish and the same age as each other,' Jules reminded her sharply. 'And now you're much older and even more foolish and gullible to boot. You're not in love, for fuck's sake. You haven't had a fuck for far too long, that's the long and the short of it.' Forget cloud nine. Viv was in cloud cuckoo land.

Julia had spent the next day on the phone, email, Facebook and Twitter, attending to her worldwide fan and friendship base, which had been somewhat neglected of late. She'd also been incubating a niggle of guilt over the manner in which she had greeted Viv's news.

Which explains why, just out of Liverpool Street, Viv's mobile rings. She sees the name of the caller and debates for a second, but she hasn't the intestinal fortitude for an argument at this point in time. Especially about doing something she has no intention of being talked out of doing. Moments later she listens to Julia's energetic voice message.

'Viv? Are you by any chance with your shiny new friend? You tend to be sentimental and trusting, remember? These are admirable characteristics, but they're not advantageous here. Protect thyself. *Know what I mean?*'

Viv reflects that Jules is capable of being both selfish and unselfish in rather larger measure than most people. In this respect, although not in many others, she resembles her goddaughter Daisy. But while Jules may be self-centred she is also self-aware, and strong on irony. Self-awareness is not one of Daisy's strong points. Not in any guise. Perhaps this will alter as she grows older. Particularly if she were to have a child.

Since their lunch in the Lebanese restaurant Daisy has gone quiet. She hasn't come over to dump her stuff, and Viv's studiedly casual emails and texts have been answered in the most cursory fashion. This is not unusual. Where communication with her parents is concerned, Daisy has always had a tendency to blow hot and cold.

Viv has scrupulously avoided the touchy subjects of Daisy's forward plans and her state of mind, but she can't help feeling the present situation is an especially worrying one, even given Daisy's bulging dossier of personal crises. Her unpredictable daughter may well find anything her mother says at this time irritating and intrusive. Might implicit questions have wormed their way into those carefully worded messages?

Viv is doing everything in her power to prevent herself from thinking about what she is doing. The reason for this train journey, and its possible (probable?) outcome. If a tree fell on the line, or if the train should suddenly be derailed, would her dominant feeling be relief? There might be a moment of deliverance, but she suspects it would be brief. What would replace it? Disappointment? You can say that again. A definite sense, she might tell Joy, of anti-climax.

As the outskirts of Chelmsford loom, Viv springs to her feet. She is at the doors before the train slows to a stop – train doors, she has heard, do sometimes jam. A surprising number of people are getting off at Chelmsford. She doubts if anyone is planning on doing the same thing as her. They might be planning on doing something comparable, but not in a similar *configuration*. Nor, she is quite sure, would they suspect her (this inoffensive woman in late middle age) of being about to do anything of the kind.

Is she the only one whose knees are knocking? Suppose Dev is not here; how long should she wait? People are heading purposefully towards the exit, down a flight of steps. She goes with the flow, and emerges into a foyer. Glass roof over Victorian brickwork.

And lo, there is Dev standing by the doors. Instead of a suit he's wearing a puffer jacket over tracksuit pants and trainers. If it weren't for those movie-star looks he'd be indistinguishable from the crowd. He hasn't seen her yet, and she hangs back to observe him: yes, every bit the eyeful she remembers. This is something of a relief. She had wondered if her perception of Dev was too heavily influenced by deprivation.

He is extending his hand again and Viv, with a jolt of déjà vu, realises she is expected to shake it. She had been fixated on his smooth skin. The thick, lustrous hair, the aquiline nose, those *beaux yeux*...

'Welcome to Chelmsford, Vivien,' his deep voice is saying, with a meaningful emphasis that prompts a small tingle to traverse her spine. 'You are looking very smart today, I see. You are wearing a hat. I think you have upstaged me. I was wrong not to dress up for this occasion. But you were quite right to do so, I am thinking.'

Does this sound reproachful? Upstaged. Dress up. This occasion. Is he feeling inadequate? Might that lead to a difficulty? Some men being, you hear, easily thrown off message. And in any case, given the unorthodox nature of *this occasion*, Dev probably doesn't need much of a reason to be thrown off message.

I should concentrate on keeping things unthreatening and everyday. That is, as far as possible under the circumstances, which are not at all everyday.

'Silly of me.' A friendly, self-deprecating smile. 'You see, I some-how always imagined Chelmsford might be a hat-and-gloves type of destination. I've never had any reason to come here before.' Does this strike the right note? Or is it a bit of a put-down? 'But I'm very glad to have such a good reason now.'

This sounds like something the Queen might have said had she journeyed here on a comparable mission. Which she wouldn't, or not in any realistic scenario. Perhaps in a satirical sketch ...

Dev takes this seriously. 'You have never paid a visit to this part of the world before? Contrary to your mental pic-ture, I think it is more casual. Informality is the keynote.' His view seems to be confirmed by the locals scurrying past them. Moreover, just as no men gave her a second glance at Liverpool Street, Dev doesn't appear to be on the receiving end of any obvious double-takes from the women Viv has been furtively monitoring as they pass.

Their libidos must be freakishly unresponsive to a display of male perfection. Unless it's just me. She sneaks another assessing look. No. No way is it just me. Of course, most of the women are striding along with their heads down, as if to avoid dog poo on the pavement, which is probably why they don't look twice at this mind-blowing figure of a man at my side. Who is actually quite short in real life, she registers.

'Is something the matter, Vivien?' They are still standing, marooned in the station.

'Something the matter?' Whatever gave him this idea?

'I think you are feeling concerned about something. Or perhaps it is critical? You are thinking that I am underdressed. You would prefer I did not blend in with the crowd.'

'Concerned? *Critical?* I wouldn't say you blended in with the crowd, Dev. Not in the slightest, quite frankly.' This might be mis-interpreted. She looks around for other people from the subconti-nent, but there seem to be none around.

'And I'm feeling anything but critical, as a matter of fact.' Is this too forward? 'I was just preoccupied, I suppose. With how –' she turns to him impulsively, quashing an impulse to grasp his hand, 'extraordinary life is.'

'*Extraordinary*, Vivien?' He looks disconcerted.

'Well, how it is sometimes, in a nice way, when it takes you by surprise.' Better not try to explain. 'But it does look as if it might rain. Should we perhaps get our skates on?'

'Fortunately, there is no need for skates as I have a car. I discovered a temporary parking bay. It is next to some building works around the corner.' He gestures in that direction. 'I take it that you enjoy formal occasions as a rule, Vivien.'

What a curious non-sequitur. And it seems to be less of a question than an assumption. An unwarranted one, too. What can have inspired it? Was it her silly remark about hats and gloves?

'Formal? As a rule? No, not much. Not at all, really.' She detects a strong odour of displeasure. 'That is, not entirely, Dev. I used to, but these days I don't get much practice. I hardly ever go to anything that would call itself a formal occasion. Apart from funerals, that is.'

He gives her a keen glance. 'But with more practice, I think you would enjoy them. In improved circumstances you would recover your former enthusiasm.'

It seems important to him, so she smiles encouragingly. They are walking side by side. No, Dev is not a tall man. He is below average height. Which is fine. She's only five three and a half, which these days is also appreciably shorter than average. She decides he is perhaps three inches taller than her, at most. Three, or maybe two and a half.

'Do you prefer to wear high-heeled shoes with your evening gowns, Vivien?'

What a strange question. Could he be a mind reader? Do I possess such an artefact as an evening gown? 'Well, I don't wear – *gowns* – all that often, to be honest.'

I never say *to be honest*; what is the matter with me? 'Certainly not those awful stiletto heels. I never thought those instruments of torture would come back, but they have.' Of course, some men find them very sexy. Might he have a fetish? 'Why, do *you* like high heels, Dev?'

'They are nice for elegant occasions. Stiletto heels no, certainly not, but you would not be taller than me in more modest heels, I have the distinct impression.'

So, that's what was worrying him. 'Oh no, I'm sure I wouldn't be.' She gives him another sunny smile. 'So, we'll be just the right height for all those black-tie balls and glamorous premières, won't we?'

Rather to her surprise, Dev responds to this with several emphatic nods. 'Yes, indeed. We will be finely matched as such a couple, Vivien.' He stops at a small white car and unlocks it with a remote.

As a couple. Isn't this rather a presumptuous phrase to use, at this juncture? Or am I being too literal? Maybe I'm taking his throwaway remarks too seriously. She slips into the passenger seat. There's no room for her bulky bag on the floor, so she puts it on her lap. Dev hasn't seemed the type to make throwaway remarks. Or light-hearted ones, for that matter. But perhaps this is just shyness. He doesn't present as a gregarious personality. Anything but, really.

Still, neither does he appear to suffer from a self-confidence deficit. Having so much sex appeal, no doubt he is used to people – to women – making the running. Hitting on him, as Joy would say.

Viv marvels again. How astonishing life is. How extraordinarily *unforeseeable*. If it hadn't been for the sex drought with my husband, and his lack of affection, I wouldn't be here now, sitting in a very confined space with a stranger (who is also rather strange), something I haven't done for years. Sitting extremely close to this improbably attractive yet curiously phlegmatic man as he concentrates on the road and gives his undivided attention to changing gears.

Does this mean that the rift with my husband has turned out to have beneficial side effects? Or would I rather it hadn't happened, and I was sitting comfortably beside Geoff in our own car? They are speeding through sober streets of houses, in a suburban area still quite close to the station. 'Dev, where is it we're going to, exactly?'

'We are going to the house, as was arranged previously between us, Vivien.'

'*Your* house? Where you live?'

'I have done.' He shrugs. 'It is not far at all. Don't worry, Vivien, sit back and relax, and I will tell you when we have reached our destination.'

Viv shrugs too, internally. He seems set on being reticent. Or perhaps he is constitutionally secretive. She is resolved to live in the moment. Even if the moment, of itself, seems to be generating a degree of stress that is increasing incrementally. She feels as though she has been borne up bodily and is now hurtling towards an unknown destiny. A mise en scène, she has to admit, that is more or less accurate.

What is the internet dating etiquette? Do not meet until you have established some relationship through texting and talking on the phone. Meet in public places until you feel confident about the person. And if not, always tell someone where you are going.

But this is not internet dating, and Dev has been vetted. Presumably. Up to a point. And Viv's instinct tells her there is nothing threatening about him. Then again, didn't Joy think her husband was unthreatening when she married him? That Mr Ronnie, all bark and no bite, Joy thought. How wrong was that. Whereas Dev has not exhibited any bark at all, and as for bite …

The rows of small two-storey houses lining the street look the same as they did five minutes ago. Neat and unremarkable. The streets are almost empty. Where are the inhabitants? It's like one of Geoff's sci-fi stories, where they have been vaporised by some invading power.

Dev pulls up outside a beige house, indistinguishable from its neighbours. The curtains are closed, Viv observes, upstairs and down. Pebbledash walls, and a front door the shade of Geoff's new jacket – dung. The passive, unsettling ambience of a Hitchcock movie crawls into her mind.

'What did I tell you?' her escort is saying in a reassuringly normal voice, if mesmerising can be in any way normal. 'It took next to no time. We are there already, Vivien.' We may be there already, matey, she hears Jules mutter, but there's no *there* here. Know what I mean?

Dev is unlocking the door with a key from a large bunch. After a moment's internal debate, Viv follows him over the threshold. He closes the door firmly behind her, and the outside world – unsettlingly quiet or reassuringly ordinary, take your pick – disappears.

The small hall is dark and stuffy. There's a strong smell of disinfectant. The doors of the two front rooms off the hall are open, and she can see they are empty. The house, like the vacant street, appears to be unoccupied. She blinks.

'Dev ...'

He has switched on the light in the hall and is heading up a narrow staircase. She stands at the foot of the stairs, perplexed. 'But there's nobody *living* here, Dev. What's happened to all the *furniture?*'

He turns round. 'Don't worry, nothing has happened to it.' She hesitates. Could he be an estate agent? A burglar? But there's nothing to steal. He comes back down and taps her on the shoulder. 'Do we have any need of a nest of occasional tables and a sofa, right at this moment? Or a chest of drawers? There is a bed upstairs. That is the object of the exercise, I am thinking. It is all we need at this moment, isn't it?'

Viv feels an agitated thrill. This moment. *All we need.* Dev is certainly not given to beating about the bush. No settling glass of wine – well, he probably doesn't drink. No cup of tea. Not even any

118

preparatory small talk. The object of the exercise is upstairs. A bed. But this is precisely what I have travelled here for, isn't it?

She follows him slowly up the stairs, aware that with each step her comfort zone is receding further into the distance. He turns into a small room off the landing. An open plastic venetian blind admits some shafts of sombre daylight. This room too is empty, apart from a grey carpet that gives out a faint odour of carpet cleaner. And lying on it is a mattress.

Viv's eyes zero in on it as she parks her bag, hat and gloves in the corner. It is a thin-looking mattress, probably foam, draped with blue sheets. A pile of folded khaki blankets has been placed at one end. The sheets have been smoothed out and tucked in, she notes. Could Dev be a squatter?

She hears herself say, 'This is a bit no-frills, isn't it? Are you camping here? I was expecting a four-poster at least.' It sounds surprisingly sprightly. Much more confident than she feels.

He is unzipping his jacket. 'No, you are right, Vivien. This is not a country house hotel.' She thinks this might be his first witty remark. Was it intentional? 'It is better to start off in a modest fashion, and then we can leave it behind us. We can look back on it all and share a hearty laugh.'

Dev and a hearty laugh would seem to be mutually exclusive. Is he trying to put her at ease? She's never felt less at ease since she was the sole woman on a train travelling through Turkey when she was twenty-two. At least there the perils were readily identifiable.

'I have already taken a hot shower,' he is saying, 'immediately before setting out to meet you. But on the assumption that you may feel inclined to do the same thing, Vivien, I have put out a clean towel.' She turns her head reflexively. 'No, not in here. It is hanging in the bathroom next door. I expect you will feel more comfortable if you freshen up.'

Sure enough, there are two neatly folded white towels on the bathroom rail. He selects one and hands it to her. 'This one,' a slight emphasis, 'is for your use.' He gives her shoulder another dispassionate pat. Up close, she detects tangy notes of pine and peppermint. She observes two mid-range bottles of aftershave and men's cologne.

'Unlike many English houses, there is a plentiful supply of hot water, and the water pressure is excellent. You do not need to hold back. Come in when you are ready, Vivien. You will feel more at home performing your hygiene routine in private, I am expecting.'

He closes the door behind him and she's left standing, rooted to the spot. The utilitarian bathroom is compact, as an estate agent would put it, with a shower over the bath. Everything is perfectly (fastidiously?) clean. She registers the green of the tiles. Jade, popular in the 1970s. She too had showered before leaving the house. But a freshen up, as Dev put it, might be advisable. What they called at school a targeted wash.

She remembers her bag, still on the bedroom floor. The door is now closed. She pushes it open, with caution. Dev is sitting cross-legged on the mattress.

'You are back already, Vivien.' He sounds put out. How can you have performed your hygiene routine with any thoroughness, is the implication. 'You are ready?'

'No, of course I'm not ready,' she retorts, quite tartly. But the minute she removes her clothes in the bathroom the butterflies return. A crowd of them, swarming in.

Her body is within the normal range and in better shape than many. But the truth of the matter is inescapable: she's in her sixties, and nudity is pitiless. It conceals nothing and leaves nothing to the imagination. She regards herself in the mirror. I am not normally an insecure person. But this is an abnormal state of affairs, even though I voluntarily signed up to it. Some challenges were to be expected, and I did expect them. Just not these specific ones.

There are two options: I can go through with this, or I can do a runner. I can put my clothes back on and run downstairs and out the front door and no one, except Dev, need be any the wiser. *Men are hard-wired.* But Dev told me himself, emphatically, that he was looking for someone older. He wasn't lying, I'm pretty sure about that. Unless I am seriously deluded. Which, of course, is perfectly possible.

The heating, if any, has not been turned on. She is shivering, and decides to have a shower after all while she mulls this over. Dev is right about the water, it's hot and plentiful. There's a new cake of Imperial Leather in the soap dish. He must have purchased it for *this occasion.* The detail is rather touching.

The water pressure is so strong she can't avoid getting much of her hair wet. That's something I forgot. Next time I'll bring a shower cap. Next time? We haven't even had a first time yet. She scrubs herself with the skimpy towel.

In for a penny, in for a pound. May as well be hanged for a sheep as a lamb. Viv has been familiar with both sayings since early childhood. They're among her mother Judith's favourite maxims. She looks inside the bathroom cabinet. No hair dryer. No traces of anything feminine, either, just the basics: hairbrush, shaving cream, toothbrush and toothpaste. Has Dev's wife, assuming he has one, done a bunk and looted everything? Are they selling the house? On the lower shelf she spots a lone hair-grip with a daisy decoration. A vital clue. Is there a daughter somewhere? Aged, perhaps, between seven and eleven?

Viv rubs her unruly hair with the damp towel and drags a comb through it. She uses the mouthwash and sprays perfume on her throat and, as an afterthought, on her cleavage. Should she put on her underwear? Black and lacy, purchased in one of her attempts to revitalise Geoff. Of course, it would only postpone the inevitable. But this could be helpful, and men have a well-known thing about sexy lingerie. Most bodies, and all *non-youthful* bodies, look better in pretty, well-designed underclothes. Perhaps she should have invested in the transformative properties of a black negligee?

She dons the black bra and French knickers. Having no recourse to a negligee or a dressing gown, she picks up the other towel. It's marginally dryer. She wraps it around herself and tucks it in. She pushes the bedroom door open – no point knocking – and finds Dev sitting in the same position. He has removed his jacket, shoes and socks, leaving the white shirt tucked into his tracksuit pants.

'You are wearing your towel, Vivien,' he says, surprised. Neutrally, she thinks.

'It's your towel, actually.'

'*Mine?*' He sounds scandalised.

'Well, they're both yours technically, aren't they? But your one was less damp. Not much, but every bit counts in a crisis.' She's unsure what is driving this strained levity. It might be an attempt to undercut his solemnity. Or to conceal the fact that she finds herself suddenly, and she fears visibly, shaking. Whereas Dev looks expressionless and untroubled. He could be about to do anything, or nothing at all.

Nor does he look as if he has noticed anything about me, apart from the fact that I'm wearing his towel. Is that something to be thankful for? Or is it the opposite?

He gets to his feet. 'You would prefer to have the light switched off, I am thinking.' She nods. Could this mean it is dawning on him that I have cold feet, in more ways than one? He has closed the venetian blind and the room is (thanks for small mercies) murky.

'You've still got your clothes on, I see,' she says.

An infinitesimal pause. Then, 'That is because I thought you would like to undress me, Vivien.'

Had he pronounced such a thing in the cafe, or possibly even in the car, it might have had an effect not unlike that of an electric shock. Now, in this airless room, the words seem to have lost their potency. The deep yet strangely impersonal voice washes over her like muzak. But with the unexpected fringe benefit of soothing her nerves, or at least damping them down. Like his towel, which is still clamped around her.

'Oh,' she says. 'Did you?' Is this what she'd like? She assumes it must be. In the recent past her fantasies tended to begin with her unknotting his tie. But this was always preceded by a long, swoon-inducing kiss. Dev, it would seem, does not do kissing.

With cold fingers that are cooperative, if lacking in zeal, she unbuttons his shirt. He stands passively as she eases his arms out of it. She makes a mental note: this must be what it's like to undress a shop-window dummy. Underneath he is wearing a T-shirt. Without being prompted, she rolls it up and over his head.

His chest is smooth and hairless, not at all like Geoff's. Viv has always appreciated chest hair, but according to Daisy it is deeply unfashionable. Dev's chest is baby-smooth. Might he have had laser treatment? Or perhaps there was never anything much there to begin with.

The damp towel is still precariously in place. This might be an appropriate time to let it drop. But Dev shows no reaction, either to the manoeuvre itself or the result, so she pushes on. She thinks (and briefly considers saying): I've started, so I'll finish. She guides his tracksuit pants down past his hips. He steps out of them with no comment, nor any evident physical response. Could he be in some kind of Eastern trance? More likely he's thinking he has been undressed with too much practical haste and not enough caressing eroticism.

He's wearing low-rise Calvin Klein trunks. They are a close fit, but Viv is up to the task of getting them down. Yet she feels unmoved as she performs the operation. Joy's phrase 'grasp the nettle' keeps recurring, a disconcerting hindrance. She avoids grasping it out of, she can only suppose, some inbuilt perversity. Now, what is it that you plan to tell me I would like to do next?

She will not be kept in the dark for long, as Dev appears to throw off some of his inertia. 'I think you would like to arouse me now, Vivien,' he says. And she feels a nascent stir, in spite of everything.

He guides her hand to his groin.

11

THE AFTERMATH

Afterwards, Viv discerns a surprising change in Dev's demeanour. In the car he's bordering on chatty, initiating fresh topics of conversation in a way she would almost call breezy. Although when she surveys these topics, having found a seat on the crowded train and composed herself sufficiently to think about anything, she realises they were variations on a single theme: glamorous upmarket vacations. Romantic resorts in the Bahamas, luxury cruises and exclusive, long-distance train journeys.

On these subjects his interest had expanded to embrace Viv and her views. Had she ever embarked on a leisurely ocean cruise? Never, was the terse response. What about an exotic train excursion, such as the Orient Express or the Trans-Siberian railway?

Not even the Ghan, Viv had replied curtly. An Australian train, she explained with reluctance. Julia had travelled on the Ghan through the Red Centre, from Adelaide to Darwin, a couple of years ago. With her brother Max, Viv recalled. They had sent postcards that looked suitably exotic, although Viv did not disclose this.

Her lack of enthusiasm had not deterred Dev. A long, relaxing sea cruise could be very pleasurable, he suggested, in the right company. Very delightful indeed. With gourmet cuisine and sophisticated cocktail parties, and en-suite jacuzzi tubs. For two, in their luxury cabin, he added.

It might be delightful and relaxing, Viv had conceded, in the right company. In the wrong company it might be very boring. She thought she had said this rather pointedly and with emphasis. Too subtle, she decided, as Dev went on to remark that these days boredom could be kept at bay. Cruise ships featured celebrity guest speakers on topics of the moment, and sparkling on-board entertainment. Guests could dance the night away to world-famous headline entertainers like the beautiful American singer Diana Krall, for example.

Viv chose not to comment on this as they pulled up. 'You mustn't feel I'd like you to get out of the car to see me off, Dev,' she'd said. Without a further glance at the driver she had made a beeline for the newly inviting bowels of Chelmsford Station.

Analysing her feelings as she sits in the train, Viv hits on the exact phrase. High dudgeon is what I am in, at this precise moment. I'm not sure I have ever been in it before. Certainly not to this extent. The fact that it is my own fault is neither here nor there.

She broods over this. Actually, it's not my fault. I might reasonably be accused of having been somewhat *rash*, but the point is that another person has just behaved very badly. In a particular type of situation, a type that benefits from some inter-personal skills, however rudimentary, somebody else has behaved with scarcely a nod to the proprieties.

Why did I go along with it, without saying anything? She shelves this question for the time being. It requires some stringent self-scrutiny of the kind she does not feel up to right now. Julia, she has a fair idea, will want to take the question and run with it. Jules will say things along the lines of: you need to own your own problem. Or: it takes two to tango.

When she switches her phone back on, she finds three texts waiting for her. She scrolls down to the earliest. It's from Daisy, and had been sent nearly two hours earlier. *Ok if I come for suppr with jules mon nite? xx*

The next one is from her mother. *Hi, dear. Can you give me a ring? Are you coming down soon? We should discuss Daisy's problems; I'm wondering if it would be a good idea for me to slip her some moolah?*

Viv knows that it would have taken her mother's arthritic fingers several minutes to compose this message, and that it would have involved multiple mistakes, painstakingly corrected. It had taken Judith some considerable time to learn the ins and outs of her smartphone, particularly how to create capitals and the location of apostrophes, brackets and semi-colons, but once a modest proficiency had been reached she took to texting with gusto. Although more trouble, arguably, than emailing or even picking up the phone, it makes her feel up-to-date, her daughter thinks, and tech-savvy.

Viv is accustomed to suffering pangs of guilt about her mother. They are mitigated to some extent by the fact, accepted by family and health workers alike, that at ninety-one Judith still has all her marbles (or nearly all) and knows she has them. She is independent to a pig-headed degree. She insists on living alone and does not wish anyone to put themselves out for her.

Least of all her daughter, who looks with disbelief at the third and most recent message. It is from Dev, and dispatched only minutes ago. *Hi Vivien! I trust you enjoyed our little tryst?! We must have a 'repeat performance' at the earliest opportunity, and make future plans!*

Like hell we must, Viv expostulates, loudly enough to get a reaction from the young woman sitting diagonally opposite, with her feet on the seat and wearing earphones.

Julia is spending a few days with friends in Oxford and would certainly have visited Viv's mother, of whom she is fond. No doubt they took the opportunity to discuss the Daisy situation. This would explain Judith's reference to slipping Daisy some money. Her professorial pension has allowed Judith to be comfortably off, but with the expenses of her old age she is living only a whisker within her means. Although she has occasionally mentioned a little something salted away, and likes to give her granddaughter cheques for Christmas and birthday, Viv doubts if the little something is much more than it sounds.

She calls her mother. A soporific male voice answers. This always gives Viv a jolt, but the explanation is benign, as it usually has been in recent years. Judith is being given her massage, a highlight of her week. Viv leaves a message. Judith will be too sleepy to talk for the rest of the day, and will retire to bed early.

The conversation with Jules about Dev, a conversation that Viv is, on balance, rather desirous of having, will have to wait.

Chelmsford leaves her with a lingering hangover. The recurring erotic fantasies, with Dev as the prime mover, have been dislodged. She finds it hard to believe she indulged in them at all, since her mental picture of Dev is now divested, magically, of any trace of sensuality. Daydreams have been supplanted by affront and disbelief. Viv can't recall having had such oppressive and burdensome feelings for years.

Joy's quilting circle presents an opportunity to give the burdens an airing. Joy is always a reliable sounding-board, unencumbered by what Viv sees as the baggage of a repressed middle-class English upbringing. Even if Viv's own upbringing was less typical or repressed, in some respects, than most.

The kitchen is a useful refuge for a chat away from prying ears. Apart from some hammering, the atmosphere down the hall is appreciably quieter than usual. It could almost be said to be muted. This can only be due to one thing: the inaugural appearance of Mr Jackson Adeyemi, the security guard. Mr Jackson's unveiling had been low-key, but did not lack its moment of drama. As Joy escorted him in, after a stern warning ('He is a shy gentleman, you girls, and he doesn't want anybody to take any notice of him. *Okay?*') he had collided with a corner of the wooden frame on which the star quilt – destined to be auctioned for the local primary school – was stretched out. The whole edifice would have collapsed if he hadn't executed a surprisingly agile save. Much, Viv imagined, as he might bring down a felon.

Closer inspection of the frame (formerly a double bed) revealed loose slats and a previous break secured imperfectly with glue and picture wire. That pretty quilt better come off double-quick so he could fix this problem, Mr Jackson announced in a soft (and relatively non-judgemental) voice, nodding for emphasis, because those repairs weren't done by a lady who knew what she was doing.

While he attends to this, Viv follows Joy into the kitchen, ostensibly to help her make a pot of tea. She has just outlined Dev's unorthodox approach to intimacy. It hasn't escaped her notice that Joy is wearing bright cerise lipstick today, not her usual custom, and a form-fitting dress in rose brocade from Oxfam. Joy likes her clothes snug. Today's dress is extra-snug around the pressure points.

Joy, who doesn't hold with electric jugs, is putting a large kettle of water on the gas. She has been left in no doubt that the recent occasion had not lived up to her friend's best, or even worst, imaginings. It was a fiasco. A unilateral performance, to put it more kindly than Viv felt disposed to put it.

Viv chooses to skirt over the delicacies by deft use of generalities. 'He hadn't a clue how to *relate* to a woman. No idea how to go about it. And if that was the only problem, I suppose you could deal with it – well, perhaps you could, over time – but he wasn't interested in my role in the equation. He didn't appear to be aware that I might *have* a role.' She considers this and adds, 'Other than that of facilitator.'

'It was all about *him*, right?' Joy knows that her role is that of reinforcer. 'He told you what things he wanted done to *him*. Just one damn thing after another.'

'Exactly. One damn thing after another. And he told me what to do in some – detail. Which I won't go into.'

'You *won't*? Well, Lord have mercy.'

Viv is not swayed. This, she thinks, may be the closest she has ever come to kissing and telling. Even if there was no kissing on this occasion. She says, 'I honestly think it never occurred to him to think about what *I* might want. Or how to bring that about. Or if it *did* occur – which I genuinely doubt, by the way, since there was not a glimmer of it – he wasn't interested in following it up.'

Joy is hovering over the kettle. Viv senses she is anxious to be out of there and back with the action.

'He sure didn't know how to give a girl a good time, honey.'

'He didn't give a *stuff* about what kind of time to give a girl.'

'Give *that* restaurant a miss from now on, huh? Only one crummy dish on the menu there. Fast food and no pig pickin' cake for dessert.'

Viv has a liking for Joy's pig pickin' cake, made with vanilla pudding and mandarin oranges. 'No dessert at all,' she says.

'Over and done before you could say Jack Robinson.' Joy spoons leaves into a teapot in the shape of a church. Viv enjoys her friend's use of faded British idioms, as well as genuine (and invented) ones from Joy's Louisiana childhood.

Joy shoots her a shrewd look. 'You acted like everything was hunky-dory, right?' She stirs the tea leaves.

'I suppose I did act like that. I'm not usually so passive. Or was it passive-aggressive? If so, it was much too nuanced.'

'Did you fake?'

Viv winces. 'I'm not sure he'd have noticed if I had.'

'Maybe he doesn't know it's possible. Know what I mean?' Viv assumes this is rhetorical until Joy says, 'That Mr Ronnie, he acted like he didn't know. Remember that thing they have?'

'Do you mean a penis or Asperger's?' Viv is familiar with Joy's views, as well as many of her beliefs. 'True, something on the spectrum might explain a lot.'

It wouldn't explain the empty house with nothing in it, Joy points out with asperity. Not even a proper *bed* to lie in. Joy, who likes a ruffled valance and deep upholstery, wrinkles her nose in distaste. She can't for the life of her understand why her friend didn't make more of an effort to get to the bottom of all that.

Viv doesn't understand it either. She can only think that she wasn't firing on all cylinders. Not quite herself. Quite who she was, though, is a puzzle. Several days after the event, she will still be turning this question over in her mind.

A text arrives from Martin Glover. Viv and Geoff are in the kitchen compiling a list for tonight's dinner with Daisy and Julia. It's Geoff's turn to do the shopping. Viv feels a touch of warmth towards him, possibly engendered by her conscience. When he's gone she goes up to the shed and reads the message: *Hi V. How did you feel about the meeting? D seemed v happy. MG.*

She calls the Discretion Agency. D may have been v happy, she tells Martin, but it was v unsatisfactory from my perspective. It was a toe-curling debacle, to cut a long story short.

'Dear me. Toe-curling? That *is* bad.' Martin sounds concerned and surprised. 'Is there anything you feel you need to tell me?'

'Just possibly. You see—' Viv pauses. She has been deliberating how she should convey this awkward matter to Martin. Deliberating without reaching any constructive conclusion. She embarks cautiously. 'Dev told me that I was his first introduction. I don't know what he said to you, but I have a feeling he may not be very experienced. At least, not with – not in the area of …'

It was a whole lot easier telling Joy. What had she said to her? Something direct and to the point. 'He seemed to think the way to go about enacting things to his satisfaction was to issue a series of instructions. Maybe he thought he was being helpful about things, but it—'

'It didn't assist things to evolve?'

'Exactly. There wasn't any – and I do mean *any*, Martin – attempt to make those things less … mechanical. Or one-sided. For example, it didn't seem to have occurred to him that I might like a little preparatory romancing, for want of a better word. I don't mean candles and wine or pretending we didn't know why we were there, but …'

Why we were there triggers a renewed onslaught of visual memories. 'And where we *were*, that's another unfortunate aspect.'

'Where were you?' Martin asks gently.

'Well, here's the thing, we were in an empty house in Chelmsford. Empty except for a mattress on the floor. It was all rather – minimalist, really.' Viv is mortified to feel herself, without warning, struggling with emotion.

'It sounds like a right shambles all round, if you ask me.'

'It was, a bit.' An alarming unsteadiness. 'Can I call you back?'

'Certainly you can. Or you could stay on the line and endure me banging on for a moment.' She nods into the phone, swallowing. 'I don't want you to be discouraged by one disagreeable encounter, Vivien. It sounds as if I need to say something to Dev, have an informal chat, man to man. It sounds like he is going about things the wrong way, and we need to avoid—'

Feeling stronger, Viv interrupts. 'Oh, I wouldn't want you to do that. I'm sure it would be humiliating for him to know I told you he was, you know—' how might Daisy put it? 'a dud bang.

And he might not be one at all with someone else, it might have been just me.'

'I rather doubt it. This sounds more like a pattern of behaviour. Perhaps an ingrained dud habit. And the matter of the bed needs addressing. As well as the venue.'

'All the same, I really would prefer—'

'Did you find him attractive, at all?'

'Oh, yes,' Viv says, 'I was bowled over by him, to begin with. But then it went out like a light. And now you could say I'm disenchanted to an equivalent degree.'

'Would you prefer to talk to him yourself?'

'*Me?*'

'Something does need to be said,' Martin says firmly. 'If you want to have a crack at it first, I wouldn't discourage you. It might be beneficial to air your grievances. Since you were the one impacted by his behaviour, so to speak.'

'Beneficial?' She thinks about this.

'Certainly for Dev. But not only him. It might be useful for you as well. To redress the balance of power, to some extent.'

That's an interesting idea. 'I've had three texts from him. Which I ignored.'

'Ah.'

'Yes. Pretty gutless, wasn't it? We could talk on the phone, I suppose. Or possibly meet in a cafe.' Not *that* one. One with decent coffee. 'Well. I suppose I could have a think ...'

'He's very keen to continue,' says Martin, 'but I take it that's not on the table.'

'It's off the table,' says Viv, quite heatedly, 'and on the floor. Just like the mattress.'

She is climbing the stairs to the top deck of the bus when her phone rings. This is her afternoon for volunteer work as a reading coach to disadvantaged and mainly refugee children, and as such is off limits to callers.

Julia has timed it carefully so as to snare Viv en route. 'I thought you might have something you needed to tell me,' Jules says, in a more ingratiating echo of Martin Glover. 'Before tonight,' she adds. Tonight she is coming over with Daisy. Viv has already taken an implication from this joint visit. There may well be an item of moment to discuss.

There have been times when Julia's position as Daisy's god-mother has enabled some privileged information to come her way, ahead (and sometimes well in advance of) Daisy's birth mother. Viv has never resented this. There were periods in her own adolescence and later as a young woman when she would have liked an older female confidante. Judith was assiduous in her duty of affection, but she was not always easy. Viv is no Judith. Still, experience has taught her that a wise intermediary can, on occasion, relieve a degree of maternal pressure.

Jules would maintain that having no kids of her own precludes her from being the fount of anything much, and most especially of all (or any) wisdom. Viv would say that this enables a useful degree of objectivity. Over the whole issue of children she thinks she has detected, from time to time, an undercurrent. It could be regret. Or is she imagining it? Jules has never said a word, either way.

Regardless, Viv believes that experience has refined Julia into someone who is, not more cynical exactly, but wiser than most in the ways of the world. She has come to value Julia's judgement about many things, and not only in the family sphere.

Geoff would put it differently. He would say that Jules has a head on her shoulders. If she weren't an opera singer she'd be a politician, in his opinion. Or if things didn't go so well she'd be a real-estate agent. Or a used-car saleswoman.

Viv lurches towards the front seat of the bus. The top deck is empty, apart from a handful of passengers texting or listening to music. The conversation with Julia lasts for the duration of the bus ride. Jules allows her to get to the end of her narrative without overt interruption, apart from the occasional expressive sound. She has a repertoire of non-verbal responses ranging across at least two octaves. Viv can generally interpret these with no trouble.

The recital draws to a close. Jules snorts. 'Well, *what* a surprise. No prizes for guessing what he's after. You've been taken for the proverbial ride, Viv. He's looking for a sugar mummy.' No sooner are the words spoken than Viv knows they are spot on.

'All that talk about high-heeled shoes and glamorous cruises. He just wants to swan around the world as a rich woman's handbag.'

'A rich *older* woman's handbag,' says Viv.

'That's the bitter truth of it, I'm afraid. When you met, were you by any chance wearing your Tiffany necklace?'

Jules thinks that Martin Glover should be appraised of this additional information, since Dev is unlikely to have disclosed the aspirations he may be harbouring. Mr Glover – who, Viv seems to believe, is of the opinion that he is performing a public service, even if it's only a niche one – would probably like to know about these.

'I can tell this has come as a body blow and you're feeling suitably chastened, Viv, so I shall lay off haranguing you about anything else pertaining.'

Having said this, Julia proceeds to go on about it at some length. The fact that no one had any inkling of Viv's whereabouts. The fact that she had put herself at some dodgy man's mercy in an empty house. Really and truly, for a woman your age (sorry) this kind of malarkey is just not on.

'And then there's the whole business, let's not err on the side of refinement, of your bum-sucking behaviour. In real life you're no pushover. Where did this spring from? Was it that you were grateful for having him served up on a plate, so gorgeous and sexy and so much younger, and you didn't want to hurt his feelings? Did you feel beholden to a man of colour, out of misplaced guilt? These are pertinent questions, you know.'

The cross-examination is unnecessary. Viv already finds these questions troubling. 'I have to say, Viv,' Jules adds, 'when I saw you after you'd just met him, you looked like you were incubating a vibrator.'

Viv says she wouldn't recognise one if she tripped over it.

'Well, it's not too late to give one a try. It might save you a whole load of money and grief, going forward.' Julia has never been averse to telling it like it is.

12

DAISY COMES TO DINNER

Tonight Daisy will turn up nearly an hour late, which is customary and surprises no one. But Julia has had to show up on time all her working life or risk the sky falling in. She arrives on the knocker, a polite five minutes after the hour. She is, she says, constitutionally unable to be late. Tonight, had she been constitutionally able, she might have wished to delay her arrival. Almost before she has been divested of her coat, and barely before she has taken a grip on her cocktail, Viv has pounced.

Yes, Viv is right, Daisy will have some news to impart, but Jules feels honour bound not to impart it in advance. And yes, it does have to do with where Daisy is going to live. In answer to a rapid follow-up query, Jules assumes an expression that Viv rates as shifty.

Yes, it also concerns the baby question, that's true, and yes, it does look as if Daisy may have reached some decisions in these areas. Yes, they are constructive decisions. Well, at least, Jules concedes after the briefest of pauses, they are constructive *up to a point*. It depends where you're coming from, she says.

Hasn't Daisy made these decisions rather fast? Viv asks, with a nervous glance at her husband. Isn't there a danger of rushing into things? Geoff weighs in here, saying reasonably that as they don't yet know what the decisions are, since Jules is refusing to tell them, it is pointless to concern oneself about their nature and provenance.

They might even, he says, be thoroughly sensible and unobjectionable decisions. His tone would have sounded unconvincing to the most objective of listeners, and his words fall on deaf ears.

Think how she rushed into those other unfortunate liaisons. Viv is pursuing a train of thought of her own and picturing Jasper, Mohammed and Bruce (a cousin of Julia's) among others. And Marco too, of course; let's not forget him. The cause of all the present angst.

'Let's look on the bright side,' says Geoff. 'It's been hardly more than a couple of weeks since the break-up. Far too soon for anyone else to be on the scene.'

Daisy's parents snatch surreptitious looks, independently, at their friend. Julia may be good at keeping her mouth shut when she deems it morally incumbent, but hers is an expressive face. Even when she is calmly sipping one of Geoff's cocktails, her wide eyes, violet-tinged and uncannily reminiscent (people have said) of Elizabeth Taylor's, are a giveaway.

She turns to Viv. 'I'm not saying anything about it. I told you that.'

'Is it someone we know?' Viv experiences a surge of apprehension. 'Just say yes or no. You don't even need to *say* anything. You can nod, or shake your head.'

'Or stand on it,' says Geoff.

'It is. Isn't it?' Viv gives her friend a beseeching look, while ransacking her mind for names and faces. 'Just nod if it—'

'Oh, for God's sake,' Geoff sighs, putting his hand over hers and then taking it away again. 'We haven't got long to wait before the full horror is revealed.' At which Jules gives an enigmatic smile.

Viv is riffling through her mental filing cabinet for names and faces, trying to call to mind the participants and approximate circumstances of each break-up. They hadn't all been what you'd call full-on entanglements, or even full-on dissolutions; some had flared and faded away like a firework. There one day and gone the next. Mohammed, she was inclined to think, whom she had rather liked (although there were tricky cultural differences) fell into that category. And also an upper-class twit called Florian. *Surely* Daisy wouldn't have re-ignited ...

'Is it one of her old flames?'

Jules makes an involuntary and almost infinitesimal movement. It is spotted by Viv and construed, somewhat misleadingly it will turn out, as a negative.

'So, it's not a former boyfr—'

Jules interrupts. 'Look Viv, may we talk about something else, *please?* I'm being self-protective here, in a caring and, yes, *moral* way. Let's discuss theatre, films or books. What are you reading? Or if you don't feel up to that, what would we do about Islamic Fundamentalism, if we were in power?'

She sees that her friend is about to open her mouth again. 'All right, I'll tell you this much: it's not an old boyfriend, okay? Not exactly. And that's my last word on the subject. Daisy will be here any minute.'

'And for all we know she'll have changed her mind twice since you spoke to her anyway,' Geoff says sensibly.

But Viv heard two of Julia's words, and they may as well have been up there in lights. Only a vague couple of words but they are ringing bells inside her head. Alarm bells. Loud ones. *Not exactly.*

'It's someone she's known for a long time, isn't it?' says Viv slowly, trying to come to grips with the germ of an idea. Jules puts her hands over her ears. 'But not been *involved* with.' Viv looks at Geoff. They are both thinking of the same person, and not at all sure what this might imply. Neither of them wants to think about the subject, or to take it any further, at this moment.

They talk about politicians, and then about films, but in a desultory way. By the time Daisy does arrive not too long afterwards, and first-course plates have been laid down (dips from the Greek deli) a flimsy wisp of tension is hanging over the table. In her mind,

Daisy's mother has several pieces of a potential scenario waiting, like a patchwork quilt, to be assembled. None is ideal, and none (sadly) involves early student romances she had favoured. All are puzzling. But some are worse, and some more puzzling, than others.

Aware that a mother's scrutiny can be a source of irritation in itself, and an inflammatory one at that, she is endeavouring not to gaze at Daisy. Her daughter's clothes are always dramatic and independent of fashion. Tonight she's wearing a long plaid skirt with a high-necked, ruffled blouse and a dark velvet waistcoat. She looks stylish – like someone in an Edwardian romcom, her mother thinks with a loving concern that is painful – and lovely as usual, although also rather tired and pale.

The main course is salmon baked with a Middle-Eastern crust. This is a recent discovery, passed on by a foodie friend who saw it on a cooking show. The crust is a fragrant mix of spices bound with olive oil. Viv is pleased with it.

After an appreciative interval in which the constituents of the crust (an unthreatening topic) are dissected and discussed, Viv murmurs, 'So, darling. Any news on anything? Have you thought about where you might relocate?'

She knows Geoff disapproves of this opening gambit. Geoff is of the opinion that it's always advisable to let Daisy take things at her own pace. Her pace can be glacial, however, and Viv doesn't think she can stand much more suspense. She prefers to take the direct approach, even though experience has told her that, in common with helpful suggestions about life in general, it may be counterproductive.

Geoff pours more wine as Daisy exchanges a glance with her godmother. A complicit glance containing some abeyant humour. This is likely to be a curly conversation because there are delicate issues involved. Not that Daisy has ever let her parents' approval, or otherwise, change her behaviour, or even influence it overmuch, as they would be the first to acknowledge.

If there is anyone whose opinion can carry some, and on occasion some real, weight with Daisy, it is Jules. Daisy takes notice of what she thinks, and her parents know it. Julia's relationship with her goddaughter has been an unexpected pleasure; one of those rare gifts, as she has said to Viv, that goes on giving. And it has not been competitive, not the two-edged sword that it might have been.

Still, the potential to cut both ways has always been there. And might, Jules is thinking, be here right now. She has no idea how Viv or Geoff (perhaps particularly Geoff) is going to receive this.

'I've moved in with Adrian,' Daisy remarks negligently. Her parents look up from their plates. Adrian is the name that had sprung independently and unprompted into both minds. Adrian: lazy, louche, funny, irresponsible. Good-looking, not gainfully employed. Drug-dabbling, profligate, gay. The name that ticks all boxes.

'Ah, Adrian,' Viv murmurs. And waits, but nothing is forthcoming. 'Well, he's been a very good friend. Remind me, where does he live again?'

'Where he's always lived, in Flood Street, Mum. Chelsea. Remember?'

'Does he have a spare room?'

'Yes, of course he has a spare room. His parents have got *zillions*. He's got spare rooms coming out of his ears. I'll have my own studio. He's been rattling around in there for months not knowing what to do with himself.' Daisy spears some sprouting broccoli. 'This is really good, Mum.'

'He hasn't always lived alone, has he?' Viv asks, tentatively.

'No, of course not, he shared the house with Henry. Remember Heggers? His twin? We had a brief thing at uni. He was my first real boyfriend, actually, or second. A *very* brief thing. You probably don't remember him, he's the straight one of the family. A real pain in the butt. He got married in June, so he moved out to his own place.'

'Yes, I do remember him. Surprisingly well, since it was – how long ago? Getting on for twenty years?' She bites her tongue.

'Heggers. Yes, cherubic with blond curly hair. I thought he was terribly sweet.'

Ouch. He was a pain in the butt. Second bite of the tongue. 'Isn't that funny, Geoff, I had no idea Heggers was Adrian's brother. They're clearly not identical twins. Must be fraternal. Did you know he was related to Adrian?'

'I don't even recall the bastard,' says Geoff. 'So, who is Adrian's *editor?*' Geoff knows, along with Viv, that Adrian is reputed to have been writing a novel ever since his brief appearance at uni (Leeds). 'Or is he still a wannabe dilettante?' He aims a weak, forgive-me grin at his daughter.

Daisy has never indicated that she harbours any illusions about Adrian's industry or his singleness of purpose. 'Oh, he's still finding himself,' she says. 'You know how it is with the idle rich, Dad. Even though there may not be anything to find.'

'Words out of my mouth. So, he's still living off his parents. Well, that's not surprising. He's only nearly *forty*, isn't he?' Under the table, Viv gives Geoff a warning kick. She knows Daisy is perfectly cognisant of the fact that her father has no time for Adrian, and is moderately amused by this. But it's better that he doesn't overdo it.

'Of course, what he really, really wants to be is a poet,' Daisy murmurs indulgently, knowing this is a line guaranteed to wind her father up. 'He had a poem published once. Or claims to, I'm not sure anyone ever saw it.'

'Don't you have to have been born in the nineteenth century to be a poet? Or aged nineteen?' This gets a dutiful dad's joke laugh, though one with a cautious underlay. Geoff goes on, 'Does he do anything in the daytime, apart from wake up?'

Daisy appears to consider. 'Therapy. He does analysis. And he's a dedicated *flâneur*. That takes up a lot of time. If there's any left over he works on the novel. He's nearly finished it, you know. For the past five years.'

A lull descends on the table, a clink of knives and forks. Viv is relieved that her husband has had the residual good sense to retreat. Along with him, she knows this subject is not yet exhausted. There is more to come.

Julia feels she should be helping out. She steps in. 'Of course, if you're going to be a poet and *flâneur* – and nothing wrong with that if you can afford it,' – or your parents can, adds Geoff – '*if* you are going to be one of these, and why not make it both while you're about it, then Chelsea's not a bad stamping ground.' She glances at Viv and Geoff. 'Although it was so much more boho forty years ago, wasn't it? Never affordable for the likes of us.'

Daisy has always had a sense of theatre. 'Anyway, whatever. We're going to try for a baby. I thought I probably should tell you, so it didn't come as a life-threatening anaphylactic shock or something. That's if I'm not barren, and if anything actually happens.'

The sound of cutlery on china ceases abruptly. In the hush, Viv can hear herself chewing, which she always finds disconcerting.

'I tried the idea out for size on Jules first,' Daisy resumes laconically, 'and she didn't keel over.' Her phone pings. She takes it out and glances at it.

Jules is trying to maintain an appearance of normality, sawing into the skin of her salmon (good omega-3) rather over-industriously.

'*We're* going to try for a baby? Is there another half of the equation?' Geoff is demanding, while directing a hostile look at Julia. 'And if so, who? Or what?' I think we should be told, he adds, in a last-ditch attempt at whimsy. Viv knows it also follows a last-hope question.

That hope is promptly demolished. 'Who? Adrian and me, of course. Who else?' Daisy's face is wary.

'Adrian? Really, darling?' Instead of fielding a bolt from the blue, Viv might be canvassing Daisy's views on reality TV. 'Do you think that's ... But how would you ...'

Her attempts to conceal her consternation are made easier (if only marginally) because the groundwork had been laid (*not exactly*) and is now confirmed. She feels she should be participating in the conversation more, to support Daisy through this. It is a rocky road to tread, and has now turned into a regular minefield. 'I mean, how would you, you know, go about it?'

'How would we *go about it*, Mum?' Daisy looks at Jules, and giggles. 'In the usual way, of course. How do you think?'

Her parents respond, in kneejerk unison, 'But Adrian's gay.'

'So? It doesn't mean he can't be a father. Or *does* it?' This question is posed in a newly belligerent tone.

'Well, no, it doesn't, of course,' Viv says immediately. 'Not if he's up to it.' The double entendre was inadvertent, and gets a snort out of Daisy. 'But …' She grinds to a halt. There are so many ifs and buts around the issue she's unsure where to start.

'And if he's up to being a father full stop,' says Geoff grimly.

Jules puts down her knife. 'I don't think the idea is that he would be a *traditional* father, necessarily.' She looks at Daisy for confirmation. 'He'd be more the *enabler*, the one who helps it to happen. Which, as matters stand, could be convenient.'

'The enabler who then drops out of the picture. Or takes a back seat,' says Viv, hoping she has stated this in such a casual way as to mask, or at least muffle, a confused wish. 'Is that the general idea, Daisy? I mean, if it happened according to plan, what would you do then? Do you think you would continue to live there independently? Or are you not thinking that far ahead at this stage?'

'*Independently*? How do you mean?'

'Sharing the house but living separately is what she means.' Geoff is visibly clenching his teeth.

'Relax, Dad. We're not planning to shack up together.' Viv experiences a flood of partial liberation. 'We're not proposing to go all retro on you. It's not going to be mum, dad and the kids and a formica-and-lino kitchen. Sorry to disappoint you guys.'

Viv is reminded of an old colouring book of Daisy's, with pictures of jolly domestic scenes from different decades. It must have lodged in Daisy's mind. The smiling fifties mother wearing a ging-ham apron and brandishing a dishcloth.

'It's not like this will be Adrian's Damascene conversion. It'll most likely be a one-off. Or like, you know – however many one-offs it takes.' A grimace, followed by a grin. 'He's never going to switch over to shagging women on a permanent basis.'

Daisy gives her parents a challenging stare before adding, in a markedly lighter tone, 'Unless, of course, the whole experience is a wild ecstatic epiphany. It might bring in its train transports of bliss beyond imagining. He's had phases of being ambi, so he knows what to do. He was engaged to a woman once.' She pauses for breath. 'But he's so unreasonable he won't even *consider* sexual reorientation therapy, can you believe that?'

Daisy's delivery is invariably rapid and emphatic. The words are coming at breakneck speed. 'Look, he's always wanted children. He wants to play an active role.' Viv's heart sinks. 'Well, he thinks he *might* want to. In any case, this way he might get a child, I'll have a great place to live and work, the baby, if any, will have a relationship with its father, and we could afford a nanny if we—'

'So, the sperm donor would consider extending his enabling role?' Geoff interrupts from a slumped position. 'He'd consider contribut-ing financially to the upbringing of any offspring, would he?' He's breathing noisily, a sure sign he is having difficulty restraining himself.

His daughter's hackles are also raised. 'He's not going to be *just* the sperm donor, Dad, haven't you listened to anything? He'll be a normal father. Kind of. We're going to—' She hesitates, takes pity on him. 'We're going to try conceiving in the same way you did. Or like I assume you did, not having been there at the time.'

'Ever heard of a turkey baster?' Geoff mutters under his breath.

'Just suck it up, Dad, okay?' Daisy looks at her watch and raps out a quick text on her phone.

Viv gives Geoff another jab on the shin. She says, without con-viction, 'I can see why this idea might seem to have a lot of inbuilt, instant solutions and advantages, darling. But there are rather a lot of issues, aren't there? To think about. You would have to be … careful of … things.'

'What about AIDS, for Christ's sake?' demands Geoff, voicing one of these *things*. 'And all the other unmentionables?'

'You're so last century, Dad. He's getting himself thoroughly checked out. And he's been off drugs for –' Daisy shrugs, 'nearly a year. He only ever tinkered with them. He was never a real addict.'

'Oh, only a *pretend* one. So that's all right then.'

'Dad, if you can't deal with it can you just bugger off and fuck yourself?' Daisy says, mildly.

All that rough trade, Viv is thinking. 'But he has been rather promiscuous, hasn't he, darling?' There have been lurid Adrian stories doing the rounds for years, involving antics that these days sound positively passé. Sailors. Hampstead Heath. Tangier. Public lavatories.

'Don't stress, he'll definitely suspend all his gross-out activities,' Daisy grins, 'for the duration.' Now that the worst is over she is visibly more relaxed. She drains her glass and extends it, like an olive branch, to her father for a top-up.

'Could you be sure of that?' Viv asks. 'What if the duration became – you know, unexpectedly long?' It hasn't escaped her notice that they are using different tenses in this evasive discussion (and Daisy is not normally given to euphemisms). Where she and Geoff are saying could or would, Daisy is saying can and will. She has made up her mind. This is merely a formality to put us in the picture. She's really determined to *do* this. Daisy and Adrian. Daisy, Adrian, grandchild.

'He's cool with whatever it takes, Mum. Look, I know there are minor downsides, okay? But he's given me his word. He's given me,' funereal voice, 'a solemn undertaking. We've discussed everything.' She smiles at Viv and Jules, a blithe, sunny smile. It places her suddenly and poignantly, in her mother's eyes, in the full bloom

145

of youth's heedless optimism. 'We've covered all the bases. Pretty much every downside you could think of.'

Her parents doubt that. Each thinks they could rustle up a whole bunch of downsides that have not occurred to Daisy.

'His *word?*' Geoff mutters. I wouldn't trust him as far as I could kick him, is the unmissable implication. And Viv finds she has some sympathy with it. To be honest (an annoying phrase she is more drawn to than ever before) she identifies with it more than she cares to admit.

13

DIFFICULT CONVERSATIONS

In the sweaty environs of the gym, Viv is contemplating daily life. Its problems seem to have expanded lately. Trying to come to grips with these takes her mind off the boredom of the repetitions. As she moves from the treadmill to the rowing machine she is in deep thought – deep in what Joy calls the cocoon of middle-class worry – about Daisy and her future. And also, in the wake of a brief exchange at breakfast this morning, about Geoff's opinion of Julia.

Last night the doorbell rang twice, just after Daisy had declined ice cream with her fruit salad. That would be Adrian, he'd been drinking nearby in Primrose Hill, she explained casually. At Heggers' place. He was coming to pick her up.

'Does Heggers live in Primrose Hill?' Viv asked. She was feeling slightly punch-drunk, and knew this sensation would endure for some time.

'Yeah, with Venetia, his child bride. They're child*less* – but going at it hammer and tongs, so probably not for long,' Daisy responded fluently, on her way to the front door. 'We're all having a race to the finish.' There was the sound, rather unnerving to those left behind at the table, of unrestrained laughter in the hall. Then Daisy returned leading Adrian by the hand.

Neither Viv, Geoff nor Jules had set eyes on Adrian for some time. Not since the wedding of Daisy's best friend Alyse seven years ago. Daisy's parents were forcibly reminded of his impact as he surged, dripping, through the doorway, apologising for bringing the warring elements inside (It's a *cyclone* out there, people!) and kissing the women with every appearance of pleasure (What a treat – you guys haven't changed a bit, how do you *do* it?) before shaking Geoff's manifestly reluctant hand.

If he had any inkling of Geoff's feelings, and Viv guessed he had every inkling, he didn't show it. He was behaving with the relaxed social ease that a very expensive education gives you, she thought, albeit to a flagrant degree. She had forgotten quite what a force of nature Adrian was. Charismatic in that risky way, like the Rolling Stones before they really went to seed. In his case, though, this was shot through with racy humour. A satirical attitude could derail a good many prejudices but not, she feared, her husband's. His visceral antipathy would be glaringly obvious to anyone.

Adrian's flamboyant brand of rakishness might be dated, but you could see, only too well, how it might appeal to the impressible of both sexes. Viv left Geoff out of this – his unimpressibility was never in doubt – but where did it leave Daisy? Watching Adrian, Viv felt that he compelled you to take up a position. You were either for him or against. Did one really want such a polarising figure on the fringes of one's family?

On the fringes? What am I thinking? He's potentially right in there. She caught Julia's eye. Jules was consuming a small helping of fruit salad, a teaspoon at a time. She wore a bland expression that reminded Viv, distractingly, of Dev.

'We're not staying,' Daisy warned, but Adrian had pulled up another chair and was lounging, with his elbows (leather patches on a chunky rollneck sweater) on the table. He looked like a rather dangerous male model. Viv put a plate in front of him. Would he like some fruit salad and ice cream?

'No, he wouldn't,' said Daisy promptly, 'he's already eaten.' But he was already helping himself (Green tea and fig and honey? How divine. Both, please, Vivien. Excess in all things!) and dumping dollops on Daisy's plate for good measure.

'Come on, darling, it'll do you good. We need to build you up for the ordeal that may lie ahead. She's gorgeous, right?' directed at the table, 'but she's a bit too skinny, wouldn't you say?' He surveyed them all nonchalantly. 'So, what do you think of our little *plan*? Do you love it, or does it give you the screaming heebie-jeebs?' His eyes rested on Geoff for a second, before reverting swiftly to Viv.

'Don't bring that up, it's mean,' Daisy interrupted, with her mouth full. 'It's all a bit overwhelming and revolutionary, they need time to get used to it.' She saw her father's face. 'Or grin and bear it and get *over* it, hopefully, and move on.'

Geoff reached for the coffee plunger in the moment's silence that followed. He regarded Adrian through narrowed eyes. 'The roads are slippery. Are you proposing to drive to – where is it – Chelsea?' He poured Adrian a long black. 'The police have been cracking down on boozers around here.'

'Dad, you're regressing,' Daisy remonstrated at once. 'You don't do that anymore, remember? Not to your grown-up daughter's mature friends.' Viv thought this was quite restrained, considering. She knew what Geoff was thinking: but you're my little girl, and you always will be. She knew this because she was thinking the same thing.

Adrian looked unperturbed. Geoff shouldn't worry because he was behaving himself now, being boringly abstemious and beyond reproach. He was gearing himself up for the mature, grown-up (a wink at Daisy) responsibilities life may be conspiring to throw at him. Now he was a potential baby daddy he was desperate to become a role model, as Daisy would confirm. He'd go down with the ship. He was thinking of buying a business shirt and voting.

He swilled his coffee and licked the last skerrick of ice cream off his spoon. Observing this, Daisy dragged him out of the chair he was showing every sign of having settled into. 'Nobody wants to discuss the plan right now except you. At least,' she grinned, 'I expect they're itching to discuss it but they can't, not with your big ears flapping. Come on, we're going home.'

Daisy proceeded to kiss each of her parents in an unusually tender manner that conveyed a degree of compunction. Viv wondered if *going home* had pierced Geoff in the same way. To the heart, most probably, she felt.

Jules would explain why the plan was a good idea much better than she could, Daisy informed her mother loudly in the hall, as Adrian helped her into her coat. Jules, in response to Geoff's glare, said she would stay for a short debrief. No more drinks because she had a wardrobe fitting tomorrow.

'He assured me he would drive carefully,' Viv told her husband, as they drew up armchairs around the fire in the sitting room. She thought that Geoff (pouring himself a large brandy) looked more shattered than she felt. All she could say for certain about her state of mind was that she felt vaguely unsettled. Which was enough to be going on with.

Geoff dumped the brandy balloon on the coffee table and put his head in his hands. 'Can you explain to me using words of one syllable how this is a good idea, Jules, because I can't see it. Quite frankly it sounds like a recipe for disaster.'

Julia said she thought they had to try very hard to see it from Daisy's point of view. Daisy's pov was driven by the biological clock. This was proof positive of God's fundamental misogyny, but they were stuck with it. Here was an old friend (a groan from Geoff) who was conveniently on tap, as it were. Someone Daisy knew inside out and loved (a prolonged groan) – loved *platonically*, Geoff – someone loaded, moreover, who was willing, indeed very keen, to become a father—

'You mean a *baby daddy*.'

'Forget that, it's just the ghastly current term they use.'

'Who's *gay*, moreover—'

'Who doesn't present as particularly gay,' Jules said. 'He was looking very Ralphy Lauren, I thought. Of course, that may have been deliberate.'

Geoff, who'd been holding himself in check, exploded. 'Who gives a fuck how he presents? For fuck's sake – if it quacks like a duck and does ducky things, and it's a bloody layabout to boot ...' He swilled his brandy.

Jules said the Geoff she knew and loved (platonically) was not normally homophobic or prone to vulgarisms. This was something of a special situation, she understood that, but Geoff had to be prepared to meet it halfway.

'God knows I'm trying. I'm trying to meet it *so* bloody halfway I'm crashing into myself. But why the hell do they have to—? Will you explain *that* to me, Jules? Why can't he just go into one of those places where they have porno magazines full of rubber and—'

'Oh, for crying out loud, Geoff.' Now it was Jules's turn to be exasperated. 'Be sensible – why would they have rubber porn in sperm donor places? Look, Adrian's a very dishy man, whatever side of the fence you happen to sit on. They've probably been secretly lusting after each other for years. I think Daisy sees that side of it as a bit of a lark.'

Secretly lusting? *A bit of a lark?* That was *it*, Geoff said wearily, he'd had enough, he was going to bed. He wasn't up to any more debriefing, he might do things he'd regret later. He'd leave them to it. They'd be much happier without his inhibiting presence.

'So, you find Adrian *dishy*, do you, Jules?' yelled from the landing. '*That* follows.' Viv toyed with the idea of going after him. She hovered indecisively, then sat down again.

Jules looked contrite. 'I'm sorry, Viv. That didn't go well. Poor Geoff, he can't cope with the idea of them having sex, can he?' Viv said that was understandable. A lot of men found the idea of their daughter having sex difficult, even at the best of times. Even with a charming, ideal young man who met all their preconceived criteria. The kind Daisy had never brought home – or not since Heggers.

'Heggers? That pain in the arse?' It had been a rackety evening, but Jules was still quick on the uptake. Well, it might be tricky for men like Geoff, she supposed, for all sorts of reasons one didn't necessarily want to go into now. Then there was the added prospect of having Adrian as the father of his grandchild. Not his son-in-law, not his daughter's boyfriend or partner – how would you introduce him, apart from anything else?

'Like he said, as Daisy's baby daddy,' said Viv shortly. She thought: he will never care how we introduce him. Or what we think of him either. 'Did you try to talk her out of it?'

Jules said she'd had to wing it when Daisy arrived with her news. She soon realised that Daisy had already made up her mind, and what she was looking for was validation.

'Did you validate, then?'

Jules lifted placating hands. 'What can you do? Daisy's an adult, and she's well and truly her own person.' This was undeniable, Viv had to admit. 'It's not ideal, she'd be the first to agree with that, but it's a pragmatic course of action. She's decided to be proactive about getting something she really wants, instead of blindly relying on chance, or *fate* if you like.'

'And risk leaving it too late.' Like I did, for her brother or sister.

'Let's face it, Viv, your Daisy is a very determined young woman. She may be her own person, but she's her mother's daughter. As indeed are you; never forget that.'

Viv had always tended to think of Daisy as a being apart, and herself as similarly removed from her own mother. But she and Judith must have contributed something to Daisy's character. More than she took into account?

Of course, the present situation could change, Jules continued. Daisy might think better of it, or she might meet someone better. They might find they were hopeless at living together. They might be hopeless at getting it *on* together. Technical hitches of this ilk were on the cards.

She lifted her hair. 'There could be any number of spanners in the works, that's the truth of the matter, Viv. And even if they *do* get it on together—'

'The object of the exercise may not eventuate,' Viv said dourly, 'and she may not get pregnant at all.'

The truth of the matter, she was inclined to think, was that Jules had stopped short of outright encouragement but had been supportive. And she couldn't argue with that. Although, to be honest, she was trying to cope with an unfamiliar feeling of solidarity with her husband.

Geoff had been sound asleep and emitting bellicose snores when she came to bed. He was taciturn at breakfast, to start with. But then he'd asked, quite aggressively, about the rest of her conversation with Julia. No doubt Jules had managed to wriggle out of any semblance of responsibility for this lunacy?

Well, it was a bit unclear, Viv said. It sounded as if Jules had avoided giving any advice because she knew Daisy didn't want to hear any and wouldn't have taken it anyway. And you couldn't blame—

'She wouldn't have advised against it,' Geoff interrupted loudly. 'She would have egged Daisy on.'

'What makes you say that?'

'Because this crazy business with Adrian is the kind of tawdry alternative set-up Jules finds irresistible.'

'Rather unorthodox, do you mean? What makes you think she finds—'

'Oh, she's drawn to it. Jules always had a nose for dirty laundry. You're not attracted to that stuff, so you don't notice it, but she is. That's the difference between you.'

He left the table, clattering his breakfast dishes into the dish-washer. Viv had stared after him, taken aback by this outburst. Geoff had always had trouble with Jules's more libertarian views, and this development with Adrian had made him overreact. It would blow over.

And how would Geoff feel if the object of Daisy's exercise does not eventuate, she wonders, as she waits for an unfit elderly man to dis-engage himself from the abdominal-crunch machine. She is near-ing the end of the circuit and doesn't mind waiting. She dislikes most gym machines, this one in particular.

As she hooks her shins in position her phone vibrates: Martin Glover. It comes as a pleasant reprieve. In the changing room she calls Martin back. He is pleased to relate he has another candidate for her appraisal. Not a younger model this time. Well, that's a blessed relief, says Viv. No, it's someone her own age. Seems like an agreeable chap. A lawyer.

A *lawyer?*

Does that surprise you? It does rather, but then again Viv doesn't know why it should. She can't think of any reason why law-yers shouldn't avail themselves of Discretion's services, any more than people in hospitality, like Dev.

Or any more than artsy-fartsy types, says Martin equably. So I can pass on your number? You're not one of those who would kill all the lawyers? Certainly not, she says. Not all of them.

Speaking of Dev, has she managed to talk to him yet, by any chance?

No, but she'll do it today, if Martin still thinks it's a good idea. Because there's something else she hadn't told him. Something a friend pointed out. This friend has a nose for – Viv substitutes uncon-ventionality for dirty laundry. The friend thinks that Dev is not look-ing for something on the side. He's looking for a sugar mummy.

Of course, this was never going to work with me, she explains. I'm not nearly wealthy enough to haul my toy boy off on endless luxury cruises. And I wouldn't want to if I was. In fact, I can't think of anything worse, *to be honest*.

Martin says he can see this match-up was not made in heaven. He and Dev need to talk this through, clearly. It's sounding very much as if Dev would do better elsewhere. No doubt there are women actively interested in this kind of arrangement, but he doesn't think any of them have ever fetched up at his modest facility.

Maybe in that case I wouldn't need to broach the physical aspect after all, Viv suggests, hopefully.

Now there's a thought, says Martin. Important as the physical side is, the sugar-mummy aspect is more of an overarching problem, isn't it? Which lets us off the other hook. A two-pronged assault might be too much for the poor chap, all in one go. It might be best left for me to tackle, in due course.

Viv is not completely convinced, but she nods into the phone. Dev would get his money back if he left the agency, she assumes. After all, he hasn't had much of a bang for his bucks. Martin agrees a refund would be only right. He'd hold on to a minor percentage for admin. And to cover the work done to date.

To cover his one unsuccessful introduction, Viv says. It sounds forlorn. She is about to put her phone back in her pocket when it pings with another message. It's Dev. Well, of course, it would be. It's a sign. A sign that I am not yet quite off this particular hook. Even though I don't believe in signs. She calls him back before she can renege on the impulse.

'Vivien!' The voice on the other end of the phone vibrates with annoyance. 'This is my fourth attempt to contact you. You are very hard to connect with, Vivien. It is a week since we last saw each other. We are needing to make another appointment in the very near future.'

She recoils, and swallows. 'I'm sorry, Dev, I really am, but I don't think you and I have any future.' She is impressed by her own directness.

'Why would you make such an assertion, Vivien?' He sounds astonished.

Be resolute. 'Because you and I are not – I'm afraid I don't think we are very well suited. It's nothing to do with either of us, it's just one of those things.'

'On the contrary, Vivien, I feel we are very well suited. I want to show you a brochure that will convince you of this. Definitely.'

'A brochure?'

'I have it in my hand.' She hears a rustle of paper. 'It is from my local travel agent. It depicts a transatlantic voyage to New York on the *Queen Mary 2*. There are lavishly appointed bedroom suites, each with its own balcony overlooking the ocean.'

'Dev—'

'There is a planetarium on board. And a spa club, which offers the personal pampering you have been longing for, with innovative and indulgent treatments by a qualified—'

'*Dev!*' She stops just short of shouting down the phone. 'Please will you kindly *listen* to me? I'm not that kind of person. I haven't been longing for pampering spa treatments—'

'It caters for all kinds of person, Vivien, you can be sure of that. There is a well-equipped library for those seeking quiet meditation, and a ballroom with elegant ambience and high ceilings …'

When she was the parent of a two-year-old, Viv was told that lowering the voice could be more effective than yelling. 'I don't want to go on that voyage, Dev.' She enunciates slowly and clearly. 'Or any voyage. Or any train journey. And even if I did want to, *I couldn't possibly afford it.*' She lays heavy stress on the last half of this sentence.

'But it is quite brief, and your estranged husband would certainly—'

'Look, Dev, my husband – who is not estranged, by the way, or not *as such* –' she hears her voice rising again, 'certainly would *not* agree to cough up enough dough for me to take a sybaritic holiday with my lover. But that's not the point. The point is, Martin Glover feels you are unlikely to find the person you're looking for at his agency. It's the wrong place for you.' She draws breath and adds lamely, 'He wants to talk to you about giving you your money back. Most of it, I should think. Nearly all, with any luck.'

'You have been talking about me with Mr Martin Glover?' Dev sounds agitated.

'Well, only a *little*.' She feels irrationally guilty. 'He wanted to know … he inquired how – how it had gone, so I, ah, I tried to explain.' She hopes the guilt is irrational rather than the opposite.

'To explain *what*? What did you tell him, Vivien?'

'What I've been trying to tell you. You know, that we weren't suited and I wasn't right for you.' Should she mention the physical side after all? 'And,' dropping her voice again, '*vice versa*.'

'But this is not appropriate. It is not the right thing to do at all!' Dev's voice rings in her ear excitedly. 'It is talking out of school, Vivien!'

'Yes, I know it is, and I'm really sorry about that, but I couldn't seem to avoid it.' No, it would be a major mistake to bring up the physical side. It would unleash a whole new can of worms.

Hurriedly, 'I have to go now, Dev. I'm sure there is a filthy rich, elegant woman out there who is up for any number of glamorous junkets and pampering treatments, and who can bankroll them at the stroke of a pen. Or –' such people would do this via the internet, wouldn't they? – 'the click of a mouse. Or her secretary would. I am not that woman, but I sincerely hope you find the one who is.' She ends the call with a decisive stroke of the thumb.

14

DISGUISES

To Julia's way of thinking, an opera production is a feat of engineering. It resembles in some respects the soaring arc of a bridge (the Sydney Harbour Bridge for preference) where every rivet plays an essential supporting role. If one sequence of rivets fails, the bridge will not collapse and nor will the production, but both will be threatened. Should many fail, collapse is inevitable. Collapse, in the case of an opera, meaning bad reviews and the ignominy of public failure.

Like Viv, Julia is dealing with life-changing issues. Following a fallow period she has been catapulted into the heart of the action. This time it was unexpected, but that apart it's nothing new. She's used to a pattern of sudden changes; it has been the way of her working life since the early days. For the immediate future her parallel lives, professional and personal, will be defined by her role as the Old Countess.

A compact but central role, as those around her feel honour bound to repeat. These people include her costume designer, milliner, wigmaker and dressmaker. And her director, who will intercept her before she leaves wardrobe after lengthy consultations on gowns (four), wigs (two), shoes (three pairs) and make-up (three looks – one being a ghost).

She will not be in the best frame of mind to be intercepted. Wardrobe had her measurements on file from last time, but as it turns out they're not altogether accurate. Last time was several years ago. The dreaded words *put on weight* hover, but are not mentioned until Julia, never one to beat about the bush, pulls them from the air.

'I have, haven't I? It's your pursed lips. Don't spare me, Marj.' The fitting room has expansive and unforgiving mirrors.

Marjorie Mackintosh, the fitter, herself a short, wide woman (her girth having expanded considerably more than Julia's since their first encounter nearly, God help us, four decades ago) is scrutinising the tape measure encircling Julia's hips.

'Only minor adjustments, dear,' she murmurs, 'just an inch or so here and there. You have retained your figure amazingly well, and a great deal better than most.'

Julia would like to know the identities of the *most*. She can make educated guesses, but knows better than to ask. Discretion on the part of wardrobe is a given. Even more than wigs and make-up, wardrobe is privy to intimate knowledge, especially when there is a long-standing relationship with a diva. Both parties in the relationship have aged at the same rate, but only one has stood in front of the other with her defences down, and revealed her physical (and sometimes personal) vulnerabilities.

Returning to sing at Covent Garden is a homecoming of sorts, and coming across Marjorie Mackintosh is a bonus akin to running into a long-lost cousin, or even a second mother. When they first met, and the young Julia was a long way from home and singing regularly here, the community was like family. There were certain highly personal concerns she felt unable to discuss with new friends, such as Vivien Quarry. Some of these she confided to her dresser, though not in exhaustive detail. But she knows Marj will not have forgotten them.

These are subjects kept close to the chest since those early, insecure days. But there are matters today, related matters, that Julia is tempted to share with Marj. Quite strongly tempted, although she resists. Her prevailing impulse is to protect herself, and anything likely to engender inner turmoil is best avoided when one is already being stretched to the limit.

'So, dear, how are you feeling in yourself?' Marjorie restricts herself to asking, and Julia replies that, overall, she's fine. They share a speaking glance, and a hug.

It occurs to Julia that Viv would feel at home among the racks of garments, the sewing machines and ironing tables. Every task is one strand of a complex web that underpins a singer's eventual appearance in front of the audience. The central aim being, always, to boost the singer's well-being: her wigs must fit securely, her shoes must be comfortable, she needs to inhabit her garments as if they were her own.

Costumes, wigs, make-up – the cunning elements of disguise are the visual keys to a singer's transformation. In spite of her director's positive presence, Julia is brooding. She has approved the sketches of her gowns (faux eighteenth-century with contemporary riffs, says the designer) with some private reservations. She needs to go away and think these over.

She will make her first appearance in a full-length gown and a long cloak trimmed with ermine. Somewhat heavy for a spring day in St Petersburg, but she's not worried about that. The costume for the crucial second-act scene, the one that culminates in the Countess's demise, is another matter.

It is a form-fitting creation. Unsuitably so? A ruffled nightgown in black silk and lace, full-length, high-necked (mercifully) and long-sleeved (ditto). But also clinging, from below the bust. This is potentially troubling. Initially it will be screened by a beautiful if filmy peignoir, but before she reclines onto the chaise longue (only to rise up in terror and fall back in a lifeless swoon) the negligee will be off her shoulders.

Would this slinky gown be flattering, or the opposite? She is not convinced by Marjorie Mackintosh's reassurances that it's not revealing, and she can wear foundation garments (Marj's term) underneath. It – the wretched weight creep – might be small, and have arisen over several years, but it's concerning. How did it happen?

Julia knows how most of it happened, only too well. Only a few weeks ago she was singing in Sydney, where the food is fresh and first-rate (when you know where to go) and her brother Max, whom she saw a lot of and who knows where to go, is a gourmet. Her Dido was not called upon to wear anything tight, and she let her guard down. There were some delicious meals. Too many scrumptious dinners. Even a few ill-advised (and incautious) late breakfasts.

Which brings to mind her brother's impending divorce. Her sister-in-law has sent Julia a long email she has put off reading. It will only be, she has predicted to Viv, a litany of complaints about Max. And probably with an undercurrent of resentment towards her. Although Julia has always bent over backwards to be nice to her, as she's sure Viv would attest.

This bittersweet train of thought comes to an abrupt halt as Emils introduces Yuri Dutka, the Ukrainian star who will sing the demanding male lead role of Herman. Julia is warm and gracious, though still a touch preoccupied. Yuri is in his forties. He's an affable fortress of a man, built like a brick shithouse, as her father might have said. Head and shoulders taller than the stocky Emils. And he looms over Julia. This makes her feel more petite, and takes her mind off Max's divorce and her measurements.

In his big scene with the Countess, the physical contrast between them will be to her advantage. It's harder to maintain a romantic operatic illusion with a short tenor or a particularly stout one. Not that Herman and the Countess have any romantic entanglement in this opera; very much the opposite. He's courting her granddaughter Lisa. He aims to extract the secret of the cards from the Countess and win a fortune. When he pulls a gun on her, the old lady has a cardiac arrest.

Yuri's physical envelope will assist with the believability of this outcome, jokes Emils, clapping him on the back. And it means that Lisa won't have to sing with her knees bent in their scenes together, Julia adds, lucky girl. She has had to do this herself on occasion – in unimaginative productions.

Emils plans to bolster the shock quotient further with lighting effects. Gruesome shadows will be thrown up on the walls of her boudoir, he says with relish. Grotesque, like in an old Hammer horror movie.

On his youthful shoulders the ultimate responsibility for the production in the public mind – it might be argued – is resting. Fortunately those shoulders are broad and capable, as Julia has observed. The director's concept is not always everyone's cup of tea. But she's confident Emils has no interest in shock for its own sake. Or schlock, for that matter. He's not setting this opera in an igloo or dressing his cast in cling wrap. Not like some of the look-at-me tyros she has known.

Emils commandeers his star for a quick chat over coffee. Is she happy with everything? Her jewellery? Wigs and costumes? She's going to turn all heads in the opening scene. That incredible wig. The drape of that gown. Very sophisticated. *Soigné*, right? And that curvy nightdress, how about *that* then? He looks searchingly at Julia.

Among other anxieties, Julia is concerned that lacy French flounces are rather unusual embellishments for an old woman's night attire. She hasn't yet come to a decision on this costume. It is within her power to veto it altogether. She decides not to raise this now, and says instead, 'Just as well I don't have to sing a note in the first scene, from under that *badger* wig.'

The badger wig is a stunning creation, black with an off-centre white stripe. She made a show of being not entirely sure about it, but Marj and everybody else thought it was fabulous. It will echo the Countess's own hair, revealed in the deadly bedroom scene with Herman. That wig will be long and straight. Iron grey, with the distinctive white streak.

Julia doesn't have to sing in the opening scene, Emils agrees, but she must do something else instead. She must attract attention.

'You rotate your head like you're the Queen of Sheba. And the soldiers and the kids – they spring out of your way as you and Lisa make your progress through the crowd. With swishes of that sumptuous cloak. With your trademark *look*, Julia. And whoever gets impaled on that look – do they know about it!'

He monitors her reaction. Julia knows what he's getting at. It's all down to deportment, and deportment is a matter of confidence. She knows how a performer on a crowded stage can be the focus of all eyes, purely by means of her physical bearing. If that's what he wants she can deliver, no worries at all.

Emils has a to-do list longer than her arm, but instead of rushing off as she was expecting he leans towards her. He radiates purpose and intensity, and something else too. 'I need to run another thing by you, Julia.'

She detects a hint of indecision. Or it could be unease. 'Run with it, then. I'm all ears.'

'Okay, here's the thing. Your bedroom scene with Herman. This is the pivotal scene of the opera, right?' They both know she likes that. 'Well, Julia, I want there to be a moment. An unoperatic moment, when everything hangs in the balance.'

She raises her eyebrows. 'An *un*operatic moment? In my bedroom scene?'

'I mean like a metaphoric pause in the music, when everything goes kind of stunned. A critical moment. When, unexpectedly between you and Herman, and *improperly at every level*,' the bright, savvy eyes engage hers, 'there's a flicker. A gesture, maybe.'

A beat. 'Like this.' Without disengaging his eyes from Julia's he picks up her hand and brushes it against his thigh. 'And at that instant there's a mass gasp. The entire audience does a double-take. Omigod, is she really vamping him? Is she thinking of one final seduction?'

A quizzical look as Julia retracts her hand and cuts through the moment. She sits up in her chair. This is exciting. Not something she has seen or heard suggested in this opera. And yet, she can easily see how it might be ...

'And Herman gets it. Before the reality of where he is – alone with this spookily alluring old woman, in her bedroom, before the gravity of it reasserts itself – because this lady is his lover's *granny*, for God's sake – we have this ambiguous moment. Where – briefly, no more – there's a deeply inappropriate possibility hanging in the air.'

For an inappropriate moment, no more, Julia suppresses the urge to push the hair out of his eyes.

'You see the point of that shapely black nightgown? It's elegant, but also –' his eyes are again on hers, not on his hands as they trace, absently, a *pas de deux* in the air, 'also *sexy*.' He looks away, shoving his hair aside. 'Even if it *is* high-necked,' he murmurs, almost as an afterthought, with a sidelong glance.

Julia hopes the shapeliness is not too unforgiving. She gives Emils a look that is very finely judged. 'Well. Let's see. We can but try it.'

'Thank you, Julia. I really want to nail this, because it impacts everything that follows. I wouldn't have thought of suggesting it.' He avoids naming the unfortunate singer who had to pull out of the role. 'But when we cast *you* as the Countess – it was suddenly possible to think outside the square.'

Julia murmurs. 'The Parisian ruffles...'

'Right. The previous costume was very prim and proper. Like, not stunning. Think grey flannel. And then we thought: hey hey, let's give that stuffy old nightdress a makeover.'

With a wide and possibly relieved grin Emils heaves his chair back. He kisses Julia on both cheeks, over a mischievous look. The look, she thinks, is aspirational French, with associated (optional) connotations.

'I can't wait to see you in your nightie, Julia,' he says.

15

THE BULLDOG

Viv is on her way to a lunch date with a lawyer. His name (given or surname, she forgot to ask) is Drummond. It is cold and windy today but at least it's not currently raining. Drummond has suggested a small, busy restaurant in Islington which Viv, providentially, knows. Their pre-meeting texts have been brief. He has booked the table at the far end in the name, no surprises there, of Drummond. He sounds efficient and to the point, as Viv would expect from a lawyer.

Bearing in mind the sartorial gaffe she made at her first meeting with Dev, Viv has considered a few alternatives, laying them out on the bed. Geoff came in at one stage to complain about the bathroom renovations taking forever and costing the earth, and asked what on earth she thought she was doing. She said she was culling her wardrobe. Or that's what she thought she was doing, Geoff. Tossing into the bin a visibly moth-eaten sweater Oxfam wouldn't want.

'Don't throw anything out without asking me,' Geoff said, 'I might like it.' He was trying to be nice. Well, that was better than the opposite. But he didn't give her bottom a smack as he might once have done.

She decided not to attempt a sartorial statement of any kind. She would be conservative and anonymous (although this could be construed as making the statement that you are not making one).

To this end she is wearing a plain black skirt, a long-sleeved T-shirt, tapestry jerkin and black boots. She has cleaned some mud off the boots. The heels are worn down, but Drummond is unlikely to notice since, presumably, he will not be inspecting her feet.

She rejected the Tiffany necklace and silver bracelet and the sixties coat, substituting a warm jacket with a faux-fur collar and a red beret. Ageing hippy (Geoff's phrase) is not the look she's decided she wants today.

The beret was not a good idea. Sudden wind gusts keep blowing it off until she jams it in her pocket. The restaurant has a doorway inside a recessed porch, where she does a quick running repair to her hair. As she opens the door she can discern the outline of a man sitting at the end at a table for two, and he seems to be looking in her direction. Without her glasses she can't see him clearly.

He stands up when she arrives and they smile a polite greeting. Only when she has sat down and hung her bag over the back of the chair do they really look at each other.

And then there is a disorientating and most uncomfortable pause, as it dawns on both of them that they have met before. They have, in fact, had dealings, midway between the personal and impersonal, on a regular basis once every six months, over a period of years.

The look of bemused horror on the face of the gentleman now seated opposite Viv (elderly, she would have to say, and cadaverous) in a navy yachting blazer is the opposite of his professional expression. Quite unlike the look in his eyes as he bends over her in a dental mask and explores her gums with an array of implements. He looks quite different without his white coat and away from his practice in Cavendish Square, behind John Lewis.

Viv's eyes have widened. She is visualising the waiting room of the practice in question. Alongside predictable journals such as *Country Life* and *Architectural Digest*, there are often a few copies of the *Spectator* and *Private Eye*. It was in this very waiting room that she first saw the ad for the Discretion Agency.

'Well, I'll be—' She restrains herself from performing a hammy action like reeling back in the chair. 'You're Mr Byron Blake, my periodontist.' Her laugh sounds forced. 'You're a *dontist*, not a law-yer. Unless you're holding down two jobs. It's jaw-jaw, not law-law!'

As an off-the-cuff effort she thinks this is rather good. But Mr Blake is plainly not amused. She suspects he finds it either juvenile or mildly offensive, and perhaps both. He has a long lugubrious face and pronounced bags under the eyes, which she hadn't taken in during their periods of close contact.

'And you are Vivien er, ah ...' A dull red flush is spreading upwards from his neck.

'Quarry.'

'Oh yes, I'm so sorry. How silly of me. Vivien Quarry, of course you are. Yes.'

'Can you believe this? We're in London, not some parish-pump backwater where everyone knows everyone. What a mind-boggling coincidence.'

'Yes, extraordinary. An astounding coincidence. Really, most astonishing.'

Like the synonyms, the conversation (if you can call it that) seems to be exhausted. It is immediately obvious to Viv, and she trusts to Mr Blake as well, that any development of their relation-ship into an alternative province would be quite out of the question. While cordial, their dealings have always been purely professional. The habit is far too ingrained.

Besides, there's something about a person knowing the interior of one's mouth so intimately that would make the possibility of them knowing about another *unrelated* area somehow ...

This train of thought is interrupted by the arrival of the wait-ress. She delivers the menus into their eager, outstretched hands. Rarely, Viv imagines, can two people have fallen upon their menus with such palpable relief. As if they were life buoys thrown to the drowning. She looks at the hovering waitress and then at Mr Blake.

'I suppose we'd better order something since we're here?' At least eating would give them something constructive to do. 'Or do you think we should just – cut our losses, and flee from the scene of the crime?' She laughs. 'Not that any crime has been committed.' Or, indeed, is likely to be.

Mr Blake, so capable in the dental arena – one of the top men, it is said – seems to be verging on comatose with mortification. He gives a one-word reply in a low voice without looking at her. Was it a yes or a no? And which proposition did it address?

He is now bent over the table, poring over his menu as if it were a map of hidden treasure. Or a particularly inaccessible receding gum. Is discomfort making him hungry? Viv herself has temporarily lost her appetite.

'Can I get you some drinks while you are making a decision?' the waitress asks. She has a placid face and strong Eastern European accent and appears not to have noticed anything amiss. The mention of drinks seems to bring Mr Blake to his senses. He sits up and takes belated charge of the situation. 'We – yes, that's right. We'd better have a fortifying drink.' He extracts a pair of bi-focals from his top pocket. 'What would you like, er, ah …'

'It's still Vivien. I don't usually drink wine at lunch but I think I'd love a rather large glass of something. Anything, really. As long as it's inebriating.'

He traverses the short list rapidly, with his forefinger. 'Would a pinot noir suit you? That might do the trick.' She nods, rather too vigorously.

'Well, er, Vivien,' he says, 'so here we are, adrift on an open sea.' It sounds falsely hearty, as well as desperate. She fears his brief impersonation of a man in charge may be about to unravel.

'Up shit creek without a paddle,' she echoes. This is a colloquial phrase of Julia's. 'Or a compass, either.' Too much nautical already. Pull yourself together, woman. 'Of course, Martin – that's Martin Glover, from the *agency* –' she leans towards Mr Blake and delivers this loaded word in a whisper, in case he would rather it were not mentioned aloud, 'he wasn't to know I was one of your patients. And how could he? He thought you were a lawyer. Lawyers have clients, not patients.'

The words *agency* and *lawyer*, even though they couldn't have been overheard, cause Mr Blake to flinch twice. Viv is curious about the extent of his double life. Or triple, if you add the stratagem of his false identity. She says briskly, 'So, Mr Blake, we've caught each other out in a little escapade. Do you think most people going to the Discretion Agency would give a –' better not say *false*, it sounds vaguely criminal – 'would give a *different* name?'

Her companion blinks rapidly, as if he finds this a confronting question. 'You know, I really wouldn't know. Perhaps they do. I was only given your Christian name. I thought this was how they do things. I'm afraid I didn't think to ask for your surname.'

His strangled expression and halting delivery suggests this might have been a sound thing to have asked for. Viv is in agreement.

'Well,' she says bracingly, 'it's a shame you didn't ask Martin Glover. My surname is relatively unusual, so it might have helped avoid this unfortunate turn of events. It wouldn't have helped *me* to ask him, of course, because you gave the agency a pseudonym.'

Too confrontational? 'I must admit, a friend did strongly suggest I should take your course and adopt an alias. Do you think it's an advisable precaution? At the start, I mean.'

And this should have been phrased better. The *start*. It could be construed as a hint that she might not be averse to something further. She sneaks a glance at Mr Blake.

He is shaking his head. 'I really couldn't say. I haven't spoken to anyone else on this subject. Only Glover, really.'

His face wears a harassed, hunted look. The kind that someone who has just parachuted into a field of cannibals might wear.

Viv says she hasn't confided in anyone else either, apart from a couple of friends. 'Neither of them is a patient of yours,' she adds reassuringly. Mr Blake wipes his face with his napkin. 'Martin Glover did say that most people on his books are doing this kind of thing for the first time. I found that quite cheering.'

'Yes, it is rather. Yes.'

They have each polished off their first glass of wine in no time at all. Mr Blake pours another, in a hurry. Instead of abating, the flush has spread to his cheeks. Besides looking ill at ease he looks ill period, which is a bit of a worry. But perhaps this is his default appearance. She should have regarded him more closely while her teeth were being cleaned. Difficult though, as he was always wearing a surgical mask.

'Mr Blake, may I call you Byron?'

'Of course, please do, I should have—'

'Or perhaps you'd rather I used the name Drummond?' He appears too discomfited to reply. 'Although I suppose there's not much point in maintaining a *nom de plume*, or is it a *nom de guerre*, when the rationale has ceased to exist.' Was there a particular reason for choosing the name? 'Does Martin Glover think Drummond is your real name, Byron?'

'Ah, yes, I expect he would. Yes.'

'And he thinks you're a lawyer, too? Since I imagine you didn't wear your white coat to the interview. Or,' a smile, 'your surgical mask.'

'I imagine he must, yes.'

The topic hasn't delivered the hoped-for conversational boost, but she's not giving up on it. Their food has arrived. It's eclectic: risotto porcini for her and steak frites for him. He falls upon his plate as if he has just ended a hunger strike. Viv is hopeful that her own appetite might be returning. She also hopes the food will put something back into Mr Blake's tank. Into Drummond's tank. *Byron's.*

She persists. 'Byron, did you fancy yourself as a bit of a Drummond, then?'

This was fairly innocuous, she'd have thought, but his reaction suggests it is a deeply personal question. The high colour has spread upwards to his forehead. 'Ah. I'm afraid you have exposed my cover. I always detested my given name.'

'That's understandable. You were teased at school, I expect. Byron is alarmingly prescriptive, isn't it? Drummond is definitely more – suave. More *you*, I daresay.' This small stretch of the imagination at last produces the vestige of a smile.

'Which did you intend it to be, first or second? Or perhaps you were envisaging a standalone Drummond, like one of those entertainers who only have one name. Madonna, for example. Or Liberace.'

The mention of Madonna looks unwelcome enough; that of Liberace seems to leave him aghast. 'Not at all. No, nothing like that. It was the name of the hero of a series of books I enjoyed as a child. About a gentleman adventurer. Sapper was the author.'

'Another standalone pen name. You mean Hugh "the Bulldog" Drummond, I presume? Yes, I remember him well. Well, rather dimly at this distance. So are you Hugh, or Bulldog?'

'Well, I'm, er, ah, Drummond Cornwallis.' Byron is looking even more uncomfortable, if possible.

'Cornwallis. Another unusual name. After another book character? Or a pet? A horse? Or a hamster?'

'After Charles Cornwallis, the first Marquess; 1738 to 1805.'

'Is that right? The *first* Marquess?'

Chatting to Byron Blake is rather like pulling teeth. How very apposite. A shame she can't share the insight with others who would appreciate it. This last question, though, inspires a relative effusion.

'Cornwallis had a remarkably varied career, as you could occasionally have in those days. As an army officer and a colonial administrator. He was a British general in the American War of Independence, not altogether successfully, and afterwards served in India and in Ireland. He was a distant relative of mine.'

'Well, good heavens.'

'Admittedly, very distant.'

Clearly this is one of the Bulldog's principal outside interests. 'And the lawyer component of your persona?' Viv prompts. Gently, she hopes. 'I suppose you couldn't make yourself a *colonial* administrator, could you? Not these days, it would be asking for trouble. And gentleman adventurers are a bit thin on the ground now, too.'

She tips the whole bowl of grated parmesan on the risotto, which is bland. 'Drummond could have been in the army, like the first Marquess. In military intelligence, maybe? Or a dashing James Bond figure. Why did you decide to make him a lawyer, Byron?'

'Ah. There you are again. I'm afraid nowadays people often have preconceived ideas about soldiering. As they do about dentistry. The law is somewhat less polarising, as it were. Perhaps more feasible to a wider cross-section.'

Viv decides against voicing doubts. Did he wish he had chosen the law as a profession, then? He looks pensive. 'I'd like to have been a lawyer, I sometimes think. I perhaps would like to have taken silk, in another life.'

'Yes, I can imagine you being a very effective judge,' Viv says, although she has trouble imagining him in any occupation other than his own. 'But in this life you're a good periodontist. An exceptionally good one, in *this* life.'

Which is true. She made the statement in the hope of bucking him up. But it seems to make him, if anything, more depressed. One could explore this territory further, no question. But she decides, selfishly she fears, to solicit his opinion on something of more immediate interest to herself.

'Do you suppose Martin Glover might be a little naive, Drummond?' Her mind toys briefly with Dev. 'He seems to take you – and others – at face value. The previous person I met was a fortune hunter. He couldn't divest me of mine, as I didn't have one. But this particular ambition had slipped under Martin's radar.'

The Bulldog, as she has begun to think of him (although he looks more like a bloodhound) seems a touch less strained. The steak must be helping. And the wine. He is a good glass and a half ahead of her and his complexion can only be called florid. But perhaps it's a relief to have been unmasked? He's relaxing to some extent, to the point of initiating an interesting remark.

He agrees that being prepared to take people at face value does seem to be central to Glover's modus operandi. But he thinks that's just part of the game. Viv is intrigued to hear the business of the agency described in this way. Glover says it's not an exacting pursuit in any way, it's more of a sideline. A little amusement. He thinks Glover is playing at matchmaking, possibly rather indiscriminately. At least, that is his impression.

'Possibly rather *indiscriminately*, you think? Should we be offended?' This allows them both to have a little chuckle.

In Viv's opinion it's not matchmaking at all. 'It might be a little diversion for Martin, but what he's doing is enabling people to stay with their partners when a problematic situation has emerged. For one of them, that is.' Although I assume our situation is problematic for Geoff too. Am I right? 'Apparently his wife works with him.'

Drummond doubts she has much input. Unlike Glover she doesn't meet the applicants face to face.

'Still, you could argue that he's performing a useful social service. Even if only in a well-intentioned, gentleman-amateur kind of way.'

'One can only hope Glover is well-intentioned,' the Bulldog says pensively. They have another cautious laugh.

Viv thinks it gives people like them a framework. 'Rather than going to bars or abandoning ourselves to the internet. Or trusting in fate. I suspect fate isn't very interested in people our age, don't you?'

'Not at all, no. Much like the world in general.'

Viv thinks the Bulldog resembles an illustration of Mr Gradgrind in Dickens's *Hard Times*. Melancholy, elongated, gaunt.

Not at all Byronic, but not entirely humourless either. She wonders about his private circumstances.

'Did it take you a long time to decide to ring Martin, Drummond?'

'Good lord, yes. Years.' He ruminates on this sadly.

'You don't rush into things, as a rule?'

A rueful smile. 'Not as a rule. And what about you, Vivien?'

'About two years.' But it did take provocation. If it hadn't been for the sentence, would she ever have reached the point of taking this initiative? 'It was a slow burn, and then it accelerated in a rush. I was – jolted into action.'

She learns that she is Drummond's ninth introduction in as many months. He's not very forthcoming on the matter, and she has no desire to pry (or no desire that can't be heroically suppressed) but she gathers the enterprise has not, thus far, borne fruit. Which might be where the *possibly rather indiscriminately* comes from.

He's inclined to be choosy, she imagines? She has assumed he is her senior by a few years. We're not easy to please at our age, she goes on, let's face it. We're too fussy, aren't we? Or shall we say, too discriminating?

That sounds more palatable, he agrees. And he fears, speaking for himself, that he's set in his ways.

'Set in our tastes, perhaps.' Viv hopes she is not especially set in her ways. Of course, he will have been told she is in her late fifties. She recalls the files in Mr Byron Blake's dental surgery. They will certainly contain her date of birth. The Bulldog is not the only one to have engaged in a spot of subterfuge. She recalls that Geoff is also one of Mr Blake's patients.

They have disposed of the bottle of wine, her companion taking the lion's share, and their plates are empty. Viv declines a dessert. She looks at her watch and makes a show of surprise. Is it really this late? Lordy, hasn't the time flown?

When the bill arrives, Drummond puts his hand over it and will take no argument. As they get up the earlier awkwardness, which has never been entirely absent, returns in full. They have each other's numbers, they say. That was a most enjoyable lunch, wasn't it? *Such* an extraordinary thing to happen.

But at the door, just as Viv is on the point of diving into the cold, Drummond grasps her arm and leans over her. It reminds her of being in the dentist's chair. Which prompts another memory: she has an appointment in Mr Blake's rooms coming up before Christmas.

'I hope you might consider doing this again,' he says. 'Now that we have broken the ice.'

Viv is caught off guard. She smiles, genuinely warm as well as apologetic. 'Well. It would have been very nice. And that was a lovely lunch, I enjoyed it. But I don't really think, as I'm already your patient, that it would be – well, you know. My husband is a patient of yours too, of course. Geoff Mayberry?'

'Mum's the word,' he says. 'You're Byron's patients. Not Drummond's.'

This is rather endearing. 'In any case, we won't let this queer our pitch, will we, Byron? Because I'd hate to have to go out and find another periodontist, not at this time of life. He'd never be as good. Or as nice.' She squeezes his arm, then regrets it.

'Perhaps you could think about it, Vivien,' he says immediately.

She does think about it on the Tube, for less than ten seconds, and then dismisses it. There's no getting away from it – if *it* is assumed to mean embarking upon a sexual relationship with Mr Blake – she couldn't entertain the idea. It would be preposterous.

16

JUDITH

Joy is unusually frisky today. Viv, who is not feeling frisky herself, has already seen that her chances of a discussion about her recent lunch with the Bulldog are next to nil. Her friend has shunned her usual cowgirl-inspired wardrobe choices, and is sporting a figure-hugging top in electric green and a tight (and short) azure pencil skirt. The gossip is that Mr Jackson Adeyemi doesn't care for country or gypsy; he goes for princess.

Joy has been visiting the YMCA and Oxfam with Riley. Not round here, but in posher catchment areas. Riley, the bombshell of the group, is the main buyer of the celebrity weeklies littering the house. She often picks up model cast-offs that look like they've never been worn. Riley confides that Mr Jackson was observed descending the stairs and eating a humungous fry-up at breakfast.

This line of talk is necessarily limited to moments when neither of the principals is in the room. Joy insists that the new male presence is unobtrusive, insofar as a hunk like that can be unobtrusive in a roomful of women. Which is not at all, in Viv's opinion. But she is becoming quite fond of him, with his shyly polite manner towards everyone.

He's still learning the ropes. Joy has been giving him one-on-one tutorials, has she? For free? Joy's coyness comes as no surprise. She has never been comfortable with intimate personal disclosure, while being perfectly at ease (verging on nosy) about her friends' activities. Mr Jackson is into research, she says breezily.

'He's fixing to study the Encyclopedia.' This is *The Complete Encyclopedia of Quilting*, presented by her tenants five Christmases ago. Ondine got it off eBay, and it's a collector's item, Joy says. She has covered it in cling wrap to protect it from sticky fingers.

Viv doesn't need to be told that her friend has fallen heavily. It has been a long time coming, and no one begrudges it. Everyone, though, has their fingers crossed. No one wants Mr Jackson to turn out to be another Mr Ronnie. Although it's well known that Mr Ronnie, for all his faults, is responsible for everyone being here in the first place.

Joy's ex-husband (now vanished off the face of the earth) also happened to be a nice (initially) Nigerian. He made, or came into, a great deal of money, most of which he took with him. But before shooting through, he put the house in Joy's name. Because it lends an ambivalence to his memory this is hardly ever mentioned.

Viv's elderly mother Judith enjoys hearing news about the members of the quilting circle. Particularly about Mr Jackson's arrival on the scene. She and Joy, and Joy's girls, bonded last summer over lunch in the West Hampstead garden and a picnic in Regent's Park. Still notoriously alert and inquisitive at ninety-one, Judith insists on being kept in the picture. She may have outlived most of her contemporaries, but her interest in other people, and especially in the vagaries of their behaviour, is undiminished. This has guaranteed a sustaining pool of friends of all ages.

About one development, though, she remains in the dark. Viv has not chosen, up to now, to keep her mother completely (or even partially) in the picture about certain vagaries of her own. Joy thinks she is being unnecessarily secretive. She's all for Viv spilling the beans. Don't keep mum about it, she says. Let your mum have a bit of a laugh at you. It's not like she has much to laugh about these days, is it?

These days Judith is Viv's captive audience. She no longer drives, although she takes the bus into Oxford, stubbornly does her own shopping and keeps up with the occasional movie. But when Viv visits, which she does religiously once a fortnight, her mother pre-fers to stay put. Their habit is to talk over a stiff aperitif in front of the fire before watching something on TV.

On this overnight visit there is a lot of ground, potentially, to cover. Viv has been weighing up the pros and cons. Does she or does she not put Judith in the picture? She has no doubt that her mother would listen with an open mind. In comparison with friends' surviving mothers she can only admire Judith's forth-right modernity.

As a child she thought her mother possessed an almost clini-cal objectivity and detachment. She later revised this to a clinical detachment allied to, and sometimes on a collision course with, a powerful (and unstoppable) sensuality. Over time, she has found this to be a comparatively unusual combination.

However, Judith's mental stamina, as expressed through her attention span, is not what it was. It may well be that her energy level will preclude discussing any family business beyond her granddaughter's activities. She knows all about the circumstances of Daisy's break-up with Marco but nothing yet, her daughter has assumed, about Adrian. In this belief Viv is mistaken.

'Did I ever meet this one?' Judith asks, frowning in concentra-tion. Viv has put down a tray of drinks and olives and is stoking the fire. She likes doing this; it takes her back to camping with the Girl Guides. She is nonplussed by the question.

She looks at her mother's shoulder-length but very sparse white hair. 'You mean Marco?' The areas of exposed pink scalp, and the backs of her mother's hands, knotted and wrinkled, dappled with age spots, never fail to move her.

'No, of course I don't mean Marco,' Judith says, very testily. 'I met Marco a hundred times, as you know. And I didn't like him any more than you did. I thought he was fundamentally selfish, which was confirmed. I'm talking about the new one.'

'Adrian?' An impatient nod. 'Oh, I didn't think you – I'm not sure, Mum. You may have met him years ago, they've been friends since university.' Viv notices, rather late in the piece, that several snaps of Daisy and Marco – on a beach in Greece, eating pizza, all dressed up at someone else's wedding – have been removed from the crowded line-up of framed photos on the mantelpiece.

'Show me what he looks like.' Viv hasn't brought along a photograph. She promises to rectify this next time. She's fairly sure that Adrian appears in the group photo she has of Daisy's friend Alyse's wedding. He hasn't changed much in seven years.

'Or better still, she can bring him down to see me. She shouldn't dilly-dally. I might drop off the perch in the meantime.'

It's unlike Judith to say something like this. Viv doesn't want to hear it. 'Mum—'

'You don't like him either, Vivi,' her mother says, with a probing tilt of the head.

Viv takes her time. Even though liking someone is dangerously close to a feeling or an impulse, and therefore not entirely subject to the empirical evidence valued by her mother, she is aware that Judith allows this to be important.

'I don't *dislike* him, I couldn't say that. He's extremely personable. Good company, charming. It's all the other baggage that complicates the issue.'

'Being gay and good-for-nothing,' Judith says, eyebrows raised ironically.

'Well. That counts for something, I suppose.'

'It all depends on what Daisy is using him for, doesn't it?'

Viv has had cause during her life to marvel at her mother's scientific knack of getting to the heart of the matter. Getting to it by means of bypassing the normal human distractions of irrationality and emotion. She hasn't always admired the bottomless capacity for dispassion that is so fundamental to her mother's character, but as she has grown older she has come to appreciate it more. For its comparative rarity as much as anything else.

Growing up, especially in the awkward teenage years, she had cause to writhe under the laser beam of her mother's scrutiny. It no longer has the power to mortify, or even to greatly disconcert. But the accompanying little smile with its hint of complacency, sometimes bordering on triumph, can still rankle, on occasion. This is one of those occasions.

'I'm not sure that Daisy is *using* him any more than he's using Daisy,' Viv says with a touch of asperity. She adjusts the rug on Judith's knees, and digs industriously at the fire. 'They may well cancel each other out when it comes to mutual exploitation.' After a short wait for her mother to interject, she adds, 'That's what makes the situation so difficult to comment on, in any useful way. Or to have much of a view on at all, really.'

'I'm sure Geoff has a view,' says her mother. When she smiles her face creases into a thousand wrinkles. This also never fails to tug at her daughter's heart. For so long, Judith's face was unlined and seemed scarcely to alter. It was only after Stefan's unexpected death twelve years ago that she began to age, in Viv's eyes, almost overnight.

'Yes, Geoff has a view and it's dim. You might say it's entirely negative,' Viv says. They nod with mutual understanding of Geoff and his views. 'He thinks Adrian is trouble with a capital T. Daisy's stuff-up to end them all, he said this morning. All the fucking cock-ups, he said.' This is accompanied by a grin at her mother.

'Of course he did. Prince Charming-and-gay is irrelevant. He wants Mr Straight-down-the-line reliable. He's her father.'

And I am her mother. Why should this always be so much more complicated? It's because I know exactly where she's coming from.

Because I can empathise in ways Geoff just can't. And yet I can't deny that I also understand where he's coming from.

Her mother's next question takes her by surprise. 'Is this going to be a marital problem for you both?' Here is a wide-open invitation, if she wants to take it.

In two minds about the matter as she has been for some time, she says, 'Oh, I don't know, Mum. A lot depends on Geoff's self-control. And on what happens in the long term.' She reviews this. 'And I daresay in the short term too. And, no doubt, in the medium.'

'Are you seeing anyone else, at the moment?'

I'm a tolerably grown-up woman, and I can still be ambushed by my mother. She can still stop me in my tracks and bowl me over with her acuity. Well, what am I waiting for? At least it will give her something new to think about. And it will take the heat off Daisy.

Viv swills the last of her drink. 'Funny you should say that, Mum. I *have* seen one or two lately. I've been going to an agency.'

Leaving this ripe fruit hanging for a minute, she repairs to the kitchen and removes the tray of cheesy vegetarian lasagne that has been bubbling away in the oven. She brought it from home, and the leftovers will give her mother another two easy suppers. Judith likes to eat early in front of the television, with a DVD playing and a tray table across her lap. She has become a big fan of boxed-set dramas, and especially enjoys Scandi-noir thrillers and political intrigues. Viv recycles the pile and replenishes it when she visits. But her news has guaranteed the TV will stay off tonight.

Tonight there's nothing wrong with Judith's attention span. She listens with the trained academic focus that has never left her, and without interrupting. Her response may be non-judgemental but it's not impartial; her daughter's well-being is at stake.

And being Judith, physical gratification is right up there when it comes to well-being. In her estimation it ranks higher, Viv has long suspected, than the profound satisfactions on offer from any other source. From intellectual or artistic sources and even, her daughter would venture to say, with mixed feelings, the mystical (but never mythical) rewards of motherhood.

Her mother's advice in this general area had commenced when Viv turned thirteen. If you were not giving and receiving sexual pleasure, and if (and *only* if, was the conscientious proviso) you regarded this as a deprivation, then Judith was in no doubt about your course of action: you were entitled to do something about it. Indeed, you would be at fault if you did not, and had only yourself to blame. Sexual frustration was profoundly debilitating, Judith said.

These ideas were viewed as daringly subversive at school. They gained Viv much cachet among her friends, imbued as they were with various eye-rolling factors. One of these factors, in the young Viv's eyes, was nothing but a brazen attempt to legitimise what she, protective of her kindly, repressed father, saw as nonstop serial adultery.

On the face of it, Judith had nowhere near as much in common with her second husband (the electrician and jazz violinist) as her first (the professor of medicine). But no one who knew her and Stefan, and especially Viv who saw them together more than most, could be in any doubt that they hit it off in other ways. Ways that made their differences irrelevant. It fostered a durable union that survived Stefan's explosive temperament (explained away by Judith as artistic) and continued until his death.

This evening Viv can see more clearly than before how her own attitudes, together with her behaviour, have been informed by Judith's views. It occurs to her now as she looks at her mother, and it's an entertaining thought as well as being faintly worrying, that the Discretion Agency might have been designed with Judith Quarry in mind.

Not that anyone introduced to her now could have the slightest idea of how she used to be before Stefan came along. No idea that she was once a seductive and, Viv would have to concede, predatory woman. No idea, furthermore, that this little old lady, increasingly deaf, white-haired and shuffling, harboured a volcanic interest in sex and a catalogue of provocative opinions. None of which, in her daughter's estimation, have significantly diminished with age.

They wouldn't have the slightest idea, Viv reflects, unless they thought to look into her eyes. Gimlet-eyed might have been written with my mother in mind. They may be pale and watery now, but behind them lurks an iron-willed personality that age has not wearied nor the years substantially condemned. Although the manipulative side of her personality has (arguably) mellowed.

Viv doesn't tell Judith what prompted her to contact the Discretion Agency in the first place. She expects her mother to draw her own conclusion, and that this will be in the appropriate ballpark. Judith is charmed not only that the agency exists, but that society has evolved in such a way as to enable its existence. Dedicated as it is, she says approvingly, to giving partnered women who need it a helping hand.

Viv feels bound to point out that the hand of succour is extended to the deprived partnered of both sexes. She remembers Martin saying there is an imbalance. Too many men, and he needs to attract more women.

'Too many men is an advantage for you,' Judith responds at once. She thinks the imbalance is symptomatic of Discretion's novelty. Society will adjust, and once the word gets out there will likely be a balance. Down the ages entrenched patriarchies have always catered for the needs of men, she continues, climbing on this favoured hobby-horse with virtual agility. In the past women have had to like it or lump it in marriage, whereas men have always had a multitude of helping hands available, chiefly the outstretched ones of prostitutes. Judith wrinkles her nose. Which has been not only grossly inequitable but ultimately degrading to both parties.

'If the Discretion Agency had been in existence before I met Stefan,' she remarks, 'I would have availed myself of its services. I'd very likely have spent a great deal of energy and much of my disposable income. Still, a by-product might have been the avoid-ance of a great deal of unpleasantness in the process.'

Viv can only agree that this might have been a very desirable by-product. Her father only lived a few years after the divorce, and was never the same. Her mother wipes her mouth with her napkin. She still likes to wear the scarlet lipstick favoured by Viv's stepfa-ther, although her hand is shaky now and her aim less accurate.

'When I met Stefan all that expenditure of time and energy into exploring *random byways* became unnecessary.' She has finished a good portion of lasagne and laid down her fork. 'I don't mean that I suddenly ceased to expend the same amount of time and energy. In fact, between ourselves, I probably spent rather more, if the truth be known.' Viv smiles. It's not the first time she has heard this par-ticular confidence.

'It was just that it ceased to be *random*. It was channelled in one direction, which was a far more efficient use of time.'

'And productive,' Viv prompts. 'In terms of well-being.' In the absence of her mother's traditional aid to well-being, an inevitable absence nothing can be done about now, she feels this nostalgic recital does her a power of good. And it is far and away her moth-er's favourite topic. Not a dialogue so much as an interior mono-logue delivered aloud.

'Oh, *yes*.' The moist, gimlet eyes are gleaming. 'Exceptionally productive. You know, Vivi my dear, after I married Stefan I was hardly ever unwell. Neither of us was, when I think about it, and physical satisfaction was almost certainly the reason. Having regu-lar relations boosts the immune system. The link will be proven eventually if it hasn't already. Whereas when I was with your poor father I always seemed to be ill with something or other, and it wasn't as if he knew nothing about medical matters, was it?'

There are more photographs of Stefan and Judith in the ground-floor apartment than there are of Stefan's children or of Daisy, Viv and Geoff. The two of them are often rumpled, always laughing or pulling faces, and Viv has long suspected that most were taken post-coitally on a camera with a timer. A large head-shot of a beaming Stefan, his hair mussed, stands on the TV close to Judith's chair.

One of several photos of their wedding, an extended family group, has pride of place on the mantelpiece. But the wedding pic-ture beside Judith's bed is of the then middle-aged pair, and Viv thinks anyone would be hard-pressed to find a just-married couple looking more aroused. She has even wondered if this one too might have been taken post-orgasm. Could the photographer have caught them emerging from a cloakroom, or a lavatory?

'Have I ever told you how I met Stefan?' The conversation is following an arc that has become increasingly familiar on recent visits. Her daughter finds it impossible not to indulge her when she is in full flight like this. Viv could recite word for word the story of Stefan coming round to rewire a brass Arts and Crafts standard lamp, a job that stretched over several days. Once this terrain has been reached, the cascade of tumultuous memories will soon tire Judith out. The way she suddenly crumples into a state of exhaus-tion reminds Viv of Daisy as a toddler.

But before she retires for the night she surprises her daughter a third time this evening by revisiting the earlier topic. She is lean-ing heavily on her stick and looking exhilarated but drained, which Viv puts down to having stayed up later than usual, as well as the reminiscent excitements of the subject matter. 'The agency hasn't distinguished itself thus far with its offerings, has it?'

'Not thus far, no. But it's early days, we shouldn't panic,' Viv says. 'Or not overmuch.'

'Perhaps you ought to think about having a little chat to – what was the name of the nice guru who runs it?'

'Martin Glover. What makes you think he's nice?'

'From the way you talk about him.'

'What kind of a chat should I have?'

'Ask him whether he has a certain *type* on his books. You don't want to waste time with any more tedious also-rans, do you?'

'I don't think a reliable screening system has yet been devised, Mum. Even for tedious random byways. What particular type did you mean?' Viv poses this question to please her mother, although she has a perfectly good idea of the qualifications she has in mind.

'The kind you haven't found in your first marriage.' Judith likes Geoff, but has never quite forgiven him for the six months Viv and the baby spent with her and Stefan, early in both marriages. She's not averse to (or too tired for) a final serve. 'What you really need now, Vivi, is the type of man who is capable of boosting a woman's immune system.'

You have to hand it to her, Viv thinks as she soaps herself down in the shower. She may be advanced in years and frail of body, but she's still capable of sending herself up. And me in the process.

The walnut sleigh bed Viv will sleep in tonight was her surprise sixteenth birthday present. She came home from school to find that her mother had moved her single bed into another room and installed this handsome piece. Double beds were nicer to sleep in, Judith said, and much more versatile. It had a pretty patchwork quilt, factory-made, as Viv now has no problem identifying, probably in India.

The bed was brought downstairs when her mother divided the house not long after Stefan's death from a sudden coronary (on the job, Viv has always suspected), creating a self-contained ground-floor flat for herself with two bedrooms and two bathrooms. Daisy was the last to stay here overnight, her presence betrayed by a tortoiseshell hair clip on the pillow and several bronze-tinged hairs in the shower. Judith's cleaner, who is forty years her junior but behaves more like an elderly retainer, knows not to bother changing the sheets when it's just family.

Viv and Geoff have shared this bed over the years. It has the comfort of long familiarity, and she usually sleeps well here. There are faded colour photos of them with Daisy on the chest of drawers. It's early for her, and Viv intends to read for an hour or more. But tonight she has trouble concentrating.

It's not true that I didn't find the right type in my first marriage. My present and only marriage, to be exact. By any account Geoff and I have had a pretty good innings. Mum might be surprised to know, although on second thoughts she's far too shrewd not to have known, that our sex life was perfectly satisfactory too, for a very long period. Until it wasn't. And now, presumably, never will be again.

She gives her husband a call on the house phone. It rings through to the message machine. His voice is still energetic, she thinks. Still virile? 'You've reached Vivien Quarry and Geoff Mayberry. Leave us a message.' She hangs up without leaving one, and dials Geoff's mobile, with the same result: 'It's Geoff Mayberry but I'm not here. Leave me a message.'

He's out. He's been out a fair bit lately. She says, 'Hi, it's me. You must be out, I didn't think you … It's all fine here. Mum's fine. Well, she's much the same. She knew all about Adrian, I guess Daisy must have told her. She took it in her stride. Or I suppose Jules might have … Anyhow, give me a call if you get this in the next hour or so. I'll be back late morning. See you then.' And she hesitates, before making a kissing noise into the phone.

Perhaps she may have hesitated too long, she thinks afterwards. It's quite possible Geoff will miss the little sound at the end of the message. Isn't that life all over? Destinies can hang on such delicate threads. Outcomes that were possibilities, changed into probabilities. Changed into inevitabilities.

Not that this is such a thread, most probably. But, she says to herself, you know what I mean.

17

ON THE HOME FRONT

Geoff did not call back. It's not particularly unusual, either for him to go out or to be uncommunicative on the subject in advance. But it taps into the conflicted mood Vivien always experiences when she drives away from her mother's house. Is it right for Judith to live alone at her age? Should she move into some form of assisted housing? Should she be in London, with them?

Where Judith is concerned, there are no easy answers; there never have been. Viv always arrives at the same conclusion, which is more of a stalemate. Basically her mother is continuing to do as she's always done: exactly what she wants. And what she wants is to stay put.

A text arrives, but it's not from Geoff. Viv is driving cautiously through the rain-lashed streets of Oxford towards the M4, heater on high, windscreen wipers at full blast, the overture to *Tannhäuser* on the radio. She glances at her phone lying on the passenger seat.

Hi V. Up to an update? M. She decides to put off responding in detail to Martin until she can give him her full attention in a more relaxing setting, and texts back, *Driving, will call later, V.*

Piotr, the good-looking Polish plumber, is back at work today tiling the shower recess in the en-suite. His paternity leave has left him visibly punch-drunk. There are dark smudges under his red-rimmed eyes. Viv admires his baby pictures and hands him a present of a musical mobile of dinosaurs, wrapped in paper covered with dinosaur cartoons. She sympathises with the sleep deficit.

'Tell Eva it's impossible to imagine when you're caught up in it, but this period does pass, trust me. And then it's gone and you can't remember it at all.'

Apart from Piotr and the cat, the warm house is empty. And the bed is unmade. 'Did you see Geoff?' she asks.

'Yes. He was here. He went out.'

She pulls the bed up with a feeling of irritation. Then makes coffee for them both, adds some biscuits for Piotr, and takes hers up to the shed. She puts on a favourite CD of old French film music that includes accordion and harmonica. Martin's number is engaged, so she texts Geoff: *I'm back. Where you?*

The agency phone is engaged for the next ten minutes. She texts Martin: *Ring when/if you ever get off phone, V.* Before any call can come through, Geoff texts back: *In a meeting.* This is curious. She writes: *What kind of a meeting?* then decides not to send it.

After another quarter of an hour her phone rings. Martin's voice. 'Sorry about that, V. Clients of an anxious disposition can be, shall we say, a little needy.'

Viv settles into the comfortable armchair and puts her feet on an old pouffe acquired on a Moroccan holiday. 'No worries, M. A little wordy too, I expect.'

'That's very insightful. Now, I'm curious to hear your verdict on D. Be as concise as you like, or as wordy. I promise not to categorise you as needy or anxious.'

'Is that binding? My verdict on D?' *Dev?* Of course, the Bulldog. 'Well, Drummond and I had lunch. He was … it was …'

'You were struck all of a heap, I gather. You knew each other from another life.' This is a relief. She had been unsure whether or what to reveal. 'Never happened before,' he says. 'Groundbreaking. An agency first.'

'Yes, amazing, wasn't it?' What did the Bulldog tell him? 'I was in the car when you texted. Coming back from visiting my mother in Oxford.'

'You have a mother? I'm envious. Mine's been gone for twenty years.'

'Mine's ninety-one and as obdurate as ever. Still insists on living alone in her house.' She hears Judith scoffing: I'm fully compos mentis and I'm perfectly all right, Vivi. Don't nag.

'One of the obstinate regiment? Independent mothers who refuse to bend to one's will?'

'You're so right, mules have nothing on them. Although I'm not sure what my will *is*, in this case.'

'You shouldn't feel guilty then,' he says. 'It sounds like she's doing what makes her happy. Keeping calm and carrying on, even if not in mint condition.'

This is comforting. 'Yes, she's not at death's door, thank heavens. Or wasn't this morning.' There's a perfunctory knock and the door flies open. A windswept Geoff looks in. She waves the phone at him. He turns away, leaving the door open. She hears him clatter down the stairs.

'Sorry, my husband just barged in, looking very bedraggled. But it's okay, he's gone again.' She gets up and closes the door.

'Ah. So the coast is clear. We can drop names?'

'With impunity. The real name of the relevant party is not Drummond, incidentally.' This, she hopes, is permissible.

No, Martin thought as much when Drummond signed on. There's a client subset, usually professional, that prefers to pay cash and remain incognito. The names they choose can be a bit of a giveaway. They tend to be somewhat over-egged, like our Mr Drummond Cornwallis. Or else they're more down to earth, like John Brown.

'I see.' So, Martin is not so naive after all. 'Do they usually give a fake occupation too?'

'That depends. For some people there's a strong fantasy element. Others are more strongly motivated,' a smile in the voice, 'by caution.'

'They could also be worried that their real profession might work against them. If they were a funeral director, for instance, or a forensic pathologist. Or a gynaecologist.' Hastily, 'Not that Drummond is any of these, by the way.'

Viv reflects uneasily on Mr Blake's ruddy countenance. Martin would enjoy knowing he was a periodontist, but it doesn't seem right to give him away. 'There's no pressing need-to-know basis here, is there, Martin?'

'I wouldn't think there's anything pressing. Shall we agree to keep mum? Let him hang on to his cover.'

Viv is relieved on Mr Blake's account. She feels protective of him.

'What I think I'm hearing from you, and don't hold back if I'm wrong, is that we don't have a tick against his name. Or rather, his pseudonym.'

'I'm afraid we don't. I do feel warm towards him, but not warm enough, if you know what I mean. Having known him in another life, as you said. It complicates matters. And then there's ...' And then there's the lugubrious Bulldog himself.

'The missing x factor. Yes, I know. Well, it won't come as a surprise, he thought you were going to give him the thumbs-down. No matter, I'm massaging what looks like a promising newcomer for you.'

'For Drummond too? I was his ninth intro, I think he said. Not an outstanding success rate, is it?'

'That's not unusual,' Martin says firmly. 'Some people are harder to match up. It can take up to two years. Three, in extreme cases. We can chalk you up as his first approval, though.'

'Except that I wasn't a favourable outcome, was I? In terms of achieving the preferred result.'

'He was philosophical about it.' Martin sounds cheerful. 'That's the way the cookie crumbles, he said, when you're of homely aspect and past your sell-by date.'

This strikes a chord. 'Oh dear. Did he really say that? It sounds so very – it sounds so *poignant*. I can relate to it.'

'Please don't relate to it for a moment, Vivien, it's got nothing to do with you. And don't worry yourself on Drummond's account, I have more introductions for him. I'm confident of achieving the preferred result in the end.'

'It's like pulling rabbits out of a hat, isn't it?' She hears Geoff shout from downstairs. How about a spot of lunch, hon? 'I'd better go, Martin. Geoff's getting restive.' Now I've outed him. He's named and shamed.

'Roger. I'll text you when the next rabbit comes through, V. Over and out.'

She puts the phone down with a touch of regret. She is expecting Geoff to be in a bad mood because his croquet game has been stymied by the weather. But he seems sanguine. They make up a salad with hard-boiled eggs.

'You've only just had coffee. I bet you had a jam doughnut,' she says. She pictures the sugary doughnut she consumed fairly recently. 'Where did you have this meeting?'

'The Scurvy Knave.'

'The Scurvy Knave? But that's a *pub*. Why on earth did you go there? It's so dark and dingy. And all that grunting-peasant decor.'

'They turn the lights on in the daytime. The coffee's perfectly drinkable with a dash of cognac.'

'With a dash of *cognac*? In the morning? What sort of meeting? With?'

'With Elizabeth Gray.'

The name rings a bell, to be followed up directly. One of Geoff's science-fiction lot. The little posse he goes to conferences and films with, the mob of crackpots as Jules calls them. 'And what were you up to last night?'

The group went to a new pizza joint in Greek Street. Good value. Authentic, white tablecloths, candles, Neapolitan music. Nice and cosy too. Proper pizza oven. Wines from Puglia and Sicily.

'You're waxing unusually enthusiastic. White tableclothes? A pizza joint? *Authentic*? You don't even like pizza. Or Neapolitan music.'

'That's an exaggeration. It all depends. These were superior. The wine, the women and the song.' He grins at her.

Was it Richie's pick? Richie is, in Viv's estimation, the only group member resembling a person interested in good food. No, he says, Elizabeth's. Her ex-boyfriend works in the kitchen. Good cook, the ex.

Viv is now retrieving from her memory an evening in the summer when the group gathered at their house for dinner. The sister of one of the crackpots came as a guest. A young, light-hearted New Zealander who laughed a lot. 'Was she the long-haired one who seemed to find everything hilarious? The *young* one?'

Geoff grins. That sounds like Eliza. Andrew's younger sister. Hasn't been in London long. She's a very vivacious girl, it's true.

'But she's so unlike Andrew. He's nothing if not turgid.'

'He's only turgid if you're not on his wavelength. He's got a brilliant mind.'

Wasn't the name Elizabeth?

Yes, but she prefers Eliza. Suits her better, too.

'Well, it's snappier, isn't it? Très on trend, as Daisy would say. *Pygmalion* was so ahead of its time. What does she do again?'

She's a web designer, says Geoff. Very bright, very talented, and stuck in a dead-end job with ridiculous hours. No security, no sick pay, no holidays. No money in it at all, needless to say. Full-time work for part-time pay. The poor girl's on her beam ends.

'And now no boyfriend either. It just gets worse and worse, doesn't it?' I ought to tone this down. 'I must say she seemed almost excessively cheerful in the face of such adversity. You have to admire it.'

Overlooking this, Geoff says he's looking into finding her a position in the IT department of his old firm. That's what they were doing this morning, going over her CV.

'That probably didn't take too long. Was it light enough in there to decipher it? While distracted by coffee and cognac?' Geoff gives her a tolerant look.

'How old was she again?'

'Oh, over thirty. Thirty-one or two.'

'Not a girl, then.'

'All right. A *young woman*.'

'You know how Daisy hates being called a girl, it's so demeaning. You don't call a man in his thirties a boy, do you? It's not as if this is very difficult to remember, Geoff. Men of your generation just can't seem to get their heads around it. They're respectful distinctions, for heaven's sake. Nothing less or more than that.'

'Don't get heated, sugar plum,' Geoff says mildly. 'It's your generation too.'

'Yes, and that's the whole point in a nutshell. Women of a certain age – and we know what *that* is – seem to be able to retrain themselves out of bad, outdated habits, and men don't. Either because they can't be bothered or they won't take them seriously. Which adds up to the same thing.'

She pulls herself up, belatedly. 'Sorry, I think I'm a bit out of sorts. It's visiting Mum that does it, every time.'

'You said she wasn't any different from usual.'

'No, she wasn't. But how much longer can she go on like this?'

'Well, let's wait until she can't, shall we, and then deal with it?'

'Here's another thing, Geoff. It's well known that women raise a problem in order to talk about it. To talk it over. Whereas men just want to grab an instant solution, usually a one-size-fits-all, and then forget about it.'

'So, you don't want to find a solution to your problems, is that it?'

'Not necessarily. I might just want to air the subject. Get it off my chest.'

'Does it ever strike you that endlessly churning over the same thing to no useful end might be pointless? Might be just a fraction neurotic?'

Viv jumps up from the table. 'No it does not,' she says hotly. 'But your compulsion to find easy solutions to things that may not be resolvable – at least not right now in the kitchen at this *very minute* – does, actually, seem borderline pathological to me, if you really want to know. Sometimes that's how it seems. As well as being pointless. And unempathetic.'

'Bloody hell,' Geoff expostulates. 'Who was the one who just said we should wait until your mother couldn't go on living in her damn house and *then* deal with the problem? Who was the one who said *that*?' He scans the room with an exaggerated expression of bafflement.

Normally this might have gone some way towards defusing the situation. But it's not a novel ploy by any means, and sometimes – not infrequently, perhaps – it makes things worse. Viv is not disposed to laugh. She's too worked up.

'I just flounced out of the kitchen,' she says in a rush, moments later, 'after picking a particularly childish quarrel with Geoff.' Then realises she's speaking over Julia's answering machine.

She texts Martin Glover. *Husband driving me round bend. Urgent remedy required. Please produce rabbit with utmost dispatch.*

18

THE LAUNCH

Julia leaves her apartment carrying a more capacious bag than usual. The designer, Marion Luce, plans a big, commanding portrait of the youthful Countess, from her days as the Venus of Moscow. The portrait will dominate the bedchamber set, and Marion asked Julia to look through old photographs for ideas. Pictures of herself as a young woman. An innocuous task on the face of it, but one that proved not quite so easy or harmless in practice.

Last night she looked through a pile of photo albums she hadn't touched for some years. She hesitated over them for nearly three hours, picking up, choosing, discarding. The exercise was something of an emotional battery and brought on a persistent, low-grade headache.

This morning she went over to the piano and took down the formal portrait of herself and her brother as teenagers. One of her treasures, the idea of it going astray is anathema. On the other hand, it is unquestionably striking. Flattering too, and the art department at the Royal Opera House is meticulous in its record-keeping. In the end she decides to have it copied, and takes it in along with several others.

Yesterday the ensemble gathered for a preliminary run-through with the conductor, Raymond Bayliss, and a répétiteur at the piano. No costumes, just a range of street attire in which Julia's studiedly casual (but very well cut) black slacks and cherry silk tunic stood out. The principals were brought forward with appropriate fanfare. Gratifying fanfare in her case: a kiss from Ray and sustained applause from the ensemble.

There were frequent stops, as Ray called a halt to adjust an inflection, emphasis or timing, but it went well. This was no surprise; no one gets to sing at one of the world's top opera houses unless they're already exceptional.

Julia was surprised to see Emils slip in and sit at the back. Directors are not normally present at the conductor's first ensemble call. She guessed that the very experienced Ray had shown unusual indulgence, as long as his young director promised to keep his mouth shut. Sure enough, Emils was silent until the very end. At which point, with Herman playing dead from his own gunshot, he was unable to contain himself.

He thanked Ray for allowing him to gatecrash his party. Even without the orchestra, without any contribution from the director, with no costumes or special effects, choreography or lighting, the singers were – he pulled up here, and Julia for one could tell he'd loved to have used an expletive – *awesome*.

Today is the director's standalone turn, where Emils presents his concept for the production. All the principals have regrouped, together with the top brass. Show and tell for the big cheeses, Julia calls these occasions.

Emils has shaved. He may even have washed his hair, although she wouldn't bet on it. Unlike her, though (floaty red chiffon scarf, black forties suit) he has not dressed for the occasion. It's the same shapeless sports coat, T-shirt and jeans. They don't detract from his confidence or his contagious fervour. With the exception of Bridie Waterstreet, the outstanding young lyric soprano from

Dublin, Julia reckons he's the youngest person present, and one of the least experienced.

Where grand opera is concerned, he announces, he is no minimalist. Meaning no chairs on empty stages, no modern dress, no gratuitous rapes. People have paid out top dollar to see an opera at Covent Garden and they'll get a blockbuster.

He strides up and down. 'Since this is a Russian take on life, it's all about love and other catastrophes. First performed in 1890, it covers the whole gamut – jealousy, greed, despair, suicide and murder – with multiple delusional behaviours on the side. So it couldn't be more contemporary.' Some laughs from the stalls.

He shows them the designer's models. They're on a large scale and complete to the last detail, with stills of filmed backgrounds: moody skies and grand mansions, fireworks, the dark heaving sea. The sets are peopled with little cut-out figures. Emils moves them about as he speaks. In her mind's eye, Julia sees a boy playing with his sister's doll's house.

'We get Tchaikovsky's trademark big scenes: high society taking the air before an April storm, a grand ball, the canal where the heartbroken Lisa throws herself.' The Lisa figurine is tipped into the water.

Lisa, granddaughter of the Countess, is the object of Herman's desire. Bridie Waterstreet, a poised and aesthetically pleasing twenty-seven, has been gazing at Emils. Whose own eyes, Julia notes when his hair is flicked aside, are now resting on Bridie.

Also watching Lisa is her betrothed, Prince Yeletsky, sung by a baritone representing Eton in the eclectic cast. His good looks (and receding chin) make him a credible aristocrat in Julia's eyes. He and Bridie have already sung together once before, in Cardiff.

Yeletsky may be an entitled nobleman, Emils says, but he's an enlightened, new-age guy. He wants to be Lisa's best friend. He's everything the impoverished, wrong-side-of-the-tracks Herman is not – and he's spurned. Looking at Bridie, Julia fears the baritone's hopes are destined to be as unrequited as those of the Prince he plays.

Emils surveys the company. 'The belief in some*one*, or some*thing*. Know the feeling? If only we can just get our hands on that person, or that thing, everything in life will be perfect. Until fate proves otherwise, right?' A bell sounds in Julia's mind. High, insistent, youthful.

He extends his arms. 'But we're not Russian. We don't need to factor in fate. We can go on believing in happily ever after.' And a second bell. Deeper, more resonant. Julia shifts in her seat. Around her, the words receive a responsive ripple.

The onlookers have been transitioning from an initial polite detachment. By the end of the rehearsal period, Julia predicts, they will be eating out of his hand. The solid masculine hand, perhaps, that is now resting on her shoulder.

'Which brings us to the foundation stone of the drama: our Countess. Whose misspent youth is wholly responsible for the darkness of the piece.' Julia inclines her head graciously.

'She is in her late *eighties*.' The note of incredulity does not go unappreciated. 'We can best imagine her as a faded movie star. Think *Sunset Boulevard* with tainted glamour.'

It is the Countess whose youthful greed set up the fate now hanging over the players. Who was told she would die when a man, driven by passion, came to demand the names of the winning cards. Who will come back from the dead as a ghost to exact her revenge.

This is the opportunity for Emils to introduce his trump card. '*Ghosts*. They've always been a logistical headache in the theatre. How the hell do you deal with them? Conjuring tricks, white robes, dry ice?' He checks out the room, to reassure himself of their attention. A redundant measure, on Julia's reckoning.

'Forget that, and bring on *cutting-edge technology*.' Julia had been so intent that she hadn't noticed some comings and goings. Technicians have contrived to beam images from one of the sets in the rehearsal room. Before their eyes, a three-dimensional church interior materialises, dressed for the Countess's funeral. Her coffin (unoccupied today) floats on a richly decorated bier against a high wall of gothic arches, flickering candles and the shadows of choristers.

Emils looks like the cat that got the cream, and no wonder. The effect is miraculous; there's an audible intake of breath. And afterwards a real buzz in the room among these people who have been there and seen everything. The general feeling is that this innovation is a master stroke. The critics will go bananas. That's if there's any justice – which is never a given.

Julia watches as Emils is surrounded. The PR chief has buttonholed him, the hierarchy are in tow. He looks unlikely to be surrendered anytime soon, so she goes off with other cast members. Including Bridie, whom she wishes to get to know. Lunch, in Julia's case, will be an unappetising salad minus dressing. But the ends, as she doesn't need to tell herself, will more than justify the means.

Julia has recognised a quality in Emils. He is adventurous, much as she is herself. Most people, she believes, lead restricted lives, held back and intimidated by their doubts and fears. She can identify with a driven young man like him because he too is programmed to regard doubts, fears and prohibitions as invitations. As challenges to surmount. Even – perhaps – as temptations. And ultimately to find them, as she herself has in her own life, a source of fulfilment and freedom.

An ultimate liberation hovers like a hologram in her subconscious. She avoids putting it into words, even in the privacy of her own mind.

19

FEELERS

Viv and Geoff are having breakfast at the kitchen table. Viv, picking her moment, demands in a strenuously neutral voice, 'Are you having an affair with Elizabeth? Eliza, I should say.' Can you demand neutrally? Doubtful, just as she has doubts about her own attitude to the answer, whatever it might be.

Geoff, who was about to eat some sugar-free muesli with fresh berries, halts the progress of the spoon in the air. 'An affair with *Eliza?* Are you off your rocker? She's younger than Daisy.'

Keep this light and humorous. 'So? I wouldn't have imagined that was an impediment. More of a massive advantage, I'd have thought.' Wrong tone. Inadvisable sarcasm.

'Oh, for crying out loud.' Geoff adds to a small heap of raisins on the edge of his bowl. 'Do you want these?' He can't understand why it's so difficult to find muesli without raisins in the supermarket.

'Well, you have been seeing rather a lot of her lately. No, I don't want them, I'm having toast. I don't like them either, if you recall. But thanks anyway.'

Viv reaches across him to the radio and switches on the news. They have tended to forgo the news lately, it's too depressing with breakfast. But a spot of depressing background commentary, she thinks, can be of assistance when one wishes to maintain a cool head.

Geoff has been helping Eliza find a new flat. An upmarket bed-sitter, or studio as they are now described. Eliza would rather not embark on another flat-sharing arrangement at her age, he has explained, and she can't afford the rent on a one-bedroom. He's been ferrying her around at odd times, after work and at the week-end. Some of these odd times have included evenings. So far the search has been unsuccessful.

'I'm curious,' Viv persists. 'What *is* your relationship with her, exactly, if it's not an affair? How would you describe it?' She thinks she has been reasonably successful in achieving the desired laid-back tone. She pours water that is just off the boil over freshly ground coffee. Coffee boiled is coffee spoiled, her mother has always maintained.

'How would I describe it,' Geoff muses, hands behind his head. 'Hmm. Is it incumbent upon me so to do?' He has put on a pedantic, donnish air with which she has a long familiarity. He also affects it when he is parodying her mother. 'Is this a compulsory question, or is it optional? Could it be multi-choice?'

'Well, for instance, is it an inter-generational friendship? Or more of a *mentoring* kind of thing? Is that how you see it?' Viv thinks she is showing admirable forbearance. She knows she has only a small window of opportunity here.

'Am I allowed to have both, or would that be too greedy?' He picks up the newspaper. They get the *Telegraph* and the *Guardian*, to do their bit in keeping print editions alive and in the interests of balance. Viv thinks balance is overrated and responsible for noth-ing ever being done, but Geoff is a great believer in it.

'Have both by all means, I'm feeling generous. So, on the men-toring front, what about the job search? Have you had any joy find-ing her something at MOP?' This is Mason Opie Pharmaceuticals, Geoff's old firm. He gives a noncommittal grunt. 'Or will you have to wait until somebody retires or expires?'

He looks up from the paper. 'No need to wait for that. They're all young in web and IT, it's a revolving door. Just like the job market of the sixties and seventies. Déjà vu all over again.'

'How convenient. There shouldn't be any further delay shepherding her through it, should there? If she's as bright as you say.'

'She's bright, all right. A very smart cookie.'

'Why didn't she get that sort of job in the first place, then?'

Insufficiently throwaway, she thinks, as this gets a no-response eyes to the ceiling. 'I guess the door's more locked than revolving when you don't have access to the old boys' network – or *until* you do.' In case this sounds too pointed, she adds, 'Or old girls', if they have any traction.'

He shrugs and opens the *Telegraph*. The window seems to have closed for the time being. Viv doesn't know where to position her feelings at present, just as she couldn't work out her attitude to the subject to begin with. There are too many imponderables.

On the mantelpiece in the kitchen is a flyer for a small group show opening in a few days. Three up-and-coming young artists in a Shoreditch gallery. One is Daisy Mayberry. Is up-and-coming the same as emerging? Does Daisy qualify as a young artist anymore? Her thirty-ninth birthday is just around the corner.

Her parents haven't seen Daisy since the dislocating dinner. Texts between her and Viv have yielded meagre grains of information: *Ade's parnts visitng. Ok but barking! Lol xx; all fine here x; houswrmng prty 2moro; workng like crazy 4 show x.* But nothing approximating the heart-to-heart her mother longs for.

A tentative query on the houswrmng prty, which Viv immediately regretted sending, generated a longer response (*small so no parents invitd sorry love you mum xoxox*), which she left on her phone instead of deleting.

I must ring her, Viv thinks, at Adrian's house. Not at his house, *their* house. The number goes, predictably, to message. Daisy changes her message nearly every week; today it's an upbeat 'Hey it's Daisy, can't answer as I'm covered in wet paint, preparing for new show at Triple G.'

Triple G is how the gallery, the Galerie Galleria Gallery, is generally known. Viv hasn't seen much of Daisy's most recent work. She has always thought her daughter's meticulous oils, small portraits in jewel-like colours, are rather at odds with her personality. Her personality, like her hair, being anything but miniature.

Her hyper-realist work has been rather out on a limb, with popular taste running more to minimalist squiggles and scrawls. But it's slowly attracting attention from the small cohort who think outside the square. Such people as Julia, who owns several pictures by her goddaughter. And in positions where they can be seen by visitors, which has led to an occasional commission and purchase.

Viv leaves a voice message. Any chance of a chat, darling? She could meet her anytime – our hectic schedules permitting. Talk over how everything's going. Work–life balance and the whole damn thing, and so forth. And say hi to Adrian, won't you?

Afterwards she wonders if this was a fraction too much. Not that Daisy would be under any misapprehensions about where she was coming from. Perhaps she should have sent love to Adrian instead of a throwaway hi. Would this be construed as a snub?

Martin Glover has contributed a new rabbit to the stew of imponderables. He has managed to expedite things, he says, in a white-knight response to her piteous cry for help. Laurence Simon Davidson is the name in full. She might like to give him the once-over. He goes by the name of Larry. No, hang on – goes by *Leary*.

'Why Leary and not Larry?' Viv is feeling pettish after her scrap with Geoff.

'Laurence Simon Davidson. LSD, Timothy Leary. Geddit?' Viv nods into the phone. 'TV director, American, fifty-four. Open as regards age, so nothing to concern you on that score. Lively, busy, interested in the arts.' With her literary leanings they might have things in common. He's an enthusiastic communicator. A not atypical American, in that way they have sometimes.

'Which way is that?'

'In that he's not overly anal.' Leary had told Martin he was putting everything out there. 'He declared full disclosure. In the spirit of which, I'll give him your pen name, shall I?'

In a conversation with Martin just previous to this one, Viv had declared her intention of hiding behind an alias for a change. It seemed like a harmless bit of fun. She had selected the name Beatrice (after Beatrice Webb) and Woolf (after Virginia). Martin had advised against Woolf. It might have unfortunate overtones, he thought.

Such as? Such as big teeth and aggression. Viv had replaced it with the less intimidating Taylor, after Elizabeth Taylor (the novelist, not the actress). She thought she might give her husband an alias too.

Leary's declaration of full disclosure need not be taken as absolute gospel, Martin suggests. A lot of what he says tends to be a bit over the top. He's a Jewish American in the Woody Allen mould.

Somewhat in that mould, Martin says, after Viv expresses a doubt. He's not married to his stepdaughter. If he was, Martin thinks this would have come out in the initial interview. Leary is not inclined to be retentive, as has already been indicated.

A text arrives from Leary soon afterwards. *Intrigued by your résumé, Beatrice.* (What had Martin told him?) Maybe they could put out some feelers. How did that sound? When Viv said it sounded fine, the next text is more informative. Longer, too.

Leary is a New Yorker, tamed & anglicised, been working in London twenty yrs. He directs series episodes & commercials. His 2nd (Eng) wife Lauren & kids Jay & Shasta are living in Dover. He is into his children's lives as much as poss but he'd have to say he & his wife are semi-estranged, although they don't plan on divorcing while the kids are still in high school. What's your spousal set-up, Bea?

After some thought, and feeling grateful for her alias, which seems to put such disclosures at a distance, Viv replies that she and her 1st husband George (after George Orwell, she omits) are still living together but she'd have to say they were distanced.

The next text asks if it'd be okay if Leary gives her a call. Like, how's today looking? Any chance of a time frame? Viv says anywhere in the next three hours is looking good. It's not long before Leary is on the line.

'Hey Beatrice! How are you doing today?' This is the first time she's been addressed as Beatrice. It feels surprisingly good. Rather liberating.

'Hi Leary. I'm doing fairly well, as far as I can tell. How about you?'

'I'm doing great. Good to make contact. I mightn't be able to talk for long, though. When I say I'm doing great I'm on the set of a crappy commercial with a bunch of prancing puppets dressed as milk cartons. OMG. What are *you* doing? Wanna trade?'

'Puppets dressed as ...' Does he mean actors? If she had to describe it, his voice does sound quite like Woody Allen's. Same accent. She can't help hoping he doesn't look the same, or at least not like Woody as he's looking these days. Weasel in the headlights, Geoff says.

'Yeah, crazy, right? There's all these new kinds of milk now, you name it they've thought of it: low fat, added calcium, added vit D, high protein, lactose free – sheesh, it's exhausting. Give me the plain white stuff we grew up with. One look at the supermarket shelf and you need to lie down. Are we spoilt for choice or not? And do we care? What are you up to, Bea?'

Viv blinks. 'Well, actually I'm making a quilt.' Is this what Beatrice Taylor would be up to? It doesn't sound quite right. But Leary seems to like it. Soothing. Calms him down already. So, she's stitching away in a darkened room with a water feature and chimes?

Hardly. With all lights blazing and Cole Porter. She's nearly finished designing it. Not that it's ever finished until it's finished. Too much finishing already, she adds, striving (fruitlessly, she fears) for matching sprightliness.

Leary says they have an old handmade quilt on the bed in Dover. Vintage USA, wedding gift, traditional ring pattern, meant to bring the happy couple good luck – cue groans and cynical laughter, am I right or am I right, Bea? So, she does that for a living, then? Nice. *Creative*. How many has she done? In the hundreds?

Not for a living, no. For the love of it. And not in the hundreds quite yet. This is her second.

Did she sell the first one?

Oh no, that's hidden away in the cupboard.

Hidden away? But that's crazy! He'd pay good money for it, he could really do with a quilt for his bed.

It's not for sale, Viv says firmly. And he wouldn't want it anyway, it's far too small, it's only a little cot quilt … She hears her voice. It sounds defensive. And evasive.

'I get you,' says Leary, who only, she imagines, gets something broadly inaccurate. 'Made a few mistakes, I guess, so you put it away. Not surprising if it was your first shot at doing the thing, right? For a grandkid, maybe? Or one on the way? Don't tell me, you got married in your early teens.'

'God no. I did it on spec.' It's necessary to change the subject while she can get a word in; she feels acutely uncomfortable with this one. Ask him about himself. 'So, what do you do when you're not filming, Leary?'

'You asked, so I'll tell you. I do *movies*. We fell in love at four and we haven't had a falling out yet. You gotta tell me right away if that's a major turn-off and we'll split before we began. Just kidding, Beatrice. Well, you know, *kinda* kidding.' A mournful, Woody-like neigh down the phone.

It's not a turn-off, Viv says, with some residual doubt. She is feeling faintly overwhelmed by Leary, and they haven't even met yet.

Well, that's good, because he's an unreconstructed movie buff. NFT? He practically lives in the place. National Film Theatre, South Bank. She ever make it down there?

Loads of times. You might have bumped into me.

I might? *Okay!* So, what do you look like? First thing comes into your head.

'Well, ah, let's see, I've got curly hair, rather a lot of it, and it's – brownish.' That is to say, it's brown *now*, with interesting highlights.

'And I'm a scrawny git with no hair. What the heck, how can we begin to describe ourselves? And why bother? Martin Glover's an insightful guy, he obviously gets that. It's very cool the way he runs the Discretion outfit. Kinda *retro*, isn't it?'

'Retro. You mean—'

'I mean the whole personal touch stuff. Genteel-cosy. Like *Midsomer Murders*, right? No photos, no fictionalised personal guff, no GSOH or SDWJM. Nice civilised English take on arranged dating. You just sit back and let someone else do the weeding and draw up the guest list.'

Viv is still deciphering the acronyms. She makes a cautious noise.

'Tells you stuff you don't want to know about yourself, yeah? When you get to see who you've been matched up with. Like, stuff no one else is gonna tell you.' The neighing laugh. 'Don't say it, we shouldn't even be talking like this, right? It's verging on treason.'

Viv makes another non-committal murmur. It might tell you more about where you sit in the open market, she suspects.

Leary thinks the no-pics policy has advantages. With everyone madly photoshopping old vac-snaps from when they were thinner and hairier and way *hotter*. And that's just the guys. Probably best you didn't see a picture of me now, we'd never've got this far.

A pause, and some muffled background noise. 'Sorry, Bea, the cartons are calling me. Get back to you soonest, set up a meeting, okay? There'll be a window of opportunity when I'm done with all this shit. Best if I text before calling? Don't want your old man on my tail. He's a cop, right? Or a rugby forward? Great to talk to you, Bea. Have a fantastic rest of the day!'

And that was that, Viv told Martin Glover when he rang to see if they'd made contact. She felt she hadn't contributed much. But she'd learnt more about Leary in a few breathless minutes than she knew, for instance, about Bulldog Drummond – and that's after seeing him twice a year for thirty years.

She realised as she was saying this that it gave Martin some clues as to the Bulldog's likely occupation. Too late, Leary's speediness was contagious. It encouraged indiscretion. She felt slightly hung over in the direct aftermath of the Leary chat.

Martin said he was wary of concluding anything much from a person's phone manner, because this could be influenced by factors such as nervousness, bravado or desperation.

'What about the urge to talk loudly and extremely fast?'

Martin had noted that. He thought it could well be a type A indication. He would await the next instalment with interest.

'Why do I feel I'm only doing this for your entertainment?'

Why? He couldn't imagine. He had set up the agency to address unmet needs. There would be by-products along the way, as is the way with any new business – you just had no way of predicting what those by-products might be. 'They are by way of being rather an unanticipated factor in your case, V,' he added.

'You can call me Beatrice if you like,' she said. Martin said he wasn't sure if he would like, as he'd become used to thinking of her as something else and he tended to be a creature of habit. But he thought the name suited her so he'd give it a try.

Viv used to think twice about answering the phone when she was working in the shed, and for a time turned it off altogether. Lately though, in case it's Discretion, or her mother, or (a long shot) Daisy to say she's having second thoughts and has quit living at Adrian's, she checks the caller. Seeing it's Jules (with whom they are booked for dinner tonight) she picks up.

Jules says she's going to be a jerk, Viv, as if you didn't know, and cancel tonight. Unless they want lettuce leaves weighed and measured. She is on her crash diet, on account of being obliged to expose her feminine form to hordes of strangers over several nights in the very near future, in the full *horreur* of a slinky nightgown and filmy negligee.

A slinky nightgown? Viv thought the role was that of an autocratic eighteenth-century Russian Countess who was very long in the tooth.

That's roughly accurate, Jules says. But the director wishes to hint that the old girl isn't past it. Indeed, that she still has quite a bit of it in her. Quite a broad hint, in fact; he is having her give her granddaughter's homicidal boyfriend the glad eye.

Is Jules sure she's rehearsing the right opera?

As far as I know, Jules says. It came as a surprise, I must admit. Of course, we shouldn't forget that the Countess was a rip-roaring femme fatale in her day. Emils thinks the idea that she should still be alluring in her late eighties is not *completely* beyond the bounds of possibility, Viv. Isn't that a reassuring thought?

Yes, yes, says her friend, tolerantly. Now, this *wunderkind* director – when you say he's young …

Twenty-eight.

That *is* young. Even younger than Geoff's bubbly new buddy, Eliza. And what is his aspect?

Stocky. Dresses like a hobo, looks like he sleeps under the bridge. Forgets to shave. Cuts his hair with shears. Probably has back hair.

Not a pin-up, then?

Not for those still stubbornly wedded to conventional norms, Jules should imagine. Of average height.

Height being possibly the only area he would be average in?

Quite possibly, yes, but the jury's still out. Suffice to say he was in possession of sound, old-style sex appeal. The type that has no truck with men's grooming aids and is tied to energy, originality and brilliance. Oh, and charm and charisma, Viv. There would be holograms on stage, did she mention that?

'Are you all right, Jules?' Viv asks.

'What's that supposed to mean?'

'You're not losing your head, are you? You're not in danger of falling into a May–December that can only end in bitter tears?'

'A late-onset cougar crush? January–December might be more like it,' replies Jules, with vigour. 'Alas and alack, and all that.'

'You haven't answered my carefully couched question.'

'I assumed it was rhetorical. I'm not quite off my trolley, Viv. You know me.'

Do I? That's a moot point. 'Some people have been known to indulge in these things, Jules,' she says, 'however well you think you know them. What they choose to do can take you by surprise.' My activities, for instance. 'I know, you don't have to tell me – you're not like some people. But still.'

'I think you may have in mind people like Geoff. So, what's the latest? Are they or aren't they?'

Viv says she put this very question this morning. 'He protested. But she's younger than Daisy, he ejaculated. Which I pointed out was never an obstacle to achievement.'

'Quite the opposite.'

'Exactly what I said.'

'He didn't *ejaculate* his protest – my God, how that takes one back – too much?'

'It sounded genuine to my trusting if morbidly suspicious ear.'

'There's a word for a male cougar,' Jules remarks. 'I asked around wardrobe. They see things, so they know. The word is *manther*. Quite good, isn't it?'

'It should be better known. We must do our bit to make it happen.'

A fractional pause. 'You believed him then, did you, Viv?'

'I know it sounds unlikely, and the word gullible is on the tip of your tongue – but oddly enough, I did. You see, Geoff's really quite a – he has strong views on whether things are *appropriate* or not. Quite conventional views.'

'You mean he's a straitlaced moralist? Well, we've always known that. It's why he's having so much trouble with Daisy. However,' Jules yawns, and Viv pictures her stretched out like a cat on her chaise longue, 'people can say one thing all their lives and do another. We've always known that, too. And, dare I say it, Geoff is probably no different.'

But *you* are different, Viv reflects to herself. And not only because you are famous. You don't fall into the common trap of saying one thing and doing another, because you haven't made your moral position clear in any hard and fast way. Which is quite a pragmatic and sensible way of going about things. Although Geoff would claim you never had a moral position in the first place.

A long acquaintance with Julia's career habits tells Viv that until the première their friendship is effectively on hold. Her social calendar has a heavy black line drawn through it, as everything in her life is subordinated to the demands of preparation. It's no exaggeration to say that for the immediate future Jules will eat, sleep and live the opera. She will diet, practise and exercise more than usual. She will rehearse until the entire piece, words and score, are imprinted on her mind.

It is startling, then, to hear that Max is arriving from Melbourne in a fortnight's time, halfway through the rehearsal period. Viv can only think that Jules's complaints about the brevity and insignificance of her role are not the exaggeration she had supposed. Then again, perhaps not, as Jules explains that her brother's divorce has turned nasty. Predictably, with Pat engaging a lawyer in order to secure, Jules declares more in annoyance than surprise, a one-sided settlement.

Max had been adamant about not going down the legal route. However, his sister was able to persuade him (putty in my hands, Viv) that he needed professional help to represent him against vested interests that were not, she believed, entirely disinterested.

'And once you are forced to drag in the snouts, it's on for one and all. Max loathes this sort of haggling. He finds talk about money and possessions distressing at the best of times. He's coming over to get away from it.'

But he haggles for a living, Viv objects.

'That's a frivolous remark, and unworthy of you. Max is an art dealer. He works for the love of it. He's a connoisseur, an entrepreneur. He represents *artists*.'

Wouldn't it be terribly disruptive of her preparation, to have him under her feet?

Jules scoffs. Disruptive? Not a bit of it, she wants him to come. In some ways Viv finds this more surprising than the fact that he is coming at all.

20

DEVELOPMENTS

Since Leary's first call there have been three more texting sessions (just touching base; how are you doing, Bea?; what's new?) and another phone conversation to set up a meeting, which has been cancelled and rescheduled twice. He's had a new TV series dumped in his lap owing to the director being indisposed – read drying out in rehab, Bea – and he's working 24/7. But a drink this week might be on the cards.

He asked if she'd read his blog yet. It had started off as a movie diary listing every film he'd seen since the age of ten. But now it had five thousand followers and he was thinking of going down the self-publishing route. Into enemy territory, right, Bea? You could get a whole bunch of exposure through social media, as she'd know.

Viv felt a twinge of unease. It wasn't just a movie diary, then? No, it had totally morphed. It was more of a typical rubbish life in progress. Or hopefully not so typical. Work, therapy, love life. The revealing stuff, like sexual hang-ups and gross-out personal fantasies, you know? People really picked up on that. It went viral.

Leary had picked up on Viv's visceral reaction to this. Just kidding, Beatrice, don't freak! So, she hadn't *Googled* him already? Disbelief echoed down the phone. No, Viv admitted faintly, it hadn't occurred to her. But she would, definitely. She'd go and do it, right away.

He'd Googled her, of course. He'd been tickled pink when her name came up along with a whole bunch of photos. Like, dozens. Hey, she was a celebrity! She was *the* Beatrice Taylor. But then he started getting anxious. Her hair was like, you know, *oldie-worldie?* Back-combed and bouffant? Yikes! Her clothes were a worry too. Seriously matronly.

And by the end of the sequence he was ready to call Discretion, because she was way out of his ballpark, age-wise. That's when it dawned on him who *the* Beatrice Taylor was. Aunt Bee! From *The Andy Griffith Show*!

'Nineteen-sixties. Well before we were sentient beings, right? All the pics were of the actress who played her, now starring in the great big telly series in the sky. Talk about a letdown!' And Leary had let out an explosive, very unWoody-like cackle.

How priceless, Viv said. She apologised for not being famous, and for dashing his hopes.

No big deal, he joked. He supposed he'd get over it eventually.

At least, I hope he was joking, Viv tells Joy. With Julia's bracing society temporarily unavailable, Joy is Viv's confidante of choice. But she is proving less willing than usual to take up the slack. It might be her imagination, but Viv feels the atmosphere at Joy's to be constrained. Bursts of laughter that generally punctuate the afternoon are absent. Today the vibe is subdued.

Joy has been noticeably introspective all afternoon. She's wearing one of her swirling skirts with Cuban-heeled boots, their first outing for a while. When Viv said she thought Mr Jackson didn't like country, Joy shrugged indifferently. Viv has raised the subject of Leary, a fellow American, in the hope of bringing her out of herself.

It only works to a limited extent. New Yorkers aren't like other Americans, Joy responds without enthusiasm, as Viv ought to know.

They should secede from the rest of the country, like Scotland's trying to do, and Catalonia. They're way more pushy and they're into wisecracking the entire time.

'Even to think about them tires me right out,' she says. 'They spend all their money on being analysed. They want to analyse every little thing. Blah blah blah. Yada yada yada.' That does sound a bit like Leary, Viv agrees.

A search of Leary's name had brought up lists of TV programs he had directed, going back years. Episodes of familiar series and soaps, and others she'd never heard of. It also yielded his blog, *Celluloid Antihero*. Viv was now one of his five thousand-plus followers, though she doubted if she'd turn into a regular.

Towards the end of her time in publishing, authors had been urged to self-publicise with blogs and Twitter. Other than their efforts, this might be the first blog she had ever looked at. She'd speed-read a few sections. It was written in punchy grabs often unencumbered with a verb or traditional structure, like some airport bestsellers. Viv had edited the books of a popular crime writer with a similar style.

Still, Leary's blog was quite a fun read. He lampooned academic film critics for their lazy refusal to re-evaluate sacred cows, such as crap like *Vertigo*. He sent up other movie buffs, a tribe of bearded loonies who emerged from the underworld to infiltrate the NFT and more obscure film venues. Viv imagined them as resembling, in some respects, Geoff's sci-fi cronies.

Did Martin Glover know about Leary's blog? Woven into the narrative were references to some (largely fruitless) internet dating. His increasingly hopeless dates were likened to dysfunctional characters in Ealing comedies. Leary's work, as well as his ongoing therapy, bore ingenious comparison to the plots of disaster movies.

'He sees connections between films and everyday life that escape many people,' Viv tells Joy later, in the sewing room. 'He sees his life as a slow-motion train wreck with horrible special effects.'

She thought Joy had been listening with half an ear. But Joy surprises her by saying that she thinks Viv ought to try him out. All that surplus energy New Yorkers have, it's better for it to have an outlet or it can go crazy and cause trouble. All men are *wacko*, right? It just depends what his brand of wacko is. And if Viv can put up with it.

She is looking over at Mr Jackson with a frown as she makes this remark. He is sitting by himself at the far end with his broad shoulders hunched, working away quietly. Viv wouldn't say Joy's expression is hostile; nor would she say it is fond. All Viv can get out of her today on the subject is that he's only here on appro. It's shape up or ship out.

Viv wonders how Mr Jackson's wackiness evinces itself. Is it his conduct in the house? The bedroom? Joy's demeanour tells her it would be counterproductive to pursue this now. But Viv is not the only one who senses something is out of kilter. She has seen unreadable glances passing between Ondine and Joy. Ondine, she recalls, was the one who introduced Mr Jackson.

His grey head of tight curly hair is bent over his work, a simple border of red and white triangles. This will be added to the quilt being made by Ondine and Yasmin, from Yasmin's appliquéd design of the local high street. Yasmin from Somalia has had no formal education, and Viv thinks she is far and away the most talented person in the room.

She watches as Mr Jackson approaches Ondine for help with the sewing machine. He is masculine without being intrusively macho, she thinks. He blends in with the group almost as if he's one of them. And a little later he takes Riley's crying baby, Reuben, and plays with him.

On her way out Viv contrives a small fishing experiment. Riley has just settled Reuben down for his nap in the crowded hall. Viv has never found Riley, the youngest member of the household, to be unduly hampered by discretion. 'Miss Joy seems a bit down today, Riley,' she says in a low voice, since the door to the hall is always left open. 'Is something troubling her? Has anything happened?'

Riley, whose beauty, Viv believes, is comparatively rare in that it is free of artifice, opens up right away. She too keeps her voice confidential. 'No, but it's been really *weird* the last few days. They're being sort of too polite, you know? Like they don't know each other.'

That *is* weird, Viv says.

'Yeah, everyone's noticed it. It's like they've had a terrible fight but they haven't? He's such a sweet guy too, he's so sweet to Reuben and all the kids. And so nice to her, you know?' Riley looks wistful. What more could you want, is the subtext, than someone who's nice to you? She shakes her long braids, which rattle against each other. Viv admires what she does with her hair, and has had conversations about how she achieves it. Today it's styled in cornrows and threaded with colourful beads.

'It must be a private thing,' Viv concludes. But something makes her persist. 'There's been nothing out of the ordinary? Nothing like, *wacko*? That you can think of?'

No, nothing. Everyone's been talking about it. Well, everyone except Ondine.

Ondine hasn't said anything?

Not a thing. But she's her best friend, isn't she? She knows what's going on, Riley's sure of that. Viv glances back through the open door. Her sightline allows a partial view of Ondine, diagonally opposite. Ondine is serious, almost studious. Nice-looking, gay but never been particularly interested in following it up, according to Joy. She's talking to Yasmin, whose English is slowly improving. Both are bent over the outspread quilt. They exude collaborative concentration.

'Well,' Viv says, 'it's early days, isn't it? I suppose it'll straighten itself out. Let's hope so, anyway.'

'Yeah, that's what we all hope.'

Another text from Leary. Viv peruses it cautiously. *Grovelling apols Bea but date night on hold for a bit, hopefully not forever. Convent series switching focus to enable more creative opps (producer-speak) eg lead nun now transgender.*

The previous helmer being holed up in rehab, Leary's been landed with the whole enchilada. Prev locations junked & he's been dragged outta town for intensive rewrite recce. Then it's back to the real (??) world, so she mustn't think she's off-leash.

'I'm off-leash and on the loose,' Viv tells Martin Glover. With a glimmer of relief, it can't be denied.

His response is prompt. In that case, they can keep the pot on a rolling boil as there's another rabbit he'd set aside for a rainy day. Viv says she's shocked. Wouldn't that be tantamount to two-timing? Martin doesn't think it would be tantamount to anything of that nature. She claims to be raring to go, doesn't she? And she and Mr Davidson haven't actually managed to make contact yet. Not face to face.

'Well, it's hard to find time for a social whirl in his walk of life, I gather. You may be unfamiliar with the TV business, Martin? I can reveal that they're all on drugs. Everything happens last-minute. It's madly full-on and worryingly crisis-ridden.'

Geoff is out again. He left the house after breakfast. Back on the real-estate treadmill, he explained with a grin. Damsel in distress and all that. Viv is about to leave for her volunteering work at Tower Hamlets. She slings a bag over her shoulder and descends the stairs, while holding the phone to her ear and winding a thick woollen scarf round her neck with her free hand.

The new rabbit calls himself Thomas Daunt, although Martin doubts whether that name is an exact match with the one on his birth certificate. 'He's a minister, so he's quite likely to be covering his tracks.'

'He's in the *Cabinet*?'

'No, no, just a minister of religion. Anglican, of course.'

'Of course. The other side wouldn't be sympathetic to this sort of caper, would they? You're having me on.'

'No, it's God's truth. He says he's a vicar, in point of fact.'

'A *vicar*? Isn't that verging on the – burlesque?'

Martin says he's not the first such specimen to cross his path. 'He's a struggling priest, as they mostly are these days, he tells me. And he keeps a low profile since his first divorce, so I think any *risqués* would be negligible—'

'His *first* divorce? Am I hearing aright? And what sort of *risqués* can you possibly be thinking of?'

'Well, I don't think paparazzi would be an issue.'

'You don't, don't you? I'm relieved to hear it.' Viv shoves open the front door, which is sticking, and negotiates the steps. 'What about the *risqué* of him being publicly defrocked?'

'I think they abolished defrocking for adultery. These days it's only resorted to for the more heinous crimes. In any case, I'm not sure frocks are worn much anymore.'

'He can't be struggling that much, to afford your fees.'

'He led me to understand his wife is fairly cashed-up.'

'His *wife*? He's using her *money*? Has he told her?'

Martin says he shouldn't have said that, and she should forget he ever said it. He might have dreamt it, anyway. He has always had an annoying tendency to dream little snatches of conversation, and it's hard to know if they're true or not.

Viv admits to having a similar tendency. 'How on earth did he get on your books?'

'He fits the Agency's specifications, put it that way. His case is not as straightforward as it may sound on first hearing. You could say he's a postmodern type of priest. Divorced with a second family – a younger wife and toddler.'

'That sounds *entirely* straightforward to me, if you really want to know.' By now, Viv is briskly on her way to the Tube, which will connect her to a bus. 'I can't think why you—'

'And this has given rise to some unforeseen complications. I'm inclined to think you should give him a chance to explain for himself. Every case is different, you know. He doesn't present as a rip-roaring sleaze. More as a hapless chump who's dug a hole for himself, through a fairly standard combination of carelessness and moral turpitude.'

'Martin, I've got zero interest in getting involved with a morally turpid vicar who has a wife and young child, and quite possibly causing a scan—'

'Shall we say his status as a husband has been non-functional for some time.'

'How old is he?' Viv takes long strides, frowning into the wind.

'Let me see. Your age. Fifty-seven.'

'That's not my age, Martin. It's the age you gave me. Remember?'

'Well, give or take. Be reasonable.'

Be reasonable? Viv gives vent to a laugh, prolonged and uninhibited, which has been building up over the past few minutes. She only just avoids a collision with an irate woman pushing twins in a double pram and taking up most of the pavement.

'You're sounding like my husband. He's always telling me to be reasonable.'

A mere two days later, following an exchange of pleasantries, she is about to be furnished with an account of the hole that the Reverend Thomas Daunt – who has no truck with formality, just call me Tom – has dug for himself. They are in a smart cafe (a former greasy spoon given the bog-standard tourist-friendly half-timbered look in the early noughties, he explains, and rebranded a brasserie) in Westminster.

Tom had said he wouldn't be wearing a dog collar, because he is off duty. But Viv identifies him without any trouble. Martin had described him as looking something like the late Bob Mitchum.

'*Robert* Mitchum? The actor?' Viv exclaimed. 'Why didn't you say that before?'

A younger, more reptilian version.

'More *reptilian*?'

Well, somewhat more.

'But that's absurd, Martin. Mitchum is not at all reptilian.'

Sorry, he thought the word he wanted might be saturnine. Saturnine yet also sensitive. A trifle over-sensitive? Perhaps a touch fleshy.

'Does he have a cleft chin?'

Martin thought not. Perhaps a bit of double chin instead.

'Younger than Bob Mitchum when he was what age?"

Well, than when he was older. When he died. Martin said he'd never been a dab hand at describing people. Vivien should ditch the idea that the Rev Daunt looked like anyone, and meet him with no preconceptions.

So, in spite of considerable misgivings, Viv is keeping a resolutely open mind for the time being. She and Tom Daunt are sitting with a side view of the door, at his suggestion. So, they can keep the hoi polloi under surveillance, he says surprisingly, in a rich and deep baritone.

Viv pictures his sermons resonating under soaring arches. Although these days congregations are said to be thin on the ground, so perhaps the pews are sparsely populated. She is interested to hear that (as an Associate Rector, she thinks he said) he works in and around the East End. In that case he would know of the Tower Hamlets school where she volunteers? He gives an absent nod. Viv, whose ears are pricked, chalks this up as noteworthy.

Tom is an urbane, worldly man with an impressive head of dark hair and a firm handshake. A tall man whose primary drive, she would predict, is physical. Viv is aware of making this assumption in a non-evidence-based way, but thinks her mother would concur. Without her glasses she can see what Martin meant. A passing resemblance to Robert Mitchum: slight, but encouraging. He has a similar air of indolence, but with the beginnings of a double chin. His thick black hair curls over the (non-clerical) collar and cravat, and he has heavy sideburns.

She can see no grey around the temples. According to Joy, who claims to know about such things, any white male over fifty who's not showing any grey is doing something about it. Joy also says long sideburns are a sign of a narcissism.

Viv is having difficulty ridding herself of the saurian image prompted by Martin Glover's description. Tom Daunt has prominent, heavy-lidded eyes that, while resembling those of Bob Mitchum (and classically bedroom) do conjure up lizards or turtles, once the suggestion has been planted. The Reverend's eyes, though, have pronounced bags under them. This does differentiate them from most reptiles, in her mind.

But if saturnine describes someone moodily mysterious who doesn't give much away, Martin's assessment is off-beam. Tom Daunt seems prepared to give quite a lot away, over coffee, and to do this unprompted and willingly.

'The advantage of hiring a service provider,' he says, 'is that we already know each other's *motivating driver*. We don't have to hide the fact that we're both trapped in a web of hideous circumstances.'

'Well, *hideous* might be a little too—'

'Well, I shouldn't presume to speak for you. Or the specificity of your spouse.' A curly smile. 'Sketch in your situation for me. How would you describe it, if not hideous? Frustrating, oppressive, intractable? Suburban? Violent?'

Viv senses he would prefer to be drinking a good claret. Bowls of nuts and mixed olives are on the table at his instigation. They're a bit at odds, in her view, with the coffee. Some olives are stuffed with anchovies, others with feta and chilli. She considers her situation.

'All I think I need to explain is that it's been a long-term relationship and—'

'Explain no more,' he interrupts. 'Long-term relationships.' It's a phrase and a statement redolent of bitter experience. He gives a derisive snort. 'We all know about *them*. I think I can confidently say that I am not unfamiliar with some and probably most of the problems *they* pose.'

'But your present one is fairly short-term, isn't it? So far, at least.'

'Short, yes. Decidedly not sweet.' The heavy lids droop. 'But my first marriage endured for a quarter-century. Endured being the operative word. And produced four moderately acceptable children.'

He coughs. 'Be on your guard against that chilli, won't you? It's lethal. Yes, I admit everything. The break-up, while *not* unprovoked, was all my own bloody work. I plummeted in lust, rent asunder the temple – aka the family home – and from that day forward all was rack and ruination.'

So far so straightforward, Viv is thinking. 'The temptress with whom you plummeted was younger?' She toys with saying, *and rich*, but refrains.

'In a nutshell, affirmative. Male, stale and midlife is the cliché. Perhaps you are familiar with this nefarious beast?'

'I do have a nodding acquaintance with it, yes.' They exchange a grimace. His curved mouth, she thinks, is marginally like that of Mitchum's, but more sardonic.

'The temptress was in her mid-thirties. Lissom and alluring, at *that* stage. German. Her dulcet tones were a dead ringer for Dietrich's.'

Viv nods. 'Accents can be very potent, can't they? Like cheap music. I'm a sucker for the French, myself. Like Charles Azna—'

'Well, each to his own. Or hers. And I should add, as it's of some import – she was up the duff.'

'Do you mean before or after you met?'

Another grimace. 'Funny you should say that. After, she claimed. *But only just.*' She'd led him to believe it was *safe* to proceed. Tom looks rather wild-eyed. He'd had it with progeny and didn't want any more. Or expect to have, he adds darkly. He was obliged to hurtle into his second stab at matrimony unwisely and with unseemly haste.

'I'm at my wits' end, frankly. Or beyond.' He puts his head in his hands. Viv, who has a strong chilli tolerance, takes another couple of olives. She sees him gazing at the well-stocked bar. 'I'm easy, but would you rather have something stronger? I expect re-living this is a bit on the harrowing—'

A groan. 'Better not. Trying not to drink in daylight on weekdays.' He'd taken up the gaspers again after twenty years when the situation got on top of him. Now he was trying to kick that ruddy habit all over again. He gets up. 'Sorry, Beatrice, let me get *you* something.'

'No no, please sit down, I'm fine.' Viv had forgotten she was Beatrice. 'There's a Costa next door, we should have gone there, out of reach of temptation. Look, Tom, it's not surprising that such a young woman would want children of her own, is it? Forgive me, but I don't quite see the problem. Why are you here?'

'Let me enlighten you,' Tom says tersely. 'Since producing the kid, she – Sabrina, to give the girl a name – has become completely unrecognisable.'

'It's not that unusual to change, after giving birth. Do you mean visually, or—'

'She's *let herself go.*' His full-body shudder strikes Viv as involuntary. After a pause he adds, 'Literally, I mean. And that's a chivalrous *understatement*, if I may say so.' Viv chooses not to respond to this. 'She eats like a horse. She's developed an antipathy towards me, won't have me anywhere near her.'

'What about the baby?' Viv asks, concerned.

'Don't worry about *that*, it's not a baby now. That's not the problem. She's besotted with it.'

'It's just you she can't abide. Well, that's a relief, isn't it? In a manner of speaking?'

He breathes in deeply. 'It's like *Lysistrata* at our place, Beatrice. Except we're not in a play, it's not funny and there's no happy ending. And divorce is out of the question. And please refrain from sentences ending in "just desserts".'

'That's rotten luck, Tom, but the odds are there's a light at the end of the tunnel. Maybe Sabrina will go on a strict diet and her libido will bounce back. It's probably something as simple as postnatal depression. After all, the baby is still young.'

An exasperated look. 'I told you, it's not a baby. It's two, for God's sake.'

Viv suppresses a laugh. 'Perhaps it's an unusually severe case. It can be protracted.'

'Rubbish, of course it's not. It's me she can't stand. She's perfectly normal with everybody else. Apart from the – the *parishioners*. She loathes them. Which is understandable enough.'

'Is divorce really out of the question, then? I mean, I do see—'

'I don't think you do see. Of course it is. *Lord* yes. It would be tabloid heaven. My bloody *subjects* would go berserk. They'd lynch me. You have to appreciate the hoo-ha that was unleashed when I took up with her.'

There was some unspeakable trolling on Facebook and Twitter. Hellish things were said. His ex-wife had been popular, she'd lavished good works all over the joint, whereas Sabrina is not into do-gooding, to put it mildly. Into *hausfrauing* is more like it. And the ethnic thing didn't help. It's all Brexit down there. He gestures, arms spread. You know, *around* there.

'Around the East End? I don't think so.' Viv thinks about the parents and staff she knows *around* there.

'You'd be surprised.'

'I would.' After a pause, 'If you don't mind my saying, why doesn't Sabrina want to divorce *you?*' According to Martin she doesn't need money, she remembers.

He mops his brow with a large handkerchief adorned with a photo of Big Ben. 'Don't worry, I'm trying to bring it on. Subtly. But whatever she thinks I want she does the opposite. And there's another thing.'

His hair falls forward, giving him a moody and rather fetching Byronic look. 'The other *maddening* thing being that she's developed a close friendship with a ghastly female jockey who's around all the time.'

'How close?'

'God knows. That would be all I need.' He yanks a fob watch from his pocket.

'Is there a service coming on?'

'I'm all right for a bit. Evensong threatens.' An eye-roll. 'Total waste of time because there'll only be three ancient takers. That's if they haven't died on one.'

'Would they notice if one didn't show up?' Viv says. 'Assuming they're still upright?'

Her high spirits are persisting in the face of some conflicted feelings about this man. Disbelief and aversion on one hand, tempered on the other by a physical attraction she would be the first to admit is perverse. The sensations seem to be co-existing without difficulty. The reason is that nothing is at stake here, she thinks. Not my feelings or his or, it would seem, anyone else's.

Were she to be questioned at this juncture, she thinks that she just might, on balance, opt for giving the Rev Daunt a go. At least she could close her eyes and think of Robert Mitchum. Which had to be better than a poke in the eye with a sharp stick, as Jules might observe. The idea of shagging a vicar: it's just too much for human frailty to resist. In Viv's present disposition, at any rate.

21

HOLOGRAMS

Julia is in the interesting position of rehearsing with a hologram. Her three Hollywood moments, as Emils calls them, will be the legendary high points of the production, to be filmed in a set in the rehearsal room and beamed onto the stage. There is a climactic third, in the final seconds of the opera, but they don't need to think about that one just now.

Julia estimates her director's stubble is four days old and doubts if he's changed his clothes for two of them. 'What's happening is an optical illusion,' he says. 'It will look like you're out there in front of the audience, Julia, but you're actually in the rehearsal room. Cool, huh?'

The technology for these elaborate stage effects is quite new. Neither Julia nor Yuri Dutka, the hefty Ukrainian singing Herman, is familiar with the process. Yuri in particular, as a keen photographer, is very taken with it. The stage action will be screened on a monitor so Julia will be able to see the conductor and hear the orchestra.

She already knows what's coming. For the first segment she has to lie in a coffin on a bier, and she is finding this unexpectedly troubling. Later she will ask herself why a seasoned old pro like herself should have had this reaction. Realistically though, being laid out as an old woman in a casket, in a burial shroud, arms folded, face waxen and bloodless, playing dead – wouldn't that give anyone the creeps? And it can only get worse, because for this early rehearsal she's in a plain gown and not made up as a corpse.

A gothic church – an atmospheric little set – sits in one corner of the vast rehearsal space behind the stage. The scene follows the Countess's demise after Herman, desperate for the secret of the cards, has pulled a gun on her. Later that night, he is prowling in his bedroom seeing nightmarish visions. The music is agitated. He thinks he hears chanting – or is it the wind howling?

The hologram is Herman's hallucination, and the film will be shot from his pov, like a dream sequence. He sings: *Drawn by an unknown force, I enter the shrouded church.* The camera moves towards the draped walls and flickering shadows.

The old woman lies in the coffin, immobile, lifeless. The picture floats before his eyes. The camera closes in on the remorseless face of the dead Countess whose death he has caused. And like a shock in a horror film, one eye opens and closes in a gruesome wink. *Away, terrible vision!* On stage, the ethereal hologram dissolves like magic.

They go through the brief sequence, with Yuri onstage in Herman's bedroom and Julia laid out in the rehearsal room, flanked by cameras. It's a piano rehearsal today, no orchestra. But Ray Bayliss is there, along with Marion Luce the set designer, both taking a keen professional interest. This is new to them too.

For the first hologram Julia won't be able to see the screen because her eyes are closed in death. Her eye movement must be timed to the split-second. 'And Julia,' adds Emils, displaying the sensitivity that has helped propel him into the position he's in now, directing an opera at Covent Garden at the age of twenty-eight, 'remember this. You're only in there before you *rise again*. In only a matter of seconds – nothing like three days.'

Julia is working at suppressing her discomfort. Which is, as she repeats to herself, perfectly natural. And she wears her most beguiling smile for her young director. Who, Ray claims, is quite besotted with her already.

When they repair to the canteen for a lunch break they discover burritos and tacos. The caterer adopts different culinary themes from time to time to please the international clientele. Today it's in honour of the Mexican Day of the Dead, which happens to fall on Sunday. How appropriate, says Julia.

Back in the rehearsal room they feel they're getting the hang of hologram procedure. In the second one the Countess's ghost is required to sing a few lines. She will be in her funeral weeds after rising from the dead.

She'll be a vision in white, Emils tells her, having exited the coffin with the help of two assistants and stepped in front of a plain dark screen. She will take three slow steps, precisely measured and timed. On stage, it will look like her ghost is gliding through Herman's bedroom door.

The rehearsal gets underway. Herman has just had his nightmare vision. He hears the Countess's cane tapping at the window. The ominous music rises. Even with the lone piano it's dramatic, suggesting cyclonic winds howling.

I am terrified. I hear steps. The door opens. No, I can't bear it! Herman rushes to close his bedroom door as the music crashes around him. He reels backwards. In the hologram's eerie shimmer, a spectre is revealed in the doorway. The ghost of the Old Countess.

Emils has been standing at Julia's side. 'Keep it short, simple, dramatic.' He moves away. She steps forward.

I have come, against my will, to fulfil your request. Save Lisa, marry her, and three cards will win in succession. Three. Seven. Ace! In a daze, Herman repeats the names of the cards. Whereupon the apparition dissolves and the scene ends. 'Stunning, Julia,' says Emils, and hugs her.

He is still fizzing with exhilaration as he sprints out of the rehearsal room into the auditorium to compare notes with his assistant director. To consult with Ray and have a word with Yuri. To identify problems and answer questions. To deliberate, evaluate, and watch three more run-throughs from different parts of the auditorium.

The scattered onlookers in the front stalls, including the conductor and designer, one or two company bigwigs and a few technicians and stagehands, have erupted in spontaneous applause. Remarkable, they agree, an extraordinary, chilling effect. Spine-tingling.

'Running *two* now, are we?' The sound of unoperatic (and rather ruttish) laughter echoes in Viv's ear. 'Into threesomes, is it?'

Julia is doing an efficient job of banishing from her mind the recent stresses of impersonating the mortal remains of a Countess. She has delayed the onset of a pedicure in order to take Viv's call. She's hesitating over an opalescent white and the wine-dark red she usually goes for.

Off-mike, Viv hears her say: 'Shall we go all pure and pearly for a change?' There is a short pause while Jules removes her footwear. Viv doesn't usually bother with pedicures in winter. After all, Geoff is unlikely to notice. Following this exchange, however, she will drop into the local nail bar and after much indecision have her toenails painted a shade called twilight violet.

She knew perfectly well that she shouldn't have called, but the urge to tell Jules about the Rev Daunt was too strong. The spirit was willing, but the flesh was (far too) weak. Her friend's reaction does not disappoint.

'You cannot be serious. Not content with a hyperventilating Yank you've got a goatish vicar in your sights?'

'The spitting image of Robert Mitchum, no less.' An acceptable degree of poetic licence, in Viv's book.

Down the phone line she hears the indistinct instruction: 'Straight across, not too short.' Then, 'You haven't signed up with

Central Casting by mistake, Viv? Martin Thingo's not producing the Xmas panto at the London Palladium? Mother *Goose*, perhaps?'

'We're meeting next week,' Viv murmurs. She explains that Leary is on hold, for the time being, on account of the helmer being in rehab and Leary out of town on a recce. The helmer is the director and a recce is a location survey, she adds.

'Tell me something I didn't know. Well, no worries – when he hits town again he'll be able to join in. The more the merrier, eh? And the priapic priest is planning to entertain you in the vicarage? While the frigid wife's in the kitchen frying the bratwurst? They're all rigged up with CCTV cameras, you know, Viv, to stop fundamentalist nutters getting in. You'd better wear a burqa.'

No need for that, Viv says complacently. I'm going to Paris instead. He has an apartment in the Marais. Two bedrooms, he said, so we can play it by ear. Just to put your worries at rest.

'Two bedrooms in the Marais? On a *vicar's* salary?' Another snorting laugh. Viv extends the phone to arm's length. Jules's voice is at full operatic projection. 'Do you have any idea what they earn?'

'Well, I think it might be his German wife's ...'

'What an accommodating little German *frau* he must have, to be sure. What's his excuse for the Paris junket? They don't get any time off, I read in the paper. They're on call 24/7. And they mostly have more than one parish, what with the ancient fan base dwindling by the second.'

Viv had seen the same article. Jules shouldn't believe everything she reads in the paper. He has to go to a conference—

'A *conference*? Of parish priests? You know, Viv, these kinds of delusions might be a sign of early onset—'

'There are no presumptions,' Viv interrupts in turn. 'He's a man of the cloth, Jules. You can't get much sounder than that.' This is delivered with forceful confidence, concealing a high degree of doubt. Jules's observations have tapped into certain suspicions already in place.

Balls. He wasn't wearing a dog collar, and he doesn't sound remotely like any priest of Julia's acquaintance. Which is admittedly limited, but no more than Viv's. Speaking of balls, she says, Viv hasn't forgotten the *pelvic floor refresher course* next week? What with all this new-found excitement going on in her life. The doc was very insistent they go.

Two years ago, at Nerida Clifford's instigation, various of her patients had signed up for a specialised exercise class. It involved the rhythmic clenching of internal muscles of the pelvic floor, in multiple repetitions, and was designed to improve bladder performance now and in perpetuity. Purely precautionary, Dr Clifford had advised. But it had beneficial side effects in other, unrelated activities. These were not to be sneezed at.

Viv and Julia had performed their routines dutifully to start with, but both had admitted subsequent lapses. All the more reason to take them up again with renewed rigour, Jules says, bearing in mind the beneficial side effects. Especially since Viv would seem to be on the verge of resuming her activities in this sphere.

Viv is surprised at Jules's insistence. Surprised also that her friend has time to think of her pelvic floor at all, given everything else going on in her life. But she doesn't expend much energy or thought on this, given what is going on in her own.

The last time she went to Paris was with a female friend to see the reopened Picasso Museum. The idea of going to the city of light and romance with a new male friend (even if her feelings about him are mixed) is appealing. As is the prospect of a couple of nights away from Geoff in an apartment in the Marais. Whichever room she sleeps in.

Joy, who is not disposed to indulge Viv by discussing this any further, and whose disposition remains as resolutely surly as it has been recently, is unimpressed by her friend's behaviour and incensed by the vicar's. She wouldn't be caught dead in *his* church.

Who does he think he is, telling people what they ought to be doing? He's a tosser, just mark her words.

But Viv sees a harmony in the timing of upcoming events. The little Paris jaunt will slot neatly into the week before Daisy's gallery opening. Almost as if it might have been divinely ordained.

22

THE REV

Viv will find it impossible to relate the Paris story in full. Not to Jules or Joy, not to Martin Glover. Certain details are just too toe-curling.

She had texted Nerida Clifford: *Swanning off to Paree for your birthday. Just so you know.* A woman of few words, the doctor had responded: *Roger.*

I'm going to Paris for a day or two, Viv remarked airily to Geoff. It was indeed Nerida's birthday about now, and there had been innocent trips (with and without partners) to Paris, Bruges and Lyons in previous years. Nerida had been lent an apartment in the Marais by one of her wealthy patients, Viv extemporised, a two-bedder, before remembering that to explain too much was a giveaway. It was arguably worse than not explaining at all.

No matter, in any case. She had been finding her husband's behaviour increasingly irritating and irrational. Eliza was being set up with an IT job in Geoff's old firm after Christmas, and she could now afford a one-bedroom instead of a studio. There would be an interim period when she couldn't quite afford it, and Geoff would provide a bridging loan.

The two of them seemed to spend hours drinking herbal tea (which Geoff had always loathed) and poring over real-estate listings on their computers at the kitchen table. Beyond that, the exact nature of their relationship remained obscure.

The plan was to take the Eurostar and connect with Tom Daunt at the end of day one of the two-day conference being held somewhere near the Petit Palais. The apartment was convenient to Bastille and the Place des Vosges. A favourite area of Viv's; she and Geoff had stayed nearby in a small hotel on several occasions.

The forecast for Paris was cold but dry. *Layering* is the way to go, and take the bare minimum – Julia's perennial travel advice was embedded in the psyche. Viv knew Julia's idea of the bare minimum differed from her own, but had thrown in a layer or two for versatility.

Apart from a fleeting moment of doubt on the train (nothing that couldn't be brushed off and swept aside) she was treating this escapade as a bit of fun. Her mood could be described as happy-go-lucky and hang the consequences. Not that there should be any. The Rev Daunt might have a wife and young child, but it was clear (and morally reassuring) that his marriage was in meltdown. Unless he was an actor of Shakespearean calibre, and Viv didn't think this was a realistic possibility, his state of disarray was genuine.

Viv had told Martin Glover she was ambivalent about the Reverend, but Paris, Bob Mitchum and the existence of two bedrooms had tipped the scales. She stopped short of asking Martin whether he believed the Rev was the genuine article; she intended to do some covert research of her own in Paris.

The train was on time. The city wove its usual spell. The walk from Bastille was quick and easy. Viv pulled her case along two sides of the beguiling Place des Vosges, pausing to admire the symmetry of its arches and look into lighted restaurant windows.

She found the address in a charming, winding street. Close to a bakery (perfect for breakfast), bistros and bars, on the top floor of a walk-up. By the time she pressed the bell she was disposed to find anything pleasing, not excluding the person – not much more than a stranger – who opened the door of what she recognised as a formal Parisian apartment of a certain type. Sedate, with parquet floors and the kind of gilded furniture she usually disliked. Here on exotic territory the curved legs and padded brocades struck her as quite agreeable. Glass doors (French, naturally) gave a view of the street and a miniature balcony with iron railings.

The Rev was in mufti again. Jeans, this time, teamed with desert boots and an Aran sweater. There were signs of his occupancy. An overflowing ashtray sat on a side table with flimsy legs, next to a wine glass and a bottle of burgundy with a fancy label. Nearly empty, she noticed.

Good of her to come, he said. A kiss on both cheeks, which produced a responsive tingle. He smelled, not unpleasantly, of wine. Glad to see she travelled light. His wife was one of *those women* who couldn't go anywhere without fifty-two hatboxes, not that they ever went anywhere these days. Viv could have taken an earlier train. He'd absconded from the conference, which was as deadly as all of their ilk.

Viv found herself disposed to overlook 'those women'. Was the conference about doctrinal matters? Something like that, he hadn't taken much notice. 'A blessed relief to be off the ruddy isle of xenophobes, isn't it?' he said. 'This is a tolerable bolthole. At least it doesn't freeze your nuts off. Can't do anything about the chi-chi furnishings, I'm afraid.'

Very tolerable indeed as boltholes went, Viv agreed. He seemed more relaxed than in London, but with the same ration of attitude. In her present mood Viv was feeling sufficiently amiable for two.

The small bedrooms opened off the hall. A mirror image of each other, each with a spindly-legged armchair, a bow-fronted chest of drawers and a double bed. White, with gilt decoration. An open leather holdall with a jumble of clothing, files and folders was parked in one. Nearby, draped (ostentatiously?) over the chair was a clerical shirt and collar. Tom put her case in the other room, without comment. Viv gave him marks for this.

He didn't have a say in the decor, then? The eyes under the heavy lids rolled. She had to be joking. They rented the place out in summer to other grisly nouveaus like themselves. *They?* The in-laws of course, he said, who do you think?

That would be why the flat was so impersonal. The only photo was on the mantelpiece: an ornamental, willowy young woman with her head thrown back and the sullen expression of a catwalk model. Sabrina, presumably, before the post-baby alterations. Tom turned it to the wall with a dismissive snort.

A gesture at the bathroom. 'Do you want to have a pee or anything? Powder your nose? But don't make yourself too much at home. The plan is to get the hell out of here asap. Could you use some exotic booze? I've booked an early dinner round the corner. Nice little place. Any problems with any of that?'

Not so you'd notice, Viv said.

And it wasn't the evening that would be the problem. Although admittedly the quantity of booze put away in the course of it was (almost certainly) unwise. It was not responsible for what took place afterwards, not by any means, but it did exert some influence.

It was far more than Viv had put away in one sitting for a great many years. Kicked off by two cocktails apiece in a darkened basement done up like a speakeasy, then a stroll through lamplit streets to a cobblestoned cul-de-sac. There at the far end was the archetypal bistro, dimly lit, complete with flowers and pink tablecloths.

Viv thought of Nerida Clifford, her alibi. This is exactly what the doctor ordered, she told Tom Daunt blithely. She planned to tell her husband the very same thing, and without the slightest qualm.

After the arrival of the second bottle it wasn't too much of a stretch to see Bob Mitchum slouching opposite. The eyes, the black hair and heavy sideburns, the ironic air. Not when viewed through half-closed eyes in the candlelight, which minimised discrepancies. And in the glow produced by good wine, which Tom was knocking back with even less restraint than she was.

Since their views on most things were diametrically opposed, the conversation tended to relapse into a chain of political wrangles. Cynicism was the Rev's position of choice – rather, Viv imagined, as it might have been that of the actor he resembled. The clerical conference was off-limits. For God's *sake!* He'd rather talk about government policy on the disabled or the worried well. This jokey remark made an impression. Viv memorised it for later.

In spite of her attempts to deflect it, the subject of his disastrous marriage wouldn't go away. While she could imagine tunnel-vision being of value in some occupations, such as finding the cure for a flesh-eating disease, she told him, in a dinner situation it was less appealing. He was unhealthily obsessed. He needed to get a life.

'What do you think *this* is?' he demanded. 'It's called getting out more. It's just bloody hard to get away from the insidious effect of the wretched woman. Permeates everything.'

'It can't be all her though, can it?'

'Don't be ridiculous. Of course it damn well can,' he said. Quite cheerfully, she thought.

He made it clear he didn't want to answer questions about the priesthood. He couldn't remember what misguided whim made him choose the ministry in the first place. The suggestion that he'd had a vocation met with an incredulous curl of the lip. So, would he go so far as to describe himself as an unbeliever, then?

'What do you think? They're all covert atheists. Well, you'd have to be, wouldn't you? They just sweep it under the carpet. Or under the clerical skirt.'

Well then, why had he entered the priesthood in the first place? In a word.

'You want one word? Too easy. Sinecure,' he said succinctly.

Viv, whose mind was buzzing in spite of a prodigious intake of alcohol, was now convinced that the Rev component of the Daunt persona was fraudulent. She decided to save this intriguing subject for breakfast. In the back of her mind, and becoming more insistent by the minute, were two questions. Did she want the fling to commence at the end of the evening? And was its commencement even feasible? This became even more relevant after the digestifs arrived. A double measure of Armagnac for him, a single Amaretto for her.

In the event, the first question was settled without an operative word being spoken. A quick but decisive kiss outside the restaurant in the chill of a gathering mist, and a walk (in a relatively straight line) back to the apartment, arm in arm (Paris was *delectable*, Geoff). Once inside the drawing room they tore off their clothes in the dark, leaving them where they fell, and headed straight for the bedroom Tom had already staked out.

When they had been in bed naked for a few minutes, Viv's earlier doubts as to feasibility were shown to be well founded. Wouldn't you know, she imagined telling her confidantes. She expected that she might feel at liberty to disclose something along these lines.

The situation was made more awkward, potentially, by the fact that she and Tom Daunt did not know each other very well. And apart from a degree of physical attraction, which she regarded as rather irrational, she could think of nothing they had in common. We didn't really get on at all was the sum total of what she would later feel able to disclose.

Humour, normally an invaluable resource, seemed out of reach. It was difficult to gauge what might be an appropriate level at such a critical moment. Viv did her best to smooth things over.

'It's entirely understandable, Tom,' she murmured. 'You must be sozzled. I know I am. I'm completely legless, quite frankly. But it couldn't matter less – please don't give it another thought. We can have another go in the morning.' Or try something else, she would have liked to say, if she'd known him better.

He stopped, she felt, just short of saying shut the fuck up, Pollyanna. 'Don't bang on about it, Beatrice, for Christ's sake. I've got the bugger's measure.'

A rather mystifying phrase, until she grasped what the measure might be. He swung his legs out of bed and started fumbling around on the floor on his hands and knees. Various items were tossed out of the hold-all, accompanied by some exasperated swearing. Then she heard the crackle of foil. Was he removing something from his wash bag? He went into the bathroom. She heard a tap running.

'Thirty minutes at the outside,' he said, returning. 'We can chill out and talk among ourselves.'

'Or quarrel and bicker. Anything I can do to ...'

'No, it'll do it itself. Do you mind if I smoke?'

'I think I do mind,' she said. It might distract him from keeping her awake and on the ball. But the next thirty minutes did not drag. Whatever his shortcomings, the Rev was a man who understood about outcomes needing to be constructed from the ground up. And alcohol, happily, hadn't dulled his grip on the knowledge, or grasp of the process. Although the words grip and grasp were too ...

A pleasant momentum was being reached when Viv found herself jerked back into the previous moment by a hard poke in the side. Tom gave a satisfied grunt.

'Shall we?' he said.

But just as the next stage had been smoothly effected it came to an abrupt halt as he pronounced very clearly in her ear, 'Holy shit!' Then followed it up with '*Fucking hell!*' Viv found this only slightly puzzling, if unnecessarily loud, as her ear was ringing. But then she realised that he had collapsed onto her with a long, expelled breath. Not only that, he appeared to be paralysed.

Agitated thoughts raced through her mind. Maybe the tablet was too strong, or it interacted badly with alcohol? Or he had taken the wrong one in the dark? They'd eaten nuts at the bar – perhaps it was a peanut allergy. Did he have an epipen with him? It couldn't be *botulism*, could it – they had chosen different dishes and there were forms that were almost instantaneously fatal.

Could it be that he had expired on the job, before the job was fully underway? This did happen, you heard, and mainly to men. If so, how on earth would she deal with it? She couldn't reach anything. Worse still, she couldn't move. Did the in-laws employ a cleaner? If not, they mightn't be found for days.

At that precise moment she absorbed the existence of voices from the living room. One guttural, the other higher pitched. In the moment that followed Tom had a resurgence of energy. He withdrew, rolled off smartly and dragged the sheet up over their heads, causing the continental quilt to slide off the bed. Viv, who thought she had never been so relieved in her life, was moved to admire his sangfroid.

Just then the overhead light in their room snapped on and she heard two people barge into the room. Beside her, Tom whispered, 'Don't move. And don't say a *bloody thing.*'

'Sabrina? Tim?' A woman's voice, strongly accented but alarmingly distinct. Viv, aware she was not quite all there, was confused.

Tom spoke up from under the sheet in a commendably normal voice: 'Gunther and Lorelei. Shouldn't you be cruising in the Balearics?'

Two raised, excitable voices replied at once. Food-poisoning had broken out and the cruise had been aborted. '*Schrecklich!*' The woman again, in an altered tone: 'Sabrina?'

The sheet had come adrift at the other end, exposing Viv's feet and shins. She heard a fevered exchange in German. They've seen my toes with the twilight violet nail polish. Not Sabrina's colour. Not her elegant toes. Not her youthful ankles.

She froze as the sheet was eased down a little way to expose her face. Both visitors reacted with shocked exclamations. The thickset, bald man, who must be Gunther, let out a loud profanity Viv identified from her schoolgirl German.

The woman Lorelei, also portly and wearing an expensive full-length fur coat, bore down on her, quivering with indignation. Discarded lingerie – black, lacy – dangled from a forefinger. Gunther was brandishing other incriminating articles. The framed photo of his daughter that had been turned to the wall. His son-in-law's underpants.

His eyes bulged as they fell on the priestly shirt and collar on the back of the chair. '*Der Bruder!*' he hissed at Lorelei. '*Der Zwillingsbruder!* Tom? Is you? You are here?'

Lorelei cried, 'Where iss your *wife?*' Her husband seized the clerical garb and dumped it on the bed. '*Verzieh dich!* Get out! You – *out!*' Viv took this to mean her. She didn't move. She was unwilling to expose her nudity to the gaze of hostile others. Besides, she was feeling some solidarity with Tom.

His in-laws still couldn't see his face. This, together with the sound of his own shouting, seemed to galvanise Gunther. He grabbed the edge of the sheet in both hands. 'And *you* get off! *Sofort! Gleich!*' A brief tug-of-war ensued. His wife helped out by snatching the other corner.

Suddenly Lorelei gasped and uttered a small scream, staggering backwards. Viv also jumped. The sheet had come away, exposing their two bodies – butt naked to the sky, as Joy would say. And more pertinently, a vertiginous erection.

Viv would retain near-total recall of this excruciating happening. At first it was one of those rare moments, an unlikely example of bipartisanship – of *team spirit*, she might almost have said – when she and Lorelei, two otherwise irreconcilable women, were as one. Both were transfixed, even if only for a split-second. It was as if neither had ever set eyes on an erect penis before.

But the moment of female solidarity dissolved in a flash. Gunther, who Viv judged to be the same age as his son-in-law, or possibly younger, and whose attitude to the engorged member was less nuanced, let out an animalistic growl. He lunged forward, right hand outstretched like a grappling hook.

Tom had spun side-on with his knees up. He had no chance of taking evasive action. Viv reacted with an inarticulate noise of empathy as his fine head of hair detached from its moorings and came away in his father-in-law's outraged claw. He let out a grunt of pain. The success of this manoeuvre (something, Viv guessed, that Gunther might have longed to do for the duration of his daughter's marriage) caused him to lose his balance and topple forward.

He landed heavily between the two of them, his substantial bulk cannoning into Viv and temporarily incapacitating her companion. Viv recoiled as the luxuriant hairpiece flew out of his hand and smacked her (surprisingly sharply, given the short distance travelled) in the left eye.

She was still processing this when she recoiled a second time. It dawned on her that her face was being slapped. This had never happened before, although she'd seen it happen countless times in the movies, or on TV. She was being slapped by Tom's mother-in-law, an enraged, muscular woman who was a good decade younger than her.

Viv's stomach heaved. It was partly the emotional toll of successive physical impacts, partly the wine, and it was not to be ignored. Her body was on display; she'd been hit by a flying toupee and slapped; she felt impervious to any further shame. She clambered out of bed as rapidly as possible and brushed past Lorelei's furry coat, feeling its owner recoil from her in turn.

At least I can still say I've never been spat on, she thought as she proceeded, left eye watering, to vomit up the better part of the evening's excellent dinner. In a short space of time the rest would be disgorged. There wasn't much point at this juncture, but she grabbed two towels to cover herself.

Tom's cock knocked into her as they collided in the entrance to the narrow bathroom. He groaned. 'Get out of the bloody *way*, Beatrice!' He looks quite different with almost no hair on top, Viv thought distractedly, even though the rugged sideburns are intact. She heard him lock himself inside.

While she would be able to recall this blood-curdling sequence in its entirety (and in unwanted clarity of detail), the minutes that immediately ensued were more like a bad dream. The kind of nasty, nightmarish episode in which you are naked in the company of two expensively dressed people who have an exceptionally low opinion of you, and are not troubling to hide it.

Tom still hadn't emerged from the bathroom when she stumbled out of the apartment into the street. And with a mixture of luck and desperation she must have managed to locate the small hotel where she and Geoff had stayed, because she woke up in one of their rooms next morning.

Not that she'd slept much. A sick headache, nausea and sundry aches and pains saw to that. In the long reaches of the night she felt her subconscious might be trying to say something. If nothing is at stake, she thought it was trying to say, what exactly is the point?

Before leaving the hotel the next morning she plastered make-up on her injuries. Her face was swollen. She had a black eye and some light bruising on the bridge of the nose. It must be whiplash. She could just make out the shadow of a palm print on her right cheek.

Geoff is out playing croquet when she arrives home. Eliza has joined the club as a beginner. When they come in they are keen to hear all about Paris. 'How *was* it?' Eliza asks. She looks fresh-faced and pretty. Paris sounds *so* divine. She's simply busting to go.

Both women glance at Geoff, who is filling the jug. 'Oh, Paris was delectable,' says Viv coolly. Her face feels stiff and sore. Geoff thought she was staying for two nights – was Nerida called back for an emergency? This has happened before.

What a bummer. You should've stayed on and painted the town red, says Eliza. Shouldn't she, Geoff?

Viv's husband looks at her more closely. 'Are you all right, sweetie pie? You seem rather peaky. In fact, a bit pale and wan.'

Eliza laughs. *Wan?* Wan monster hangover, more likely. Double bummer! She hopes Viv at least had *wan* scrummy French dinner to make it all worthwhile! Viv feels her gorge rising yet again. She mumbles an excuse and heads for the en-suite bathroom. It has now been renovated, and is freshly sparkling. Rather like Eliza, she thinks sourly.

'I decided not to stay on for the optional second. It was just a one-night stand,' she tells Martin Glover. 'And not even quite that, to be scrupulously honest.'

Anything go particularly pear-shaped?

Everything, really. She and the Rev were basically incompatible, you know how it is, and she should have known better because she already knew how it was before she went. Their politics were violently opposed, among other things. She'd developed a terrible stomach upset.

Not that he's a Reverend, by the way, that's his twin Bruder. Tom is actually an MP called Tim Daunt. Viv had glimpsed a House of Commons pass, or something of that nature, as she scrabbled around under Tim's parents-in-law's well-shod feet, endeavouring to retrieve her garments.

'Incidentally, Martin, he wasn't in the *least* like Bob Mitchum, either.'

Martin says he's sorry about that, but it's one of those things. He'll try not to make comparisons in future. They can be invidious. Or is it odious? Human interactions are at bottom unknowable, aren't they?

'You can say that again. Invidious, odious, and unknowable at bottom. Covers all bases.'

Well, he says, I don't think Mr Davidson looks like anyone except himself.

Leary had texted Viv in the train. He'd be back in the land of the halfway living the day after tomorrow. Viv read this with a feeling of exhaustion.

23

INTER-GENERATIONAL DIALOGUES

Julia has been having an early evening drink in a cosy room. She has chosen a red-wine spritzer, unusually, but since she's the one doing the pouring it comprises mainly soda water with a dash for colour and flavour.

Her companion is Bridie Waterstreet, who as yet has no need to think of her figure and is polishing off a second glass of full-strength red. Bridie is the strawberry-blonde Irish soprano playing Lisa, the Countess's granddaughter.

They have three scenes together, fairly brief encounters in terms of time. But Julia is well aware of her position as a role model, and is happy to act as a mentor and confidante. As a diva in the last years of a stellar career, Julia Jefferies is held in high esteem (bordering on awe, in some cases) by those just embarking on theirs. Especially aspirational young sopranos.

It's easy to like Bridie, who is sweet, unaffected and reverential, almost (but not quite, since this is a generous arc) to a fault. She is also very pretty, which Julia has noticed Emils Liepins also observing. Julia doesn't resent this. It would be exceedingly foolish to do that, as well as pointless, and she is far too experienced and worldly to waste her emotional energy on matters she can do nothing about.

Besides, such concerns are effectively irrelevant. She has other things, as Viv might say (although not in this context), on the back burner.

Julia has invited Bridie to her apartment for a drink. They are seated side by side on a sofa in front of the fire – gas with look-alike coals, so realistic that Bridie, admiring everything, the pictures, the furniture – thought at first it was real. Their drinks, olives and quickly assembled smoked salmon and pesto on crispy pita bites (which will double as Julia's supper) are set out on a coffee table in front of them. The pale silk curtains are drawn. The softly glowing atmosphere is conducive to relaxed confidences.

They have covered Bridie's impressive career path. Where she has already been, and where her teacher would like her to go. Julia's views have been sought, respectfully, and received with deference. And now they are discussing names.

Names, for singers as well as actors, have an importance that is not to be brushed aside. Who knew whether Anna Maria Kalogeropoulou or Frances Gumm would have gone as far as Maria Callas or Judy Garland? Would Norma Jeane Mortenson ever have scaled the heights of Marilyn Monroe?

The subject came up because Bridie has confided dissatisfaction with her birth name. Too late to change it now, isn't it, Julia? And anyway, she says charmingly, it would *mortify* her parents. But – Bridie Waterstreet. It sounds so prosaic. So *unoperatic*, she says in her light, delightful brogue. It's like a road beside a river. Or a blowzy character in Dickens.

Bridie Waterstreet is a perfectly good name, Julia interpolates firmly. It is pictorial, with a rhythm and lilt – like your voice, Bridie – which is what you want as a singer. Not only is it unusual – unusual *without* being peculiar, Julia stresses – it lodges in the mind, and you want that.

It's too late to change it anyway. You are well on your way now, and your public already knows you as Bridie. Julia knows that the phrases *well on your way*, and in particular *your public*, have an importance that far outweighs their component parts. Bridie does not miss them.

'Had *I* been christened Bridie Waterstreet,' Julia says, 'I wouldn't have changed my name.'

Bridie turns to look at Julia. Her eyes widen. 'Did you ...'

'I did, as it so happens, very early on. I went from June Jeffs to Julia Jefferies at the suggestion of my first singing teacher in Melbourne. She thought June was naff, and she didn't like two single syllables together. Julia Jeffs wasn't much better, so we lengthened them both.'

Julia's eyes have an absent look. 'Funny how you almost forget things like that. It was such a big deal at the time, yet now I hardly ever think of it. A name evolves into its own symbol, in a way, doesn't it? It becomes so familiar over the course of a career that you could say it becomes an entity in itself. My brother still sometimes calls me June.' She smiles. 'In unguarded moments.'

She turns to her young colleague. 'But she was right, my teacher, don't you think, when she said that Julia Jefferies was more harmonious?'

'Oh yes,' Bridie is eager to agree. 'She was. Definitely.'

Julia steers the conversation towards another area, which will bring her within spitting distance of the topic she intends to cover tonight. Towards the opera and Bridie's feelings about making her debut at the Royal Opera House. Her excitement is contained, in Julia's presence, because she is a professional and wishes to behave like a composed young woman with some experience behind her.

There is a fine line between confidence and anxiety, as Julia recalls very well. She made her own debut there at twenty-six, a year younger than Bridie, with a now-legendary director. And Emils Liepins, down the line, has a very fair chance of becoming another.

She diverts Bridie by musing over the difference between hetero and homosexual directors. Homosexuals can perhaps have more empathy, heteros more intuition. But some combine both qualities. Emils, for instance, falls into this category …

Unprompted, Bridie feels secure enough to share some of Emils' suggestions. What he has told her she needs to focus on and bring out in her role. She hasn't had many comparisons yet, she knows that, but she hasn't worked with a director who's anything like him before.

He's such an enthusiast, Bridie says, with a matter-of-fact frown. He has an overview that's quite, you know, *visionary?* And yet he's so kind of unpretentious and *normal.* You know – that hair. And those clothes! Do you find that, Julia? You must have worked with hundreds of directors.

Julia sees through the attempts at level-headed detachment. She has discerned that Bridie is in a state of nascent hero-worship, a condition Julia knows is not too far removed from falling head over heels. The memory of this condition, its intoxication – and the reckless extremes it can trigger – has never left her. At the moment (for other reasons that are accelerating by the day) this is in the forefront of Julia's mind.

She agrees that their young director is quite something. She contrives to remark, subtly and without emphasis (in fact, to remark almost in passing) that Emils is in the early stages of a brilliant career that will take him all over the world and place in his path innumerable temptations. To emphasise gently that among his tasks as a director is to draw the best performances out of his principals. Every one of them, whatever their age, the older woman smiles. And the capacity to enthuse and to beguile is a huge help in this endeavour.

Julia talks a little about directors she has known. She touches on what she calls the art of *intellectual seduction,* possessed by the top practitioners, and prosecuted upon their targets. This, she tells Bridie, is world's best practice. It can't be taught. It's either innate, or it doesn't happen.

All the best directors have it, in her experience. Almost universally. And sometimes, the ones you would least expect. Ones that might seem at first so – Julia shrugs, with evident disbelief – *ordinary*.

'That ability to enthral and captivate. It can bowl you over, you know,' she says pensively, to the air. 'Emils has it, of course.' She turns to her companion, and confides with a sigh, 'I have felt it myself.'

She is aware that the young woman sitting next to her is somewhat bowled over to hear this but far too polite to express it. Seduction, even if only of an intellectual nature, is not something she will have associated with Julia.

'Oh, yes, Bridie,' were it not for the name, you might have thought Julia was talking to herself, 'I have imagined myself in love countless times.' Julia raises her shining, well-coiffed head. 'Reciprocally, of *course*, and that is their genius. Later, when the season comes to an end and everyone disperses to the far corners of the globe, I've had to come back down to earth.'

She laughs wryly. 'Sometimes with a thud. And I've realised the mutual enchantment was just another part of the production. A very lovely part, but a mirage.'

Bridie pushes her long, shining hair behind her shoulders. On her best behaviour, she has nodded and listened to all this with an earnest expression. However, her role model knows only too well that understanding the reasons for certain phenomena only goes so far.

I've done my level best to spell it out, Julia tells herself. Where the oblivious young are concerned, one is powerless beyond a certain point. If their minds are set on a certain course, nothing anyone can say will deter them. Their minds? Who do I think I'm kidding? It has nothing to do with their minds. As I should know better than anyone. The insecure, almost *deranged* extremes it can trigger...

Within easy reach on the coffee table are books and magazines in two well organised piles. On top of one is a catalogue from the current show at the Max Jeffs Gallery in Melbourne. Julia points it out.

'My brother's art gallery,' she says. 'He didn't change his name, of course. No need. Max Jeffs is also two single syllables, but we all thought that on him it sounded just fine. What do *you* think?'

'Oh, I agree,' says Bridie. 'I think it sounds absolutely fine. It's an authoritative name for an art dealer.' This answer, she is pleased to see, receives Julia's tick of approval.

Triple G, a very different type of art gallery, is Viv's midday destination this Tuesday. At Shoreditch's Galerie Galleria Gallery, three emerging artists – a collage photographer, a painter, and a sculptor who works with found objects – are delivering their work today for the group show that opens on Friday at 6pm. Among them is Daisy Mayberry, the maverick painter of miniature portraits, who has suggested that her mother meet her for lunch after she has unloaded her paintings.

Her mother discovers on arrival that Daisy has branched out recently into what she and the gallery director hope may prove to be a more lucrative field. There are four paintings of male nudes, front on, larger than her usual portraits and similarly hyper-realist.

'Adrian's suggestion, I don't need to tell you,' Daisy grins. 'You don't like them, do you? Dad will *hate* them.'

'It's *certainly* not that I don't like them,' Viv says stoutly. She is trying to suppress an unwanted flashback. 'It's just that they're – well, rather breathtaking. They make quite a statement.' They laugh.

The gallery is made up of three rooms, white windowless cubes, identical and intersecting. The plain white walls will show off Daisy's twelve brilliantly coloured pictures effectively. Her cube is the middle one. When Viv arrived, Daisy, in distressed grey dungarees that managed to look stylish, was walking round it with another woman. They were holding up her pictures at differing heights on the walls. Some to be hung with a yard of space around them, the nudes to be grouped together for greater impact.

'There won't be a hope in hell of talking at the opening, Mum,' Daisy is saying. 'It'll be a bunfight. That's if you can bear to endure it, of course,' she adds. They have repaired to an organic cafe across the road. Salads containing a number of esoteric ingredients have been ordered.

Daisy's opening gambit was unexpected and has Viv full of anticipation. She tries not to imbue it with too much significance so as not to meet with a sledgehammer of disappointment. But Daisy did refer to *talking*. Viv makes a mental note: be sensible, do not barge in, allow Daisy to introduce any sensitive subject. Which seems to include a wide range of possibilities.

'Oh, of course I'm coming, darling. You couldn't pay me to stay away.' The invitation to the opening is in a prominent spot on the mantelpiece at West Hampstead. 'Dad will certainly want to come too.'

'His *bête noire* will be there, remember.' Daisy pulls a satirical face. 'So, how's he been? Has he mellowed at all about anything, or is that a pigs-might-fly question? Or wouldn't you know?'

'Well ...' This was expected, but Viv is still unsure how to reply. 'He's – I'm sure he'll get used to things eventually.' However, she's not at all sure he will and neither, she imagines, is his daughter. She wants to ask a follow-up question, but the area is strewn with pitfalls.

'I suppose he can come as long as he doesn't make a scene. Although there'll be such a scrum no one would notice anyway.' Daisy seems cheerful on the surface, but her mother senses she has something on her mind.

Daisy takes a sip of coconut water. 'Did Judith tell you I took Adrian down to see her at the weekend?' Judith dislikes words like *granny*, which denote a precise, or limiting, relationship.

She glances at her mother. A sidelong glance. This is a safe topic, Viv would think, or safe-*ish*, and does enable smooth entry into an area that may be more slippery. Sure enough, Judith had mentioned Daisy and Adrian's visit yesterday, on the phone.

Viv smiles. 'Adrian won her over. She found him extremely engaging. As you'd expect. She also thought his *genes* – I don't mean denim – were sound. In terms of IQ and EQ. And his level of attractiveness, of course.' This level being of paramount interest to Daisy's grandmother. Judith had also been of the opinion that gayness was not, in the main, transferable genetically, but Viv thinks it wiser not to say this.

She is surprised that Daisy doesn't make a follow-up comment. She becomes conscious that her daughter is watching her through lowered lashes. This is unusual in itself, because Daisy is not a guarded person. She's habitually upfront. But her mother, who thinks (possibly erroneously) that she can read her like the proverbial book, is in no doubt that she is being furtively observed. Assessed, almost.

As it turns out, it's more of a reassessment. Viv is on the point of filling the lengthening pause when Daisy says, with a studied casualness that is also unlike her, 'So how's it going with the dating agency, Mum? Have you met anyone yet?'

Viv's glass (iced mango green tea) had been en route to her lips. She puts it down on the table, more heavily than she intended.

'Judith said she thought I ought to know.' Daisy's eyebrows have gone skywards. 'Don't have a fit, Adrian wasn't in the room. He'd gone out for takeaway. That was unusually *tactful* of the old girl, considering, wasn't it?'

Viv gropes for words, but finds she is at a loss for them. If ever a woman were honest to a fault, yet brimful of ingenuous guile …

'No doubt she's plotting to tell him next time,' she says grimly.

'Just keep Dad away from her door. Unless –' a wary grin, 'you're planning on telling him anytime soon?'

Viv folds her arms and rocks backwards and forwards.

'Come on, Mum, I don't disapprove. Not in the *least*, Mum. You're probably doing the right thing. The *sensible* thing. Stop rocking.'

Viv stops, and takes a steadying breath. She knew it wasn't a sensible thing to tell Judith. Telling her, in fact, was a crazy thing to have done. A *stupid* thing. She hears herself sounding heated.

Yeah, well, it's done now, Daisy tells her, in an amused tone that strikes Viv, even in the state she's in, as novel. Not unlike a mother soothing a child.

'Anyhow, what's the latest?' Daisy asks. Gaily, Viv thinks, in the old sense of the word, but in a slightly hectic version of the old sense. 'Judith couldn't remember the details. Except she was adamant you hadn't met Mr Right yet.'

Viv says, 'I suppose you've spoken to Jules, have you?'

Jules was being very cautious and loyal, says Daisy, also cautiously. Three or four intros, she thought, but she didn't think oil had been struck. A TV director sounded promising.

Not *that* cautious and loyal, Viv thinks. But given her divided loyalties, entirely understandable. At least she hadn't mentioned the vicar. A silence falls, in which the small noises of the cafe sound unnaturally loud.

'Are you planning to get divorced, Mum?'

Viv sees that her daughter's expression, which she had thought inscrutable or ambiguous, is the result of a strenuous attempt to show no emotion.

'No, darling, that's really not the plan.'

'So, *why*? I mean – you know, all of a sudden …'

'At my age?'

'Well, yes.' The raised eyebrows, the attempt to be composed and ironic. Viv sees through it now. 'After, you know, Mum, all this time.'

Viv travels back five decades, a journey she has often taken. Her mother has just told her of an affair she is having. *Why*, her daughter had asked. Why didn't she tell her father? The second, unspoken *why* was, in effect, what her own daughter is now asking. And how had the cool-headed, rigorously truthful yet guileful Judith put it? She needed something Vivien's father could not give her.

'Long marriages go through stages,' Viv says, feeling her way. 'I know it must sound bizarre, but the problem is I'm – not getting something that I need. I used to have it, I had it until quite recently, and I've been missing it.'

Daisy's earnest look is not one her mother has witnessed with any frequency. Viv does not and could not know that it is oddly reminiscent of the look on Bridie Waterstreet's face as she listened to her mentor, Julia Jefferies, subtly recommending against an inadvisable affair of the heart. Daisy too is listening earnestly, but like Bridie she is not, perhaps, grasping the picture in its entirety.

'You mean, you're not having sex, Mum.'

Viv detects a resolute effort to embrace the concept not only of having, but of having had. Also of *wanting to have*, an arguably bigger challenge than the rest. She touches her daughter's hand. 'You're being very understanding,' she murmurs. 'These things aren't easy with parents, I know.'

She can tell that Daisy has another question, of the what-was-the-last-straw variety. The question is there, but Daisy may not be happy asking it and may not really want to know the answer. And may be better off not knowing.

Viv would bend over backwards not to bring about a rift between Daisy and her father. Or rather, extend the rift that already exists. She thinks it would be best if Daisy, whose feminist credentials are as staunch as her mother's, is not told exactly what prompted Viv's engagement with the Discretion Agency.

'I just came to realise that the situation was unlikely to change,' she says. 'And I decided to do something about it rather than sit about and do nothing.'

'Well done, Mum. I hope it works out.' Viv sees Daisy hesitate, and reach a reluctant decision. 'Is he – is Dad having an affair?'

Viv had expected this. 'Oddly enough, no. I shouldn't say oddly enough – I just mean I don't think so. Although admittedly he has been spending time with the younger sister of a friend from the sci-fi group. She broke up with her boyfriend and he's been helping her find a flat and a job and so on. But—'

'How young?' Daisy leans forward.

'Early thirties.'

'Jes-us.'

'I know it sounds – but I honestly don't think …'

Daisy breathes in deeply. 'It doesn't sound good, Mum. Quite frankly.'

'No, I know it doesn't.'

'So, what would you do if you fell for someone? Just as a passing thought.'

'I'm not looking for that' – only for a little romance, in passing – 'and I really don't think it's likely to happen. At my age,' she adds, in the unlikely event Daisy hasn't factored this in.

They pause to order coffee and two slices of Middle Eastern lemon and almond cake. Then Daisy further surprises her.

'In a spirit of *quid pro quo*, Mum, we're doing okay and Adrian's passed his tests.'

'He's doing a course?'

'No, Mum. His *tests*. He's as clean as a whistle.'

'Well, that's good news,' Viv says, mostly meaning it. 'But I might ask you the same question. What would *you* do, darling, if you fell for someone?'

Daisy stares at her, rather as if her mother has suddenly become the village idiot. 'What do you think I'd do? I'm a free agent. I'm not *marrying* Adrian.'

'No, but – living with him, or in the same house as him – it won't cramp your style?'

'Of course it won't. I'm as free as a bird, Mum. I'll carry on as normal.'

'I see,' Viv says, quashing doubts.

'He knows that. And the same goes for him.'

'But he's not going to carry on as normal, as free as a bird, while you're – you know, while you're trying to conceive?'

'You got it, Mum, he's going to be entirely faithful to me while that's going on.' A broad grin. 'I told you, this is just a laterally thought out, *interim* solution to the baby question. Or possible solution.'

'Yes, I see,' says her mother again.

'He's great fun, you know. We have loads of laughs; it's like living with your best girlfriend. Except,' a gleam, picked up by Viv, 'it's not *quite* like that. Do you know what I mean?' She clearly thinks her mother doesn't have much of a clue.

'Actually I think I might, just a little,' Viv murmurs. It might resemble, in some respects, the rollicking times she, Geoff and Jules had when they shared Julia's flat. Or, and this is a more uneasy resemblance, when she and Geoff, explosive new lovers, were alone in their room.

Daisy says nonchalantly, 'Don't stress, I'm keeping my eyes peeled for viable alternatives.' She shoots a meaningful look at her mother. 'Just like you are, Mum.'

Viv arrives home to find Geoff and Eliza holed up yet again in the kitchen. She greets Eliza with every appearance of pleasure. Indeed, were it not for a negative cast in the back of her mind, an aggravation she traces directly back to her mother rather than anything else, she thinks she could be quite kindly disposed to her.

Eliza jumps out of her seat and gives Viv an enthusiastic hug. 'Great to see you!' Brilliant timing, because they just found her a flat. *Whoop de do!* A tiny little bolthole, but really quite pretty.

The word bolthole gives rise to another unpleasant memory. 'Light, too, and not far from here,' Eliza continues. Isn't that amazing? If only it weren't four in the afternoon they could be breaking out the champagne.

We might even defy the four o'clock curfew, says Geoff, eyeing Viv gingerly, if we had any on the ice. Which we don't.

What bad management, says Viv, who has resolved to put Paris behind her and wouldn't mind a glass of champagne herself just now. Shall we have some wine instead? What have we got, Geoff? She'd very much like to vent her feelings about her mother's behaviour too, but as this is out of the question she sits down and asks questions about the new flat instead.

Eliza likes white, so they crack open a bottle of Pinot Gris. She is stoked to hear about Daisy's show. What an incredibly talented daughter you both have. She would love to see her work and meet her sometime – would it be possible to gatecrash the opening, or would that be absolutely not done?

What do you think, hon? A swift glance between Geoff and Viv, with Daisy as the complicated subtext. Viv nods. We could probably smuggle you in, Lize, says Geoff.

No need to smuggle, says Viv, briskly, *Lize* will be lost in the crowd anyway. But she's sure Daisy would enjoy meeting her, too. Her airy glance meets a matching one from her husband.

All these exciting things on the horizon, says Eliza. 'Geoff is acting as guarantor on the flat until the new job comes through and I'm solvent at last. Isn't that sweet of him?' She looks at him, not a million miles (had she or anyone present known) from the way Bridie Waterstreet has been looking at Emils Liepins. Viv takes it in with, she is surprised to find, a feeling that is more or less neutral.

The flattering attention of the opposite sex, especially the undivided interest of a youthful acolyte. She can't blame Geoff for lapping it up. Most people would, although Viv thinks she herself might find it tedious after a while. Eliza, with her abundant locks and eager manner, reminds Viv of a silky terrier straining at the leash.

She decides to take her second glass of wine upstairs. 'I'm going to leave you to it. I must go and call my mother.'

'Wow, is your *mother* still—' Eliza stops short.

'Yes, still alive and kicking at ninety-one. Must be hard for you to believe. But people are living so much longer these days.'

'She's in a home, is she?'

'She most certainly is,' smiles Viv. 'Her own home.'

When Judith eventually answers the phone, she sounds all in. 'Are you okay, Mum?'

'Yes, I'm perfectly well, thank you.' This is predictable.

'You sound a bit tired, that's all. Did you have a big day?' A big day, for her mother, might be the bus into Oxford and, less frequently now, a film.

'Whatever makes you think that?' The thin voice is querulous.

'Why don't you have supper and an early night?'

'I'm quite all right, dear, for Pete's sake don't fuss. Was there anything else?'

Viv shelves her conversation plan. Her plan of attack, as it would unwisely have been. It was her fault, anyway. She's had a lifetime to get to know her mother; nothing she does now should surprise her. Judith deals the cards according to her lights and never on impulse. She weighs things up, determines, and only then does she act.

It's just that Judith's particular lights, in the eyes of her daughter, don't conform in many respects to those of others. Her mother's influence makes her aware that this is untidy thinking. *Woolly*, Judith would witheringly call it.

Untidy it may be, and woolly, but Viv has found that codes of ethics that differ markedly from one's own are always hard to handle. Hard to comprehend, even over a lifetime.

She stares at her phone. Her hand hovers over it. Then she puts it away, out of sight, and spreads out her quilt. It's still unfinished, but evolving.

24

LEARY

Viv is standing on the crowded platform at Finchley Road, having let one overloaded train go past. There are delays due to repair work on the line. She is standing here in response to a text from Leary.

Hey B. Any chance of a quick drink, like N.O.W? Bar in Greek St circa 6?

As she peered at it with, she wouldn't pretend otherwise, a certain reluctance, the front door had slammed downstairs. Footsteps, and Eliza's voice. She made a quick decision. *Okay.* She looked at her watch. She had roughly three-quarters of an hour.

Great. I'll be the scary dude in a hoodie. Kidding – boring geek in baseball cap. He gave her the street number and a name: Greek to Me. Viv had grabbed a black top and thrown a coat over the rest of her work gear.

On the packed Tube a young man gives her his seat, something she always has mixed feelings about but is grateful for overall. She performs a cursory operation with lipstick and powder. The next station is Green Park, where she will need to get off and walk or change to the Piccadilly Line. Fast walking will probably be quicker than Tube or bus. Anything to get out of here. The crush in the streets will be more bearable. Bag over shoulder, she marches resolutely up the escalator.

Viv has some misgivings about coming face to face with Leary, but on the plus side a drink will either clear them up or enable a painless getaway. As she exits the station, on impulse, she texts Martin Glover. *Going off to meet Leary for a drink Soho 6. No great expectations. Any advice gratefully accepted.*

The phone rings promptly. 'What sort of advice did you have in mind?'

'Well, I don't know, do I?' she replies. 'That's why I was asking.'

'I don't think it's my place to give you advice, Beatrice.'

'But if it *were* your place, Martin, what advice would you give?'

'If it *were* my place, I'd probably say: do what your instinct tells you. I have great faith in instincts.'

'I'll try to do that but I think my instincts may have seized up. It's freezing.' She had come out without her gloves. She tucks in her scarf and tugs her coat tightly round her. A wind has come up. Nasty, brutish, and attacking in short, savage gusts.

'Are you in the street?'

'Yes. Piccadilly. Along with thousands of fellow sufferers. How did you know?'

'I think what gave it away was all the cars, buses and fire engines screeching and hooting.'

'Okay.'

'Are you warm enough?' he asks.

'Not really. But I should probably trudge off gently into the good night, or I'll be very late. Although the night doesn't seem all that good at the moment.'

'Well, my other advice is to order a hot toddy. Don't—' The traffic is louder than ever. Now there's a deafening ambulance siren.

She shouts. 'What did you say?' She can't hear a thing. But maybe he didn't say a thing, she can't be sure. 'Did you say *don't*?'

'You're only going for a drink, you said.'

'I did, yes.'

'Well. That's all right then, isn't it?'

'Don't *what?*'

'Don't do anything against your best instincts, Beatrice.'

She hurries away, walking extra rapidly to shut out the wind and anything else she doesn't want to let in.

She nearly misses Greek to Me. Apart from the number on the door she wouldn't have known she was there, the nameplate is so discreet. But once inside, she can see through engraved glass doors that it's crowded and buzzing. There's a personable young woman in a reception area taking names. It must be some sort of club.

She gives her name. The receptionist scans up and down the list with the kind of elongated, immaculately painted forefinger Viv could never aspire to. Is it real or stuck on by one of those false-nail salons? She smells of something fashionable, perhaps suede or licorice, reminding Viv that she hasn't any perfume with her.

Whose guest was she again? Funny, she's saying, I can't see you here.

Viv does a mental somersault. 'Sorry. *Sorry* – did I just say I was Vivien Quarry? I must be going bonkers, that's not my name at all. It's my mother's name. I'm Beatrice Taylor. Senior moment.' She rolls her eyes. 'Stupid of me.'

And she's the guest of?

'I'm the guest of Leary – oh God, what *the fuck* is Leary's name? He's in TV, I've got a – a script meeting with him. Actually, Leary's not his real name either. Sorry again, I'm having a complete mental block. Or a total meltdown might be more like it.'

Now the girl is giving her a pitying look. 'It's all right, I've found you. Beatrice Taylor is right here. You're *Laurence Davidson's* guest,' a tinkling laugh, 'for future reference, Beatrice.' And Viv is waved through the glass doors, feeling very foolish.

At least it's warm and welcoming. Lots of etched mirrors, framed cartoons, masses of celebrity photos, comfortable armchairs and sofas. A bar and plenty of people drinking cocktails. It's bigger than it looks, a long room full of nooks and crannies. Viv screws up her eyes, and identifies what looks like a baseball cap on a blurry figure in an alcove with bay windows. She gives a tentative wave, but can't tell whether the figure has seen her or not.

She catches a passing glimpse of herself in an ornate Venetian mirror from early last century. The glass has lots of cracks and worn patches. Her face is pink from the cold and her hair is a mess. She should have dashed into the cloakroom for a quick touch-up.

'Beatrice?' The man in the cap has lurched into focus. He jumps out of his armchair. A middle-aged white man, in a black leather jacket and jeans. Tallish, lean, wire-rimmed spectacles. He exudes a harassed sort of energy, as Viv had anticipated. He shakes her hand vigorously, and in a seamless move plants a kiss on her icy cheek.

'Guess I can take off my ID now.' He whips off the cap to reveal thinning sandy hair standing on end. It looks wiry, like the rest of him. 'Hey, you look like you're totally knackered like me and you're frozen solid.'

He gives the chair opposite him a hospitable pat and hangs her coat on a Victorian hat stand in front of the window. It wouldn't look out of place in Julia's flat. Between their chairs is a table with a canvas satchel lying on it; his script bag, Viv assumes.

'I tried for a seat in front of a fire,' he scans the room, 'but they were all taken. Bribery, threats, intimidation – nothing worked. What are all these guys *doing* here? Why aren't they still in the office? You have to ask yourself these searching questions, right?'

His attention, jokey and restless, switches to her. 'This is a searching look. Can I call you Bea?' He continues without pause. 'They do New York-style cocktails here.' He indicates his over-sized glass. 'The real deal, none of your cheapskate London thimbles. Wanna try my martini? Shaken not stirred. Award-winning Aussie barman Adam, best in town. What'll you have? You name it, he'll do it.'

It feels like a major decision, one Viv feels incapable of making just now. 'I'll have what you're having. Or, Leary, wait—' He has sprung to his feet. 'Better still, a hot toddy.'

He shakes his head. 'Not possible. This is a strict no-toddy zone. Pain of severe penalties. But one of Adam's mind-blowing martinis'll warm you up. What do they say? Warm the cockles. Know where they're located, Bea?'

'Somewhere in the heart, I believe.'

'Okay! Very appropriate for our purposes, right? Vodka or gin? Olive or twist?'

'Uh – gin. With a twist. Please.'

'Hendrick's, Bombay Sapphire, or they have these great new craft—'

'Surprise me,' she murmurs, smiling. She sinks into the arm-chair and is strongly tempted to close her eyes. Leary has vanished. Does he have a hyperactive disorder? Perhaps this is a requirement for directing armies of people in TV dramas. He's already exchang-ing badinage with the barman.

She locates the ladies, heads for it and attends to her hair. She needs another visit to Ramona. And it's only a matter of days since she was hit by a hairpiece and had her face slapped. The whiplash has gone, and the black eye, but there's still a faint shadow on the cheek.

She applies more powder but the result looks cakey and has to be rubbed off with a damp tissue. She tells herself she must be more grown-up and organised. Must keep foundation in my bag for just this sort of emergency. And a travel-sized perfume. Not that this encounter is an emergency, it's more of a – she realises she was about to think, a nuisance. It's more of a – *distraction*. But a distraction from what?

Leary's back waiting for her, and on his feet again. He thought she'd stood him up, for a moment there. Written him off as a crap date. He was getting all geared up to skol her martini and stagger outta there. Then – *phew!* – he saw her coat.

He smiles. 'Hey, you fixed your hair.' Rather a sweet smile, she has to admit.

'Insofar as it's fixable,' she says. 'My hair is …' what was Ramona's word? 'It has a mind of its own.'

'Don't knock it when you've got it. I always wanted an afro. My feminine side. Shoulda been more of that, my wife used to say. When we were still speaking.'

All the darting back and forth has prompted him to remove his jacket, revealing a check lumberjack shirt, flannel, with a rather stylish black wool waistcoat. He's very fit-looking. One of those men with corded muscles whose slight build is deceptive. High metabolic rate. His canvas bag jogs Viv's memory.

'Oh, Leary – I had to tell the young woman on the door we were having a script meeting. Just in case she mentions it.'

'Is that right? A script meeting, huh? Why, did she give you the third degree?'

'I'm afraid I couldn't – summon up your surname, in the heat of the moment. Well – in the bitterly cold moment. I had to bluff my way in.'

He looks her up and down. 'I'd pass you as a screenwriter, Bea. You could've said we were checking each other out for – what does Discretion Agency say? For *discreet* purposes.'

'I didn't want to shock her.'

He laughs. 'But she found your name in the end, right?'

'Yes – she just couldn't find it,' a disingenuous smile, 'initially.'

'So, what's the show we're having a meeting about? In case she grills us separately. Let's say it's a *Dangerous Liaisons* remake. Easy to remember if we're put on the spot. So, Bea – tell me about yourself, as they say in speed dating. Ever tried speed dating?'

'Lordy, no.'

'Good move. Sheesh, it's crazy. So fast you're moved on before you get to first base. First conversational base. But you read my ravings?'

'Your ...'

'Blog. My blog.'

'Oh yes.'

'What do you say? Biggest crock of shit since Dianetics?'

'I like all the skirmishes with the bearded nerds. But I didn't read every word,' Viv says. 'I didn't have enough of a clear week stretching ahead.'

He shakes his head. 'We're crazy-busy people, right? Time-poor, rich in golden dreams. More on them later, if time. But you know a bit about me and I know nothing much about you, except you're an ace quilter. See, I'm a glass-half-full kinda guy. They said you used to be in publishing, back in the day. How much fun was that?'

They must mean Martin. She tells Leary some anecdotes, edited for a man who, it's not hard to see, has a short attention span. Famous literary feuds. Authorial brushes with plagiarism and other iniquitous practices.

This strikes a chord. Iniquitous practices? Tell him about it. Except whatever she can tell him about authors has nothing on producers. Insanity, it's a lifestyle choice. Like when they're also financing the show and want to direct it instead of you. And rewrite the story and change the ending. More of that later, time permitting. He's got a mountain of script notes to do tonight.

On cue, his mobile rings. It's in a leather case hanging off his belt. He listens, raps out a reply Viv can't follow.

'Sorry, Bea. I should be good and turn it off, right?' He doesn't, however. So, he says, don't they say the books biz is in deep shit? Self-publishing's the way to go. Bypass the middlemen, ditch those ruthless exploiters of struggling writers. A grin. He's sure she wasn't one of those jerks.

He leans forward and clinks her glass. 'Enough shop talk already. Time to put our cards on the table. What's it all about, Bea? What are we doing here?'

'You mean, besides talking shop and enjoying these ace marti-nis? Is there something more pressing we ought to be doing?' She's nearly halfway through her drink and feeling more kindly disposed to a situation that is not too onerous, aside from being something of a conversational battery.

Leary has pale eyebrows, pale reddish skin and sharp features. If she had to pick an animal it would be a fox. Yasmin's jumpy red fox in Joy's stories, with a pointed, questioning nose, sniffing the air. What would she remind him of? Jules once told her she was like a koala. A dazed and confused one, presumably. Up a gum tree.

She is aware of being dissected by a pair of narrow, inquisitive eyes of a yellow shade of green. Leary is saying, with a shake of the head, 'I'm being up-front here because time's not on our side. The old wingèd chariot's hurrying by. Isn't that right, Beatrice?'

'Do you mean in terms of our lifespan?' Or does he want to leave already? 'Can't we find time to finish our drinks?' She sees he's fin-ished his. 'But if it's not on your side, there's not much anyone can do about it. Please don't let me keep you from—'

He interrupts. 'Sorry Bea, I'm a suitable case for treatment, you're not the first to tell me that. I guess what I'm looking to get from you is a progress report. We're here to size each other up, right?'

No point in arguing with that.

'The puppet-master at the agency thought we might get on. So, what do *we* think? Are we getting on yet?'

Was that what Martin thought, that they would get on? 'Must I answer that right now, Leary? Are there dire consequences if I need to mull it over?'

'I'm too impatient, is that what you're saying?'

'Well, aren't these questions a bit premature? I'm not sure you're really –' what was it Daisy used say about Marco? 'in the *moment*, here—'

He stalls her with a hand. 'Yeah, yeah, okay. Moving actors around is what I do, Bea. I get people to *do* stuff. Solve problems, take shortcuts.' The sweet smile again. 'I guess I forget how to have a regular conversation and impersonate a halfway normal person. How about you ask the questions for a bit?'

Viv moves her chair back a little. Unobtrusively, she hopes. Leary's not a big man, but he takes up more personal space than most. Her own feels as if it's being systematically – but not irresistibly – invaded.

'We've only been here – what,' she looks at her watch, 'half an hour? Far too soon to have formulated a non-superficial decision. Can we put it on the back burner? You could tell me about this pilot you're doing.' That's several sentences in succession, she thinks. Not bad going.

He surprises her by springing from his chair, saying there's one decision that does have to be made. They need refills. Two's his limit. Guard the chair. He puts his bag on it. He's wearing black trainers with a silver and blue trim.

Viv gets up. 'Please let me—' But he's on his way.

The concept of impersonating a halfway normal person brings her husband to mind. In relation to Leary, Geoff's familiarity is reassuring. I've known him for so long. And I still live with him ...

She pulls out her phone to text Geoff, then remembers the sci-fi gang are going to the original *Blade Runner*. At the NFT, coincidentally. The director's cut, she thinks he said, which was longer than the released version.

This might interest Leary. Take his mind off analysing whether or not they're getting on, something on which she has no view right this minute. Or not one she can readily discern. No real interest either? She shelves this thought as he returns with two brimming martinis. Not a drop spilled, he says, how's that for steady hands?

Blade Runner? Brilliant movie. Seminal. He can't believe she never saw it. He thought everyone ingested it with their mother's milk, like *The Sound of Music*. Viv says she's never seen that either. Leary puts his hands over his ears.

'It's not the director's cut they're showing tonight,' he says, 'it's the *final* cut. Big difference, Bea. It's the only version Ridley Scott had complete control over. Issued fifteen years after the director's cut, ten years after the international cut that followed the theatrical cut that came after the work print.'

'I had no idea.'

'Uh-huh. You'll be examined on this. If you don't pass you'll be kept in. See how dudes who need a life can make a lifetime study of this movie?'

Up to a point, Viv says. She watches the couple nearest to them, two smartly dressed young people who can't keep their hands off each other, while Leary tells her why Ridley hadn't had complete control of the director's cut in spite of being the director.

Leary is drumming his fingers on the table. She realises a little late that his recital has come to an end. 'Sorry,' she says, 'I think I must have gone into a bit of a dream.'

Leary draws a cartoon face on the table with his index finger. His nails are blunt and bitten, unlike those of the receptionist. The face has a downcast mouth.

'My apology emoji, Bea. I've been known to hypnotise people into submission. An involuntary reflex. My therapist's always telling me it can drive people nuts. Women in particular it can drive really nuts. The upside is, it can be treated, she says.'

'No, I'm sure it's a healthy reaction to str—'

'To multi-tasking's what you were going to say, right?' A grin. 'Like watching *Network* to recover from off-their-faces who want to helm your show for you. Instead of shooting yourself dead on camera like Peter Finch.' She did see *Network*?

Yes, and she can see how watching it might work to sublimate fury and frustration.

'Good one.' Leary is wearing a watch that may be the biggest (and ugliest) she has ever seen. He glances at it. 'Well, at least you'll be able to set George straight.'

George? She casts around.

'Your husband, Bea. Remember him? Set him straight about the movie. That's if you're still speaking. Do you still speak?'

George Orwell, of course. Leary doesn't need to know his surname, does he? Should it be George Taylor? 'Well, we do, but we're not – not close.'

'Still sleeping in the same bed?'

Where this might once have been considered private, she supposes it's not anymore. Not under these circumstances. 'Yes, but—'

'No sex, right?'

Unquestionably, she would once have considered this privileged information. She shakes her head.

'Sorry to be nosy. Need-to-know basis, I guess. You're looking for a physical relationship, sex with no strings, right? Like, how often do you envision? Once a week?'

'Well, uh – I hadn't really thought …' Is it refreshing, Leary's directness? It's not entirely off-putting, in a strange sort of way.

'You *hadn't?*' A look of disbelief.

'Not quite that far, no.' Better think now. 'Once a week sounds about right.'

She's reminded of her interview with Martin. How it removed the burden of the intimate from the personal. But shouldn't *this* conversation be on a more intimate basis, since I'm having it with someone I might actually—

'And where do you envision it?'

'Where?'

'If it was with *me*, say.' The amused look again. 'Would you want to go to a hotel, or is my place okay? Assuming yours is out of bounds. George is likely to show up, right? I'm guessing he wouldn't be too thrilled to meet me. Or am I wrong there?' He regards her with his head tilted and a pixie-like expression.

'No, you're right there, he wouldn't.' Viv feels the conversation getting away from her. Leaving her behind, leaving her somewhere else entirely. 'Where do you live, Leary?'

'Bachelor pad in Clerkenwell. My wife couldn't care less if she saw five women in bed with me, but the family's in Dover so it's quite safe.'

Viv tries to catch up. 'I see.'

'You've met other guys from the agency, right? Does your husband know what you're doing? Does he know you're *here*?'

This is something Viv has been thinking about lately, fairly long and hard. 'He doesn't, no. But I probably ought to tell him, soon ...' These are weighty matters.

'Isn't he gonna want to know how you're so knowledgeable about *Blade Runner* all of a sudden?' He laughs. She joins in, uneasily.

Another sudden change of subject. Studies show it's women who routinely make the decisions about dating, did she know that? It's women who decide if there's going to *be* a second date.

Viv finds this dubious. She'd have thought it was a joint decision.

'Nope. Wrong. Majority of young women decide within ten seconds of first meeting on the basis of chemistry and don't change their minds.'

'You're talking about *young* women? That may well be different ...'

He grins. 'Your call, Bea. Still too soon to formulate a non-superficial response? We could toss a coin?'

'How about we just go away and think about it?'

'Go away and *think* about it?' The fingers are drumming again. That's not what directors like to do, she can tell.

'You think about it, and then decide if you want to follow it up. It's not some arcane tribal ritual,' Viv says. Reasonably, she thinks. 'It may not be what you're accustomed to doing, but it's what centuries of cultural conditioning and ingrained Anglo-Saxon reserve have instilled.'

'I'm all for the arcane tribal instinct, Bea. Beats dancing round each other with endless drinks and dinners, right?'

Instinct. Do what it tells you. Even if Leary reminds me of a fox, he does have a sense of humour, a reasonably G one, and I suppose he's not unattractive, in a way. Is that enough to—

'Bea! Are you in a trance here? Have I done you in?'

What is my best instinct telling me? 'We've only had one meeting so far,' she says. 'That's not much, is it? Drinks and dinners don't have to be *endless.* Can't we just – see what happens?'

He throws up his hands. 'We both know what we're looking for, right? Someone we quite like the look of, not a lame brain, who's available, no strings, who may turn out to be compatible. So, let's make a decision here. Do we take things any further?'

'Could we discuss it over a follow-up meeting?'

'I thought we already did the discussing *and* the meeting.' He shakes his head. 'There's a good script in here, Bea. We're grown-ups, right?'

Their expressions of good-humoured exasperation, Viv thinks, must be nearly identical. She sails in. 'Since we're being so up-front, Leary: why aren't you looking for someone younger?'

'Someone *younger?*' A rueful look. 'Why am I not like other guys, is that what you're saying?' Yeah, well. It hadn't worked for him, okay? So, he told the agency he was more open. Same way she did, he guesses.

Maybe not quite the same way.

'Look, Bea,' he says. 'We've done Act One. Act Two, we risk a tryout. Act Three, worst scenario, you quit the disaster movie. Kinda like *The Truman Show.* Tell me you saw that.'

That and *The Purple Rose of Cairo,* what's more, where she steps out of the screen. See, I'm not a complete ignoramus, Viv says.

'So, we head off into the sunset with no game plan under our belt, is that it?'

At least he doesn't seem resentful. He helps her into her coat. On their way out, the young woman on the door smiles and hopes they had a good meeting. Inconclusive, Leary tells her. The script may have potential. It just needs writing.

We're going away and thinking about it, Viv adds. Has she been a bit craven over this? As he holds the door open against the icy blast, Leary says, 'Shall we road test a kiss?'

Viv thinks she has never been asked that, or not in such a way. The kiss is more prolonged than casual, and they stand in the street pressed tightly against each other. It's the first such kiss she can remember having for many years. Tom – *Tim* – Daunt wasn't really into long kissing. And George and I – *Geoff* and I stopped sharing kisses of that kind a very long time ago.

Geoff won't be back for hours, and Viv doesn't feel like going home to an empty house. Instead, she ducks out of the cold into a welcoming little trattoria. Candles and pink tablecloths. A little too reminiscent of another restaurant in the Marais? She shrugs off this thought as she is led by a hospitable waiter to a small corner table.

She orders a glass of vermentino from Sardinia, dons her reading glasses and studies the menu. She asks for a tricolore salad followed by penne Siciliano, places her book on the table with a candle on each side, and puts her phone next to it. Then she sits back to evaluate.

What was missing from the encounter with Leary, she decides, was any element of excitement. Even before she'd met him, shouldn't there have been something? A certain frisson at the prospect?

And then, the kiss. It was – how was it? Experimental. Nice, but inconclusive. Nice, but not *that* nice. Not an immune-system booster. There was no *romance* about the whole process. But then, she tells herself, romance is a notoriously woolly concept. When it's absent it's just that: formless. Whereas when it's there you know all about it, rather like love. You can identify and describe it with delight.

Am I wanting the impossible from an arrangement such as this, which by its nature is the antithesis of romantic? Could romance ever develop from such a negative base? Or is that what it does all the time?

It's quite unreasonable even to be thinking in such a fashion, under the circumstances. She's certain that Leary, for example, would not be thinking along anything like these lines. The first course has arrived, and Viv opens her book. Instead of turning the page she eyes her phone. Should she send a short bulletin?

Without giving this impulse time to cohere into an objection, she texts: *Had two large drinks. Want interim report?* She's not expecting an answer necessarily, but one flies right back. *Do you want a chat?*

She calls back, right away. She's not on the street again, is she? Martin asks immediately.

'No, I hived off the street into a little bistro. They were two of the biggest martinis you ever saw. Biggest and most dangerous.'

'But you got away,' Martin says.

'Leary revealed the barman was the best in London.'

Martin says he could do with a dangerous martini right now. What's stopping him? He says the absence of key ingredients, such as gin or vermouth, is stopping him. He'll have another glass of claret instead.

They reawakened a sybaritic instinct, she says. Always there, but latent. 'I know how you like your instincts.'

They should be let out on occasion, Martin thinks. One wouldn't want them to atrophy.

One would not. Have mine atrophied lately? Perhaps a touch, Viv says, to be honest. What is the state of yours?

Not the healthiest they've ever been. Although he'd hesitate to say they've withered away entirely.

'I daresay they're just waiting to be reactivated.' Viv says she hasn't gone home yet because – well, partly because George is at the movies with friends. Did she say George? She meant Geoff. She tells Martin about the confusion over her alias. 'And then I topped it by not being able to remember Leary's surname.'

'It sounds like you had a nice time with him.'

She considers. The drinks were nice, definitely. And he was nice too – if a trifle souped up. A trifle? 'I think he has a manic streak, Martin. I made the mistake of mentioning *Blade Runner*, the film George is going to, and I couldn't stop him. It was as if he'd been injected with a truth drug and it all came pouring out.'

Leary had an exhausting effect. She realised she was faint with hunger after she left the club. That was when she was seduced by welcoming lights and people eating things, and was lured inside.

'A better outcome than seduced and abandoned.'

'Yes, and with better food.'

What was she having?

The main course has arrived. She describes it. 'Sorry, I'm probably interrupting your dinner. You should have told me to desist from this inane chatter.'

He says she's not interrupting anything. He hasn't started yet.

So, what's he going to have?

Steak and kidney pie.

'Really? Ambitious. Leftovers, or is it your turn to cook?'

Her imagination, or was there a hesitation? 'I'm on my own. It's heating up in the oven. In fact –' she hears something in the background, 'there's the buzzer. Signal to take it out.'

'I can eat pasta with a fork. But I should probably let you—'

No, it's all right, once he's extricated the dish he can eat it with a fork as well. She can carry on with the inanity while he gets it out of the oven.

Viv toils over what is still in her mind. 'Martin, tell me this. Do you think *romance* has any place here? I mean, you must have had a lot of experience observing people in all kinds of permutations. In your opinion, can it start up from nothing? I mean, if there's not a skerrick of rapport, after a certain point? Don't forget the oven gloves.'

There is a lengthy pause. She imagines him lifting out a pie and putting it on the kitchen table, with mustard and a pepper grinder standing by.

'Did you or your wife make the pie?'

'It's a bought one. Quite good, though.' Another pause as she pictures him dishing out a portion. 'You were asking about romance.' She nods into the phone. 'Tricky, isn't it? Theoretically, of course, it has to be possible for it to start up from nothing.'

'It's the chicken and egg, isn't it? Leary's the kind of person who wants instant solutions. Or in their absence, a rapid advance towards a resolution situation.'

'That's a common male trait, one is led to believe.'

'Massively enlarged in film directors, I daresay. All those problems swarming round, that you have to solve instantly and get out of the way.' She hears something crunchy. 'Is it nice, the pie? I hope you're having some greens with it.'

It's nice, yes, and he made a salad. Returning to the romance question, was this something Viv had decided she wanted?

Well. Viv knows she hadn't *said* she wanted it. Not initially. And besides, it was probably unrealistic to expect ...

Another pause, while they continue eating.

'Still on the problem of absent romance,' he says, sounding unusually tentative.

'Yes?' she prompts.

'One wouldn't want to say it could never start from scratch.'

'No, one wouldn't. On the other hand ...'

'On the other hand, if there's not a skerrick by a certain point, maybe the odds are against it. I think that's what I would say.'

'Yes,' Viv says. 'That's more or less my feeling, too.'

25

THE PORTRAIT

Unknown to each other, Viv and Julia are both in Covent Garden at the same time, but with different objectives. Viv is combing the shops for a portable dressing gown, light enough to fold into a tote bag. She has decided that what she needs is a classic negligee, preferably black. And something silky to wear underneath, perhaps a satin slip with shoestring straps. For once, she finds the two items on her shopping list, more or less as designated.

Leary is keen to progress their liaison, as soon as problems around the transgender nun, now the Mother Superior, have been ironed out. Viv is not sure she can get her head around Leary or progress their liaison, but Joy thinks she should keep her head right out of it. At least he's not a fake vicar. And he's the only ship on the horizon, right?

Julia has been through Marjorie Mackintosh's hands and arrived at the piano rehearsal primed for action. Today is her big scene with Yuri. Her nightdress is not quite ready so she is wearing a rehearsal skirt, a plain cotton gown in similar style, with a lightweight robe. Marj, who knows Julia likes support and something to push against when she sings, has given her a structured bodice.

Already in position in the rehearsal room is the set of the Countess's bedchamber: a shadowy candlelit room in grand classical style. Outside the tall windows, moonlight illuminates a stormy sea. The Countess's gowns are displayed on stands. And dominating the room is a huge portrait from the days when she was known throughout Russia as the Moscow Venus.

Although she knew it would be there, Julia is unprepared for the impact. They hadn't bothered with any of the alternatives she brought in. They had just used her teenage photograph, and reinvented it.

Staring down at her is a remarkable likeness of June Jeffs as a young girl on the cusp of womanhood. Arresting, rouged, her hair in elaborate ringlets. The dark hair is bisected at the crown, dramatically, by a slash of white. The chin has a provocative tilt, as if challenging the onlooker to a duel.

The smoky eyes are not those of an ingénue. She wears an off-the-shoulder scarlet evening dress, cut low, with a tight bodice and flowing skirt, and an equally sensational necklace of emeralds and diamonds. It's like a Gainsborough portrait.

Emils is transfixed. 'It's bloody breathtaking.' A bloody marvel, Yuri concurs, shaking his head. Julia says she wouldn't mind that bloody necklace.

It has caught her unawares and she has to conceal the fact that she is shaken. It's not every day you encounter a stunning portrait of yourself as you once were. Although you never looked exactly like that, in truth, because it is informed by artistic licence. The fact that you are now in your late sixties (although everyone believes you to be only in the mid) lends a further lack of clarity to your feelings.

'At least the stripe will identify me. In case nobody knows who it's meant to be.' The men scoff. It's obvious who it is.

Emils watches her. Smiling, hands on his hips. He's about to take her and Yuri through their moves, to piano accompaniment. Complicated moves, crucial timing, to be teamed with singing of the greatest delicacy and finesse. The fusion of these will need to be embedded. The portrait perfectly sets up what is to come between them.

Yuri first. The scene opens as Herman arrives. He is riveted by the portrait. *I cannot tear my eyes away from that terrible, fascinating face. I stare at it with hatred, and yet my eyes cannot get their fill …*

The Old Countess enters the bedchamber after the ball, escorted by her entourage of female attendants. Julia emerges from behind a screen wearing her second wig, the Countess's own hair: long, iron grey with the white streak. Her night attire appears dignified and funereal at first, draped with a black peignoir.

A chaise longue in rococo style is positioned under the portrait. The Countess dismisses her servants and reclines upon it, mesmerised by her own image and memories (poignant, troubling) of her youth.

This is Julia's great moment: *Je crains de lui parler la nuit.* A famous aria from the Countess's youth, and Tchaikovsky's homage to an earlier French opera. She rises to her feet, and very slowly – '*molto grave*, Julia' – she begins her dance movements. A frail old woman, observed only, as she believes, by the ironic eyes of her younger self.

Behind her a slow-motion film is projected on the tall windows. The soft-focus outlines of men and women in wigs and elegant costumes. Dancers, long dead but unforgotten, revolving in her mind. The simplicity of what she sings is deceptive. It requires formidable technique. Total vocal and emotional control, the result of a lifetime of training.

In order to maintain her equilibrium, to be at one remove from the emotion of the words (and the unsettling effect of the portrait) Julia will sing slightly outside of herself. This is the moment the Countess reveals the fragility behind the facade. It is a lament for the past, and for her lost youth.

I'm afraid to speak to him at night
I hear too clearly what he says

he tells me: I love you, and I feel
— in spite of myself — I feel
my heart, which beats
which beats …

The peignoir slips from her shoulders as she reclines. She continues her reverie (*'pianissimo* now, Julia') softly, as in a dream. Almost imperceptibly, the last word fades away. It trembles and dies on the air. Her eyes close as Herman emerges from the background. His stealthy figure approaches. *Don't be frightened!* The Countess awakens, with a start.

Emils demonstrates, with the lightest of touches on her upper arm. 'You are initially in dread, Julia, of this staring, threatening man. You have seen him before. You had a fearful premonition.'

I have come to ask a favour …

'As he continues to sing, your history kicks in. You make a gesture. It's not a flirtatious move, but it's subtly erotic. You invite him. You indicate the space next to you, and he obeys. You are a dark presence, Julia. A bird of prey. You are totally aware of each other.'

You can make my whole life happy.

It won't cost you anything—

'For a moment,' Emils says, 'we need to think — and almost believe — that this is the start of a love duet. The Countess listens. And as she responds to his words, she leans towards him. Leans into him. And she puts out her hand — make your hand old and spidery, Julia — on his leg as he sings …'

If you ever knew the feeling of love
If you remember the ardour and passion of young blood
If you ever smiled at a child, or felt your heart beat in your breast
I beg of you, by all you hold sacred — reveal your secret!

'Your hand is making a move up his thigh. You must time this right, Julia,' Emils cautions, 'or all of us are in very deep shit.'

This breaks the tension. They relax, and regroup. 'And then comes Herman's fatal error.'

What good is it to you?

You are old, you will die soon.

Emils' hand guides Julia's elbow. 'She repudiates him for those words.' Enraged, quivering, the Countess rises from the chaise. As she brandishes her stick, Herman pulls out his pistol.

Old witch! I'll make you answer!

She falls back, and expires from shock. Compared with many deaths Julia has undergone in her operatic career, this one almost qualifies as run of the mill. It appals Herman, but for a darker reason: she has died before revealing the secret of the cards. Bridie Waterstreet as Lisa enters, to be greeted by the sight of her dead grandmother. The scene ends.

They run through it again, twice. The director appears casual and relaxed, hands in his pockets, listening and watching with ears and eyes that miss nothing. Between each break other key people surround the singers. The language coach, the assistant conductor, the movement director, the choreographer.

Rehearsing a difficult scene for the first time is demanding enough. The nuances of this one are exceptionally tricky. But the work is cathartic in the way, only semi-explicable, of all great art. As Julia puts it at lunch: 'The way it seizes your feelings, puts them through the wringer and shreds them. And then reassembles them in a new and improved version. It's what keeps us all going, isn't it? What else is there in life, when it comes down to it?'

She glances at Bridie. 'Of course, there's always love.' This is by way of being a simple, throwaway line. Almost, but not quite.

Bridie shares a special smile with her. 'You were simply wonderful, Julia.' Contriving, Julia notes, to sit on the banquette next to Emils.

26

A REVELATION OR TWO

Leary has been texting sprightly messages once or twice daily. *What's up, B? Omg I'm snowed under. No change. Transgender issue causing papal ructions. Still snowing.*

Still snowing arrived during Viv's meeting with Daisy, but was not read until afterwards. The latest one came when she was shopping for new nightwear: *Hey. Watch this space. Upcoming wop.*

Viv has responded in a sprightly way too, while contriving to be non-specific about outcomes. She is reluctant to think about where an upcoming window of opportunity might lead. At the same time she is disinclined to mention Leary in any further communication with Martin. Which hasn't come up, as there has been no further communication with Martin since their conversation a few days ago.

Julia's attachment to her goddaughter is beyond doubt. But Daisy, like her mother, has grown up in tandem with Julia's career and knows the rules. Jules was never going to make it to the opening of her show and it's no surprise when she phones to cry off, with apologies. No surprise either that she will opt out of Daisy's birthday celebrations the following week. They'll have a humdinger of a party instead, after the closing night of *The Queen of Spades*. Daisy says she's not at all sure turning thirty-nine is anything to celebrate.

Her godmother tells her that from any objective perspective the age of thirty-nine is sheer heaven. You're young enough to have every possibility in front of you, and old enough to know what you're doing.

'Did *you* know what you were doing at thirty-nine?' Daisy demands, and then regrets it. A rubbish question on any reckoning. By the age of thirty-nine Julia Jefferies was a world-famous name. Daisy Mayberry, who is similarly passionate about her art, hasn't abandoned such soaring ambitions, although she is aware of doubts creeping in.

She says, 'Don't answer that, it was a dumb question. You knew exactly what you were doing. You were well on your way, in every respect.'

Jules feels for her. 'Only in some,' she replies.

A slight equivocation prompts Daisy to pursue this. It propels her to ask something she last asked as a teenager, and has often toyed with asking again. She has always chickened out at the last minute, in large part out of respect for Julia's privacy. Why this time should have been any different, she will reflect afterwards, she couldn't say.

'Did you ever consider having children?'

Jules answers casually. 'It wasn't possible with my career. As I've told you before.'

There is something pat about this that suggests many rehearsals and much repetition. It is both too automatic and too evasive for Daisy today. 'Didn't you ever take any risks?'

This time there is a pause on the phone, quite a lengthy one, as Julia weighs this up. Where her goddaughter is concerned she wishes to play with a straight bat. 'I took risks. I had an abortion once. Between ourselves, of course.' They have a longstanding agreement where sensitive matters are concerned.

'Of course.' Daisy, who is astounded, sounds like she takes this information in her stride.

'After that I never took any more risks. Ever.'

'Right.' Daisy proceeds to put another toe in the water. 'Were you tempted at all? To go ahead?'

'No. I wasn't tempted for one moment. It wasn't possible.' A fractional beat. 'Or desirable. I knew that.'

Daisy tosses caution to the wind. 'Why not?'

'Usual reasons,' says Jules, lightly. 'No money, too young, wrong time.' A Hollywood accent: 'Wouldn't have fitted in with my *skedule*.'

Daisy is being fobbed off and she knows it. She changes tack. 'What about the guy? What did he think about it?'

For a moment she thinks they have been cut off. Then Jules says, without expression, 'He thought nothing because I didn't tell him.'

'You didn't?' This seems to go against everything Daisy knows about Julia.

'I dealt with it myself. It was better that way, I thought.'

There is something in Jules's tone that Daisy can't identify. 'Didn't you have a relationship with him? Who *was* he? Was he just –' a grin, 'a ship in the night? Or don't you remember?'

Another pause. 'Oh, I remember.' It's quite plain, even over the phone, that Jules is not prepared to say anything more.

Something strikes Daisy. She is silenced, almost, by the implications. The possibilities. 'Jules – it wasn't *Dad*, was it?'

Julia expostulates. '*Geoff*? Allah preserve us. What on earth gave you that idea?'

'You would tell me?'

'Of course I would.' But she probably wouldn't, Daisy thinks.

At Daisy's show, as with most small art openings in a confined space, there are no in-depth conversations. They are precluded by wall-to-wall sound in the three uninsulated white cubes, and an Aeolian wind harp and percussion (played by two of Daisy's musician friends) in the background.

With a table of inferior red and warm white wine and a two-hour time limit, it's like a cut-price wedding, Viv says to Geoff and Eliza, only with three hugely disparate guest lists. The mood is positive. Those in Daisy's camp feel her work puts the others in the shade – and not only because the others are dark and hers are bright and glowing.

She is surrounded, like a bride, by gushing well-wishers. Her portraits have become more political lately. Pensive studies of refugees silhouetted against brilliant backgrounds: a Syrian mother and child, an Iraqi girl, a couple from Yemen. Daisy met all of them through Viv's volunteer network.

Already two of the male nudes have red stickers. One would be Julia's; she sent word that she wanted one. Geoff finds them confrontational. They're too in your face, he says.

'Can't be too in your face for the likes of us girls. Can they, Vivien?' Eliza laughs. Viv catches her husband's eye. He dislikes noisy, crowded gatherings like this.

Adrian is the most dashing male in the room in Viv's view, as she feels he would be in many other rooms and views. Being taller than average and considerably more extrovert he is easy to track as he navigates the crowd. He's decked out in a floppy yellow bow tie with black spots, black shirt and a bespoke, three-piece denim suit (distressed). He's introducing himself to everyone as the artist's muse and willy model.

'If you care to look closely you can see the cocks are all the same,' he's saying to the throng around the nudes. 'I'm looking into organ transplants for variety. Have to keep rivals out of the studio. You know how it is with artists and their models.'

He has discovered a vicious vein of hetero-jealousy he never knew existed, although it must have been latent. Eliza is hanging onto every word. Geoff can't hear most of them, which is a relief to Viv.

Adrian spots them. 'Doesn't your daughter look *fabulous* tonight? I'm basking in reflected glory. Don't you just love the cutting-edge new work? She's going to be a name, right up there with Bacon and Freud. You heard it here first.'

He brings a couple forward as Geoff retreats. 'You remember Daisy's old flame, don't you, Vivien? Henry, my more respectable twin – he's in insider trading – and his gorgeous pouting wife, Venetia. They *adore* the refugee pictures. They want to commission one of themselves dressed as asylum seekers, but Daisy's being very po-faced about it.'

Heggers has evolved into a bluff, generic type. There are vestiges of the old charm, although Viv finds herself immune to it and is rapidly revising her former opinion. She feels her phone vibrate. A text from Leary. She replaces the phone in her jacket pocket without reading it.

Adrian keeps it snappy. He looks to his right. 'Gotta go rescue the tortured artiste from the clutches of those *terminal bores*. I'll bring them over for your assessment.' A glance at the nudes. 'Just keep in the forefront of your minds, bold, confrontational, *figurative* art is not quite their thing. Along with art in general.'

Eliza grabs Geoff's arm. 'Wow, was that Daisy's boyfriend?' Viv sees her husband flinch. She glimpses the terminal bores, a faded, inoffensive-looking couple of around their own age talking to Daisy. Soon afterwards she and Geoff are being introduced to them: Macaulay and Ruth.

Viv becomes aware that Ruth is regarding her fixedly. It seems an inappropriate glance to receive from someone she has only just met and knows nothing about: intense, but with an obscure subtext. She can't begin to think what it is trying to convey. The dilapidated husband Macaulay, however, seems to be completely out of it. Pickled, probably.

And now Ruth is offering her a business card and saying, most surprisingly, 'It would be lovely if you and I might meet for coffee.'

The voice is earnest and slightly strained, and it dawns on Viv who they must be. She gives Ruth a vigorous nod, but before she

289

can reply they have been buttonholed and swept away. Viv puts the card in her bag. She is trying to decode, retrospectively, the message of Ruth's glance. She thinks she might have a fairly good idea of what it was trying to convey: fellow-feeling, and a measure of relief.

'Who the hell were *they?*' Geoff asks. 'Friends of yours?'

Daisy reaches them. She is indeed looking fabulous, hair piled up, her denim suit coordinating with that of her companion (as her mother has decided to call him) – yellow bow tie, long pencil skirt and jacket over a black shirt.

There are hugs, a special one for Joy who has just arrived unaccompanied (Mr Jackson works five nights out of seven, Viv recalls; assuming he has not been shipped out) and a quick intro to Eliza. Daisy allots her a tight smile.

'Sorry, I did try to warn you but I was ambushed,' she tells her parents loudly. 'What did you make of them? Adrian says they should bring back the guillotine. But they're actually quite harmless. Lord Mac's as deaf as a post as well as permanently paralytic, so he wouldn't've heard a word anyway.'

Lord? Viv hopes she misheard. 'They're Lord and Lady Frensham,' Daisy says with disdain. 'I thought you knew. Antediluvian, isn't it?'

The titles are confusing on several fronts. And rather unwelcome, overall. 'Does that mean Adrian and Heggers are *Hons?*' Viv asks her daughter. Evidently it does. Heggers will be a Lord eventually.

'Nothing to stop him renouncing it,' Geoff says.

'Oh, he'd never do that. He can't wait for his dad to peg out. Lucky he came out first, wasn't it?'

It's too crowded to see any of the work properly, although they make a half-hearted effort to push through into the other rooms. But Geoff in particular, who has a low tolerance of bad wine, noisy gatherings and art (other than his daughter's) of less than museum quality, is desperate to get out of there. They will return another day, when Daisy says they're quite likely to have the gallery to themselves. She waves them off with, Viv fears, a touch of relief.

They take refuge in an Indian restaurant down the street. It's nearly empty, which might be a bad sign. Viv can tell Joy wants to talk, so she sits next to her.

Her husband, who is grumpy on several counts, asks for drinks before the menus arrive. A bottle of house white and cold beers for him and Eliza. Large bottles. Should be an improvement on the bilge you were just swilling, Lize, he says to her. Although she hadn't seemed to mind, Viv noted, and neither had Joy. Being younger they probably didn't notice what they were swilling.

Geoff's mind hasn't moved on. He reaches for his beer. 'God send me patience,' he groans, to no one in particular. 'Why can't she get herself a proper man?' Viv, sitting opposite Eliza, can't quite reach his leg to kick him. She shakes her head, frowning.

Joy is looking puzzled. Does he mean Daisy? Nothing improper about that fella, in her opinion. He's *hot*. Probably loaded too.

Eliza agrees. A hottie *and* an Honourable, hey! Probably with a stately pile. What more do you want, Geoff? And what a dress sense! She and Joy high five each other.

'A hottie?' Geoff echoes. Viv hopes the other two diners are out of earshot. 'Are you out of your mind? Turkey cock's more like it.'

'Geoff—' Viv interrupts, midway, but he takes no notice. What has he told Eliza? Probably nothing.

'*Dress sense?*' he's repeating incredulously. 'He's as camp as a row of tents.'

Eliza and Joy roll their eyes. 'You can't tell anything by what guys wear these days, Geoff,' Eliza scolds, with a headmistressy shake of the head. 'Can you, Vivien?'

Joy chimes in. 'They're *all* interested in their wardrobe, believe me.' She too glances at Viv. Like Lady Frensham, she's trying to telegraph something. Again, Viv has no idea what it might be. 'Some of those macho guys, they have as many clothes as us. More, I'm not kidding. They're worried about things *going* with things or *not* going, and stuff clashing, you know?'

'That's right, Geoff, I'm afraid you're *way* behind the times,' Eliza giggles. 'They're all caring and sensitive now and they all use moisturisers.' She clinks glasses with everyone. 'Cheers.'

'And not just aftershave, honey – *cologne*,' says Joy. 'Spicy lime and pomegranate, with woody notes—'

'Sensual fragrance sprays—'

'For the manly, waxed chest. Excuse me, Geoff,' Joy leers, 'but your wife needs you to play major catch-up here. Just saying.' She and Eliza, who appear to be bonding over this, burst into gales of laughter.

'For fuck's sake,' Geoff explodes. 'He's gay, period. Is that *simple* enough for you?'

A little taken aback, the two of them look at Viv, whose face is resolutely vacant. Then back at Geoff. Well, they say, okay. *So?*

Joy shrugs. 'What's that got to do with the price of fish?'

'Who gives a rat's anyway?' asks Eliza. 'This is the twenty-first century, you know, Geoff. LGBTIQXYZ or whatever, what's it matter? Gender fluidity rules. People chop and change all the time, no one gives a fuck about rigid sexual orientation anymore.'

She takes a copious swig of beer. '*Young* people, anyway.' She grins at Joy. 'Maybe it's different for—'

This riles Geoff. 'There's no need to lecture me about passing social fads. Nor is there any need to patronise.' Eliza's eyes widen. An uneasy silence settles on the table.

Joy breaks it. 'Whatever. It was still nice to be there and see Daisy's work. Especially the full frontals, right?' She and Eliza snigger.

'I never would've guessed his parents were *lords*, would you?' Eliza persists. 'They sounded hoity-toity, but they looked quite dowdy and ordinary.'

'It costs mega-bucks to look as dowdy as that, honey,' Joy sighs. 'I sure hope they buy up big. *I'd* snap up every one of her pictures and put them on my wall, if I could.'

'Yes, she's incredibly talented and beautiful and cool,' Eliza agrees brightly. A sly glance at Geoff. 'And her boyfriend's cool too, I don't care what you say. *And* well connected. Don't you just hate her?'

Viv, who is still extremely annoyed with Geoff, realises she hasn't said a thing for some time. And any chance of Geoff and Eliza getting in a huddle and enabling her to speak quietly to Joy on personal matters seems to be receding.

A platter of mixed appetisers is placed in the centre of the table. Reaching for a samosa, Viv feels her phone buzz again. She slides it onto her lap and glances down, aware of Joy's eyes on her. It's Martin this time. The message is short and to the point. A single question mark. She chews the samosa. It's very dry.

Joy nudges Viv, and leans towards Eliza. 'That cute accent you have, honey,' she says in a cooing voice. 'It's not from here, right? Is it Aussie?'

'Kiwi, if you *don't* mind,' Eliza protests, as Viv slips out and heads for the WC. It's unisex, and not far from their table.

Martin is number six on her favourites list, after Geoff, Daisy, Judith, Jules and Joy. She hits the button. He picks up immediately. 'Is it Vivien, or is it Beatrice?'

'I think it's both.' She keeps her voice low. 'I haven't heard from you for days.' She is in a very small and badly lit loo. It's spotlessly clean, though. She puts the lid down and sits on it.

'I could say the same thing.'

'Three days at least.'

'Is it that long? You sound very fuzzy. Are you underwater?'

'I'm in the loo at an Indian restaurant. You couldn't swing a cat in here.'

'Is there a particular reason for talking in there, then? Other than – efficacy?'

'Efficacy doesn't come into it; I didn't want to be overheard.'

'You're not alone?'

'I'm with my husband, his young female friend, who's a New Zealander, and my friend from Louisiana.'

'Your husband and his friend,' he says.

'That's right.'

'And you and yours.'

'Mine's Joy, my quilting friend. What did your question refer to?' she asks.

'My question?'

'Your question *mark*.'

'I'd been wondering how you were.' A noncommittal tone.

'Had you?'

'And wondering,' more briskly, 'whether you had anything to report. Any developments or firm conclusions, one way or the other.'

No, there had been no developments. And no conclusions, firm or otherwise. 'Leary's working 24/7. He's been texting, though. He's an indefatigable texter, you can say that about him. He last texted half an hour ago but I haven't read it yet.'

'You haven't?' A pause. 'No thoughts, then?'

'I think I should go back to the table. They might think something untoward's happened. The samosa I had wasn't up to much.'

'I meant, thoughts about Mr Davidson.'

The door handle rattles. 'Someone's trying to get in.' She flushes the toilet, which makes a surprisingly loud noise. 'No thoughts right now, no.' She doesn't want to think about Leary. 'Other than – well, I suppose we ought to have another meeting. It would be lily-livered not to, wouldn't it? Given he's a director who likes to *resolve* things quickly.'

'I'm not sure that *ought* should come into it,' Martin says. 'Or lily-livered. You probably shouldn't let yourself be rushed into anything, Beatrice.'

'The type of thing I might regret later, you mean? Another Dauntish escapade?'

'Something like that. Are you feeling—' he stops mid-sentence. 'Would you like me to line up another rabbit? Is that what you're leaning towards?'

Another pause. Viv says, 'Perhaps I am leaning towards that, I'm not entirely …'

'I get the sense that now isn't the time?'

'No I'd better let that poor person in before they have an accident. Should I flush the toilet a second time?'

'Your call. It might add to the verisimilitude.'

'Yes it might do that. Well, I suppose I'd better go.'

The cistern thunders again. Waiting outside the door and frowning is the female half of the other couple of diners. Viv mutters an apology and returns to the table, where the appetisers have been replaced by a selection of oily curries.

Eliza has moved on to white wine. She's telling Joy the plot of a new sci-fi film involving rogue algorithms. Geoff is joining in, looking less peevish, and is on his second beer. The bottle of house white is nearly empty. Viv toys with desultory forkfuls as Eliza and Joy clean up their plates. They must look as if they're enjoying it, Joy urges, for the waiter's sake. The poor sap's hovering anxiously outside the kitchen.

Eliza is enviably slim and seems to have a gargantuan appetite. When she announces that what she'd like now more than *almost* anything is some kulfi, preferably mango though she'd settle for pistachio, Joy gives Viv another surreptitious prod. Sorry to spoil the party, guys, but she's got an early start in the morning. Viv says she's feeling slightly queasy and she'll go with her.

Geoff looks concerned. 'Take the car, hon.' He rummages for his keys. No need, she assures him. She can always Uber. She just needs a bit of fresh air.

Joy doesn't care for fast walking. She and Viv saunter towards the Tube, heads down and hands in pockets. With a heavy cloud cover it's not as cold as it was and the street is almost deserted. Joy mutters, 'Geoff's girlfriend's quite a nice little thing but she's got an eating disorder, right? Can't be anorexia. Must be bulimia.'

'Might be just a racing metabolism. I don't know if she *is* his girlfr—'

'Born yesterday, were you?'

'Probably was. So.' She gives Joy a probing look. 'How's it all going?'

Joy is reticent about personal matters until she needs to get something off her chest. 'That Mr Jackson Adeyemi,' she says, with an upward inflection. 'Think back to when you first saw him. Did you say to yourself, there's something *off* about that fella? You tell me the honest truth, now.'

Viv tells her no, she definitely did not say anything like that to herself. She thought he seemed very decent. She liked him.

Nothing different that made you think, *uh-oh*, what fresh shit is that damn-fool woman getting herself into now?

Well, he *was* different, Viv supposed, in that he was a burly security guard who was interested in learning to quilt and didn't mind being the only man in a group of women. That was unusual in a good way, she thought.

'With a group of women.' Joy shakes her head. 'That should've told me a bunch of important stuff straight off, shouldn't it?'

'Well, I don't know. Should it?' Where is this heading?

'And it was Ondine. *She* introduced him. *That* should've told me something.'

'Like *what*?' Viv is genuinely perplexed.

'She goes to those clubs, you know?'

Viv has only the haziest idea of the nature of those clubs. She goes over the previous conversation in the restaurant. 'Is it that he's got a thing about his clothes matching,' she asks at last. 'Or clashing? Maybe he's just colour blind.'

Ha-ha. Right. He did bring a truckload, so Joy let him have the big old closet that had been Mr Ronnie's. He moved all his stuff in there.

Yes, Viv encourages. Hurry up and get to the point, for God's sake.

Well, one evening she'd had a little poke around. Joy looks defensive. Like you do when you don't know much about them. First up, under some tracksuits, she found a blonde wig. Maybe a bit of leftover fancy dress, she thought. Then, in the back of a drawer, she found make-up. Shocking pink lipsticks. Lord have mercy!

Then a dress. Must've been made to measure, with his size. And two pairs of high heels, hidden behind his work boots. She laid them all out on the bed when he came home from work on Saturday morning. That was before last week's quilting circle.

Viv is not unduly surprised to hear this news. Joy draws an indignant breath. Well, it sure surprised the hell out of her.

How did Mr Jackson respond?

'He said playing lady dress-ups was like, his hobby. He said he got a kick out of it and it was only a bit of fun.' Joy exudes disbelief. Hobby. A kick. *Fun.* She blows out her cheeks.

The majority of cross-dressers are straight, Viv says. Or so she gathers. Apart from this, does he behave normally? In other ways?

Apart from this he delivers, she is given to understand. But that's a big apart from, Joy adds darkly. Viv can see how it might have been a surprise, and Joy's girls probably don't need to know about it just yet. But does it really matter? On balance? This is what Joy needs to weigh up. Given all the things that *could* be wrong with a man.

Joy says it's easy for Viv to say. 'You haven't got one sleeping in your bed that likes to go out all dressed up like a tart. Your problem is you've got one sleeping in your bed that doesn't *do* anything.'

Viv acknowledges the truth of this. Has Joy seen Mr Jackson all dressed up yet?

Joy utters a small scream, giving rise to an uncomfortable mental image. *Yet?* No, Joy has not. And she's not going to, either.

Bearing in mind Martin's recent advice, Viv counsels her friend not to rush into anything. She should let herself go off the boil for a bit and then see how she feels.

Joy says she didn't rush into anything. She didn't rush into stabbing him multiple times with the carving knife, did she? It's a nasty shock for any woman, and she's just trying to get her head around it, you know? Why hadn't he said something before he moved in, to test the water?

Viv says that in her experience, men tend to avoid introducing any topic that their gut feeling tells them will not be well received. Until they can't see any alternative, she adds, thinking of Geoff.

'He said his gut feeling told him how I was most likely gonna be about it,' Joy says fluently. 'I was gonna be like, it sucks, but maybe I'd get used to it. I was like, no way, baby. Only way I'm gonna get used to *that* is when it doesn't happen.' Joy bats her eyelashes. 'Lordy. These men.'

'These men,' Viv agrees. 'You know, I hate to strike a defeatist note, but things like that seem to be more of a psychological compulsion than a choice.'

'That's just psychological crap. Know what he said yesterday? When I'd got used to it I could come with him, and we could have a girls' night out. Ha *hahhh*!' She dabs at her eyes with her gloved hand.

Viv says, 'That would be fun. I'll come with you.'

She's not joking, but they both laugh immoderately as they disappear into the Tube.

27

JULIA

Viv doesn't look at Leary's text until the next morning. And then only after he sends a follow-up. *Thurs cool?*

She reads his message of the night before. *Hey B, wide open window likely Thurs. Lunch my place? Whadda you say? Whole pm free. Mulled it over yet? Lx*

Thursday is far away. In five days, anything could happen. She replies: *Will pencil in Thurs.* Equivocal enough? After some hesitation, she adds, *B.* And after further hesitation, *x.* His response flies back: *Cool. Big X.*

She puts the phone out of sight, behind a bundle of material scraps, and prepares to start work. It rings almost immediately. Her mother, asking about Daisy's show. Daisy and Adrian are bringing her up to see it next week, for Daisy's birthday. Then they can all have an early dinner and she can stay the night. This arrangement is presented by Judith as a given.

Geoff sitting down at the same table as Adrian? In your dreams, says Viv. For the moment, anyhow. She knows that her mother, while deploring it, will be intrigued to hear that Adrian is the younger son of the Earl of Frensham. She drops this in.

Frensham, muses Judith. Near the Scottish border, she thinks. If Daisy and Adrian *should* become pregnant (Viv enjoys her mother's stringent efforts to keep abreast of social and linguistic trends) her understanding is that the child, as the offspring of the second son, will not be entitled to use the Hon.

Viv pre-empts her next remark. So, we're in the clear, she says. Hons can have undesirable airs of entitlement.

Exactly, Vivi. The rule applies whether or not the parents are married, Judith thinks.

Don't use the m word in Geoff's hearing, Viv warns. At this, Judith asks whether she herself has met any halfway satisfactory man yet? None at all, Viv replies firmly. She has already decided not to say another word on this subject.

Her mother, in vigorous form this morning, is not so easily put off. Is she in touch with anyone? Has she any follow-up appointments? Is there any new *intro* on the cards? Viv answers all questions with a flat negative. Having resolved to say nothing more, she hears herself remark, 'It's too late now, but I do wish you hadn't told Daisy about the agency.'

'What makes you say that?' Her mother sounds curious and faintly injured.

'Because I wanted it kept private.'

'Really, dear? Why?'

'Oh, I don't know, Mother. Just a tedious, bourgeois preference.'

'It's nothing to be ashamed of, you know, Vivi. On the contrary—'

'Yes, yes, I know all that.'

'You told *me*, didn't you?'

And how stupid was that? 'Yes I did, but I assumed – silly of me – you'd keep it to yourself.'

'Assumptions that are neither informed nor evidence-based—'

'—are unreliable, inadvisable and not worth the candle. Yes, I do remember that, Mum.'

'Daisy is a very strong and freethinking person. I have always thought it's most important for a daughter to see her mother in another light. As a woman who happens to be her mother.'

'Instead of a mother who happens to be a woman.'

Somewhat to Viv's surprise, Judith finds this joke amusing. 'Have you consulted your guru – what was his name?'

'Martin Glover.'

'About lifting his game,' says her mother. 'He's not coming up with the goods, Vivi. Not only has he not produced a credible prospect, they would seem to have dried up altogether. Are you quite sure you're getting value for money?'

'It's all cool, Mum, don't worry about it.' Cool. Must be Leary's subliminal influence. She knows she is not meeting her mother's expectations here. She maintains a steely resolve. 'If and when I have something to report, in terms of a credible introduction, I'll be sure to let you know.'

If and when. Not the right phrase. There's something wrong with it, but the nature of its wrongness is not something Viv feels inclined to explore right now. Either in dialogue with her mother, or with herself.

Viv did not expect to be sitting in Julia's flower-filled flat again before the season of *The Queen of Spades* had come to an end, much less before it had even commenced. But early Sunday evening, after the quilting circle, she makes her way to Bloomsbury. Jules had suggested she might like to drop by for a drink on her way home.

The atmosphere at Joy's had eased a little, Viv felt. Mr Jackson was still in residence. She was relieved to see him working away, a placid presence at the end of the room. Joy told her he was minding his p's and q's.

Did this mean he was abstaining from lady dress-ups? You can bet your sweet life it does, Joy replied grimly, and he'll go right on abstaining if he knows what's good for him.

Viv provides a rundown on this while Julia mixes gin and tonic. For Jules this means diet tonic with lemon and a thimbleful. If Joy thinks abstention will work in the long term, she opines, she has another think coming.

Jules is tranquil on the surface, but Viv senses a restive underlay. She puts this down to pre-season nerves. Rehearsals are going well, however, and Jules has lost five pounds to date, mainly in the target area of the midriff. This has obliged her costume cutter Marj Mackenzie to make small adjustments to the Countess's distinctive nightdress. In addition, Jules has instigated (insisted on, Viv imagines) a few adjustments of her own, with the designer's compliance. A dropped waistline and a diagonal ruffle will be more elegant and decidedly more flattering, she feels.

She is having a copy made for herself. A sexy black nightie being one of those wardrobe staples that never goes astray. Viv concurs. She tells Jules about the plain satin slip she recently bought herself. Simpler and less dramatic, but it should serve the purpose.

And do we have a purpose waiting in the wings, Jules inquires. Not a concrete one as yet, her friend concedes, but it's as well to be prepared. As she says this, she experiences a bout of severe internal fluttering. She asks the same question, on the assumption (informed and evidence-based, this time) that any answer will be as evasive as her own.

However, Jules throws in a surprising embellishment. 'But at some point in the *not* too distant future, I fully expect to whip it off its hanger.' She strokes the bridge of her nose. 'Wasn't there a hyper-speedy TV director?'

'Only one meeting and it was a dead end.' Does this constitute a decision just arrived at? 'And don't I recall a spunky young opera director?'

Jules smiles. He has stolen one heart already. That of the eager young debutante at the Garden, poor little Bridie Waterstreet.

One and a half hearts, perhaps? queries Viv. And shouldn't the other half know better? Does know better, says Jules. But nature will have her wicked way.

She has put out similar nibbles to those she offered Bridie: mixed olives and crisp pita bites with low-cal toppings. The flat is cosy and fragrant. The feathery white sofa induces a state of restfulness. Were it not for a latent jittery sensation Viv would feel pleasantly relaxed. She is aware, on some level she doesn't care to investigate, that this is linked to the mention of black nightclothes. She asks if Max is still coming.

Jules raises her eyebrows. 'Of course he is. He arrives tomorrow.' This seems to plunge her into a chasm of deep thought. Instead of sitting next to Viv on the sofa she has placed herself in an armchair opposite. Backlit as usual. The light from three lamps and the fire's red coals is soft and glowing.

In a quick, decisive movement Jules clicks her feet together on the floor and leans forward. She positions her left forearm across the waist, rests her right elbow on the back of her left hand and supports her chin in her right. For someone who prides herself on the elegance of her posture, this awkward pose is notable. While it is Viv's first inkling they are not having the cosy drink she had imagined, she has no inkling that her friend is about to detonate a bombshell.

'Vivi, there's something I haven't told you.' Julia's right hand moves up to stroke her own cheek. 'I don't think I ever told you how I met Max.' Her hand brushes her face in a caress.

Afterwards, Viv will always associate this conversation with the tango music playing softly in the background. Astor Piazzolla's *Oblivion*.

Viv sits on the Central Line heading for Mile End and the school where she volunteers every Monday. On her lap is an unopened novel. She looks at her watch. Max might be just arriving. He might have reached Bloomsbury already. She is still profoundly affected by what she heard last night. It wasn't so much a conversation as a soliloquy, before an audience of one. Once again, she revisits it.

'How you *met* him?' she had echoed. 'But Max is your brother.'

'Yes, but we didn't grow up together, you see. I was an only child.' Julia's eyes are in the shade and unreadable. 'Or so I thought.' Jules had thought she was an only child until she was fourteen, when her parents divorced. 'They timed the split for when I was at boarding school, so I was cushioned from it. To some extent.'

Viv remembered passing references to their parents' divorces when she and Julia were still getting to know each other. But they were both in their early twenties at the time and had other things on their minds – pressing, age-related matters that were more germane and far more engrossing. Apart from recounting how June Jeffs had become Julia Jefferies, Viv's new friend was reticent about her background.

Since then, Viv had subscribed to the belief that it takes a certain temperament to brood endlessly over family shortcomings. Neither of them had showed that inclination. She thought they recognised this in each other, and respected it. It would take another forty years before she discerned the limits of those perceptions.

Did the divorce come as a shock? Strangely enough no, Jules said. Not really. She thought she must have anticipated it, deep down. 'What happened afterwards, though, estranged me from my father. Dramatically, in a way I'd never imagined. But it did make me very close to my mother, for the rest of her life.'

The teenage Julia had been well aware of a coolness in her parents' marriage, although unlike Viv she was not taken into her mother's confidence. After the divorce her father, a doctor, moved to work in Mount Macedon, a country town north-west of Melbourne. The arrangement was for Julia to stay with her father during the school holidays. And after Christmas she came for a prolonged visit. She would stay at Mount Macedon until the end of the summer.

'Nothing,' she said, her violet eyes fixed on Viv, 'had prepared me for what I found there.' She broke off abruptly and looked away. For a moment Viv suspected her of playing this for all it was worth.

She revised the thought almost before it took shape; Jules was drawing the story out because she found the telling of it difficult.

Later that night it would occur to Viv that she may never have told it to anyone before. Later still, she would discover Jules had in fact confided in her trusted agent, Malcolm Foster, and (in a slightly modified version) her dresser, Marjorie Mackintosh. I had to tell *someone*, Viv, or they'd have had to section me. Viv heard this admission with a spark of hurt.

Whether or not the developing suspense was deliberate or unconscious, it was working. Viv was on the edge of the sofa, hands on her knees. It must have been a full minute before Jules resumed.

Her father had picked her up from their old house, and driven for nearly an hour and a half to the small town in a mountainous rural area. On the way, he told her he was living there with another woman whose name was Catherine Templeman. He had known Catherine for a long time, and he hoped June would come to like her.

'He'd known her since at least a year before I was born, as it turned out,' Jules said dryly. She was thunderstruck to see the evidence of this long association. Her father and Catherine were living in a Federation-style house (1907, vaguely Arts and Crafts, rather rambling and fine) with timber verandahs on two storeys. Every room was filled with photographs. Photos of her father with Catherine Templeman and a third person. A child. A boy.

'I think I hardly said hello to Catherine. She was just an indeterminate woman of Dad's age. Although later I discovered she was also a doctor, and I realised she was quite a stunner. But on that first day I was like a feral animal, roaming all over the house. I was in a fervour, staring at all the photos. My father kissing the baby, the three of them in various contexts. I was completely mesmerised.'

Jules disentangled her arms. 'Sorry, Viv, but we're going to need another drink.' She went to the cabinet, pouring herself only a slightly stiffer measure than before. She resumed her pose. Viv, as she had done countless times in the past, admired her willpower.

'I asked no questions about the boy. I know it seems incredible, Viv, in this day and age when everything's out in the open, but I actually think no one said anything. Nothing at all.'

Two days later, he turned up. He came home from boarding school and they were introduced to each other. They had the same surname. He was Max Jeffs.

Jules's face had turned very pale.

I must try to keep this on an even keel, Viv thought, for her sake. My reaction must be matter-of-fact and unruffled. 'How amazing, Jules,' she said quietly. 'What a shock that must have been for you. How old *was* he, exactly?'

'Fifteen. He was very dashing at that age. Very dazzling, Viv. As you can imagine. Only three months older than me.'

'Three months. And so – how did you both react?'

Jules got up and stood in front of the fireplace, with her back to Viv. She stood still, in silence, drink in hand, her head bowed. 'We were angry. I can't tell you how unbelievably, how *identically* angry we were. We were incandescent with rage. How could they have done this? Been so craven. How could they never have said a word? Even my mother didn't know.'

Viv heard Julia's deep breaths. *Incandescent.* She pictured two fiery young dragons. 'Was it a bonding experience?'

'*Bonding?*' There was another silence. It extended, to the point where Viv, hardly daring to breathe, began to wonder if she had said something tactless. Something offensive.

When Jules turned round she seemed almost unaware of Viv's presence. Her eyes were dreamy and abstracted. 'You could say that. Yes, I think you could say it was bonding.'

'What happened then?' Viv asked carefully. This was untrodden territory. 'I mean, with your father and Catherine?'

'Oh, *them?*' With contempt. 'We just turned our backs on them and lived our own life.'

The house was close to hill farms and cleared bushlike parkland. They had abandoned the house and gone off every day, on bikes or on foot, taking picnics. Swimming in creeks and waterholes, climbing rocky outcrops. Often stealing wine or beer from the fridge and wrapping it in wet newspaper.

'We were intoxicated at all times. Sometimes in both ways at once.' Colour had flooded back into Julia's cheeks.

Viv was unsure how to interpret this. 'They didn't – your father and Catherine ...'

'Didn't what?'

'They just – let you do your thing? Turned a blind eye?'

Jules's head jerked up. 'We were unstoppable, Viv. You need to realise that. You would've had to lock us away. And they were both at work, most of the time. I think they were vastly relieved we were –' a fleeting grin, the first for a while, 'getting on.'

Viv got up and went to the piano. She picked up the framed photograph of Julia and Max. An arresting study of two dark-haired, strikingly beautiful children. That was how she had always thought of them. But of course, they weren't children. Every inch of her skin prickled.

Jules was watching her. 'That was taken on my birthday, just before we had to go back to school. We dressed up and went to Melbourne by train, and had it done. So we would have a proper, sophisticated record. A grown-up photograph of ourselves together, how we wanted to be. To last until next time. As it has always done.'

Next time. Viv was aware that this had acquired a new meaning. *From now on*, was what it meant. This was the implication. She made no attempt to come to terms with it, not yet. It was enough just to take this in.

'Those weeks. They were a turning point?'

'They were seminal. The entire summer.'

307

'Was it *the* turning point of your life?'

'Of course it was. And, you'd have to add, the discovery of singing. That I could sing, and make a crust from it. They were the two turning points.'

She unwound her arms, rotated her shoulders and arched her neck. 'I thought I needed to tell you this, Viv. Before he gets here. Because now – with this new stage of life, with the divorce – it's time. And because I wanted to.'

All the premières. All the phone calls and flowers. 'It never waned, did it?'

'It never waned. We were irreplaceable, you see.'

Viv did see, clearly. And perhaps had always seen, when they were together. She nodded. 'He did marry.'

'He tried. We both did. He had children. And that's a great thing, for both of us.'

'Any marriage was never going to work though, was it?'

Jules lifted her hair. It gleamed as it fell. 'We were each other's first, and we will be the last. We always knew that.'

This was what it was like – to see someone through new eyes. It wasn't hard to look at this woman and see the girl. Not if you had known her for most of her life. If you believed you had known her.

Viv could discern the template: June Jeffs as she was, glowing and ardent. Max Jeffs at fifteen, already tall and classically handsome. Two creatures in the bloom of youth. Enraptured. It didn't take much imagination to picture it, or to understand.

'I understand it, Jules,' she said.

Viv was familiar with a particular expression. A playful one, full of incipient mischief. It had served Jules well, over the years. It settled now on her face. 'My God, Viv, am I glad to have this hulking bloody elephant off my chest. Believe me, I didn't want to wait until my hand was forced. I was always dying to tell you. I just couldn't quite— You do understand that too, don't you?'

And she does. But a sore point will remain in place. If only a pinprick.

Viv puts her unread book away and leaves the station. She strives to reboot her mind. A short time from now she must concentrate on helping children learn to read, in a way that will not put them off. In a way that will empower them. Ignoring the drizzle, she takes long, swift strides towards the school.

But her delinquent mind refuses to move forward. It lingers on them, on Jules and Max. Lingers with a protective tenderness. You can know someone intimately, for so many years, yet in all that time know nothing about the seminal emotional experience of her life. The turning point that would affect everything to come. Although I always did have an unformed knowledge. I always knew there was something she wasn't telling me.

Odds are, they have the perfect cover from now on. No one will think twice. She wonders if it can be hidden from Geoff. If Geoff ever suspected, it would confirm his worst convictions.

Oblivion. To be, for so long, oblivious.

The school rings with children's voices. Shouts, yells, high screams of laughter. Is there anything else I am oblivious about?

28

VIV

It's Tuesday morning. Viv picks up her mobile and glances at her favourites. Before she can think twice, her thumb has connected of its own accord with number six. It is answered straight off. 'You again.' A light stress, not unwelcoming.

'I'm afraid so. Sorry about that. I'm wrestling with an issue, Martin. A matter of contemporary etiquette. Do you mind if I ask your opinion?' She puts her feet up on the work table, having cleared a space. 'You may want to consult your wife.'

'No,' a pause, 'that's what I'm here for.' Genial. 'One of the things, at any rate.' Nice timing, and an altered intonation.

'But you don't know what it is. You might think it's quite trivial.'

'That's just as well. I tend not to deal with things of any great import before lunch. So, what's happened now?'

He must think I'm a walking disaster area. 'Well, it hasn't happened yet. It's supposed to be happening on Thursday. I should really deal with it myself, and impersonate a halfway normal person, without bothering you.' A halfway normal person? I'm impersonating Leary.

'You can feel free to bother me at any time. I doubt if there's such a thing as halfway normal. Or normal at all, for that matter.'

Could this be the root of the problem? 'No, perhaps that's …'

'And a lot of things are subjective. It may well be that I don't find it a bother.' This is encouraging. 'Whatever it happens to be.' Is that ambiguous again, or am I imagining it?

'Is it acceptable to withdraw from a relationship – well, nothing like that, more of a passing acquaintanceship, by text? Before anything has happened? But I suppose *that's* likely to be subjective as well.'

'I shouldn't have thought *that* was very subjective, Beatrice.'

She laughs. 'No, you're right, *that's* pretty clear-cut. But the thing is, it – I mean *that* – is scheduled to happen around lunchtime on Thursday, or after lunch. Potentially, I mean. Although I may have let it sound as if I was going to go along with it.'

Just to clarify, we are talking about Mr Davidson? Martin had sensed he wasn't floating her boat.

'No, but he might have thought he was. I'm sure he'd float plenty of other people's, though, so please don't write him off. I suppose I could just tell him that I've fallen for a hot new intro. Whereas I keep telling myself that I ought to give him more of a go.'

'Is that what you're feeling you'd like, Beatrice?'

'What I'm feeling I'd like?' What am I feeling? Confused and all at sea might cover it. If they don't live together, Martin and his wife must be separated. Is that a viable assumption?

'A hot new intro,' he's saying neutrally. 'I can try to arrange that.' It sounds offhand. 'If you think it would be a good idea.'

'A good idea?' Offhand to match. Why is this so infernally difficult? Nothing for it. Confront the fear head on. 'Well actually, Martin, I don't think I *do* think that. That it's a good idea, I mean. You see, I don't ...'

There is an extended pause. Extended, and confronting. Then she hears him exhale in what sounds like a sigh. Of what? Irritation? Resignation? Or something else?

'Beatrice,' a definite hesitation, unless this is a contradiction in terms, 'lately I've been wondering if it might be more helpful to talk about this in person.'

Wondering lately. While on the diffident side, this allows a lift of the heart. 'In *person?* Is that allowed, in the rules?'

'Well, I don't think it's explicitly forbidden. In any case, I make the rules, and I can bend them.'

'How very convenient.' There was just the one meeting. Since then, there have been only phone conversations. 'It's ages since we met, isn't it? Although I think I might be able to pick you out from a police line-up, in a good light. But would you recognise me?'

'In all probability, I think. There'd be more of a chance if you wore that red hat. That's if you haven't lost it after all these weeks.'

'It might be helpful to meet, as you say. Were you thinking, for instance, of a quick coffee somewhere?'

'I was thinking of something a bit longer than a coffee. More along the lines of a drink in a pub.'

'A long drink might be more helpful.'

'That's what I thought. We'd better make a plan. When is good for you?'

'This week might be good. Or did you mean earlier than that?'

'Earlier might be preferable on the whole, I thought. Later today, for instance?'

Viv says she's supposed to be doing something later today, but she could bend the rules. They arrange to meet in a pub near Green Park Tube at five-thirty. It's quiet, Martin says, and defiantly unfashionable. Six stops on the Jubilee, not too hard for you to get to. She'd forgotten he knew where she lives. He lives, she discovers, in Parsons Green.

'I'm meeting someone for a drink, so I might be late,' Viv tells Geoff at lunch. 'Are you in for dinner?' Green salad and a plate of beetroot and feta is at one end of the table. Geoff's laptop is set up at the other end. He's been working on an article for the online fanzine.

'I'll be in,' he says. 'But don't feel you've got to rush back. I can get myself something.' He doesn't ask who she's meeting, she notices.

He gives the salad a toss. What is he working on, she asks. A review of the new movie Lize was talking about. The one featuring robot-activated algorithm viruses that run amok and colonise computers, he reminds her, causing worldwide chaos. Based on a novel that was a runaway bestseller.

'A dystopian farce, is it?'

Not at all, it's deadly serious. It's a wake-up call for sleepwalkers. He serves her some salad. 'What are we going to do about Daisy's birthday?'

'Well, that depends on you, to some extent. Mum's coming down to see her show. She wants to stay over. She wants us all to have dinner. I told her this is probably not likely to—'

Geoff snorts. '*All* includes Adrian, I assume.'

'Exactly.' Viv taps his hand. 'You know, Geoff, it's not going to go away.'

A groan.

'I mean, it's not going away imminently. I don't mean it won't go away in the long run, necessarily. But in the short run, do you think you might be able to grin and bear it? Or if that's too unrealistic, hide it behind a mask of grim stoicism? You don't want not to see her, do you?'

He shrugs. 'Of course I want to see her. It's him I don't want to see. I've got an atavistic aversion to him. Why does he have to be included in everything?'

'Because he's—' Viv hesitates, 'her *partner*. At least for now. And because it's what she wants. Can you work on it? I mean, you worked on your atavistic aversion to Mum, didn't you? For my sake. You conceal that very well, I think. By and large.'

'Do I? Thanks.'

'People who don't know you would never pick up on it.'

A grin, and a sigh. 'All right, I'll work on my stoicism. But whatever else you want to say about Judith, she's not a poncy twit. It's not that I dislike her, I respect her. She's a very able woman, not a dissipated wastrel. You can't help but admire her ferocious capacity to get her own way.'

Viv thinks this is as far as he is prepared to go in smoothing the waters. 'Max arrived yesterday,' she says. It's nearly a year since they last saw him. She pictures Max. Still a striking man. She used to think of him as remote, but she's prepared to reassess this in the light of new evidence. Her idea of Max Jeffs has undergone a fundamental change, along with that of his half-sister, her lifelong friend Julia Jefferies.

'A bit strange, isn't it?' Geoff remarks. 'The idea of having anyone to stay while she's still rehearsing. Jules must be mellowing in her old age.'

Viv sees him wishing he could bite this back. 'Something we should all consider doing in our *old age*, perhaps?' There have been fewer clangers, but she's not prepared to let anything pass. 'Of course, Max is not just anyone.'

How long is he staying this time?

'Oh, for quite a while, I think. His daughter does most of the running of the galleries these days.' It's as well to start laying the groundwork. 'Max is the closest family Jules has. They've always got on so well, and he has the perfect London base. Now he's divorced, he's planning to be here more. A whole lot more, she says.'

Geoff surprises her by saying he always wished for a sister. Max and Jules are lucky to have such a lot in common, aren't they? They get on much better than most siblings he's come across. Than most married couples, for that matter. I don't mean us, sweet pea, he adds, with an evasive grin.

Viv looks at him. She's tempted to say something banal (yet apposite) about sex rearing its head and complicating everything. But it's too apposite, and too close to the bone. Instead she says yes, he's quite right. Jules and Max have the perfect relationship.

And she and Geoff are able to laugh it off. Their amusement is genuine and mutual, but derives from different sources. It comes at its subject from tangents, touching at times but not merging. As will be the way with us, she feels, into the future.

Viv works through the afternoon with an intensity she hasn't experienced for a while. All year she has been working on this patchwork quilt, and now the end is in sight. There's a satisfying symmetry of colours and patterns in the design. Compared with the results achieved by people like Joy or Yasmin (who's in a different league) she has a long way to go, but progress has been made.

The pleasure she feels in her work, the *flow*, keeps safely at bay the competing feelings she doesn't care to analyse. Immediately after this morning's phone call she put her red hat on the bed so as not to forget it. An hour before leaving she changes out of her work clothes, and after a moment's consideration opts for what she wore to her first interview with Martin Glover. The suit will have a chance to recapture its insouciance. And keeping out the cold will be that old faithful, the voluminous sixties overcoat her husband dislikes.

On the point of leaving, almost as an afterthought (in fact, not wishing to give it another thought at all) she picks up the straw tote instead of her usual bag. Which still, as it happens, contains various items that accompanied her on recent journeys to Chelmsford and to Paris. Many of them travel-sized and packed in a wash bag, together with the recent black purchases. She places two paperbacks on top to hide what lies beneath.

At the appointed time Viv is at the pub in a lane behind Green Park. She doesn't bother with being a polite five minutes late. The door opens into a simple, shabby bar with a sprinkling, as Martin had indicated, of unfashionable patrons. The kind of neighbourhood drinking hole that has nearly vanished, especially in that area. No TV, no fruit machines, no music. Nothing changed or spruced up, she would guess, for more than half a century.

All afternoon she has been aware of an internal stasis that is almost a concern in itself. It's unnatural how becalmed I feel. The calm before the storm? There is ample potential for getting this whole thing massively wrong.

She finds Martin Glover out the back in the snuggery. There is an electric heater – not a real fire, that's too much to hope for, but with bright and cheerful flames. The small room is lined with age-speckled prints and photos of London before and after the Second World War. He is the sole occupant, reclining on a worn leather chesterfield. He's not reading, but there's a book on the table at his elbow, next to an untouched beer and a packet of cashews.

Viv takes in a series of impressions. A white male with grey receding hair, brown eyes behind tortoiseshell glasses, and a touch of middle-aged spread. She observes a face with a prominent high-bridged nose. The mouth has a wry curve that suggests its owner is attuned to the humour of life, and not unfamiliar with its downsides. His clothes look comfortable and well worn. A tweed jacket over a fawn crew-necked sweater, blue shirt and brown corduroys. Although they have only met once, she is struck by how familiar he looks.

He seems to be gazing at the wall, although possibly not seeing it, and her other immediate impression, arriving directly on the heels of the first ones, is of a man in deep and possibly troubling thought. She stands in the doorway, taking all this in. While also remembering to take in the deep and steadying breaths Julia would advise.

'Martin,' she says.

He looks up. 'Vivien. You're here.' He gets to his feet and the worried expression creases into a smile that, she thinks, is very much in the moment. But the moment is rapidly followed by another, this time of uncertainty. It's mutual. They regard each other.

'Well,' he says. He comes over and kisses her slowly on both cheeks, lightly grasping her shoulders. Pensive kisses, she thinks. Contemplative. From someone becalmed, like me.

He picks up her hands and rubs them. 'You're freezing. Did you forget your gloves?'

'There was rather a lot on my mind,' she says. 'Although it was trying to convince me there wasn't.'

'Mine was convincing me of the opposite, rather too successfully. That's a large coat for a small person. Is it an old favourite?'

'It's a battered relic from the sixties. They were called swagger coats. George – that's Geoff, my husband – thinks it should be put on the scrap heap.'

He relinquishes her hands and takes it. 'And you wore that hat. It's a trilby, isn't it? I've become quite partial to it, in its absence. Come and sit down, and talk to me reassuringly, Beatrice.'

'Do you need reassuring?' She touches his arm. 'When I came in, I did think you looked worried.'

'Did you?' He's still holding her coat. 'I think I was worried, among other things, that you might have changed, or I'd got you wrong. But you're just as I remember, Vivien.' He shakes his head, as if to throw something off. 'It's rather a relief.'

'It *is* a relief, isn't it? I was worried too, in case you'd turned into someone else. I don't know what I would have done. It would have been really quite –' she thinks this over rapidly, and opts for the truth, 'really quite unbearable.'

They are still standing facing each other. 'Good lord,' he says, 'you've been left stranded without a drink. What would you like? Gin and tonic? White wine? They do a warming Tuscan red here. Nice and chewy.'

She watches as he drapes her coat over the back of the sofa, keeping the hem off the floor. She's still grounded in that pervasive calm. An unfamiliar feeling, lately. But it feels entirely natural. Nonetheless she perches cautiously on the edge of the sofa, hands on her knees. How I was sitting when Julia told me about the love of her life.

When he returns with her glass of red wine she says, 'What about the other things you were worried about? That's if you feel you can tell me.'

He sits next to her, close but not touching, and stretches out his long legs. Her eyes are drawn to them: solid male limbs in brown corduroy trousers. There's something endearing about them. And also, she can't deny it, something unexpectedly erotic. She resists an urge to place her hand on his thigh. 'Your worries,' she prompts.

'I'm not sure I can call them to mind now,' he says. 'It's a bit like trying to remember a dream. When you wake up and find it's gone for good.'

She looks at a photo of a horse-drawn cart alongside cars in Regent Street. It was taken in January 1939. Those people were on the verge of life-changing events. 'How did you know about this pub?'

'It's near a hospital where my wife used to come for treatment. I spent quite a lot of time here at one stage.'

'Where she used to come?'

He takes a long, meditative drink before tackling this question. His wife, Ursula, suffers from a form of dementia. They set up the agency as a joint business, a way of working together from home for as long as possible. Which in the end didn't turn out to be very long. She has been in a home for two years, and doesn't recognise him or their two daughters.

'She said she thought the agency would be a neat way – neat was her word, she's from Boston, originally – for me to meet someone else, eventually. She was practical and she liked to face up to all eventualities. But I didn't consider that option, and nor did I ever think of meeting anyone else that way. Funny, isn't it?'

He takes another long drink. He's sitting on Viv's right, with his left hand on the edge of the sofa between them. Like her, he's wearing a wedding ring. This time she doesn't resist the urge. She puts her hand over his. He responds immediately, with a decisive shake of the head.

'Beatrice, I'd better tell you now that I do have one more introduction, because I don't think it can wait.' He grasps her hand before she can snatch it away. 'I didn't intend to introduce him. In fact, it didn't occur to me at all, but in the end he left me with no alternative. He overrode all my objections and all those worries.'

He drains his beer. 'Here's the thing. He's a balding cove with glasses. Hopelessly uncool, as his daughters say. Way past his prime, needs to drink less, exercise more and lose some weight.' He turns. 'Is he remotely feasible, or am I a deluded idiot?'

Everything is all at once at stake and Viv's heart has speeded up. 'I wouldn't say he's past anything much, to be honest. Will you please stop me using that phrase? It's a bad habit I've got into lately. It's all these strange men you've been introducing me to.'

'I did work quite hard to – match you up, you know, Beatrice.' The quizzical look again.

'Then there's something I need to ask. It's important. Did you think I would be compatible with any of the match-ups? Including Leary? May I have a nut?'

He holds her palm and tips a heap of cashews into it. 'Ah, Leary. Well, I'm afraid by then I,' a pause, 'I very much hoped not, frankly. I just wanted you to be sure you weren't.'

'I think I was sure of that before I met him. Long before. I don't know why you didn't divine it.'

'I might have divined it if you had been a little more forthcoming.'

'It was all your fault for putting me in such a difficult position. Invidious, I think the accepted word is.'

'*All* my fault? Invidious is a bit strong. Weren't you in that position of your own volition?'

'Well, it was mostly *your* volition by then. I didn't want any more introductions. Obviously I couldn't tell you why, could I? You'd have thought I was dreadfully fast.'

'I don't see that as being a problem.' Mildly, 'I'd like to have known.' He strokes his jaw. 'I did think the match-ups were – somewhat unlikely. Admittedly. Although you can never tell. You did say you found Dev very attractive. You spent some time in Chelmsford, as I recall.' He takes off his glasses. 'And you went to Paris for the weekend.'

She likes the tone of reproach. 'That's called being conscientious. I think we both were, in our different ways. Admirably dutiful, you'd have to say.'

'I'd have feared it was severely unethical otherwise. And against the rules.'

'But luckily you make the rules and are allowed to bend them.'

'And we *are* both consenting adults.' He raises his eyebrows a fraction.

'That should mean we're in the clear, shouldn't it? With the combination of bending and consenting?'

'With that combination I'd be very surprised if anyone would prosecute.'

'Even if they did, my feeling is we'd get off with community service. At our age.' She's older than him, she suspects.

'Or with a caution. Although at our age they might even waive that.'

Men are hard-wired. She finishes off her glass of wine, which delivers a dose of Dutch courage. 'Are you younger than me, Martin?'

'I'm sixty-three. But don't worry – that's if it's in any respect a worry. I remember you saying something to that effect about your husband. It's negligible, as well as irrelevant. Besides, you look much younger than me.'

Is he just saying that? 'I'm saying that because it's true, Vivien, in case you're wondering. And also because I think you are lovely.'

She feels herself blush. No one has said anything like that to her for years.

320

He says, 'Would you like another drink, now?'

'Now? Did you have an alternative in mind?'

'The alternative, I was thinking, is that we could jump in the car and go to my place, where I put a bottle of champagne in the fridge. What do you think of that as an impromptu plan?'

'As an impromptu plan? I think it's faultless.'

His car, a Honda, is in a parking garage a few minutes' walk away. Rush hour, so it won't be the quickest trip, he says. He puts her bag on the back seat and switches on the ignition. A Handel opera: *Julius Caesar*. Radio 3? No, a CD, somewhere towards the end. After that Van Morrison comes on and lasts all the way to Parsons Green.

He's a good driver. She has been watching his hands on the wheel. Large and square, sprinkled with hairs. Capable. 'Here we are,' he says. The two-storey house is in a row of terraces. He unlocks a blue door.

Only in the last minutes of the journey has she wavered. The calm has departed and some nerves have moved in. Not many, although of course they may just be an advance party. She has felt like this on other occasions, rather long ago now, when she was on the threshold of something. It wasn't apprehension, back then. It was excitement. She had forgotten the feeling.

The house is warm, with rooms opening off a corridor down the left side, and a staircase. The last time she entered a place she didn't know, it was the Rev's parents-in-law's apartment in the Marais. Before that it was Dev's empty house in Essex. But apart from a similar sense of unreality (and this is fading fast) those times had nothing in common with this one.

In the hall they heap their coats and scarves over an already cluttered hat stand. She passes a small book-lined sitting room with a flat TV and a fireplace with candlesticks on the mantelpiece. An open-plan kitchen is at the far end. The house looks relaxed and lived-in. At ease with itself, Viv thinks, like him. A wall has been knocked down to connect the kitchen with the dining room. She observes a single tablemat on the table, an outspread newspaper, a laptop, a radio, and more books in piles. In the centre of the table, with a space cleared around it, is a glass vase of dark red roses.

'Is this where you work?' she asks.

'No, I've got a study upstairs, in what used to be one of the girls' rooms. It's much less tidy than this.'

The kitchen is in a bit of a muddle, but everything looks clean. A frying pan and saucepans of various sizes are heaped up to dry on the draining board. 'I'm afraid I didn't do a big tidy up.' He has put his arm round her. 'It seemed too much like tempting fate.'

'Is that how it seemed?' She leans her head against his chest.

'Better not assume anything, I thought.'

'But you did have an impromptu plan in place. You bought those beautiful roses. And you put a bottle of champagne in the fridge.'

'I did do those things, yes, just in case. To be on the safe side.' He goes to the fridge. 'It would have been unforgiveable if you'd come and there were no roses or champagne to greet you, I thought.'

'Pink, too. And French. My favourite.' She buries her face in the soft rose petals, inhaling their scent. An old country sideboard, genuinely rather than artificially distressed, and painted pale green over cream, displays some mismatched mugs on hooks. He removes two flutes from a jumble of glasses, and a folded tea towel from the drawer.

'These haven't had an outing for quite a while.' He gives the glasses a vigorous polish. The tea towel is a faded souvenir from the Salem Museum in Massachusetts.

'There's so much we don't know about each other,' she says. But it's not daunting. The opposite, if anything.

He whips the top off the bottle (efficiently, she thinks), pours generous measures with no spills, and returns the bottle to the fridge. There is a moment, palpable, of indecision. Their eyes meet.

'Now Vivien, we can take these into the other room.' A glance at the stairs. 'Or we could …' Perhaps it's not irresolution. Perhaps it's doubt. Or worry. In which case …

'If we go upstairs we're *there*, aren't we?' This receives a smile, but it is infused, she feels, with a certain constraint. 'Are we going too fast? Is that what you're thinking, Martin? Or is it better to – bite the bullet?'

He appears to give this some consideration. 'That's a question replete with ramifications, isn't it?' He picks up the two glasses. 'I think they're probably better dealt with in bed. On balance.' Now she thinks the smile is more whimsical.

The bedroom – Martin and Ursula's bedroom for years, she supposes, and now his – is a pastel blue with chintz curtains and a view of a wintry back garden. There are pictures on the walls and photos Viv avoids looking at, for the moment. An open door leads into a small bathroom. Some of his clothes, a shirt, a maroon sweater, are draped over a wicker armchair, one of a pair. The bed, queen-size, has a white cotton bedspread in a traditional design, perhaps French. It has been carefully made and smoothed out.

He deposits the tray on a chest of drawers. They clink their glasses and Viv takes a good swig, not a sip. As, she notices, does Martin. It goes straight to her head, which is welcome.

'I always make the bed properly,' he remarks. 'It gives that daily illusion of being tidy and organised.'

'You mean you didn't do it specially?'

'Not specially, no. But come to think of it, I did go and buy new sheets recently.' He pulls back the bedspread. 'Polar ice, the colour is. Formerly known as white.'

'Recently, did you?'

'It might have been the day after one of our conversations.'

She likes the picture this conjures up. Martin discussing the ins and outs of sheets with a shop assistant. 'Which one do you mean?'

'Possibly the long one when you were in the restaurant. Not the one in the Indian loo.'

'Do you think you might have been thinking ahead? Subconsciously, I mean.'

'I think that's a plausible hypothesis.'

'And you put the new ones on the bed. As well as getting roses and champagne.'

'Yes, I did do those things too. But as I say,' another smile, 'no major tidy up.' They are standing together at the foot of the bed, glasses in hand. Should we get in now, Viv wonders? But that would involve *undressing* …

She is almost felled by a wave of anxiety, all the stronger for being unexpected. She takes another hearty gulp of champagne, wipes the bottom of the glass on her jacket, and puts it on the empty bedside table. The other side has two big piles of books, a glass of water and a pair of reading glasses.

'That's your side, isn't it?' She hears her voice. It sounds as if she's just run up a steep hill at top speed.

He comes over and cups her face in his hands. 'I'm rather hopelessly out of the loop, you know, Vivien.'

The surge of relief she feels is almost as great as the apprehension. 'So am I. Dreadfully out of it. We can make allowances though, can't we?'

'I'm afraid you're the one who's likely to have to make them. You may have to make rather a lot. Have a top-up?'

'Oh yes, please.'

'I'll go down and fetch the bottle.' He pulls the curtains, then kisses her hair. 'Why don't you get into bed?'

She hears him clatter down the stairs. It seems to take him an age to locate the bottle and bring it back. Enough time for Viv to pop into the bathroom and freshen up. To whip off her clothes. To open the wash bag and utilise some of the contents. She leaves on the black lacy underwear she finds she had changed into, providentially, before heading out this afternoon.

When he returns she has pushed back the blankets and covered herself loosely with the sheet, which immediately brings on a disconcerting Parisian recollection. Martin refills the glasses before turning off the overhead light and switching on his reading lamp, angling it away from the bed. 'Light enough?'

She nods. He may be out of the loop, but this is not an inexperienced or insensitive man. There's enough light, however, to see that he looks preoccupied as he takes off his shoes and socks, jacket and sweater, and unbuttons his shirt. Or more likely, he's anxious.

'I couldn't care less about any allowances,' she says, but she senses he's not reassured. She sits up, allowing the sheet to fall away a little. 'I was thinking about your trousers.' He stops, on the point of removing his belt.

'I found them very sexy, when we were in the pub. I still do, only more so. May I unzip them? Or do they have fly buttons?' Her heart has taken off again, rather unnervingly. 'But first, Martin – do you think I could have a hug?' She's still having trouble with her voice. It sounds constricted.

It banishes any remnant of humour from his face. He looks appalled. 'Forgive me, darling Vivien, I'm even more out of it than I feared. Don't move.' He takes his glasses off. Geoff has called Viv plenty of pet names, but never, oddly enough, darling.

Martin tosses back the sheet and gets in beside her. What she experiences then is so unfamiliar it takes her a moment to recognise it as arousal. And we've hardly even touched, she wants to tell him. But as soon as they do, this becomes redundant information.

The Leary kiss, Viv's most recent, was nice enough but inconclusive. This is not inconclusive at all and it takes them both by surprise.

Taking trousers off from a horizontal position is never easy. It prompts a warning to do with going off the rails, unless she is more careful.

A little later, and a little indistinct: 'That's very delicious underwear. But there's a time and place for it and it needs to come off right now. You may have to—'

She doesn't, however, and this is the last halfway (or indeed anyway) coherent sentence spoken. For a longer period, it's fair to say, than either might have predicted. The minor side of Viv's mind that is aware of what is going on rather than engulfed by it tells her things are going to be quite all right.

A little later she qualifies this. They're going to be *perfectly* all right.

They had fallen deeply asleep and woken ravenous. Viv's new black slip and negligee were admired, but thought to be more suited to the tropics; a warm dressing gown was provided. They proceeded to the kitchen and made a quantity of scrambled eggs on toast, followed by hot chocolate. There was very little talking.

Viv was experiencing a sense of relief combined with emotional exhaustion. They were equally overwhelming. It's like riding a bike, you don't forget how to do it, she thought. And yet it's not like that, because you don't do it in the same way. Not the same way at all.

She texted Geoff. *Not coming back tonight. See you tomorrow. x.* This afforded her some considerable satisfaction.

When they are back in bed Martin remarks, 'I'll have to give you a partial refund, won't I, Beatrice?'

She doesn't think that will be necessary. 'After all, I had four introductions. Five, if we count you. I think that was pretty good value. *Considering* ...' Her head is resting on his outstretched arm.

'Considering?'

'Considering I didn't have to make any allowances,' she says. 'And bearing in mind other subsidiary services provided by the agency. Which I don't remember being listed in the brochure. Not even in the small print. Were they perhaps in the prospectus?'

'I'm afraid the agency doesn't run to a brochure. Or a prospectus.'

'I thought it didn't. So, what prompted them?'

'The other subsidiary services?' He props himself on an elbow and puts his glasses on to look at her. 'They're by way of being a bonus for unanticipated contingencies.'

She's back in the black satin slip, for the time being. Leary comes into her mind. She feels a throwaway affection for him. He had replied to her carefully phrased text very graciously, and added that Thurs wouldn't have been poss anyway, as the domestic-violence scenario at the convent was being expanded exponentially to include a siege.

29

RECONFIGURATIONS

'Max well, is he?'

'Firing on all cylinders.'

'Not too distracting from the daily round? All your vocal and physical exercises?' Pause. 'Just inquiring.'

'Enhancing the daily round. But thanks for the inquiry.'

'Jules, do you think there might be any chance of wangling a couple more tickets? On top of the usual?'

'Hm. Hard ask. Hen's teeth come to mind. Why, who else do you want to bring? There are two intervals, remember. Too much for Judith.'

'Much too much for Judith. And Joy doesn't care for opera. She says it would be all right if it didn't have so much singing in it.'

'It was Debussy who said that, Viv.'

'Well, Joy and Debussy are of one mind. No, I was thinking of Eliza, that's Geoff's new, possible – probable, I suppose – girlfriend. And Martin, my new lover.'

'*Come again?*'

'Well, I haven't had a chance to tell you. What with you going to ground, and everything.'

'Well, I never. Is it the Reverend or the TV director?'

'Neither of the above.'

'Good grief, Viv, you're out of control. I'll see what I can do. They won't be all together, mind.'

'No worries. Anything to keep Geoff at arm's length from Adrian.'

'Honestly, if Geoff doesn't get more of a grip he might do lasting damage.'

'Fortunately Daisy says Adrian doesn't give a rat's arse what Geoff thinks. Which helps.'

'It's the twenty-first century. Geoff needs to get himself re-birthed into it. Now, what's all this about your *lover?*'

'Well, let me see,' Viv says. 'You could say he floats my boat.'

'You could say he floats your boat for *starters*, Viv ...'

At the Sunday quilting circle Viv and Joy are planning a dinner. Joy has expressed a wish – more of a demand – to give Martin the once-over. It will have to be postponed until the week after the première, however, because Joy has a deadline over a new picture book. Yasmin is doing the pictures, as usual.

'It's about twin foxes,' Joy says shortly, in answer to Viv's query.

'And?'

'A boy and a girl.'

'Oh yes?'

'The boy wants to wear his sister's tutu to school and she wants to wear his britches,' Joy says, rapidly and rather defensively, and adds that she has plans to involve other animals. If it goes well it might become a new series. The publisher (Viv's old employer) thinks it's very timely and up-to-the-minute.

Viv looks over at Mr Jackson, who is quietly working away on his own. She is prompted to suggest they schedule the dinner for one of his nights off. 'Then the boys could give each other the once-over too.'

'You reckon they'd get on?' Joy asks. Her face, Viv thinks, is inscrutable.

'I'm sure they would.'

Joy says she'll think about it.

Viv is discussing the première with Daisy. 'We'll make sure Dad's not sitting next to Adrian.' A disgusted noise comes down the phone. 'He *is* working on reinventing himself, you know.'

'Never gonna happen.'

'I suppose you think it's not fair on Adrian.' This is disingenuous.

'Oh, he's not the problem. Adrian thinks it's a riot when Dad behaves like a toxic dinosaur. Whereas *I* think it's totally fucking unacceptable.'

'I thought perhaps Dad could bring Eliza.'

'Eliza? The trophy girlfriend? Or whatever it is he thinks he's snatched from the cradle?'

'Actually, she's quite nice. And quite a good influence. It might be easier all round if she was there. You see, darling, I'd rather like to introduce you to my new man, and—'

'Your new man? From the *agency*?'

'Mm. Well, sort of. He owns it.'

'He *owns* it? Blimey. That's very *lateral* of you, Mum. Is it legit? What's his name?'

'Of course it's legit.' And even if it wasn't ... 'He's called Martin Glover.' A rush of lust. Apart from Jules, Viv thinks it may be the first time she has pronounced his name to anyone since the significant escalation of their relations.

'That's – wow. That's great, Mum.' Saucer-eyed, she guesses. 'What's he like?'

'Oh, he's ...' Viv hasn't had to describe Martin before. Daisy wouldn't give him a second glance. 'Well, he's very bright, with a terrific sense of humour. Quirky. He's rather like you, in that he's got in inbuilt bullshit detector. He's very kind and considerate. *Attuned*, if you know what I mean. Witty, nice to be with – great fun to be with, actually.' She hesitates. 'And he's very sexy ... at least, *I* think—'

'All right, Mum, you can stop now. Didn't you say you weren't looking for romance?'

'Yes, well, I thought I wasn't.'

A pause. 'You really like him, don't you?'

'You *are* coming to the première?' Viv asks Geoff at breakfast. Coffee, toast and newspapers are spread across the table.

'I'm invited, am I?'

'Don't be silly, you know you are. As long as you promise to be civil. It's only family. Just without Mum.'

'But *with* Adrian.'

'Adrian *is* family,' she says, 'for the immediate future.'

And depending on a smorgasbord of imponderables, quite possibly for the future, period. Geoff goes through some facial contortions but, it is pleasing to see, refrains from groaning.

'Would you like to bring Lize? I think Jules could organise an extra ticket. And I'm sure Daisy would be fine with it.' She doesn't say she has already cleared both these propositions.

Geoff looks up. 'That's not such a bad idea, hon. Anything to dilute the alien slime.'

Viv feels obliged to overlook this, in view of her immediate objective. 'I thought I might do my bit there, as well. I expect you've guessed I've been seeing someone lately.' The *someone* prompts a warm feeling. My lover.

Other than tilting his head to the side, Geoff doesn't display any particular reaction. 'I thought you probably had. You've been out a fair bit, haven't you? All night, more than once.'

'Would you like to meet him?'

'Sure.'

'I'll bring him too, then. The more the merrier.'

Daisy had wanted to know when Viv was planning to introduce Judith to Martin because she wished to be on hand to observe it. 'She'll be creaming her jeans, Mum. Or whatever is the senior female equivalent.' Which had given them both cause to smile.

The mother–daughter moment took place yesterday. Viv reflects on its specificity as she drinks her coffee. 'There's another thing, Geoff, that I've been wanting to run past you.' He grunts. 'I was wondering if it wouldn't make more sense for us to start sleeping in separate bedrooms.'

A pause, while Geoff spreads marmalade thickly on a slice of toast, then munches it. They take a long look at each other. It's not divorce, but it is a point of no return. Each is regretful; each is relieved.

He says, 'I suppose it does make sense, hon. I could move into the spare room.'

'Then we wouldn't keep waking each other up. You know, when we come in late at night, and so forth.'

'Or late in the morning,' a companionable grin, 'in your case.'

'His name's Martin Glover.' A renewed rush of lust. Something has just occurred to her. Something she finds remarkable. If you take off the G …

'Retired, is he? What did he do?'

'No, he's not retired at all. Why would you think that? He runs a dating agency.' She monitors Geoff's expression. It conveys surprise, and bemusement.

30

THE PREMIÈRE

For a sense of occasion, nothing beats one of the grand opera houses of the world. Viv and Geoff have converged on Covent Garden from different directions: Viv and Martin from Parsons Green, Geoff and Eliza from West Hampstead. They meet in the Champagne Bar. They haven't had to shell out for their exceptionally expensive seats, and a degree of splurging is in order. It will be a reliable icebreaker. Not that there turns out to be too much ice to break.

There is some covert humour between Geoff and Viv as their companions are introduced. And traces of other feelings. A slight bias towards smug in Viv's case (justifiable, she believes) as her husband and lover monitor one another while ostensibly talking about the World Cup, a subject neither knows much about. But overall, a tricky situation is navigated with aplomb.

A second tranche of introductions will happen in the first interval. Max Jeffs has sent word he'll see them at curtain up. Viv is not surprised; she knows how Max is before one of Julia's performances.

Daisy and Adrian are running late (deliberately, Viv guesses). They will sit away from the others and further back from the stage; Jules said her power to acquire an extra brace of freebies could only go so far. Let the gilded couple (a phrase not repeated to Geoff) eat cake with the groundlings, she joked to Daisy's mother.

The opera world knows it is several years since Julia Jefferies last performed at the Garden. Everything is ramped up when Jules sings here, her friends tell each other. There is a heightened buzz of anticipation in the spectacular red and gold auditorium.

Julia has always maintained that those who claim they are not afraid before going on stage are lying through their expertly whitened teeth. Some people won't talk for three days before a performance. Others take homeopathic remedies for a week to calm the nerves. Julia, however, believes in allowing the nerves free rein. Without them, she says, and without your unfettered adrenaline colonising the joint, you'd risk boring everyone into an early grave.

For Viv, and for Geoff too, the occasion carries an additional tension. The tenterhooks you're on when you are close to a singer, Viv tells Martin (who is observing this for himself) are bad enough. For Max, they're almost unbearable. Viv has found she already trusts Martin sufficiently to confide such a thing.

Viv and Geoff have a nodding acquaintance with Julia's agent, Malcolm Foster. One of Julia's only chosen confidants, Viv recalls with a remnant twinge, until events forced her hand. He is seated on Geoff's other side. Viv has placed herself between Martin and Max. She is very aware of both men, in quite different ways. This is the first time she has sat next to Martin in any opera theatre. But she has been at Max's side many times at Julia's premières.

It has never failed to touch her, how Max lives through every note of his sister's performances. He is always the same: uptight and monosyllabic before the curtain rises, scarcely moving a muscle through the entire opera. He remains in his seat at intervals and only relaxes as the curtain falls.

Tonight she grasps what she had understood only imperfectly, and in part. She can see no change in his manner towards her, apart from a certain flicker in the eyes. But she has more insight now into his reticence, honed over the years.

Since Julia made the big-time, Viv and Geoff have known the privilege of premium seats and the advantage of being close to the stage. To be near the conductor as he mounts the podium and is applauded by the audience – Raymond Bayliss is a luminary and receives an ovation. To see the expressions on the singers' faces.

The set also receives applause as the curtain rises on a Moscow park. Idyllic, sunlit, crowded with pleasure-seekers. Children, army officers and citizens in their spring finery, playing and gossiping. Everyone enjoying a brief burst of April warmth before a storm.

All eyes, on stage as well as in the audience, are on the entrance of Julia Jefferies. She is unrecognisable as the Old Countess, on the arm of her granddaughter Lisa, played by twenty-seven-year-old Bridie Waterstreet, making her much-anticipated debut.

Over the years, whenever Viv has watched Julia perform she has felt as if she were watching a stranger. This time is no exception. But tonight her usual thoughts (this character is someone else, I don't know her, the whole thing is a magical illusion) are compounded. The illusion has been turned on its head.

Tonight, on stage, Julia seems to have grown taller. She has turned into an imperious old lady in an ermine cloak and an iron-grey wig slashed with a stripe of white. Forbidding, sinister and – more disturbingly – physically decrepit. She has intimidated the audience without singing a single note. How does she do it? The story unfolding in front of their eyes is enthralling, but Viv is finding it unusually hard to concentrate.

The first-act curtain follows a magnificent ball, and the arrival of the Empress Catherine the Great against a backdrop of fireworks. Max stands to let the others out, but doesn't acknowledge them or leave his seat. Julia's big scene is up next.

Viv has been impatient to introduce Martin to her daughter. And Daisy makes no bones about stage-managing it. She dispatches

Adrian to get drinks, and sends Eliza to give him a hand. She concentrates, insofar as it is possible in the crush, on her mother and on charming her mother's new man, while giving him the surreptitious once-over. She is at her best (cascading hair, long dress with an Elizabethan neckline), agreeable to everyone except her father, whom she largely ignores.

Adrian has dressed in the manner of the period, sporting a cravat and a green velvet smoking jacket. He spends time chatting up Eliza (at Daisy's instigation, Viv suspects) with a scurrilous account of what Catherine the Great got up to with her lapdogs. This relegates Geoff to the sidelines, and stokes the simmering fire. Viv observes Adrian's eyes flicking between her and Martin, Geoff and Eliza. Apart from the lewd lapdog stories, she guesses he knows very little about late eighteenth-century Russia.

Martin, however, turns out to know rather a lot since he was, Viv has discovered, a history teacher in a previous incarnation. He is absorbing the intricacies of the present situation with the comedic sensibility that, it has been rewarding to find, is a dominant trait. It also happens, she thinks, to be Adrian's. Allied in his case to a predilection for hellraising.

Daisy turns to her father as they leave the bar. 'You've morphed into quite a libertarian, haven't you, Dad? Adrian's in stitches. He really *admires* you. He thinks you and Mum are daringly bohemian for your age.'

Viv misses Geoff's expression. If Adrian knew Julia's backstory he would be even more admiring. She contrives a soothing word to her husband as they return to their seats.

Like Julia when she first set eyes on it, Viv was unprepared for the impact of the portrait dominating the second-act set of the Countess's bedchamber. Apart from the scarlet gown and the white stripe in the hair, it could almost be the girl on Julia's piano, photographed on her fifteenth birthday.

Max makes an involuntary movement. He may have known it was coming, but he couldn't have foreseen the effect. The young girl, frozen in beauty, confronting the corrupt and decayed old woman she would become. Viv finds the juxtaposition troubling. It impacts every nuance of the unfolding scene. She has no difficulty concentrating now.

As the Old Countess dredges from her memory poignant verses from her youth, as she revolves before the misty shapes of remembered friends dancing, the entire audience is as motionless as Max. The filmy peignoir slips from her shoulders, revealing the lines of a sinuous nightgown.

Raymond Bayliss controls the orchestral sound, shaping and moulding it until it is almost a secondary component of Julia's voice. And when the final spectral note of *Je crains de lui parler la nuit* shivers on the air and almost imperceptibly dies away, Viv brushes away a tear. Beside her, Max shades his eyes with a hand.

Herman emerges from the shadows. In their encounter, the Countess exudes another form of decay. A ruined sensuality, intimate and mesmerising. The audience have become voyeurs. They are half-reluctant yet riveted observers of the creepy power game unfolding before their eyes. The seductive approach of the old woman, in a black nightdress which reveals the outline of her body. The spidery hand as it moves on Herman's thigh. His revulsion.

It has never struck Viv with such force: how brave Julia is. How fearless as a performer. And fearless too, in life.

In the second interval Eliza complains she's too wrung out to talk. Is that a promise, Lize? Geoff asks, with a placatory wink. A loud group of Adrian's friends has descended on him and Daisy. The others can't locate the drinks he ordered in advance, until Daisy finds them under the name of Lord Frensham, his father.

'Not entitled to it, uses it when it suits him,' Geoff mutters to Viv, who is distracted. She has just noticed that Daisy is drinking water.

The opera ends with a third hologram. The impoverished, obsessive Herman has lost Lisa to suicide, he has provoked the death of her grandmother and been visited by the Countess's ghost – but he believes he is about to make his fortune.

He has bet on the first two cards, and won. He sings a drinking song to the assembled gamblers, a crowd of well-born officers.

What is life? It's a game.
Good and evil are only dreams,
work and honour old wives' tales.
What is true? Death alone.
The vain sea of life provides one refuge for us all.
Today, it's you! Tomorrow, I!

As he calls out the ace, the image of a great card rises from the table and hovers in the air. Herman sees before him an implacable countenance: the face he last saw in her coffin. The features of the Old Countess are superimposed not upon the ace he was expecting, but upon the queen of spades. One eye winks at him. Her revenge is complete. He shoots himself in the heart.

The curtain drops. A hush, then a thunderous roar of applause. Max is on his feet and the others follow. He looks completely done in. Viv feels the same. She touches his arm. 'She was sensational. They're ecstatic.'

They have said much the same thing to each other on many occasions over the years. Even when an audience has been less than ecstatic about a production, Max and Viv have made up for it. The post-mortems of Julia herself, on the other hand, were always ruthlessly objective.

Julia hasn't had to do anything in the third act, other than hang about for her hologram appearance. If I hadn't had to make like a crone on a playing card, she will say later, I'd be as fresh as a daisy for the curtain calls. This time there's no doubt about the audience response. Roses rain onto the stage like brightly coloured hail. The decibel rating of the cheering is off the scale.

'It made all the difference,' Viv says to Max, as they leave their seats, 'having you around for rehearsals for the first time.' His eyes, blue-violet like those of his half-sister, meet hers. They are as she has always found them: expressive, yet impenetrable.

They surge out with the crowd.

'Are all operas so incredibly tragic?' Eliza demands.

'Julia says all operas are about love,' Viv tells her, 'but some just rub it in more than others.' She chooses to omit Jules's astringent postscript: and they all end in tears. Instead, she agrees with Martin that they all end in a blooming miracle of catharsis.

From being dazed and shattered, everyone is revitalised. Together with Malcolm Foster they go round to the stage door, where the fans are massing with bouquets and autograph books. They have passes to Julia's dressing room, which is filled with flowers and cards. By the time they're admitted, Jules has had her costume and make-up removed and is her customary smart self. Max takes charge of the champagne.

Emils, the director, pops in to give Julia kisses and a hug. The length and ardour of both are unconstrained by the presence of outsiders. Viv sees a stocky young man with a tangled mass of hair (not unlike her own) and a broken nose. His evident dynamism is unchecked by a suit that looks mismatched and a crumpled tie that's coming loose. She is suddenly put in mind of her stepfather, Stefan.

Emils relinquishes his diva with evident reluctance. 'The first time we met, I told Julia the Countess was the star of the show,' he announces. 'She didn't believe me. Can you imagine that?' Julia regards him indulgently as she attends to his tie. If Viv didn't know better, she'd think she had designs.

Julia introduces him to the others by their first names, her keen eye lingering on Martin, and lastly on Max. Emils is throwing a post-performance party, small and select. My date is my brother here, she smiles.

'But Julia, I totally thought you were *my* date,' Emils protests, with a comradely grin at Max. He knows all about Julia's weather eye on his short-term objectives vis-à-vis Ms Waterstreet. And is totally undeterred, as she expected.

Only the principal singers and significant others will be admitted to the party. 'What do you have to do to be a significant other?' Geoff inquires of Max. Viv looks at him sharply. His expression is bland.

Max shrugs an elegant pinstriped shoulder. 'What makes you think I'd tell *you*?'

Parsons Green, late Sunday morning. Newspapers, magazines and an open laptop are on the dining table, along with debris testifying to a proper English fry-up. Viv and Martin are trawling through the reviews.

'"Gripping and thrilling production."'

'How about this? "ROH goes high-tech with holograms. Seniors behaving badly."'

'I can top that. "Julia Jefferies marks her welcome return to Covent Garden with a superlative sound and a shatteringly sensual performance."'

'"Yuri Dutka has a commanding presence. Bridie Waterstreet has a gleaming sound. But the stage belongs to the peerless – and fearless – Julia Jefferies."'

'That's the winner,' says Viv.

'Did he get your seal of approval?'

How much is riding on the answer? Not as much as she'd once have thought. Still …

'You can relax. Both of us liked him. He's quite a cool guy, we thought.'

Both of us. We thought. 'I couldn't help noticing, darling, that you were drinking water in the interval.'

'We weren't planning on telling you quite yet. It's extremely early days.' A sigh. 'Nothing gets past your eagle eye, does it, Mum?'

Breakfast in West Hampstead, a few days later. Coffee, toast, the *Telegraph* and the *Guardian*.

'I've got some amazing news, George.' He looks startled. 'Sorry – I meant Geoff. Fingers crossed, you are going to be a grandfather.'

A brief pause. 'It's not *that* amazing. These things happen. I thought it would.'

'I think I thought so too. Isn't that odd? I didn't want to say anything for fear of jinxing it. The cot quilt will come in useful after all.' Geoff seems to be studying something in the paper. 'But you're pleased, on the whole?'

A longer interval as he weighs things up. A grunt. Viv understands this to indicate qualified assent.

'How's *he* taking it? Assuming it's his, that is.'

'Oh, I think we can assume that. Daisy says he's over the moon.' Viv hesitates. 'She says he's boasting about being one up on Heggers and Venetia. They were having a race to the finish.'

Daisy had also said Adrian felt like he'd finally activated the full flower of his manhood. She was about to regale her mother with his follow-up remarks before she remembered who she was talking to and thought the better of it.

Geoff says, 'No doubt he thinks he's validated his existence.'

'As a male? Or by raising the quality of the gene pool?' No response. 'Is that what *you* thought?'

He looks up. 'For fuck's sake. Normal men don't think like that.' He sounds mildly amused rather than full-on irate, which is encouraging. The import of the news must be sinking in.

'Lize enjoyed the opera, didn't she? I'm glad she's such a feisty young thing. We had quite a good talk at dinner, about opera themes and prejudices. How women have such a bad time of it, and so forth.'

'Yes, I know. I was there.'

'So you were, I was forgetting.' She throws caution to the winds. 'Well, what did you think? Of Martin, I mean.' Although it's of minimal interest. Basically, I couldn't care less about anyone's opinion, yours in particular. All the same ...

'He seemed like a pleasant chap.'

Quite high praise, really. 'Yes, he is, isn't he?' He'll be coming round here after work tomorrow. There's a thought: perhaps he could stay the night. Now we have separate bedrooms, this is perfectly feasible. How daringly bohemian. Wouldn't Adrian approve?

And the new quilt is already on the bed; she put the finishing touches to it yesterday. Joy is coming over on the weekend to see it in situ. They're going out for the once-over dinner afterwards. You may as well book for four I suppose, Joy told Viv, offhandedly.

There is one other thing (of importance to Viv, but evidently not to Martin) that she wishes her husband to know.

She says casually, 'I've been meaning to tell you something, Geoff. He's a few years younger than me.'

The sentence hangs in the air between them. Invisible words, linked by invisible threads to different words that Viv and Geoff have said to each other over the years. A long time ago, or in the recent past. Forgotten, and unforgotten. Relevant, and irrelevant. Words that marked moments: moments that were mostly inconsequential, because that's how life is, but were sometimes decisive.

A small pause. Geoff looks up from his paper. 'Well, bully for you, petal.' Another beat. 'Younger, eh?' A grin. He clinks her coffee mug.

'Touché.'

ACKNOWLEDGEMENTS

My principal thanks go to Robert Gay, who put at my disposal his encyclopaedic knowledge of opera and music over many enjoyable meetings. While his enthusiasm for this project from the outset and his informed suggestions were the springboard for Julia Jefferies' fictional existence, any mistakes or howlers, naturally, are mine.

For many 'insider' insights I am most grateful to Dame Anne Evans, who generously shared her experiences and answered incessant questions with patience and warmth.

Hywel David of the Royal Opera House took me on a detailed personal tour of backstage Covent Garden that was an invaluable spur to the imagination.

For their zeal in inspiring certain aspects of Viv's experiences, I thank various friends who (together with their contributions) shall remain nameless.

Among those who read, commented or contributed in different ways, I particularly thank John Duigan, Penny Gay and Jennifer Bryce, as well as Tara Fisher, Nammi Le, Katrina Mortimer, Drusilla Modjeska, Sara Colquhoun, Anne Chisholm, Jean Deacon, Jo Smith and George Merryman.

To my agent Jane Novak for her drive, humour and unfailing belief, and to everyone at Ventura Press – Jane Curry, my perceptive editor Claire de Medici, Zoe Hale, Eleanor Reader and Sophie Hodge – for their exemplary zest and commitment – thank you all.

ABOUT THE AUTHOR

Virginia Duigan grew up in England and Australia, and apart from spells in America has contrived to live and work between the two countries. Besides freelancing in many branches of print journalism, with a strong bias towards the arts, she has written a movie, and in the more distant past had stints as a tea lady, a teacher, an ABC television interviewer and writer of children's drama series. She is the author of three other novels, most recently *The Precipice*, which was longlisted for the Miles Franklin prize.